SMALL MAN

SMALL MAN

The Storms of Time

TATE PUBLISHING
AND ENTERPRISES, LLC

Published by Tate Publishing & Enterprises, LLC
127 E. Trade Center Terrace | Mustang, Oklahoma 73064 USA
1.888.361.9473 | www.tatepublishing.com

Tate Publishing is committed to excellence in the publishing industry. The company reflects the philosophy established by the founders, based on Psalm 68:11,
"The Lord gave the word and great was the company of those who published it."

Cover design by Nino Carlo Suico
Interior design by Manolito Bastasa

Published in the United States of America

ISBN: 978-1-68187-917-8
1. Fiction / Christian / Fantasy
2. Fiction / Science Fiction / Alien Contact
15.10.27

I would like to dedicate this third book in the series of Small Man books to all my many friends at the WonderFest convention held each year in Louisville, Kentucky. Many of these friends have been instrumental in inspiring the creation of this story.

I especially would like to thank my buddy Chris Walas for his friendship and sharing with me some of the stories of his many successful projects for Hollywood movies such as the *Gremlins* and the second version of *The Fly*. Listening to him tell of his many creative projects made me picture him as the very model for my character in the Small Man series, who I have named Tack Moultrie. Thanks, Chris, and thanks again, guys and gals of WonderFest! See you next year!

Contents

1

Blue Glow

FREEZE Agent Chris Slattery was busy making a concentrated effort to make the necessary adjustments to being back at his office. The FREEZE facility was starting to grow unfamiliar to him of late, mostly because of all the traveling back and forth from Hamlet's Mill, Georgia, to Houston, and then to JPL; it just made coming back home somewhat of a strange escape from the twisted UFO investigation that had turned ugly.

The last story he'd heard and couldn't begin to believe was about the president of the United States. He was growing weary from shaking his head all the time, but this commander in chief stuff had him wondering about his sanity—everyone's sanity. The world had gone insane, and he had to believe in what was absolutely unbelievable.

He hadn't had much sleep since all the events back in Hamlet's Mill. His mind was clouded by the excitement and overwhelming series of actual events. All this stuff that he had personally been witness to made what little sleep he did get to being crammed full of dreamlike images of UFOs, aliens. Added to all that weirdness was the occasional appearance of the beautiful lady he knew as Evelyn Milford.

The powerful image, finally, of that flying saucer Tack Moultrie had been trying to convince everyone that he had seen was etched permanently in his mind. He'd actually seen it himself up close, as it rose out of the sinkhole. It had then hovered there in plane view as he watched. It then had moved forward and rose slowly up to the open air, and he could hear a humming sound—and in addition, he could feel it.

And then, over toward the Milford farm at the lake that was nearby, he could see a blue glow that shouldn't have been there, and the glow was pulsing and flashing. The glowing saucer then slowly slipped on up into the night sky above him until it was directly overhead. Eventually the saucer ship moved off into the western sky toward Evelyn's house.

Chris heard a familiar chime from the speaker of his laptop and realized that he was just sitting there doing nothing but remembering. Finally, as he sat in his office just staring at the wall, this new sound drew him back to reality and his mind returned to the present situation. An e-mail had just flashed onto the screen, and it seemed to be a new message from Jack O'Rilley. He read over the text twice and couldn't believe the unexpected good fortune that had come his way.

Just because, years ago, he'd made a friend in Jack O'Rilley while attending the WonderFest convention at Louisville, Kentucky, Jack was now providing an extremely valuable cross reference to the Hamlet's Mill case in the form of a brief account or what Jack and his buddy SiFi Bob had just witnessed in the deserts near Las Vegas. It took a while to digest it all, but what stood out were the indications that he'd been mulling over in his mind for that past few days. It was an extremely long shot, and it was a crazy idea, but…

Chris looked up from the laptop screen at his reflection in the mirror on the wall and said, "I was right. It looks more and more like it is just possible that the Hamlet's Mill saucer can change its size. It can change size." He shook his head. "And, big or small, I'm blessedly sure I know who's piloting that ship."

2

Message

Jack's message to Chris was short and simple but gave the FREEZE agent another train of thought to add to his list. Jack said that SiFi Bob had insisted that they stop off in Vegas to check out the Travis Factor. It seems that this Travis guy had some connections with one of the big plastic model companies out at Buena Vista Point. What made Chris especially interested was the information that Travis was constantly obsessed with the evil designs of something called "the New World Order." That interest, strangely enough led to the Luxor Casino in Nevada.

Back up on Freedom's Ridge, the group that had previously gathered around the president and the F-16 pilot had moved on past asking them questions that they could not answer beyond attempting to relate point by point what they had personally witnessed in their battle with the two large flying saucers. What was even more difficult for them to explain without sounding absolutely crazy, nuts, wild, and ready for the nearest loony bin was what they remembered about the third smaller saucer and their F-16 had been enveloped in a blob of green light, and how the world had somehow grown to enormous proportions in literally seconds. Then, after being in some kind of room or chamber for a while, their F-16 had been dropped or placed there on the Freedom's Ridge site, somehow, seemingly, back up to normal size.

But who is going to tell the president of the United States of America that he's full of blueberry stuffing?

3

Huge Importance

Tack Moultrie was still trying to grasp the huge importance of what he had just done to save the most important human being that was in existence at that particular time, the president of the United States of America. In order to save his life, Tack had literally shrunk him down to a tiny miniature of what he had been just minutes ago. The ship's shrink beam had successfully turned the most important man on Earth into an insect-sized doll, and that just seemed to be just too much power for one small crop duster pilot to have. Just what the president of the United States was doing out in the desert of Nevada flying around in the dark of night and obviously being chased by two UFOs that Tack had come to call king angel ships was anybody's guess.

Now, Tack Moultrie was bent on concentrating on what use to be the friendly nighttime. A very quick scan of his instrumentation and the view screens told him that the two UFOs that had been chasing him were currently, probably trying to figure what had happened to the F-16 and the weird saucer ship that had seemingly vanished from existence right before their alien eyes. Tack had decided his best bet was to get back to Hamlet's Mill, Georgia, and the safety of the sinkhole cave pronto kimosabee.

Tack Moultrie had found the UFO that he had given the name Spirit some weeks ago in a nearby wooded area. Somehow he had actually been successful in learning enough about the controls of the alien ship to actually fly it. Using some of the weird controls in front of his command seat, he had learned that he could shrink the Spirit down in size. He had learned about this strange ability of the UFO quite by accident, and he was still in the process of learning to use and understand its limitations.

He was now using what he'd learned about how to reduce the ship's size and had the ships dimensions down to approximately ten inches across. This being accomplished, he headed east into the night sky. Thus the Freedom's Ridge campfires were left far behind as were the two alien UFOs that had been chasing him. These weird saucer ships were still busy down in the valley, near the ridge, looking for him.

On the other hand, Tack's pet raccoon that he'd come to call Cisco was finally calming down from the evening's exciting adventures there in the wastelands of Nevada. The coon was slowing down his pacing back and forth on the floor of the alien ship's command deck.

Tack was currently busy thinking of all the possibilities and dangers his current lifestyle was bringing to him as the Spirit headed home to Hamlet's Mill, Georgia.

4

Prospect

Not far from the bio lab that Tack had recently been investigating from his shrunken flying saucer the same Dr. Sorocro that had escorted Agent Slattery on his recent visit to the supersecret warehouse was working with his crew, busily putting together as best they could what had once been the wreckage of the strange spacecraft recovered from Georgia State Road 432.

Dr. Sorocro stood overlooking a good deal of the pile of unknown metal parts that had been recovered from the Georgia crash site near Hamlet's Mill. A large number of pieces of the craft had been recovered from the area and moved to the secret facility at Edwards, and Sorocro had been busy at work attempting to study and identify them.

So far, a good deal of the reconstruction of the strange ship was beginning to take shape. Had these technicians and engineers been aware of all that had taken place at the Milford farm, the reassembly of the various parts would have clued them in to the fact that they were indeed working on the final escape ship that a unique female hybrid known as Quadrilla had designed and built on an artificial planet far off in another part of the galaxy.

Agent Driscoll Battey was sitting in a folding chair near that edge of the circle of crime tape, intently watching the workings of the reconstruction. With a notepad on his knee, he was busy sketching the basic shape of what he determined to be the final dimensions and shape of the craft Sorocro's people were piecing together.

Painstakingly making notations and adding various callouts to the sketch, Battey was attempting to point out some of the ideas that were popping into his head as to the purpose of some of the strange parts of the craft.

Sorocro had been at it for several hours and decided to take a break from his labor. He instructed his crew to leave the makeshift workshop for a well-deserved rest and walked over to Driscoll.

"I think we are getting close," he said. "Before long, we'll need to see if we can get a lift in here to elevate the ship enough to extend the landing legs…if, indeed, that is what those strange-looking things are."

"That's silly," Driscoll said. "What else can they be? It seems obvious to me."

"Me too, but in this business, I've found it dangerous to make that kind of leap of faith."

"I don't consider it so much of leap of faith than a sound engineering assumption."

"Yeah, well, as my old grandma use to say, 'Never ever assume anything!"

"Well, your grandma might just have a point there. I miss my grandma and all her cute sayings, not to mention her good cooking. I just hope all this work turns out to be worthwhile and that Slattery doesn't find out what we've been up to."

"If he does, it looks like everything's on my head…at least until you officially take over the project."

"Or, God forbid, Glassgow assumes command."

Both men made ugly faces at that prospect.

5

Cowboy

The Spirit streaked through the sky, making its way back to Hamlet's Mill, Georgia, as Tack watched back and forth between the read-out screens and the antics of Cisco. The coon was pacing around the command deck trying to find something to do, while down there in the dark of night in another part of the desert, Jack and Bob sat quietly in their van, racing toward Las Vegas. Like Tack, they too were unaware of the well-hidden secret facility far behind them, deep under the cooling desert floor.

Amid a series of supersecret rooms and chambers, there was a long, darkened hallway. Travis Dollman wasn't sure he liked being there in, what he'd been led to believe, was the most supersecret facility in the world. Dollman's heavy-set form turned into another even darker hallway, and the only sound he could hear was his own labored breathing. This corridor was so dark that he had to put out one hand along the left wall to help him maintain his balance. He felt the trouble with his inner ear on that side of his head return, reminding him of his childhood and his fear of dark places and of the unknown. His hand slid along the wall, steadying himself just to make sure he didn't lose his balance and fall on his face.

Finally, Travis came to the end of the hall and found a steel door with large rivets around the frame. At the right side of the door was a dimly lit keypad. Travis looked at it for a few seconds and then punched in L, A, Z, %, r, t, e, k. He could hear a tiny chime ring somewhere in the wall, and the door slid open.

He'd been in this location only once before, but it didn't take much of his thinking to take in the cabinets along one wall and the small desk piled high with books and magazines. He quickly counted four men sitting at a round table over in one corner under a flickering florescent ceiling fixture. All four of them were looking in his direction, so it wasn't hard for him to recognize the president of the United States and Douglas Bullworth. The other two guys Travis hadn't seen before.

"Well, the pyramid cowboy finally arrives," Douglas said, standing up and crossing room to shake his hand. "Been awhile. Glad you could get away." He noticed Travis looking past him at the president and the other two guys. "Of course you know the president. The tall guy is best seller writer Robert Newton Newhouse, and the other gentleman is air force pilot Tom Strine."

Travis nodded to the group and said, "Well, I don't really know the president, but I recognize him. It's an honor to meet you, Mr. President."

President King nodded and gave Travis a brief weak smile. "Pleased to meet you, Mr. Dollman." He stepped forward a little and continued, "We were hoping you could assist Captain Strine and I in coming up with some kind of…let's call it a solution to a problem that we find ourselves in the middle of."

"Come on over and join our little group, Travis," Douglas said, shuffling back over to the small table.

The president took Travis by the shoulder and guided him toward a chair. "Someday, over more pleasant circumstances, Mr. Dollman, I'd like to take the tour of the Great Pyramid with you."

Travis sat down in the empty chair, and Joshua moved back behind Tom.

Travis, in turn, looked up at the president and then at the faces around the table. Finally his eye settled on Robert Newton Newhouse. "I've read several of your books, Mr. Newhouse. You've definitely got a gift in storytellin'."

"Well, Mr. Dollman, it just so happens that storytellin' is what this little get-together is all about." Newhouse forced a smile.

"Yeah," Bullworth threw in, "and even though this story is worth tellin', it's never to be repeated. There's a best seller in here for sure, but no one would believe it—not even your most devoted science fiction fan."

The president rolled his eyes and moved to sit down in the empty chair next to Tom.

"Well," Travis sighed, "you've managed to get my attention. Not that it takes more than meetin' the president of the United States in a basement in the same neighborhood as the Little a Lee Inn to get my attention, don't cha know?

"Tell him what you saw, Robert." Bullworth nodded to Newhouse.

Newhouse pushed back his chair, stood up, and said, "I talk better standin' up."

Travis too pushed back, away from the table slightly so he could follow Newhouse as he started pacing back and forth around the room telling his account of what had just happened out near Area 6451.

"We were camped out on Freedom's Ridge, overlooking the secret area down near Groom Lake."

"Area 6451..." Travis chimed in.

"So it's been called, though, of course, according to the air force, there is no such place." Bullworth smiled a wicked little smile.

6

Maroon

Faster than the time it takes to scan a map of the US of A, from way out close to 6451 back to a tiny little town in Georgia, Professor Balboa called and asked Chris to pick him up at the Orlando Tradesentral Hotel. Not long after, they were headed out to the Orlando International Airport. Once Chris had turned in the keys to his rental, they stopped in at the lounge to have a couple of drinks.

They sat at the bar, and Balboa placed his briefcase in front of him. "I've read this and reread it, and I've made some notes and observations." He opened the briefcase and took out a maroon folder marked Is There a Quadrilla? "My notes are on the blue sheets."

Chris picked up the folder and thumbed through the file. "Nice work. Looks like you've made quite a bit of progress."

The bartender brought their drinks, and Jesse squeezed the lemon into his glass. "They usually make these things too sweet for me," he said.

Chris sipped his vodka Collins and read through several pages. "I like what you've done here in describing all the different shapes of UFOs that have been seen." Realizing what he'd just said out loud, Chris cut his eyes up to scan around the bar to see if anyone picked up on the fact that he was talking about UFOs—in a public place. Everyone within hearing range was too preoccupied to care. That's the way it was in this modern age, of noisy video games, and people who were unconscious of how loud their conversations were.

"Yes, it's very interesting how skeptics use the fact that these unidentifieds come in a variety of sizes and shapes seems to prove that they can't be real. I got this from Professor Glasgow's book on the subject."

"Professor Glasgow?"

Jesse sipped his drink. "Ooooo, I made it a little too sour. Should have tasted it first. Yes, Glasgow, he's an arrogant slob. Has the audacity to call himself a scientific. He's one of the noted scientists that claim that global warming is a fact, not just a theory."

"You about finished with your drink? I need to get out to the flight line and check out the Red River Queen before we head back to Hamlet's Mill."

"Sounds good to me?"

It took them the better part of 90 minutes to get back into the air and on their way, and like Chris had promised, it was a quiet, smooth ride.

After Chris got through with all the tower takeoff talk on the radio, Jesse was the first one to speak. "I'm glad I stopped off at that EPOTEK lab in Houston," he said. "You know, Chris, those EPOTEK people are going in so many different directions at once, it leaves my head spinning."

"All American institutions are like that ever since the computer did away with paperwork," Chris said.

"And real managers that have some practical experience, I have to add."

"E-mail—shucks, it was supposed to make communications better."

"And it only made it easier to be vague. They don't even bother to put dates and times on their messages." Jesse squinted out the front window.

"So, what did you find out in all that stuff in your folder that we can use?"

"Not much, but on the plane, I met this guy named Baldwin, and we got to talkin' about aircraft and rockets. Eventually, I decided to get his views on UFOs, and he recommended I read Professor Glasgow's book."

"Oh, like Glasgow's views can be trusted at all."

"You know him. I can tell."

"Not as well as Battey does. He's one of Battey's heroes…or used to be."

"Well, Chris, if you will indulge me for a moment, I was about to tell you about Glasgow and his list of UFO shapes and sizes. In regard to the descriptions of UFOs, Glasgow says that no two reports describe exactly the same kind of UFO. This isn't true. It is only a generalization, and his book is full of them. He goes on to say that there are dozens of types of saucers, resembling each other as little turnips do to comets. He has that much right, but so what? Do all of our human vehicles appear the same? Is a unicycle anything like a bulldozer? Is a Cessna 150 anything like a F-117 stealth fighter? It's a cheep shot and not even close to relevant.

"When he gets to the shape of the vehicles, he says that the descriptions of flying saucers vary widely when it comes to their shape. Sometimes, it appears as a circular disk, like a saucer. At different times and places the saucer will display a small protrusion in the center like a knob on a kettle. It can be elliptical… sometimes shaped like a bean or a flattened sphere. Then there are some that look like a circular base supporting a dome-like superstructure. Sometimes a sphere, surrounded by a central platform is described, you know, like Saturn and its rings. The saucers can be long and thin like a cigar or a tapered sphere like a teardrop. Some of them are spindle-shaped, with or without knobs on the end, and it can even appear as a triple-decked form like a stack of plates."

"That's quite a variety of stuff," Chris said. "And I don't suppose they are all the same size…"

"Ah"—Jesse smiled—"the size. Glasgow says that the saucers vary greatly in size. The estimates of the different diameters range from twenty or thirty feet to several thousand feet. And, get this, some of them suddenly increase—or decrease in size—while the observer is still watching it."

Suddenly Chris looked over at Jesse. "Professor, you just made my day. I knew it! I just knew it!"

"I thought that particular bit of information would get your attention. Now on to the different colors. Glasgow says that the saucer also varies greatly in color. It can be white, black, gray, red, blue, green, pink, yellow, silver."

"Almost any color you can think of," Chris said.

Jesse looked back at him. "You're right, just about every color there is. He says that the saucers may be luminous or dull. They may be solid color, or they can be circled by a central band of different color. Sometimes they display flashing lights of various colors. In addition, the saucer may even change color or luminosity.

"What does he say about the motion of the objects?"

"He claims that saucers display a wide variety of motions. Sometimes they travel very slowly, or very fast, approaching the speed of light. They can travel at the speed of a jet. They can zip through the sky like a meteor. They can hover motionless in one location. They can change speed or direction instantaneously. They can do the same with velocity and direction. They can move horizontally, vertically, in a straight path, or a zigzag, and like the Cheshire cat, it can vanish instantly or slowly fade away."

"That's probably because of it shrinks in size."

"The saucer's propulsion mechanism is a mystery, according to Glasgow. Sometimes they don't make a sound; sometimes they make a strange noise. Sometimes they hiss or whistle. Sometimes they roar like a jet or a rocket. Some witnesses have heard a thunderclap."

"Like a sonic boom, maybe…"

"Yeah."

7

Flying Saucer

Chris took his eyes off of the instrument panel and looked over at Jesse. "All I know is that Glasgow always refers to the UFO as a flying saucer or just saucer."

"Yeah, I noticed that. It's probably just his way of attacking those who have seen something they can't explain with their known experience." Jesse checked his seatbelt buckle.

"He's one of those so-called scientists that want to force everyone who has seen a more legitimate unidentified to be included in with the kooks who have some kind of agenda beyond getting to the truth."

"Sometimes the number of sightings will suddenly increase in a certain location. People have even seen them in groups showing a geometrical pattern, or a single object may split and multiply into a group, or a group may merge into one saucer." Jesse shook his head.

"One thing's for sure, saucers almost always appear in the air, although I have heard of them appearing on the earth's surface or in bodies of water."

"Yean. One of the most impressive accounts I've ever heard of was a saucer that landed in the sea. It was even seen to move around down there."

Chris was quiet for a moment while he made a slight course correction. After he leveled off the StarShip, he turned to Jesse and said, "How about the structure of a UFO?"

"Well"—Jesse shifted in his seat and groaned—"Glasgow contends that a saucer may be visible or invisible to the observer.

Visible, that is, to the human eye but not to the camera or radar. Or in some cases, visible to the camera or radar but not to the human eye." He waggled his hand, little finger and thumb extended. "Some saucers seem to obey the laws of gravity and inertia. Others don't.

"Doesn't he also say something about the fact that no officials in the government, or the press, church groups, major universities have ever claimed to have received any kind of communication attempts from the saucer people?"

"That's not actually true, you know. It's all in how you look at it and what you personally consider communications to be. It's also not exactly true that no saucer has ever produced intelligible visible, audible, or radio signals. This is Glasgow's own opinion. I could say that a dolphin or a whale has never attempted to communicate with a human. The fact is, as humble little old Jesse thinks, no one can say for certain that dolphins or whales or even ants have not attempted to communicate with humans."

"Well, I totally disagree with his notion that no two reports describe exactly the same kind of UFO." Chris reached up and punched a button on the console. "It's just not true. I believe it's a very broad generalization. Glasgow's book is, I fear, full of generalizations."

"Yeah, I know."

"He borders on really showing how ignorant he is when he says that long before an investigator finishes his study, he realizes that he is not dealing with one thing but with many. Now how much intellect does that statement take?"

"Are you sure you remember it right?"

"Yes, I'm sure. He says that no single phenomenon could possibly display such infinite variety. Okay, that really ticks me off. First of all, what is a single thing? It's like science fiction. Is the thing he's talking about the blob or the alien, or carpenter's version of the thing...Or, to be fair, is it like what John Campbell wrote about in Who Goes There?" Chris interjected.

"Right, John Campbell...Point is, if the inherent nature of a thing, to use Glasgow's words, is to become many things in order to survive or hide or blend in to go undetected for reasons of observation, then its very nature, its life-sustaining tactic would be to appear to be something it most certainly is not. Or maybe it's going to even appear as something strange and goofy looking in order to have witnesses who report seeing it be laughed at by such pseudo scientists as Glasgow."

"Glasgow is so much of a purist that he makes himself look ridiculous."

"I'd say that's not hard to do when one is dealing with the intellect of Professor Jesse Balboa."

Chris laughed, feeing the warm glow of the fellowship he shared with Professor Balboa.

8

Cat o' Nine Tails

Back down on the surface of Georgia, the night sky that covered the Hamlet's Mill Animal Hospital was being made even darker as the oncoming thunderstorm moved in from the southwest. Occasional streaks of violet-tinged lightning broke into the approaching darkness, accompanied by a loud eruption of thunderous clatter. Inside the main lab of the hospital, the clock on the wall was moving close to 9:30 p.m., and the sudden clap of thunder caused Doc Parks to jump up from his chair, dropping the Intelligent Discovery magazine he had been attempting to read to the floor. Quickly he moved over to the window and watched the multitude of lightning strikes illuminating the clouds as his eyes attempted to adjust to the contrast between the dark and the brilliant flashes of lightning.

Back toward the little town, the lights were still on at the Golden residence, and Kelly Golden danced down the stairs of her front porch with a bundle held tightly against her breast. She quickly made her way through the driving rain, to her blue 2008 Ford Mustang. She opened the passenger side door and placed the bundle on the seat, working the seatbelt around the blue blanket. She made attempts to arrange an opening in the bundle so that her pet cat, Theo, could breathe and also see what was going on inside the car. Once she was confident her beloved cat was secure enough for travel, she went around to the other side of the car and climbed in.

She started the engine and looked over at Theo. "I sure hope Doc Parks can figure out why you're not eating right," she said as she threw the gear shift into low. Screeching her tires and roaring down the circular drive out to the main road, she made her way out to the hospital.

....

The sky was a mass of lighting bolts as Doc Parks stepped closer to the window, rubbing his eyes. All of a sudden, the window was blasted with a gush of huge raindrops that threatened to turn into large hale stones, and Parks stepped back a little, wondering if the glass in the window could take the strain of the wind and the blast of heavy rain. As he studied the flooding rush of water running down the face of the window, he became aware of what could only be the headlights of an approaching vehicle of some kind. The fractured pattern of headlights attempting to pierce their photons through the downpour advanced toward the building, and Parks could see that, indeed, someone had been desperate enough to attempt to pay the animal hospital a visit, even at the cost of being struck by lightning, or worse.

"I wonder…" Parks gasped. He decided to meet whoever it was at the front door and offer any assistance that might be required. He headed down the darkened hallway.

Through the glass of the door up ahead, he could see the distorted image of a man figure. The door suddenly opened, and a rush of wind and water particles spilled into the reception area. Parks was wishing that he'd had the presence of mind to grab a towel as he observed the man pushing the door closed against the protests of the wind and rainstorm outside. His eyes flew wide when he recognized that the rain-drenched man was none other than Fredrick Belmont from the night of an earlier frightening storm.

"Hey, man, let's get you into my office so I can get you something to dry off with," Parks said, throwing an arm around the shivering Belmont and guiding him back down the hall toward the operating room.

Because his back was now to the front door, Parks was unaware of the headlights that flashed across the front of the building as another vehicle approached the rain-soaked building.

Kelly sat in the Mustang a few minutes and then decided to brave the pounding rain. She quickly jumped out of her car, went around to the passenger side, purchased the bundle of blanket-covered house cat, and made a dash for the front door to the animal hospital. The noise of the storm kept Parks and Belmont unaware of Kelley's presence. However, she spotted the two men up ahead and headed toward them. It was difficult to hear what they were saying, but Kelly caught a few words and realized that Belmont was one of the emergency workers that had been at the accident out on State Road 432 that Tack had been bugging everybody about. The downpour outside was making a heck of a racket on the roof, and the roaring sounds of the torrent were filtering down through the ceiling as she lost sight of the two men when they turned into a well-lighted lab. As she approached the door, she stopped in the darkness of the hall and glanced down at Theo. At that moment the sounds of the rain slacked off a bit, and she could hear more plainly what Belmont was saying to the animal doctor.

"You know that weird blue stuff I showed you last time I was here? Well, I…I…I might as well tell you. You won't believe the rest of what I've got to tell you anyway. I went out to the lake, you know near that old farm with all the buildings around that big white house…"

"Sounds like the Milford place." Kelly heard Parks say.

"Yeah, well, anyway, I threw those two bottles…jars…whatever…that you gave me…you know you used to catch all that blue stuff that the kid was bleedin'…well, I threw both of'em into that there lake…wanted to get rid of the stuff."

"Hey, Fred, I thought you wanted to get that stuff analyzed over in Atlanta."

"I did, but…well…I decided it was…well, weird…too dangerous, so I just tossed it."

Kelly decided to stay invisible and just listened to the conversation. Theo started pulling at the blanket with its left paw, and she tightened the bundle around the little animal.

"Well, the point is, Doc. I don't know anyone else to tell, I went back out to the lake the other night to see if any of that stuff had…you know…washed ashore…or somethin'…I was worrin', you know…I kinda wished I hadn't been so scared of the stuff and thrown it away…when…swear to God…I saw these two girls…young ladies, really. At first I only saw the one. Then after I followed her a spell, I saw that she was…followin' another young lady. Thing is…Doc. The lady she was followin' just walked…swear to God, she walked into the lake and…just disappeared. She didn't try to swim or struggle or anythin'. She just ducked and went right under the water, and…never came back up…"

"Wait a minute." Doc Park's voice betrayed the shock at what he had just heard. "You tellin' me you saw a girl drowning in the Milford Lake? Did the other girl see what happened? What'd she do?"

"Well, at first she didn't do nothin'. She just backed away from the lake real slow like, then she turned, and started toward where I was…so I hid from her…didn't know what else to do. Anyway, Doc, I can't figure what's goin' on. I…just—"

"And you don't know who that other girl was, the one that got away?"

"Well, yeah, that's what I wanted to tell ya. It was that gal that works at the Day Glow Inn. She's the one I talked to that night… that put those jars up in the fridge for me…I think her name's Cassy…don't know the last."

"Yeah, I've seen her around...but I don't know much about her...anything really..."

"Anyway, what should I do, Doc?"

"Don't worry about it. If she drowned, she'll turn up, and there's nothing we can do about it. She's dead. Tell ya what, I'll ask around, and if you give me your number, I'll give you a call when—and if—I find out anything about her."

Kelly had heard enough to pique her interest, and the "detective" part of her mind caused her to decide to remain quiet and sneak back out of the animal hospital before she was seen by either of the two men. The scientific part of her mind had been stimulated by what she had just heard, and this new information took prominence over what ever was wrong with Theo's eating habits. The downpour of rain had slackened off a bit as she made her way back to her car, Theo meowing in protest to her rough handling.

Once safely in the Mustang, albeit soaked to the skin, she said in a low but determined voice, "Cassy Towers...Cassy Towers... yeah...I've seen her before. She works at that stupid motel across from Maud's Restaurant." Her last word still hanging in the air, Kelly cranked up the Mustang and looked back over her shoulder as she backed out of the parking place.

9

Unfriendly

Kelly's plan that was forming in bits and pieces in her fertile mind was to head for the Day Glow Inn and see if she could catch Cassy before she went home. The storm was settling down to a less-threatening, steady downpour as the Mustang pushed its sleek form down the country road. She had no idea if Cassy lived at the inn as did old man Bailey or if she had an apartment or something near by. Also part of her plan was to check out Cassy's story and to see if Tack had anything to do with what Belmont had seen at the lake.

As Kelly approached the flickering neon sign for the Day Glow Inn, the rain began to slack off slightly. As she turned into the parking lot for the inn, she pushed her wiper blades to intermittent and looked for a parking space close to the reception office.

She glanced over at Theo, who seemed to be quite satisfied to just rest there listening to the rain that now peppered the roof of the Mustang. She then reached over and gently patted the furry crown of the feline. With a slight smile, Kelly murmured softly some reassuring words she hoped would maintain the calm state of the blanketed animal at least long enough for her to have a brief conversation with Cassy should she be so fortunate as to find her still at work.

Quickly, she opened the car door and ducked through the icy raindrops making a mad dash for the office door. Once inside, she was slightly disappointed to see no one present behind the counter. Even old man Bailey's chair was empty.

"Ms. Towers," she called out once and then again. It seemed there was no one at all working the reception area. She was just about to give up and start back to the door when she thought she heard a noise that might have been some movement back in the adjoining room. Slowly she turned, listening carefully to see if the noise might be repeated.

She tried calling out again. "Cassy. Is that you?"

"Hey, just a minute," a girl's voice cried back, and there was more noise of movement.

"No problem, I'm Kelly Golden, and I just wanted to ask you a few questions." She tried to think of something that sounded a little more official and quickly added, "Deputy Friendly said he'd seen you out near the Milford farm the other night."

Cassy came into the office drying her hair with a large white towel. "Deputy Friendly, you say?" She tied the towel around her hair an adjusted her T-shirt.

"Yes, I...well, I was out at the Milford lake myself several days ago...and...well, I sort of tripped and fell into the edge of the lake, an...well, Friendly said something about seeing you near the lake one night when he was investigating a prank call...and...he said he thought he heard someone splashing around...like you... well, he wondered if you might have fallen into the lake yourself, and I was just wondering..."

"That's strange, I thought I heard someone following me that night...but I never saw anyone." Cassy went over to the register book and quickly scanned the names. She looked up from the book at Kelly across the desk and continued, "Sounds mysterious I know, but I've been looking for my sister...Susan Towers... you know. She disappeared on the same night as that big wreck out on State Road 432...you know. No one believes there was a wreck, but my sister was supposed to be coming out to see me, and I think she was traveling with some folks that picked her up in their camper...you know, one of those big bus-like things."

Kelly's eyes were big, and she said, "Yeah, my boyfriend is absolutely sure there was a big wreck out there, and that one of the vehicles was a bus or something. He wasn't sure though, 'cause he bumped his head real bad and can't remember exactly what happened."

"Well," Cassy went on. "The other night, I saw a girl leaving Maud's…you know, across the street. I didn't get a good look at her, but something…about her…well, I thought she looked a lot like my sister, so I decided to follow her. I couldn't believe she didn't have car or anything. She just started walking down the road." Cassy stood back up straight behind the counter. When Kelly didn't say anything, she went on. "I figured that she was just going down the street to one of those houses down there, so I followed her. The next thing I knew, we were way down the road toward the Milford place. It was dark and scary. I couldn't believe how far I had followed her, but she was acting so mysterious, like she was walking in a trance or something, so I just decided to follow her no matter what. I had to find out where she was going, and next thing I knew, we were cutting through the woods. We wound up on a path I didn't even know was there…and I surely had no idea that Deputy Friendly was following me."

"So, what happened to the girl?" Kelly jumped in, betraying her excitement. "Did she finally see that you were following her?"

Cassy came around the counter and steadied herself with a hand to the wall. "No, she never gave any sign that she was aware I was even in the same world with her…and she walked through the woods straight toward the Milford Lake…and it was the weirdest thing—she walked right into the lake…and disappeared."

By this time, Kelly could barely contain her excitement and wonder at what she had just learned.

10

Drowning

Kelly talked Cassy into going with her out to Evelyn's place to see what she might know about what's been going on her property.

"I don't know." Cassy frowned as she followed Kelly out to her car. "I've never met Mrs. Milford. It might not be a good idea to tell her that I've been trespassing on her farm."

"Pooh…you weren't trespassing." Kelly moved quickly, ducking under the rain. "You were following a potential burglar…or maybe even a serial killer—who knows?" Kelly opened the passenger-side door and moved Theo into the backseat.

She motioned for Cassy to climb in, rushed around to the other side of the Mustang, climbed in, and said, "Besides, if Evelyn doesn't know about all the weird stuff that's been going on her property, it's time somebody told her." Kelly cranked up the engine. "And hearing directly from someone who's actually seen a girl drown in her precious lake…well, it's going to be very interesting to hear her side of the story—if she even has one." She paused and then looked over at Cassy. She quickly glanced into the backseat. "That's Theo, my cat," she said. And as she screeched off into the rain soaked night, she added, "Theo's not been eatin' right lately. I think he's sick."

When the blue Mustang drove up to the front of the Milford mansion, Kelly turned off the engine and looked over at Cassy. "To do this thing right, we've got to have a plan. Here's what we'll do: I'll tell Evelyn that you and I saw Deputy Friendly's patrol car parked on the side of the road by the woods, and we went to see if he needed help. We followed him out by the lake when we saw this girl jump in the lake and drown, and when Friendly wouldn't explain what was goin' on, we decided to talk to her." Kelly blinked her eyes. "Sound okay so far?"

A worried look swept across Cassy's face. She finally said, "But what if Evelyn calls the deputy and gets his side of the story? She'll know that we are…you know, up to something. She'll know that we lied about what's been going on…I just don't know…"

"Don't worry, if she knows anything, she'll either tell us or try to cover something up. Either way, we'll be able to get some answers." She opened the car door. "Come on, Cassy, let's get this thing done."

Cassy hesitated only a second, then shrugged her shoulders, and climbed out of the Mustang into the cold drizzle.

Just behind the grapevines bunched in a wild tangle of dark green, a dark figure watched as the two girls ran up to the front porch of the mansion, his eyes squinting tight to shut out the wetness streaking down his face. A light came on inside, the door opened slightly, and Kelly went through her planned discourse quickly, shaking her head, motioning to the rain and then to Cassy standing there next to her. Max watched as the two girls were admitted into the foyer of the Milford stronghold, and once they were safely out of sight, deep thought betrayed the expression on the face of the giant black man as he turned slowly and headed toward the lake. Minutes later, at the watery edge, and assured that the two young ladies would not see him, he dove into the rain-peppered waters. With mighty strokes, he swam out to the center and soon disappeared beneath the surface. Finally swimming down into the murky depths of the Milford Lake, Max held his breath as he slowly opened the topside hatchway of the Spirit's sister ship,

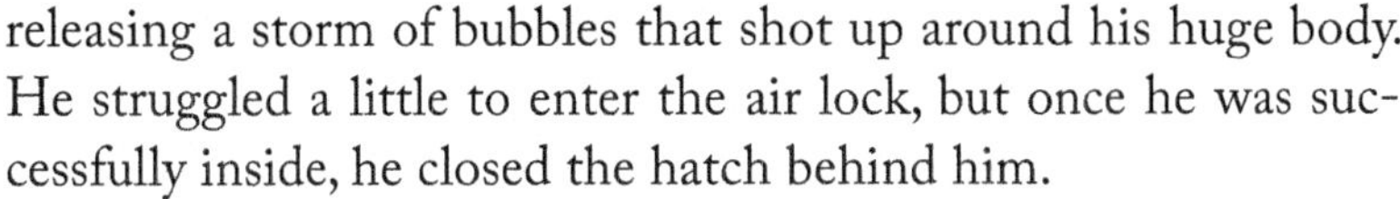

releasing a storm of bubbles that shot up around his huge body. He struggled a little to enter the air lock, but once he was successfully inside, he closed the hatch behind him.

Evelyn returned from the kitchen with an armload of towels and handed them out to the two girls, and Kelly began her prepared story. Kelly and Cassy quickly went through their planed dialogue with Mrs. Milford and managed to satisfy themselves that Evelyn's knowledge about the possible drowning event was a big, fat zero, and they found her to be totally trustworthy. They were confident that she had no knowledge of the girl at all, and this would hold at least until they were able to build up any counter-information to her side of the nonstory.

Outside the stately house, the rain began to slack off a little, and back out in the depths of the Milford Lake, the airlock hatchway of the Spirit's sister ship, again, slowly began to open, releasing a tempest of tiny bubbles. Surrounded by this storm of bubbles, a young woman floated upward from the sister ship through the dark lake waters. Breaking the rain-peppered surface, the woman swam toward the shore of the lake in the direction of the Milford mansion.

By the time the body of Susan Towers made it to the edge of the lake, Kelly and Cassy had managed to say their good-byes to Evelyn and quickly ran from the house through the rain to Kelly's waiting car and the end of the walkway.

The Mustang finally drove off through the drizzly night as Susan Towers was just climbing out of the water's edge. She had waited, waist deep, watching as the two girls left Evelyn's front porch and didn't seem to be in any hurry as she walked up toward the entrance to the Milford mansion. This visit was to be quite different from the time she'd last met with Evelyn face-to-face, the night of the big SR 432 crash. True, at that meeting she had to explain to Evelyn that she was, in fact, the alien Four that had been somehow magically transported into this Towers body. However, now, instead of the street cloths she'd been wearing that night, she was clothed in the seemingly same outfit she'd originally worn when she'd visited the Milford lady as Four... on that terrible night. The original costume had, of course, been destroyed in the crash as had her alien body. Now she wore the clothing that Max had brought in the sister ship. Max had insisted on including a full stock in the sister ship, just in case of some unforeseen event such as had happened in the unplanned for crash.

At the ornate door to the mansion, Four, now known as Quadrilla, could see that the foyer light was still illuminated, and she raised the brass knocker and let it fall twice, then once again. Seconds went by, and then the door slowly crept open to reveal a startled Evelyn Milford.

"My goodness, girl," Evelyn was finally able to stutter. "Where on earth have you been? Oh, never mind that now, just get in here out of the rain. You'll catch your death..."

Susan smiled, wiped the rain out of her eyes, and Evelyn put her arm around her, leading her inside the house.

11

Malakhim Raoth

Evelyn led Quadrilla through the foyer, through the living room toward the kitchen. "I think the best place for us is to sit at the table in the kitchen," she said. "Your cloths are soaking wet, and in here, we can get you dried off, and while you're warming up, I'll get you some dry clothes to wear."

Quadrilla looked into her eyes with a look that made Evelyn shiver. "I feel, Evelyn, that it is time bring you into my full confidence...to give you the details of all that has brought me here to your planet...your estate." She wiped the wetness from her face and let Evelyn guide her to one of the chairs by the kitchen table.

Evelyn grabbed up a towel from the back of the other chair and began patting Quadrilla's shoulders and arms. "We've plenty of time for that, my dear girl. First, we've got to get you dried off."

"No, Evelyn, I'm afraid that we do not have all that much time." Quadrilla raised her eyebrows. She had an extraordinary look about her, and Evelyn suddenly knew that she must give this strange woman her full attention.

"My number one helper, Max, has seen the girl that is the sister of this human body that I have managed to keep functioning. I learned from a lady named Maud that the body I now occupy is that of Susan Towers, the sister of Cassy Towers."

Quadrilla's words had an air of such intensity that Evelyn now realized that Quadrilla's visit was more urgent than she had previously imagined and nodded for her to proceed with her story.

"Evelyn, I must tell you the rest of the story so that you can be prepared should the king angels close in and become more of a threat to your safety. They are looking for me, and it is only a matter of time until they figure out that the water of the lake is defying their tracing devices. Once that happens, we will be forced to escape, and should we escape successfully, they, in all probability, will certainly come for you. I simply cannot let that happen."

"I don't understand" Evelyn said. ".What do you mean by 'the rest of the story'? I thought that you had been the source of the notes I have been writing to myself...the story about your planet and your escape...and your search for your son."

"That is all true," Quadrilla replied. "However, to protect you, I have held back certain details especially as concerns the king angels and what they are—why they are here, why they captured my mother, and why they created me."

"My goodness." Evelyn pulled her chair back and sat down. "Max and I have been in contact about these very things, but he has led me to believe that things were under control and proceeding as you wished."

"Yes, Tack is progressing nicely in learning how to pilot the ship I sent here as part of our escape plan, and Deltoo has reported to Max that they are developing capabilities that will serve our cause well when the king angels become more and more of a threat."

Evelyn twisted the corner of the towel that she still held in her hand, caught herself, laid it down on the table, and said, "I'm still struggling to understand just exactly who and what the king angels are. I mean, are they really angels as we read about in the Holy Bible, or is that just what you call them because they are so powerfully different from human beings?

"The name they choose to call themselves, their kind, comes from a word or words that were translated by the ancient peoples of the Earth long, long ago. In my investigation since coming to your time, your world, I have learned a little more about who they are...or, better said, what they are. Their story is a very sad one.

"In the land you call Egypt, where my mother was captured, I have since learned that there are something like three hundred years of history missing from the current knowledge that has been gathered from that time. There were people, a nation that had somehow come to live with the Egyptians as allies and friends. For many years, they lived together in harmony. A force, an evil force that still exists in this reality today, came between these two peoples and caused the Egyptians to look down on them—putting aside the fact that they had once been friends. The Egyptians became so jealous of these peoples, especially of their creative minds and the God that they worshiped that eventually they put the whole nation into brutal slavery.

"A great deliverer rose up in the ranks of the slaves. He claimed and proved in several displays that he had behind him the power of his God, and eventually, he convinced the Egyptians to let the slaves leave Egypt. The powerful happenings that this God had brought upon the land of Egypt had left the land in such a state of chaos that as the slaves were leaving Egypt, a force of men, some think creatures, came into Egypt and ruled that land for the three-hundred-year period that is missing from history.

"While Egypt was still in ruins, this force of people that the ancient scriptures designated as the Malakhim Roim took over that country and ruled until in around a three-hundred-year time period, a great king descended from one of the slaves. He helped the few remnants of the ancient Egyptians to regain their homeland. Malakhim Roim is the word that the slaves used in their written account of this evil force of people. Malakhim Roim has, in your time, been translated as the 'evil angels.' However, there is another term that is very similar to Malakhim Roim—Malakhim Raoth. Malakhim Raoth has been translated in your time and reality as the 'king shepherds.'"

"King shepherds?" Evelyn frowned. "But where did the king angels name come from?" Evelyn wrinkled her forehead. "I don't understand."

"Your confusion, Evelyn, is justified. It has been suggested by some of your scholars that a nation of people known as the king angels were misnamed because of a translation error that should have translated the word angels to the word shepherds. I have since learned that instead of the nomadic tribes known in those times as the king shepherds, these people or beings that went into Egypt after the slaves had been freed took advantage of the destruction that had left that nation in ruins." Quadrilla leaned forward and looked Evelyn directly in the eye. "I came to call these beings king angels, because that's what they called themselves. But they were mistaken. Their great knowledge of those ancient times led them to choose that name rather than the name that is translated to evil angels. They did not want to call themselves Malakhim Roim because they do not see themselves at evil...or good. They see themselves as somewhere in between, unwilling to connect themselves with the rebellion against the Supreme Creator of all things and peoples."

12

You Mean God

Evelyn's eyes grew even larger as she thought about what Quadrilla had just said. "The Creator? You mean God?"

"As I was growing up in the world of the king angels, I heard many stories of their history that I didn't understand. However, when Max and I became friends and then we brought into our confidence the little alien shape-shifter that we came to call Deltoo, between our three different experiences we began to understand some of what the king angels history could reveal to us." A trickle of water ran down the side of Quadrilla's face, and Evelyn handed her the towel.

"The Great Creator made the angels. No one really knows why, but the reality that the king angels believe and sing songs about betrays their absolute belief that this is the real truth. He made the angels in all perfection. He was determined to make them as much like himself as was possible. Because the Creator had the freedom to make choices, there being no one above him to dictate what or how he should do what he wished, he gave these angels the same freedom.

"The Malakhim Roim came about, as the history tells it, when the most beloved of those angels attempted to use his freedom to overthrow the kingdom of the Creator and convinced a third of the angels to join him. The Creator crushed this evil attempt to destroy what he had created and punished these evil angels for all time, cutting them off from his kingdom. But all this happened outside of our time. This makes our reality separate from that battle. To us, that battle is still being fought. Our lives and what we do are the results of that battle. Outside of our time limits the Creator had resolved the conflict, but we are still in the process of living it all out—and it goes on. All of the evil you see going on in your world is the result of that battle.

"The king angels are the result of a particularly weird part of that rebellion. Some of the evil angels came into this reality, to the earth, in the most ancient of times, and took human women to themselves to create hybrid beings that came to be known in the ancient scriptures as the Nephilem. Humans have believed many of these beings to be the mythological beings—giants of old that have been written about in ancient writings. Their plan was to create beings that were somewhere between human and angel in order to make good on their efforts to take over the kingdom by corrupting the human race with hybrids that would side with them against the Creator and ruin the creation. The Creator had promised a connection between him and the human race that could only come about with uncorrupted human beings. He was to take on human form and dwell for a time with the human race at the height of the birth of real civilization—a division of personification that is not understood by human standards even today. In order to make this possible, it was necessary for the Creator to destroy all, every last one of the Nephilem. To accomplish this destruction, he caused a great flood of watery masses, beyond that had ever before existed on the earth. This slushy mass did cover the entire planet Earth for many days and nights. All the Nephilem were thus successfully destroyed. However, some of the evil angels were undecided angels. They were outside of the Creator's kingdom, caught in the far reaches of space, between the evil angels and the angels that were loyal to the Creator. This segment of angelic beings is not commonly recognized by any group of human beings, nor has it been recorded in modern languages."

Quadrilla folded her hands and sighed. "The king angels, being undecided, has set them on an impossible quest. They have been searching for answers to their confusion for thousands of your years—and that is why they are here to find me, and my crew.

Evelyn was speechless. All she could do was stare back at Quadrilla and let her finish her story.

"Though the king angels believe in the Creator as a true living being, they do not like him. They do not agree with his followers, and therefore, they have doomed themselves to an unending search for an answer that has led them to attempt to recreate the Nephilem. Thus far they have been unsuccessful, but I am convinced they will never stop trying. They will also never agree with the Creator's kingdom, and therefore, they are doomed to attempt to achieve understanding by experimenting with your science. They, as do many of your fellow human beings, worship of the Creation, not the Creator.

"This is the reason they have been trying to create more hybrid beings using king angel DNA and human DNA, and I fear they won't stop there.

"I believe that in their attempts, they have accidentally created me.

"Evelyn, it seems I am very much like one of the Nephilem creatures that have been created. But is seems that I am even beyond the Nephilem creatures that they have created. Unlike the others, I found that I was able to survive—even to escape the realm of the king angels—and that makes for a very dangerous situation for you and those around you. That is why I have come to find and guide my son, Tack Moultrie.

"It is thus that I, as a superintellect, frightened the king angels. They realized that they had lost control, and thus they came to the realization that I was able to figure out the reality of my creation. More importantly, the king angels now believe that I have used my power of advanced intelligence to create the prototype spaceships to use to escape into the realm of human time constraints. Sadly, with my overwhelming drive to escape, I have thus have led the king angels into the current situation wherein we now find ourselves. Yes, Evelyn, I have unwittingly brought this terrible danger to you and all those you know, especially Tack Moultrie, my son. I fear that I have thus created the storms of time that we now must face and somehow must find a way to live through."

As Quadrilla fell into silence, Evelyn could see the tears flooding her captivating eyes.

13

The Disconnects

The FREEZE StarShip was crossing over the Florida-Georgia state line. Jesse leaned forward in his seat and looked down at a particular pattern of lights below. It wasn't a huge city, but the lights were impressive all the same.

Chris reached over, fingered a switch on the console, and tapped one of the gauges. "Professor, do you think that the UFOs can actually move faster than the speed of light?"

Jesse smiled and folded his hands together. "It's funny how the speed of light has always been one of the most fundamental numbers that we hear all the time. To the best of our knowledge, nothing that is at rest or traveling at any speed less than the speed of light can ever be made to move at the speed of light, much less faster."

"But, Professor, how can you be sure? I mean, suppose there is an unknown factor...something that we just haven't found yet?"

"When the mass of an object approaching the speed of light increases toward infinity, the object becomes shorter and shorter in the direction of travel until it loses, entirely, the dimension of length. And as far as our unidentified object is concerned, time stops. And it goes without saying that light does travel more slowly in air than it does in a vacuum."

"Makes sense."

"And photons travel even slower in water, as you might guess." He waggled his hand. "A mere 139,000 miles a second. But not one of my aging neurons ever thought for a moment that light could be slowed to the approximate velocity of a galloping horse or a snail."

"I would hope not."

"On the other hand," Jesse went on, "gravity is with us all the time, and it is everywhere. We don't even think about it."

".Until we fall down the stairs," Chris added.

"Physicists speak all the time about the gravitational constant. It's what we call the big G and is 6.67 × 10–8 cm3/g sec-2."

"What was that again?" Chris snapped his head in Jesse's direction.

"Just trust me. I'm the professor, and you're the pilot. The little g is the strength of gravity at the earth's surface. It's constant…at least it has been—until now. Now we have new ways of measuring the longest distances in the universe. We use exploding stars as the increments of our measuring stick. Now we are finding out that instead of being slowed by the aggregate gravitational pull of"—he waved his arms—"all the galaxies, stars and even the so-called dark matter behind them, the galaxies farthest away appear to be accelerating away from us.

"Accelerating?"

"I know, I know. It's crazy. It's a phenomenon that we believe exist only at astronomical scales, and it surprises us. Black holes objectify 'big' and 'strong.'"

"Objectify?"

Jesse frowned and looked at Chris over the top of his glasses. "The small ones are the remains of massive stars that collapsed in on themselves. The really big ones are the equivalent of millions of stars, sitting at the centers of galaxies like so many insatiable spiders. It has been imagined by some that black holes can be so small that they are floating by us in the park, even residing inside our homes. Such black holes might go completely undetected." He turned back to Chris, who was looking to his left out of the window. "Now, Chris, think about this. Suppose antigravity can also exist on a small, let's say human, scale. How strong might it be?"

"Just enough for you or me to float up into the sky at will, I guess."

"Yeah, and before you fall out of your seat laughing, let's wait to see what the scientists come up with to explain the large-scale antigravity force. Let's see if they can duplicate the force in a laboratory, making little shuffleboard pucks on, say, a tabletop rebound from each other in the same way that the north poles of two magnets repel each other when you push them together. And let's not forget that electricity was once no more than a laboratory curiosity."

....

The evening was progressing, and the StarShip was now over Albany, Georgia. The two men were quiet for a while listening to the whine of the engines, and then Jesse said, "Did you have a chance while you were in Orlando to work on your problem with Diane?"

"I tried to, but I don't see how I can do any good with such a short visit. Diane and I aren't getting along too well lately, and I hate to admit it, but I kind of dread going back a little more each time I go on a trip. I love her and all, but she's just so sick of my job...and I can't give it up..." He shook his head, unable to find words to finish his thought.

"That bad, huh?"

"Well, it's so bad that I've started thinking about an old boyfriend that she used to date back in college, that just maybe he's been seeing her behind my back. It would explain why lately she's been acting, you know, cold to me."

"That's too bad, Chris. I'm sorry to hear that."

Chris rubbed his hand across his face. "Yeah, I probably shouldn't talk about it. It might just be my imagination. But I guess I have to tell someone about it. If you just keep stuff like this in and never let it out, well...you know"—he waved his hands—"boom—talk about your big bangs."

"Have you talked to her about all this?"

Chris sipped his coffee and said, "Well, I used to try to talk things out with Diane, but after a while, I found that just keeping my mouth shut and letting some time pass by did more good than the usual 'What's wrong?'…'Oh nothing' routine. When we do get beyond that, it turns into that old spiral escalation bit…you know, it starts off with, 'Hey this toast is burnt,' and before you know it, she's telling me that I never liked the way she cooked, I never liked her mother, and then, you find out she's been keeping all this stuff all dammed up inside her until it all spills out like a backed-up toilet. And when it spills out, it spills out all over me."

"Yeah, I've been there. Logic just ceases to exist."

"Yeah, I've often thought the answer is to become a Vulcan, like Spock."

"But then you've got pon farr."

"Yeah, that doesn't look like too much fun either."

"Well, maybe we can settle things out at Hamlet's Mill, and you can get back to Orlando and straighten things out a little." Jesse smiled.

"I'd feel a lot better if I had your insight on some of the details. This gal Evelyn, she's got some of the keys, I'm sure of it, if I can just trust that she's leveling with me. I know it sounds crazy, but one thing's for sure. She believes what she's telling me."

Jesse nodded. "Maybe I can talk to her. Sometimes if someone is putting you on, a sound scientific ear can detect some insignificant detail that just magically opens up the whole thing so you can see the disconnects."

"I can arrange that, I'm sure."

14

Area 19

The StarShip banked and headed out to the northwest, between Cedar Town and Atlanta. "Whoa, that did something to my stomach," Jesse said."

"I've been thinking, Professor. What do you make of Evelyn's story? How could she possibly know all this stuff she comes up with? I mean, if it didn't actually happen. Some of it she says she dreams. Some of it she actually experienced. This Quadrilla. If she's not a real person, but a collection of people that Evelyn is some how in contact with, you know, through her mind, or something like that..."

Jesse's eyes lit up. "Maybe Evelyn's a remote viewer," he said, rubbing his elbow. He pulled a map of the test site out of the seat pouch. "This guy introduced me to an airline pilot who used to fly the commercial rout between Las Vegas and Salt Lake City. This guy was a scanner buff, and he had friends who piloted Janet 737s into Groom Lake and the Tonopah Test Range. But they told him they also flew somewhere else, in the Nellis Range that had an invisible eight-thousand-foot runway. They call it the Cheshire Runway—it's disguised to look like the desert, but at the last minute you can see it because they turn on the sprinklers. When it's wet, it shows up against the dry desert sand. Before you land, you have to get clearance to make sure no soviet satellites are overhead. Area 19 is controlled by the Defense Nuclear Agency; the test site doesn't even know what classified programs are located there. On the jurisdictional map, though, Area 19 is controlled by Los Alamos—and a number of people, including me, have said that Los Alamos is the place that would handle UFOs.

"This is where we start getting into some pretty wild stuff. I have a contact who used to be a contract engineer for the CIA. He was also in Vietnam and the Reagan White House. He's a spook, basically. Well, he decided he wanted to build an electromagnetic radiation detector for UFOs, but to do it, he needed to find out the correct frequencies. He got in touch with a woman who'd spoken on the radio about that very topic, and when he had lunch with her, he found out that she was a remote viewer.

"And you think that Evelyn might be one of these remote viewers? What exactly is a remote viewer?"

"It's a form of extrasensory perception. It was extensively researched by the CIA in the 1970s. At the direction of the agency, the Stanford Research Institute conducted experiments with people who were reportedly able to transport themselves mentally to distant places and report what they saw with surprising accuracy. Sometimes it's referred to as 'psychic warfare.' The practice has been written up in many respected scientific publications."

"So what did they find out about this woman remote viewer?"

"She said she'd been hired as a consultant by a certain aerospace firm. They gave her a couple of geographical coordinates, and when she went to these coordinates, she saw this gleaming underground lab. Then a door opened, and out came a gray alien. The thing that really disturbed her, though, was that the alien could see her as well. Then the alien went back through the door, and then some more aliens came out and stared at her. In all her remote-viewing experience, she said no subject had ever been able to detect her before."

"Must have scared her good, huh?"

"She decided to get out of there, but when she did, she said they were apparently able to track her—she started having computer break-ins and all this other weird stuff started happening to her. The best part is, when she reported to the company what she'd seen, they said, 'Yes, that's just what we expected. Thank you very much.'"

"So how does this remote viewing work?"

"Well, in this case, they wanted to specifically find out about Area 19. But first, they had to, what they call, 'calibrate' her. They called a guy one of them knew over in Virginia. They told him to arrange some...articles—whatever anything he could find... didn't matter what. The point is there was no way she could know what the items were that he arranged. Then they told her his address. She went there in her mind, and she said she saw a pile of rags with a yellow toy on top of it."

"Yesss?"

"The guy had put a towel in the middle of his living room and placed a yellow toy chain saw on top of it."

"I'm impressed. So If Evelyn could do that, I'm beginning to see what you mean." Chris cocked his head. "So what happened with Area 19?"

"When she was given the coordinates for Area 19, she rattled off a lot of detailed descriptions. She said that at the end of the power line, within the ring of roads, there had once been a pumped photon apparatus—which corresponded to the description of SDI laser technology. She said that an explosion had destroyed the facility, but later an underground building was constructed, with a louvered retractable roof and a circular bay for a thirty-foot disc. She said that the saucer, which had been cobbled together from a couple of other damaged UFOs, was powered by capacitors—it was a very crude system, like running an airplane with a steam engine. The disc was remotely controlled on the very short flights without any passengers. She also saw antiaircraft emplacements and lot of military and security guards to the south."

"Did she see any aliens?"

"No, no aliens, and when we gave her the coordinates for Papoose Lake, all she saw were empty hangars."

"You know, I got to study a soviet satellite photo of the Papoose Lake area. I think it was made around 1988 or there about. I didn't find evidence of any structures or land disturbances there. You can see what looked like roads and turnarounds. But I was disappointed that I couldn't find anything else. I guess I expected too much."

15

Blue Fire

The professor studied the scene ahead through the StarShip's window, took out his handkerchief, and wiped his face. "Chris, did you ever hear of blue fire?"

"Wasn't that a security condition imposed at Area 51 during the first UFO conference in Rachel?"

"Good, you have heard of it. Well, what I wanted to say is that this blue fire explored such hot topics as Los Alamos, the Tonopah Test Range, radiation gauges of southern Nevada, and radar cross-section facilities of the Mojave Desert underground bases."

"I call 'em black-budget puppeteers," Chris said.

"Yeah, it's like watching a magician."

"Yeah, I hear ya. I always look at the guy's other hand, the one that's not supposed to be doing anything."

"A wise person knows that there's secret, and then there's really secret. If you study the Manhattan Project, you learn that these guys are really clever about hiding things. The really secret facility could be fifty miles away on the other side of Groom Lake. There might be stuff so black that it's not even at Area 51.

"Ever hear of Area 6451?

Chris looked over at Balboa like he'd just said something dirty.

"Kept you in the dark about that one too, eh?"

"Drop the other slipper, Professor."

"Let's just say that I knew this…science feller. He worked for thirty years in something that he called the Secret Saucer-Duplication Program. He told me about a retired mechanical engineer in his seventies. He said he'd been employed in the design of flight simulators used to train human...yeah, I said 'human' pilots to operate aircraft that were inspired by captured extraterrestrial craft. The project was called FOGET. That stood for 'Fundamentals of Gravity Envelope Technology.' The purpose of the project, assuming you haven't the brains to figure it out, was to duplicate an alien disc that the air force had recovered from a crash."

"You're not talking about that mysterious crash near Kingman, Arizona." Chris twisted his face and bit his lip.

"May 1953, I believe."

"I'll be zonked. Battey studied that one. Said there was nothing to it. Give me a break!"

"The old man said he was speaking of under the scrutiny of his former employers, who had granted their permission for unknown reasons. Although he was now officially retired, he still received regular visits from a security officer and could lose his pension if he stepped out of line. Sounds like the people we know, doesn't it?"

"Sounds like Battey all right." Chris threw the StarShip into a steep bank that had the professor hanging to the left of his seat.

"This is StarShip 209, Gold Field," he said into his mike. "Request landing lights on the main strip."

"Does Gold Field have a night crew?"

"I called ahead, and they said they'd have someone down there to turn on the lights. It's a special case, you know."

The radio squawked back, "Gold Field operator. Roger the field lights. They'll be on in one minute. Winds from the southeast, but it's only a slight breeze. Be advised that the grass is wet. I repeat, the grass is wet."

"Understand. I'm looking for the lights."

"There they are," Jesse said, and Chris leveled off for the landing.

16

Running Scared

The StarShip came down on the grass strip, slipped to the edge of the tree line, turned, and taxied back toward the Gold Field building complex. Finally it rolled to a stop in front of the main Gold Field hangar, and Chris let the engines idle down. Jesse could feel the vibration of the props slowly dissipate until all was quiet and still, while out of the front window he could see Tack Moultrie jogging out to chock the wheels and tie down the wings to the concrete anchor pads.

The door to the StarShip swung open, and Jesse stepped down to the grass surface of the strip. He waited as Chris came out of the ship and joined him.

"How you guys doin'?" Tack smiled and held out his hand to Jesse.

"Just fine, Mir. Moultrie. Have you seen any more strange air crashes lately?"

Tack almost blushed like teenaged boy that had just been discovered to have hidden a girly magazine under his pillow. "Heck no. Things are bad enough as it is."

Chris stepped up and shook Tack's hand. "Don't worry, Tack." He winked. "If you actually saw something, we'll find out what it was and why we're not able to find any evidence."

"Well, I saw something, that's for sure. But I'm not sure what." Tack turned back to the Gold Field main Office door and motioned for the two men to follow. "Come on in and have some coffee. I'm just about ready to close up shop for the night, and I'll give you a ride to the hotel. Evelyn has your car over at the shop for servicing. Billy'll drop it off in the morning."

"Yeah, I phoned her from my office this morning just to make sure that flying direct wouldn't put a strain on my investigation." Chris shuffled along behind Balboa and Tack as they entered the office.

"Have a seat." Tack went over to the coffeepot and started pouring three coffees. "I make this stuff really black." He spun around briefly and faced the two men. "You take cream and sugar? I drink it black."

"No, black for me," Chris said.

"I'll have a little cream," Jesse nodded.

"I hope this dried stuff is okay." Tack held up a jar of creamer.

"That will be fine." Jesse plopped down on the couch.

Tack handed Chris his coffee and then Jesse. "You guys really hunt for UFOs for a living?" He shook his head. "I thought I had a weird job."

Chris sat down straddling an old wooden chair with the back against his belly. This allowed him to rest his arms on the back of the chair, and he held the coffee in both hands. He took a sip and made a face. "This stuff ought to require a permit...at least."

"Keeps me goin'." Tack sat down on the edge of the desk and waited, looking at Chris and then over in Jesse's direction.

"I'm guessing that the deal is." Chris nodded with a crooked small smile at the edge of his mouth, "First, we talk a little about UFOs, and then you take us to the hotel."

"You in hurry?" Tack gestured with his cup. "We didn't have much of a chance to talk the other day, and I just thought this was a really good opportunity...don't you think?"

"You're right, of course," Jesse said. "Here you are, the center of this...ah...investigation, and we've hardly talked to you at all..."

"And now is as good a time as any...I guess," Chris said.

"So are UFOs real, or not I mean, the air force denies that they exist. Open congressional hearings haven't been conducted. Scientists make up the lamest excuses in the world to explain credible sightings by pilots and astronauts...what's really going on? You can tell me, I'll...I'll shut up, I promise."

"You know that it's dangerous to get too close to a UFO, don't you, Tack? It's just a very dangerous thing to do. If you go too close to a UFO, you might get burned, and few ever fully recover." Jesse was lying back on the couch, resting his coffee on his belly.

"And there are a lot of people hiding out, laying low, running scared, because they don't have a choice. Doors have been closed to them. They can't find work. Their friends and neighbors avoid them. You just don't talk about UFOs. If you do, weird things can happen to you. Things in your life start going nuts. You get followed, or you think you are followed. Your life changes, and there's absolutely nothing you can do about it."

"That sounds pretty scary." Tack gulped down a swallow of the black brew.

Chris raised his cup and drank some of the wicked caffeine concentrate. "Tack, you ever heard of a guy named Ruppelt?"

"Sure, I've got his book somewhere."

"He was quite a guy." Chris shook his head and sighed.

"You knew Ruppelt?"

"The professor over there did," Chris said. "Wouldn't be here if he didn't?"

17

All the Way

"Over the years Ruppelt and I crossed paths several times," Balboa took up the conversation with Tack as his eyes scanned the notes and posters that plastered the walls of the main Gold Field Office. "When Ruppelt was forced out of the air force, it came as a shock to me." Jesse sat up on the edge of the couch. "I've no doubts at all that he was a true believer and that he died a true believer."

"Didn't sound like that in his book." Tack got up and refilled his cup.

"I don't care what his book said."

"You mean to tell me that he really took the possibility of UFOs seriously?" Tack said.

"I'm sure that he did, a lot more than he could let on. He was an air force man all the way, and he believed in the air force…and the air force believed in UFOs. The truth of it all is that the air force was trying to learn from the UFOs: how they worked, the nature of the propulsion system, why the aliens had come here in the first place—all of that.

"Tack, it may surprise you that it is believed that the air force believed in UFOs from as far back as 1947."

"You're right about that. It surprises me alright. You sure don't get that impression from the newspapers, or all the so-called scientific guys that go out of their way to make up silly stories of why those of us that have actually had a sighting are just a bunch of crazy nuts."

Chris smiled. "The Air Technical Intelligence Center back then was based at Wright Patterson AFB in Dayton, Ohio. They were in a state of near panic after Roswell erupted."

"How come?" Tack raised an eyebrow.

"Well, contrary to their own publicity, the military was being plagued by many UFO sightings of their own, and they couldn't explain them away to themselves."

"I didn't know that," Tack said.

"Yeah, first they had a sighting over at Maxwell Air Force Base in Montgomery, Alabama."

"Alabama?"

Chris nodded. "Then, to their horror, they had a sighting smack-dab in the middle of A-bomb territory over in the White Sands proving grounds."

Tack whistled and shook his head.

"What really got them going though," Jesse joined in, "was a whole series of sightings in July 1947, at Muroc Air Base."

"Now we call it Edwards," Chris chimed in.

"Way back then it was the most top-secret air force test center in the Mojave Desert—"

"That we know of," said Chris.

Jesse nodded. "Yeah, that we know of."

Chris stood up from his chair, crossed the room, and refilled his cup. "Man, this stuff casts a mean shadow," he said and took a swallow. "Won't be sleeping too much tonight." He came back to the chair and swung his leg over like he was climbing onto the back of a horse. "What do you think, Professor, shall we tell Tack about Quadrilla?" He glanced back at Jesse over his shoulder.

"Think he can take it?" Jesse smiled like he knew a dirty punch line was coming.

Chris looked over at Tack and cocked his head slightly. "I don't know. I really don't know…but what the heck."

"What's a Quadrilla?" Tack gulped down a slug of his coffee and almost choked.

"I have been working up to a way of telling you about a… woman named Quadrilla Bowden. At least we think she's a woman."

"Yeah? Go on."

"In a way she's a gal from the future, but not only that. She is, perhaps, from another galaxy as well." Chris waited for a second to see Tack's reaction and then went on.

"You see, Tack, it's not at all like science fiction plots that deal with galactic wars treating them like world wars. Galactic wars have a size element that has never been adequately addressed by Hollywood. When Captain Kirk descended to a planet to meet the aliens, it was like visiting a small city. Reality is far different. According to Quadrilla, alien life is not limited to organic tissue but is tied directly to the creation of energy. The idea that energy is the ultimate intelligence, or the God factor, is at the core of her story.

"Who is this Quadrilla, anyway?"

"Quadrilla, if she actually exists, is one survivor of several ancient experiments that have been conducted by a multilevel removed intelligences. Translation of her name for these super-creatures comes down to something like 'fallen angels.' She and her helpers took on the whole galaxy to escape her captivity, rebelling against the massive energy source of the alien forces that controlled their grand experiment for many thousands of years."

Tack looked down into his coffee cup and then back up at Chris. "I don't understand…Where did Quadrilla come from?" Tack finished his coffee in one final gulp and stared at the bottom of the cup while he waited for the answer.

Jesse took up the progress of the story. "Quadrilla and Max were collected from earth eons ago, but time begins to have little significance to us humans because these creatures are not limited in any way by what we conceive of as time. Let us just say they were gathered from Earth during the age of the ancient Egyptian period. Actually, a more accurate description is that their genetic material, or DNA, was harvested from human captives living at that time."

Tack suddenly looked up at Chris and then Jesse and said, "Wait a minute, how do you guys know all this?"

18

Supership

Chris and Jesse looked back and forth at each other for a moment, both of them attempting to communicate mentally about how to answer Tack's question about how they knew all this information, most of which was new to the young pilot.

Chris finally decided to just play it by ear, at least until he got a better idea. "From several sources, really," he said. "We've been studying the information that we've collected over the past few weeks, and this is where we are. Somehow, your experience with the events of that stormy night have led us on this investigation into areas that are not common to UFO sightings, and we seem to be on the trail of something extraordinary. Quadrilla, Max, and Deltoo, off somewhere in the galaxy, decided not to be the victims of these fallen angels, so they began working on developing a new kind of ship, or galactic vehicle. Their story is like unto those guys that build airplanes in their garages, or the computer guys that develop some unheard-of concept in their own tiny labs. Quadrilla and her crew, if you can believe it, have, in fact, built a supership—or I should say, the prototype of one. It was the ultimate shade-tree operation—alien technology and human ingenuity."

"And…you expect me to believe that this story has something to do with my story about the accident that almost killed me…that disappeared while I was unconscious?" Tack shook his head.

"No," Chris said, "we don't expect you to believe this story. We do want you to help us find out if your story is actually what happened. There are other so-called government agencies looking into this…event. Some of these agencies will do anything to keep this thing under control, and we just wanted you to be on our side…if events start to—"

"Get out of control," Jesse finished for Chris.

"Hey, say no more. I'm on your side."

"Good," Chris said.

"Hey, Tack, you ever been to the moon?" Jesse asked, with a silly smile on his face.

Tack smiled a crooked smile back at him. "Why in the world are you asking me a question like that, Professor? Of course, I've never been to the moon…except…"

The room suddenly was extremely silent. It was getting very late, and nothing was moving in Hamlet's Mill, especially in the Gold Field hangar complex.

Chris and Jesse waited, both intently staring at Tack's young man face smiling back at them. Was he going to come clean and tell them what he'd been up to for the past four weeks?

"In my dreams," Tack finally finished. "I've always wanted to be an astronaut, and I'm really ticked off that NASA hasn't gone back to the moon. It's not like they don't have the ability. It's not like we don't need to go back, build a base there, mine helium 3…and build our space launch platform there instead of having to lift all our stuff off the high gravity of the Earth. I'd go to the moon in a minute if I could."

Chris laughed. "And bring back a load of moon rocks too, I bet."

"You betcha—a bag full."

"That meteor that you gave to Ms. Golden, it's looks a lot like the moon rocks I've seen at NASA. Where'd you get it?"

"Found it up on hill near the Milford Place," Tack lied.

"When you were looking for the UFO?"

"When I was looking for what made that bright flash when I flew over it looking for the UFO. I never saw any UFO, just some burned grass and a raccoon."

"A raccoon?"

"Yeah, a raccoon playing there in the burned grass. It was weird. It was like the little fur ball was looking for something. When he ran off, back into the woods, I found that meteor. Well, it looked like a meteor to me. So I picked it up and gave it to Kelly. I told her if I ever got to the moon, I'd exchange it for a real moon rock someday, haha."

"You plan on going to the moon, Tack?" Jesse asked.

Tack slid off of the desk and stood up. "Someday, maybe we all will. Who knows? The US space program won't always be peopled by a bunch of executive types that forget what the space program promised us devoted followers."

"I don't think the guys at NASA would take that kind of talk mildly," Chris said.

"I hope they complain in public to my face. I'd love to debate them on the subject."

Chris stood up and said, "Yes, I bet you would at that. For now, let's just head out to Maud's. I'm getting hungry for one of her famous chili dogs."

"Man, you do live dangerously." Tack laughed.

19

Say Again

Tack drove Chris and Jesse to the Day Glow Inn and dropped them off. While they were on the road in Bill's pickup, they had all participated in a continuation of the conversation about Quadrilla and Max. As he drove away from the inn, Tack's mind was buzzing like his brain was full of angry hornets.

Is it possible? he asked himself. Is the Spirit the ship that Quadrilla built to escape the fallen angels? Do they know that I went to the moon and that Kelly's moon rock is real? Man. Man. He shook his head so hard that he almost missed the turnoff for the trailer park.

As he went into the camper, Cisco was waiting by the door, looking up at him. "Man, have I got a story to tell you, buddy."

After he'd spent some time in the bathroom and washed his face with cold water in an attempt to clear up his thinking, he poured himself a cold class of milk and sat at the kitchen table, just staring into space. Images of a far-off planet with millions of workers milled around in his mind like a scene from the old silent movie Metropolis. Cisco climbed up on the table and sat back looking at Tack as if to say, "Okay, are we going to talk, or are we gonna eat?" Tack decided to talk.

"Here's the deal, Cisco. You probably know all this already, since you seem to be part of this alien experience. But I'm gonna say it anyway. Maybe putting it all into words will help me to see it more clearly myself. As I understand it now, if I can apply what I've learned so far, we have established that the people responsible for creating the Spirit ship we now enjoy, and somehow allowing it to fall into my hands, are sort of like…abductees… They came from Earth…sort of…and they are somewhat human in their appearance now, sort of…because the aliens long, long ago were experimenting with creating beings that could be sent to Earth or some other Earth-like planet or world and without the need for a lot of metamorphosis to become ambassadors or at least fit into the organic element of whatever society with which they happen to be blending into."

Cisco sat there as if listening to every word.

"Therefore,"Tack continued,"such as Mr. Sagan and others are wrong when they insist that there is no positive way aliens would look remotely like us humans. Toonwalt was right when he said, 'Never, never, never assume anything in your human arrogance, not to mention religious arrogance.' And what about Earth life arrogance? Well, I for one am convinced that we humans do not know everything, and once we realize and recognize that simple fact, we are automatically more likeable and more interesting to most other people, perhaps, even aliens."

Tack sighed deep, took a long drink from his milk, and looked up at Cisco. "So, this gal Quadrilla and her crew built the Spirit to escape the evil angels. And the Spirit is a flying saucer discovered by little old Tack Moultrie in southern Georgia one night, while trying to figure out why the local police, CIA, FBI, army, air force, marines have decided to cover up a horrible accident that almost got him killed.

"I bet if I understood it all, I'd find out that the unified field theory is behind all this."

Cisco licked his lips.

"This very special vehicle, though simple in concept, is a device that not even the energy/God/aliens were able to dream up. It's sort of like what Toonwalt called the 'janitor factor.' Here you have all these egg-head scientists standing around the blueprints on a table trying to figure out how to make an XYZ machine to conquer the speed limit of, say, the speed of light."Tack finished his milk in one gulp. "And this janitor comes along emptying the waste baskets. He looks over the shoulders of all these scientists and engineers. Then he clears his throat and suggests something simple like, 'Why don't you just use aluminum foil and steel wool to fix it?' Then he walks away. Then…all these wise men look at each other and say, in unison, 'That's it!'"

He looked down into his cup at the remaining few gulps of milk. "So, Quadrilla and Max are so human and so inhuman that they manage to think on a totally different level than do the humans or the extraterrestrial God-like aliens.

"Therefore, to escape, these, there brains, Quadrilla and Max, Deltoo, design and build the Spirit. The ship they manage to come up with is a conveyance that will allow these guys and gals… whatever, to travel from one galaxy to another, without resorting to near-light-speed propulsion methods. Instead of using energy in their engines, they simply cause the Spirit to grow in size until it is as big as a galaxy. By simply moving its own length, it is moving several billion miles. And since it can travel through space, it can move outside any environment it finds on any planet so that it can grow to the proper size. How does it do all this? By solving the unified field theory. I've read about it, and Eric has filled me in on it so that I have some basic understanding of how it works.

When both strong and weak nuclear forces, electromagnetic forces, and gravity are joined into one energy source, the laws of physics that we have been bowing down to for thousands of years no longer confine human ambitions." He got up, rinsed out his cup in the sink, and then turned to Cisco. "What do ya think, Cisco? Are these guys full of bull or what?"

Cisco just looked back and twitched his nose.

"Yeah, you're right. I'm full of bull. After all I've been through, especially what we just saw in Area 19, this story is child's play."

20

Back on a Cloud

Tack got up early the next morning and headed to the Day Glow Inn. He wanted to ask Chris some more questions about what they'd discussed the night before. He had an idea that Evelyn had contributed at least some of the material for the Quadrilla story. He planned to have an in-depth talk with Evelyn as soon as he could arrange it and work into his busy schedule, but he wanted to check out a few things with Chris before that happened.

When he got to the Day Glow, both Chris and the professor had already left, and the gal at the main office told him that they'd gone over to Maud's for breakfast.

"Hey, if you're going over that way, I'll walk with you," the girl said. "I was going for some breakfast myself."

"Sure," Tack said. "What did you say your name was again? I don't think I've ever met you before. Are you new in town?"

"Not really. I've been here for a couple of weeks. I'm Cassy Towers." She gabbed a sweater off the coat rack and joined him at the door. "You are that duster pilot out at Gold Field, aren't cha?"

"Yeah, how'd ja know that?"

"I met your girlfriend Kelly Golden the other day…and… this man…a government agent and I have been talking about the crash you were in. He's staying here at the motel. Agent Slattery mentioned your name, and I remembered it because I thought it might have been a nickname…you know, Tack for 'tachometer,' and you're a mechanic and all."

Cassy got closer and closer to him as they walked, and he got choked up a little and could only say, "Oh."

Maud's was almost empty, and there was no sign of the agent or the professor, so Tack decided to join Cassy for breakfast.

"What do ya like? I'm buyin', so you just feel free to pick out anything you want. I'm going to have a couple of eggs overeasy and a couple of sticks of beacon."

She smiled and looked down at the menu.

Tack realized that Maud herself had come over to his table and was looking down at him like she knew a secret. Tack figured that she was one of Kelly's spies, and he was going to have some explaining to do when he next saw Kelly. "Can I get you something to drink while you decide?" she asked.

"Is it too late for breakfast?"

"At Maud's it's never too late for breakfast," Cassy said. Her smile was becoming infectious. Tack really liked this new gal in town. She seemed awfully nice, and usually that meant that deep down she was eventually going to be trouble—but who cares? Tack's stepdad's voice sounded off in the back of his mind: Avoid disappointment, aim low.

"In that case, I'll have two eggs overeasy, a biscuit and gravy, some grits, and two strips of bacon." He handed her the menu and looked over at Cassy.

"I'll just have some toast and some orange juice...and some strawberry jam." She smiled up at Maud. "Have to watch the waistline, you know."

Tack watched Maud as she headed back toward the kitchen. "And coffee—black," he yelled after her.

He looked back over at Cassy. "How well do you know this Slattery Agent?" Tack asked.

"Well, we shared his room one night," she teased. "Don't get any ideas, it was the night the van got blown up, and I was scared. Chris slept in a chair."

"Hey, Cassy, that's your business. I just wondered if you knew he was here to investigate the...well, maybe you've heard about my story...maybe not."

21

Overnight

Cassy smiled back at Tack and gave him a knowing nod. "You claim there was a big accident out on the highway and that they cleaned it up like nothing happened." She reached over and took Tack's hand and squeezed it gently. "Tack, I think you did see an accident. A guy driving an emergency vehicle came to the motel that same night. He acted really scared, said he'd been shot at… or something like that. They don't send out emergency vehicles for no reason at all."

"Really, this guy was at the accident?"

"That's what I figured. He was real secretive about it. Put some kind of blue liquid in jars in our fridge overnight. It was real scary."

"Blue liquid. Man—"

"I'm not a man."

"Yes, I know, I just…well…"

Maud came back with his coffee and set it down in front of him.

"So, how do you like Hamlet's Mill?" She looked down at Cassy.

"It's a nice place, a lot quieter than what I'm used to."

"Really?"

"Well quiet, except that I'm having breakfast with a crop duster pilot that they say saw a airplane crash…that never was, and telling him about spending the night with a government agent that helped me look at some weird glowing blue stuff in the motel refrigerator?" She leaned back and pushed her hair out of her face.

"Word gets around, doesn't it?" She detected that Tack was a little disgusted with himself.

"Well, for what it's worth, I believe you."

His eyes widened. "Really?"

"Tack, that's two 'reallys' in a row." Cassy smiled a big knowing smile.

"You sound like my girlfriend." He sipped his coffee.

Cassy pouted, her bottom lip puckered out just like Kelly's. "Shucks! You've already got a girlfriend."

"Well, she's not really my girlfriend. She's just sort of...the boss's daughter, you know, and she thinks that gives her some kind of power over me."

Cassy twisted her finger around in a blond curl that threatened to fall into her eye. "And does it? I mean does she have some kind of"—she bent over close to him—"power over you?"

"And how!" He looked down into his coffee. "She drives me crazy. She hates my airplane. She hates it when I leave her out of any of my activities. She hates it when I date her sister. She hates it when I don't fight back at her dad." He looked up as Cassy. "Maybe she just hates me...and chasing after me is her way of living out her hate."

Cassy reached over and took Tack's hand again. "Sounds like she's in love to me."

Tack gulped down half of his coffee and looked over at the kitchen door as Maud came in balancing two plates. Cassy had entranced him so that he hadn't realized that Maud had even left the table. She placed the breakfasts in front of them and put some extra napkins in front of each of them.

"Yep, I think your girlfriend's got it real bad." Cassy gave a quick glance up at Maud and then put her face close to him, and he could smell her perfume. It was intoxicating.

"In love?" Tack groaned. "I don't think so. I think she's just bored with her life, and torturing me gives her something to do."

Cassy's closeness was making Tack nervous. "I don't think I would hate your airplane. What kind is it?" She pulled at her curl some more.

"You've probably never heard of it. It's called a Long-EZ. I built it myself. "

"Long EZ…sounds like a movie star from one of those, you know, girly videos." Cassy looked for his reaction.

Tack ignored the innuendo. "Come on out to the field sometime, and I'll show it to you."

"Really? Oh blast it, now you've got me saying it."

"Anyway, I'm serious, I'd love to show it to you, the Long-EZ, I mean."

Cassy laughed out loud. "If you're that serious, how about this after noon? I'll take the afternoon off, and then you can"—she did a swooping motion with her hand—"take off in your Long-EZ."

"Hey, that would be great. It's a date then."

"As close to one as I've had lately."

Tack smiled and tore into the gravy biscuit. Then he suddenly stopped in midmunch, his eyes growing very big. Then he smiled, shook his head, and said, "She's in the hospital. Ain't no way she could find out."

22

Two Clouds Too Many

It was about an hour after the noontime buzzer when Cassy drove up the Gold Field hangar in a dark-blue 59 Mustang convertible. She climbed out over the door and leaned back searching around the field for any sign of Tack. Finally, she settled her baby blue on the young pilot checking out the cutest little blue airplane she'd ever seen. When her eyes finally settled on the words Cloud 8 1/2 painted on the bullet-shaped nose, a big smile crossed her face. She quickly leaned back, looking into the rear-view mirror, and painted her lips a deeper shade of red with a little golden-red tipped cylinder, then pressed her lips together, moved away from the car, and headed out on the field toward the sleek little Rutan Long-EZ.

"This thing looks like it's been built backward," she threw her head back and laughed. "Tack, you've got to be kidding. This is your airplane?"

Tack stood up, grease all over his face, a mountain of meekness, and said, "Yeah, I know it doesn't look like much, but I built it myself."

Cassy waved her arms. "It's all wrong. The wings are on the back. The tail is in the front. And lo and behold, even the engine and prop are at the wrong end."

"I just got through with my preflight inspection, so she's ready to fly. How'd you like to take a ride in it? Maybe you'll change your mind about how wrong it is when you see how it flies."

"You mean, take a ride in this thing? Will it hold both of us?"

"Yeah, I'm sure. It'll be a little tight, but if you don't mind me sittin' in your lap, we'll do just fine."

She raised her eyebrow. "Well, it beats me sittin' in your lap, but don't you have an airplane around here that is a little more conventional and roomy that we can fly in?"

Tack turned three shades of red, glanced across the field to the old Beechcraft C-45 that was sitting over slightly behind the corner of the hanger, and said, "Well, I suppose we could kill two birds with one flight. I've been needin' to check out that Beechcraft every since Buford traded an old crop duster for it. The owner said it was flight-worthy so I recon it will do. What do ya' think—conventional and roomy enough for ya?"

"Well, I guess so. At least you won't have to sit in my lap." She laughed.

It took several minutes more for him to do the preflight of the C-45, but soon they were both snugly settled into the pilot and copilot seats, and Tack quickly worked through the checklist. When he was ready, he looked over at Cassy, winked, glanced to the right and the left of the aircraft, and shouted, "Clear!" When there was no answer from outside, he smiled at Cassy and said, "I have to do that, you know. Part of the ritual." Then he pushed the starter, and the whine of the starter motor made Cassy look over at the twirling propeller as it swung round an round and then finally picked up momentum.

He let both engines warm up for a few minutes, checked his gauges, and taxied out onto the field. Cassy leaned forward and looked through the front window as he pulled the throttles out a little and headed the C-45 out to the strip. It didn't take long for them to reach the end of the grass runway where he spun the ship around and pulled both throttles out to the full. The C-45 bounced and waggled for the first few yards as it approached take-off speed, and then it leapt into the sky. He circled the hangar area and then pulled back on the stick. The antique airplane started on its climb up to five hundred feet, and he began to notice that the Beechcraft was acting a little sluggish, perhaps because of the extra weight of Cassy's rather shapely body. He looked over at her, and she looked back at him and smiled.

"Hang on," he said and started them on their way to the crash site.

"Where are we going?" she yelled over the roar of the engines.

"I thought you might like to see the site of the accident," he yelled back.

"Good idea." She nodded.

It only took five or so minutes to reach the site, where he banked to the left in a counterclockwise turn and began to take the aircraft into a wide circle.

"This is it," he shouted, and they both let their eyes scan the site below.

When he reached level flight, just over the treetops, he put the ship into a slow climb and banked into a clockwise, wide circle. This time he gave a little more throttle so he could tighten the curve.

"You're right," Cassy said. "It sure looks like they tried to clean up a horrible crash to me. I wonder why they did that…I mean, why pretend it didn't happen. Why cover it up?"

"I don't know. It's like the authorities are trying to cover up something. It's really frustrating to be part of something like that, and nobody believes you." Tack leveled off a little and glanced at the horizon. "You've seen enough?"

"Yeah, I guess so. I don't feel so good in my tummy."

"I guess that means no stunts on the way back, huh?"

"Maybe some other time," she said, fighting back a belch.

Tack pulled the throttles out to full and went into a steep climb. When he reached 850 feet, he leveled off started back to the field.

23

Newspaper

As the C-45 was making a low pass over the treetops out at the Dove Creek Trailer Park, Chris Slattery folded up a newspaper and slipped it between the stairs of the Nova Base. Chris turned to glance up at the aircraft as it streaked in front of the puffy cumulus clouds that had been gathering all afternoon. The Beechcraft was running low and fast, and in the excitement of the flight, Cassy felt her heart thumping, and she momentarily forgot about her stomach. It was just a glance as he looked down where his camper ought to be, but Tack managed to catch a glimpse of the man in front of his camper door, and his heart skipped a few beats. It looked like Chris, but he couldn't be sure. He decided to make one more low attempt at treetop level.

In his second pass, Tack wagged the wings slightly, and Chris waved his hands, pointing at the camper. It was all so fast, Tack couldn't be sure that he'd actually seen what he thought he saw, but he was getting low on fuel, and he turned back on course to Gold Field. As he made his approach and settled to the end of the runway and taxied toward the main hangar, Cassy looked over at Tack and said against the roar of the twin engines, "Chris mentioned to me that you built the camper that you live in… some kind of portable landing tower."

"In a manner of speaking," Tack shouted back.

"Wow, you sure must have a lot of time on your hands. Can I see it sometime?"

"I don't see why not." Then he had one of those visions of Kelly swinging a hammer at his skull and wished he'd kept his mouth shut.

As the craft began to slow down a little, Tack scanned over his instruments and then taxied the C-45 up to the hangar and shut down the engine. After climbing down from the plane, Tack helped Cassy down to the grass surface.

"Thanks for the ride, Tack. That was fun." She looked over at the Long-EZ and continued, "Maybe someday I'll have the guts try your little blue bird over there, and I'll have to take back everything I said about your weird little airplane."

"It flies like a dream."Tack nodded and noticed that this beautiful girl's eyes were not looking at him directly. She was looking past him in the direction of the hangar.

"What's going on over there?" he muttered.

When Tack turned and looked behind him, he saw Buford, Bill, and Billy Dale standing at the back of Buford's old pickup looking down into the bed. They had long, sad faces, and Tack started to have a really bad feeling about the way the day was going. He headed over to the truck, and Cassy followed.

As he got to the side of the truck, the three men turned and looked at him.

Tack couldn't be sure that it was the same raccoon. It was so badly smashed up, he didn't want to look too closely.

"Didn't you say something about a raccoon following you around the other day?" Bill asked.

Tack fought back the tears that threatened to blur his vision. He could barely see what was left of the tiny fiber-optic lights around the raccoon's ear, but unless there was more than one of these little bio experiments, this road kill had to be Cisco. "Yeah, I saw him around the camper a couple of times. Took him to the vet once when I found a bad wound on its shoulder. What happened to him?"

"Some guy was here yesterday." Buford grunted. "Said he had to check with Kelly about something...ask her some questions. Came in on one of them black helicopters...swear to God. Anyway, I loaned him my truck so he could get to the hospital, and when he came back, this little guy was in the back."

"It's really weird," Billy said. "I saw this guy in Buford's truck… thought he'd stolen it or something, so I dropped in behind and followed him. This little raccoon was…I swear to God, it was chasing the truck. I've never seen a raccoon chase a truck before. Then the guy stops at a red light, the one on Magnolia and Timberland, and the coon tries to get in front of the truck." Billy looked into Tack's face. "The little guy fell off the running board, and the…truck just run over 'em."

"I just can't…!" Tack groaned. "What in the world was he tryin' to do?"

"Well, I know this sounds crazy, but it looked to me like he was trying to climb up through the window," Billy said. "Sure looked like it…but I can't imagine why a raccoon would do that. Maybe it was rabid."

"He wasn't rabid," Tack snapped back with a tone of indignity. "He was just a coon…just a dumb animal."

"Now it's just a dead animal," Bill said and spit out the toothpick he'd been chewing on.

"Yep, dead all right," Buford said. He looked up at Tack. "Sorry, son." He patted Tack on the back. "Stuff happens, you know."

24

The One

Evelyn Milford stood on her porch looking out over the landscape. She stood there for a moment just taking it all in, and then she went down the stairs and deliberately walked through her yard, crossed the road, and followed the pathway to the nearby lake.

Her bright-blue terry-cloth robe was flapping in the breeze, displaying her shapely tan legs to the morning sun as she made her way to the edge of the lake. She carried a large white bath towel with a blazing yellow cartoon sun printed in the center. She laid the towel out on the ground, stood back, and stripped off her robe. As she began to spread the towel out flat in a position that suited her, she unconsciously used the shadow of her body to help her select the best placement for absorbing the suns rays for her morning sunning ritual.

Soon she was lying there feeling and enjoying the tingly ultraviolet rays bombarding her smooth, soft flesh, and she was able to enjoy this experience for at least fifteen minutes before the gurgling sound of many bubbles near the shore of the lake brought her up to a sitting position.

She watched as the dark figure surfaced about fifty yards in front of where she sat, her sky-blue eyes following him as he swam to the edge of the lake in front of her.

Evelyn showed no apparent surprise at all as Max climbed from the water's edge and stood there looking down at her.

"What have you discovered?" she asked as though it were the most common thing in the world to sit there on the towel, talking to a very tall black man.

"Deltoo hasn't communicated with me in several hours of late. However, he has managed to speak to me in visions. Deltoo says that this, as you suspected, is the One."

Evelyn smiled and nodded. "I am pleased to hear that. The search therefore is over."

"I must agree. Quadrilla is also in agreement."

"What does Deltoo wish to be done?"

"Deltoo asks that we let events develop naturally. Intervention is no longer necessary. The One is on the proper path," Max said but stood there quietly waiting for the proper words to continue.

"Something is troubling you." Evelyn looked directly into his steel-gray eyes.

"Yes." Max hesitated. "A government agent named Battey is closing in on the truth. If he discovers that the artifact is from the moon, he will cause trouble."

"I've heard of this agent. Quadrilla warned me. He may be working with the evil angels, whether or not he is aware of it." Evelyn shifted on the towel.

"I agree. Should I address the problem?" Max let his eyes scan the horizon.

"Not yet," Evelyn said. "I'll have to consult with Quadrilla. She will know what is best. Is the prototype secure?"

"Yes." Max returned his gaze to woman on the towel. "The One keeps it hidden in the cave, and he has made arrangements for its security."

"You have spoken with the One?"

"Only to warn him of the angel's pursuit of him." Max stepped forward a few inches.

"Do you think that a wise move?"

"He has discovered the second prototype. It was important that I keep him from investigating further."

"I understand," Evelyn said, and she turned her back to Max. She held up a bottle of sunscreen and said, "Would you be so kind, Max."

Max stepped forward and began applying the lotion.

25

EPOTEK Laboratory

It was ironic that far from Gold Air Field, and farther still from the mind and knowledge of Tack Moultrie, the white-painted brick EPOTEK laboratory building located in Houston, Texas, looked very much like the British movie workshop known as Shepperton-Pinewood Studios. Those British buildings were a representation of an earlier time where, to name only one, the science fiction classic motion picture 2001, A Space Odyssey was filmed. The EPOTEK lab architects responsible for the design had placed their pride and joy just off the highway known as NASA Road. The lab currently looked deserted at that late hour and stood there like a stone, Gothic castle, in the light of the fading crescent moon.

Somewhere inside this high-tech facility, a man and a woman dressed in white lab coats sat quietly watching the monitor screen of some highly technical equipment that Tack would have scarcely have been able to identify had he been there. The scientific instrumentation they were using betrayed the innermost secrets of the surface of a strange ice-blue crystal they had been observing for several hours. The unique stone had been commanding their intense interest to the exclusion of all else, and their eyes were beginning to grow very tired to the point of losing the ability to focus properly.

"So, where did you say they found this little jewel?" the man asked, his Australian accent more than obvious.

"All Richards would say was that the investigation team found it recently at some a supersecret facility out west someplace."

"So, then, you're telling me…hummmm…that's very interesting, Zelda, my love." He busied himself with the controls of the state-of-the-art microscope. "I think I might as well go on down to 500k. There seems to be something embedded inside, and resolution isn't good enough at this magnification."

"Yeah, I can't think of a reason not to." Zelda reached for the keyboard and began punching in new coordinates.

The screens crisscrossed with the usual bars of static that signaled a drastic fluctuation of current, and when the image finally steadied, both of them let out a gasp, and their mouths fell open.

"Well, would you look at that!" the man muttered.

"Holy Moses!" the woman gasped.

The object on the monitor screen was clearly some kind of glass-like substance—an ice-blue teardrop shape, almost spherical.

"It appears to be some sort of crystal formation. It might just be…" His eyes widened slightly.

"I don't know…" She sighed.

"To me, it looks like the work of some artist…"

"I was afraid you were going to say something like that," she moaned. "I was going to say it had the look of scientific handiwork. Richards is just a long-lost associate of mine who spends a lot of his time out in this supersecret facility." She rolled her eyes. "If you get my drift." She shifted in her chair. "Hank, darling, zoom in on it a little more. I think we need to analyze this thing more carefully."

"Sure." Hank moved over toward her and began moving his fingers across the keyboard. "This baby's no toy." He adjusted the power and called up the electronic program that would make the electron scan go to a greater resolution. "I think it's time to put it on the large video screen."

"It's about time."

"Okay, ready?"

They both looked toward the end of the darkened room at the six-foot-wide video screen. The new greatly enlarged image was being scanned in, one line at a time. Their eyes grew even wider as the scan began to reveal the image of an indistinct shape. As the image cleared into a sharper focus, the shape inside the crystal, sure enough, looked more and more like the silhouette of a tiny human fetus.

"Hank, do you see what I see?" But all she heard from Hank was a gulping sound.

Both of them watched in silence as the last few lines were scanned onto the screen. Then Hank said, "Worlds of wonder down under...what have we stepped into, Zelda? You said that Richards gave you this thing?"

Zelda leaned back in her chair, crossed her arms, and began slapping her bare shoulder nervously. The fetus-shaped object inside the crystal seemed to be moving slightly.

After another loud gulping sound, Hank started studying the keyboard again, as if looking for a key function he'd forgotten.

"Richards didn't tell me much," Zelda said. "He just said he had gotten the crystal from the secret government facility—one that isn't supposed to exist. At this secret place, it is generally believed that human experimentation has been going on for a very long time, and the authorities can't seem to do anything about it."

"Seems like with Congress conducting all of these hearings, they'd put a stop to something as abhorrent as human experimentation."

Zelda made a face and said, "Yeah, seems like one party or the other would want to use this to their advantage like the Progressives did back when the War on Terror was at full tilt. They did everything in their power to make the Conservatives look bad for going after the radicals in our society like they did."

Hank was feeling suddenly proud of his Australian accent. His was the one country that poured itself out in supporting the effort to rid the world of terrorism as a way of life.

Back up on the screen, Zelda thought she saw the fetus move again. She shivered and caught her breath. "Holy mother!" she gasped.

"Hey, that's what I said, only I didn't use the word 'mother.'"

"This thing…fetus…it can't be possible that it's…it's…alive… do you think?"

"No…I don't. I've been watching it real close, and I think this crystal has some special optical properties. It makes the little object appear to move. Of course I could be wrong, I don't know anything about this crystal material. It is possible that it may have some kind of unique stasis effect…like subzero temperatures. Anyway, the electron microscope kills organic material, which means if it was alive, it's not any more. But this glass is strange stuff. It might just act as some kind of shield that can protect organic material…who knows?"

"Well, I think you're right. The thing looks dead to me… now…" Suddenly Zelda's eyes lit up. "Hank, I've…I'm having a…this is a crazy idea, but if Richards can get us another sample, we could look at it under our x-ray microscope. Using that technology, living material can be observed—without destroying it." Zelda's voice betrayed the excitement that her idea had just created.

"Wish we had thought about that earlier."

"Me too."

26

Still Alive

That same night, far away from the electron microscope lab, Chris Slattery drove down the two-lane blacktop that connected the main road to the animal health and emergency service facility just outside of Hamlet's Mill city limits. He turned to the professor and said, "Wait till you see this, Jesse. You know, Cassy, the girl I met at the motel…well, she did a little detective work on that stuff I told you about that was in the refrigerator—the blue stuff, you know? And like I told you, she knows a girl that has a pet kitten…and she drove it to the vet. While she was watching him do an examination on the kitten, it wasn't eating right or somethin'. She noticed he had this collection of antique fruit jars on a shelf in his office. Long story short, she asked him where he got the jars, and before she knew it, he'd told her this wild story about some guy that had been shot by a UFO. This made her laugh at him. She thought it was something he was just making up, but it made him get angry, and he decided to show her proof that his story was actually true. This is great. I want it to hit you cold like it did me. You can't fake stuff like this."

Jesse nodded back to Chris as he turned into the driveway and parked in front of the animal hospital. Doc Parks was standing in the hall talking to one of the guys that Chris had seen at Gold Field. "I'll do what I can, but don't get your hopes up," he was saying as Chris and Jesse walked up.

He tuned to Chris and said, "Oh, you must be the guy I talked to on the phone. Agent Slattery, is it?"

"Yeah." Chris put out his hand. "And this is Professor Balboa." He nodded to Jesse.

Chris cast a glance at the other man. "You're…Bill…I've seen you out at the field?"

"Yeah, Bill Innis. We met the other day."

"I'm good at faces, but I wasn't sure." Chris shook Bill's hand. "Got a sick pet?"

"Something like that. Got hit by a truck."

"Oh, I see. Too bad. Is it going to be all right?"

"Hard to tell."

"He's going to leave it here with me for a few days, and I'm going to try some things. I'm amazed it's still alive."

"Well," Bill said. "I was sure it was dead, but while I was wrapping the little guy in a Tater sack to bury 'im, I noticed its eyes sort of flutterin' like…so I decided to see if the doc here could do anythin' to help him out, or…if not…you know, put the little guy out of his misery." Bill tilted his head back a little. "Well, I gotta go, Doc. Let me know if there's any change in the condition of the little guy, okay? You got my number."

"Sure thing, Bill. Take it easy."

The three men watched as Bill made his way down the hall. As the door at the end of the hall swung shut, Chris and Jesse followed Doc Parks down the hall to a door where the light was spilling across the hallway. The vet put the little bundle of injured animal down on a table and said, "I gotta take care of this little guy while we talk if you don't mind."

"There's no big hurry," Chris said. "We just want to see the tape you talked about on the phone."

"Sure thing, I've got it all set up and ready to go in my office. Think you can cue it up yourself?"

"I don't think it will be a problem." Chris smiled.

The vet's office was state-of-the art with gadgets all over the place. Chris had a hard time identifying many of them. It didn't take him long to spot the machine on the shelf over in the corner of the office. He went over and pushed the Play button and then joined Jesse on the nearby couch.

"The vet's proof is on video?" Jesse asked.

"Yeah, you see, Doc Parks told me that when he works nights, he usually turns on his security cameras just in case some whacked-out druggies decide to hit the hospital for drugs."

"I get it," Jesse said. "Those drug users, they'll shoot anything to get high these days."

"Yeah," Chris said. "They'll even use animal tranquilizers. Anyway, the doc said that he checked out the night's events on the video about a week after Belmont came in to see him. Only then did he realize that he'd captured what we're about to see on this tape. Lucky for you, lucky for us, lucky for our investigation—here is the absolute proof."

"Proof is good." Jesse smiled.

The monitor screen flashed and flickered and finally lit up with a picture. First, the screen displayed a date and time, then the picture was flashed on the screen, and they could see a video version of the very office they were in.

"Oh, too bad it's only black and white," Jesse groaned.

"Doesn't matter," Chris said. "It's the story that counts—and those jars of blue stuff.

Chris went on, "The camera is located up in the west corner of the office. Of course, being a surveillance camera, it won't pan or shift angles. Hollywood calls it a locked-down camera. However, Professor, the picture is pretty good for a miniature camera. Parks said he purchased it out of a catalog entitled Things You Never Knew Existed." They both laughed.

27

Favorite Part

"Things You Never Knew Existed...I believe that I use to have one of those catalogs...sometime ago. Used to be Johnson and Johnsons, I believe." Jesse smiled. "I think I may have ordered some of my UFO books from them. You never know where a scientist is going to find his information." Jesse laughed even harder. Then he added, "Don't tell any of my scientist friends I said that."

As they watched, the video was showing on the screen the ambulance driver and the veterinarian from an overhead angle, but a wiggling bundle of some kind of animal was also visible down on the examination table. Then, briefly, a tiny, black human hand emerged from the blanket.

Fredrick Belmont was saying, "Can you stop it, Doc...the bleedin' I mean? I don't know what the kid's on, but it can't be good, him bleeding from the navel like that."

"I'll do what I can." Dillard Parks busied himself over at a cabinet. Behind him, Jesse could see some fruit jars on a shelf.

Jesse waved his hand toward the monitor, but before he could ask the question, Chris said, "Yeah, that's the jars I told you about."

Fredrick was talking. "Can you catch that stuff in a bottle or something...in case it's some special plasma or...heck, it may be his blood? If I can make it to Atlanta, maybe they can figure out what it is."

"Mister," Parks said, "I don't know what you've gotten yourself into or what this stuff is oozing out of the baby's body, but the sooner I can send you on your way, the better. This has been a crazy night. First, I'm told to help out with the victims of a terrible crash out on 432, then I'm told there ain't no crash...then you come in here with a kid bleeding Tastee Freez...I'm just a veterinarian. I help animals. I'm not a miracle worker."

Belmont watched Parks as he finished filling up the two fruit jars with the blue fluid and put a wide bandage over the child's navel. Then he looked over at Fred.

"You know that crash you was talkin' about, I was there," Fred said.

"You were involved in the crash?" Then Parks started slowly shaking his head. "There wasn't any crash...at least that's what I was told by Sheriff Gayland. He said it was all a mistake...false alarm." Dillard came over to Fred and asked him to take off his jacket and shirt. "Let's have a look at that shoulder of yours."

"False alarm my aching back," Belmont went on. "I'd seen it myself. There was fire all over the place. A bus...a big fuel truck...and something else they wouldn't let me get close to. No, I wasn't in the crash, but that night, I drove an ambulance for the Volunteer Fire Department, tryin' to help 'em out a little."

Parks shifted his glasses on his nose and held his head at an angle, studying Belmont's shoulder wound. "This isn't as bad as I thought it would be. It's not bleeding at all." The young veterinarian looked up at him. "It's more like a burn than a bullet wound." Parks reached over on his desk and picked up a jar of salve.

"A gun didn't to it. It was more like a—"

"Here, hold this."

Fred held on to the cotton pad while Parks taped it in place. "Ouch. I hate a burn. It just throbs and throbs like the devil."

"I think this salve will start to ease the pain, just try not to bump it."

"Anyway." Fred cut his eyes over at the jar of salve. "The wreck was so bad the Polk county guys were asked to help out. They asked me to drive this kid to Atlanta for 'em..." He winced as the doctor painted the wound with the amber salve. "I might as well say it, Doc. these two flying saucers have been chasing me ever since I stopped to check out this kid. Somethin' weird is happening to him. I don't think the saucers want to attract the attention of the cops. When I tried to get away from them, one of the saucers shot some kind of death ray at me. That's how I got this burn."

"Can you pause it there?" Jesse got up from the couch and moved closer to the monitor.

Chris hit the Pause button on the controller. "Death ray… Professor," Chris said. "You know what this means, don't cha? This guy was the one drivin'—"

"The white van," Jesse finished "The one at the hotel?"

"Exactly. Whatever this death ray is, it's a powerful weapon, but I don't think…no, I don't like to say I don't think. It's the opposite of what I intend to say. I don't believe that the UFO we are tracking, the one that Tack is involved with, is the source of this death ray weapon, do you?"

"Are you saying the UFOs are different—two different kinds?

"That's exactly what I'm saying. The Quadrilla papers. Evelyn's girl Four. Her story spells it out quite clearly…at least it seems clear to me now."

"I think I know where you're going with this," Jesse said. "The aliens created Quadrilla. She was a biological experiment."

"One of many."

"Right…only this experiment went wrong…or right… depending on the side you're on. Quadrilla had a unique characteristic in her way of processing information. Creative thinking. Outside the box." Jesse returned over toward the couch.

"Outside-the-universe thinking."

"Of course you're right, Chris. Box is much too small a word for what Quadrilla was capable of. She created a ship capable of traveling across hundreds, maybe millions of light-years."

"And my favorite part," Chris said, "it may actually be capable penetrating the barrier of time."

"And capable, if we can make ourselves believe it, of changing its size—both large and small—total control of the molecular world." Jesse shook his head slowly and glanced back at the monitor. "I can't believe I'm saying this. I'd be laughed out of the scientific community."

"Well, Professor, aren't they already attempting to do that."

"You are right, at least Dr. Glasgow is doing his very best to do just that."

"Glasgow," Chris groaned.

Jesse scowled and turned around to face the monitor. "Is there any more of this tape I need to see, Chris?"

"I want to see it, but right now, I don't think we have the time. I'll see if Doc Parks will let us barrow this tape."

Jesse turned to the machine and removed the cassette. "Let's see what the good doctor says."

As they came back into the operating room, Chris could see that the animal that Bill Innis had brought to Doc Parks was actually a raccoon. And it was increasingly obvious that the animal was in no way dead. Extremely weakened, maybe, but not dead.

"Hey, Doc," Chris said, "can we borrow this tape for a few days? We'll bring it right back. It's a promise."

"No problem," Parks said. "Soon as Ms. Towers told me you were interested in the tape, I made you a copy." Dillard stepped over to his desk and took a cassette from the drawer. "I got the original here, so you can keep that one if you like." He filled out a sick-on label and handed the label to Chris. "You can stick that on if you're a mind to, but I thought you might like to keep it confidential, you know, and leave it unidentified so to speak."

"Thanks, Chris said. "Good idea. We can look at this later, Professor. I want to see if we can set up a meeting with Tack and see if he knows anything about the controller that Evelyn gave me. Also, Buford Golden called this morning at the motel. He was concerned that Agent Battey was in town. I'm guessing that Battey's snooping around to get something on Tack. If I can help it, I mean to do everything I can to get in his way. What do you think, Professor?"

"I think you're right, Captain." Jesse did a fair impression of Star Trek's Scotty as he followed Chris out of Dillard's office.

28

Houston Moon Rock

Tack dropped Cassy off at the motel and fought back his tears all the way back to the trailer park. He pulled up in front of the Nova Base, switched off the Hawk's engine, and just sat there for several minutes, thinking about Cisco lying there in the back of the pickup, not moving at all.

The world just wouldn't seem the same any more with Cisco gone. It was almost like losing a brother or, at the very least, a close friend. He looked out at the driveway in front of his car—all the trailers and campers sitting there under the towering pine trees, the sky peeking through those millions of pine needles, pure and blue, a clear blue sky. It was peaceful and quiet. There were probably millions of raccoons in the world.

"No telling how many of those little guys there are on the planet," Tack said, tears streaking down his face. Once the tears got started, there was no way to hold back the salty flood. He sobbed and tried to wipe back the sorrowful river with the sleeve of his leather jacket, but it did little good. He tried to clear his vision enough to get back to the peaceful scene outside the car—the tall pine trees, the blue sky, the Nova Base. Then he saw the newspaper stuffed between the metal stairs at the trailer door. "A newspaper," he said out loud. "I don't take that liberal rag. Who the heck left me a—"

In an instant, the image he'd seen from the sky flashed through his mind. Down below he could see the man Agent Slattery, motioning toward the Nova Base. He'd motioned at the front door. It was suddenly very obvious. Chris had placed the newspaper there.

He pushed open the door to the Hawk, walked over to the front steps, and picked up the newspaper. It wasn't in the headlines, but it was prominent on the front page. And Chris had outlined the article with a ballpoint pen. There was a color photograph of the moon rock that he had given to Kelly at the top of the article. It wasn't a very good photograph, but it was good enough to convince Tack that it was unmistakably his moon rock.

Tack's keen eye scanned the name of the article. It read, "Unknown Source Finds Rare Stone."

"No, it can't be." He read on.

> Government agent claims that a stone that he found in a small Georgia town is a rare moon rock. He can't account for its appearance in Hamlet's Mill but claims that he has been on the trail of a series of unexplained UFO sightings and that the trail led him to the stone's discovery.

Tack's eyes quickly scanned the entire story and then scanned it again. "I can't believe it. Who is this Agent Battey anyway?" He looked up at the window in the camper door. He was looking at it, but not seeing it. Instead, his mind was supplying what he was seeing—the moon rock around Kelly's neck and the statement he'd just read in the story that said, "The stone is in the possession of a young girl in the small town in Georgia. Continued A2, 'Mysterious stone.'"

The hand holding the newspaper dropped down to his side, and he staggered back a few steps. His face went white, and he shook his head as if to rid himself of the last few hours of his life. He finally stumbled into the camper and stood there looking at the model of a UFO he had on a shelf by the dome stairway.

"My god," he spoke out loud, "they've found out about the moon rock!" He slapped his opened palm against his forehead.

"Jeeze, they'll trace it back to me for sure. The government will come to investigate where she got it, and she'll tell them about me. Eventually they'll find out about the Spirit, and they'll take it away from me." The newspaper slipped from his hand and fell on the edge of the console.

He paced back and forth in the Nova Base like a caged animal for a few minutes; then he stopped in front of the console. He looked down at the newspaper there draped across the computer keyboard. "Yeah, they'll come and ask a bunch of dumb questions. They're bound to find out about the cave…and then the Spirit—dang it! I don't get it. Who's this agent guy anyway… Chris must know who it is…but he had to warn me. And how did this clown find out about Kelly? If the government comes to take the moon rock away from her, she'll kick up a fuss that will attract the entire FBI. She wouldn't part with that thing if her life depended on it. Heck, my life does depend on it. Shineola!" he said and reached down for the paper.

As he stood there staring at the floor with the newspaper dangling from his fingertips, a small piece of paper slipped out from between the pages of the paper and fluttered to the floor. He bent down to retrieve what appeared to be a business card and lifted close enough to read FREEZE Christopher M. Slattery Low… Remember. As he started to slip the card into his back pocket, he noticed that there was something written on the backside of it: "Tack, Chris. Kelly's stone. It may be a target of the investigation. Get it back at all costs—quick as you can!"

29

Golden Mansion

The Golden Mansion was not what most people would call a mansion. True, Buford Golden had, over his lifetime, acquired a great deal of money, but Allison, his wife, had spent most of it on things that wouldn't last. Her objective was well founded, but her education and taste were lacking. She wanted to take Buford's success with the airfield and the crop-dusting business and all that those two exercises attracted and use them to break into the aristocracy of the Hamlet community. She was a laughingstock—only behind her back. From her perspective, she was doing just fine. But, finally, as often happens in small communities, word got back to her at one of her Wednesday-night church gatherings, and she was profoundly hurt when she realized that she was being laughed at. In her unfathomable hurt, she decided that the best thing for her to do was to leave Buford. The two girls didn't need her anymore. Their relationship with their mother had been rather shaky from the start. The two girls were totally devoted to Buford, and this left Allison very jealous. She had little in common with the girls, just as was the case between her and Buford. Finally, she just packed up and left—went back to live with her mother.

The house that was called a mansion was really just a big house. It was an old house, and because Buford wouldn't see moving out, tearing it down, and building a new one, Allison had initially settled for a series of extensive remodeling phases. The result was a really weird-looking place. But it was on a good piece of land, and it had that old-fashioned State Fair, (the original version of the film) look about it.

Most people in the community thought the Golden place was ugly. It wasn't ugly as such, just very, very different. It didn't fit in with the county board's ideas of what they wanted their town to look like, so a huge confrontation with Allison at the church social had started to build, and this eventually added to Allison's determination to get out of Hamlet's Mill for good, leaving her family, her house, and her humility behind.

Tack liked the old house. It was extremely functional, and it was, what Tack called, neat. In particular, Tack liked the fact that there were skinny little halls that led to strange little rooms. And there was a room for everything. Some rooms made no sense at all. There was one particular room that Tack liked most of all. It was up at the very top of the house, on the third floor. The staircase went right up into the middle of the room, dividing it in half. That was the first feature that made no sense. With the stairs coming right up into the center of the room, this made it necessary, for the sake of safety, to put a handrail around the back and two sides of the rectangular hole in the floor. The open end of the railing was, of course, where the stairs ended at the floor level of the room.

The second wonderful feature that made Tack's mind go into high gear was the series of little rooms along each side of the main room. One might have decided at first that these rooms were closets, but that also made no sense. The top floor was rammed right up into the roof, like an attic apartment with two gabled windows down each side. The little rooms were not square. They had drastically slanted ceilings, which forced them into a wedge shape, suitable only for piling stuff on the floor. What purpose they had served in the past or in Allison's mind was a complete mystery to everyone.

Finally, there was absolutely no furniture in the room, or in the eight little rooms. But there was a doorway in the wall at the end of the room where the stairs ended. It led to a hallway that led to a bathroom across the hall, and to the left of the bathroom was the room that Kelly occupied. Strange as it may seem, but it didn't seem strange at all to Tack's way of thinking, the opposite end of the room had a six-foot circular window with concentric circles of different colors of glass for each segment of the crystalline bull's eye. It was red in the center, then orange, then yellow, then green, and finally dark blue. When the sun hit that window in the afternoon, just before sundown, it turned the white room into a bizarre tableau of spectral light. But since there was seldom anyone on that floor, Kelly usually zipped through it with scarce notice, the entertaining quality of the effect was hardly ever noticed.

Tack had seen it once, before Judy had gone off to college, when he was waiting for her to get dressed for a date. Kelly had tried to lure him into her bedroom to examine her collection of rubber band–powered flying models she and her dad had constructed during her tomboy childhood. When he balked at the possibility of being caught by Judy in Kelly's bedroom, she had talked him, instead, into seeing the 'weird room,' as she called it.

There was no chance he'd see that room on this visit, because of three limiting factors. It was already well after sundown, he was in a big hurry to find the moon rock and make his escape, and finally, he was only about an inch tall, a really small man in the storms of time.

30

Twenty-Twenty

Before flying the Spirit to the Golden residence, Tack had made a quick call to Tammy at the hospital, and Tammy had confirmed his suspicions that they had finally let Kelly go home. Kelly's eye was completely healed, and no infection had set in. Her vision had tested out 20-20, and happily, she had returned to her own warm, little bedroom at home, with the window facing out the west side of the house toward the 150-year-old oak tree in her yard.

This old tree had a special attraction to Tack. It still had a limb conveniently located so as to allow Kelly to escape the house clandestinely if she so chose. And there were still the remnants of the old tree house that Buford had built the girls back when they were very young and things were happier and simpler. Now the tree served Kelly well when things weren't going too well between her and Buford, which seemed to be happening with increasing frequency lately.

Tack knew that Kelly was one of those fresh-air freaks that loved sleeping with the window about a third of the way open, even in the wintertime. He had decided to reduce the Spirit down to Frisbee size and attempt to fly into the open window of her bedroom when the opportune moment arrived.

He was remembering a time back when he and Kelly and Judy were little kids and played together in the tree house, well up into its larger branches of the old oak tree. But now, as he flew the Spirit up to the level of her window, all that remained of the house were the decaying remnants of a platform. It was on this platform that he carefully landed the Spirit. On the remnants of what he believed to be the most substantial piece of that platform, Tack watched and waited outside Kelly's window for her to go to bed.

He was counting on the possibility that Kelly hadn't already gone to bed. As he sat there waiting for the light to come on in Kelly's bedroom, his mind couldn't help but revisit a time past when he and Kelly were little Kids together.

One hot summer afternoon, when the cicadas were going nuts all around the countryside, the two little kids, barely aware of the fact that they were boy and girl, had played up in Kelly's new tree house, while Judy practiced her piano lesions up in her room on the opposite side of the house.

Tack had pretended to be a World War II pilot, using his portion of the little tree house as an old B-17 on a mission over Germany during World War II. Kelly wasn't at all happy with his role, not that she too didn't like airplanes, but as she was approaching that time in a little girl's life when she began to dream of white knights and castles, she, on that particular afternoon, wanted instead for the little tree house to be a tower in her father's castle.

High up in that tower, she, as a golden-haired princess, had been imprisoned by her evil father who was punishing her for attempting to escape and run away with her knight in shining armor. She'd gotten the idea from something Judy had said about Tack, and Kelly had decided to steal Judy's idea to replace her own, which was to be an airline stewardess who was really a secret agent. Her commandeering of the medieval plot had led to an obvious rivalry between the two sisters that had finally taken on the form of the current situation.

Now Kelly thought about not only about stealing the princess idea, but stealing her sister's boyfriend as well.

Eventually, back then, there had been an argument, and Tack had been banished from the Golden's Mansion, and thus Kelly's castle for the rest of that summer. Judy had eventually won control over Tack because she was the oldest of the three, and she'd used her superior age advantage to make Tack feel it was his duty to ignore her younger sister. After all, Kelly was only six. Kelly was just a little kid. Judy was eight, and Tack, being exactly between the two girls at seven, was pretty much trapped by Kelly's older sister's superior position.

This had been the situation ever since; at least it was until Judy had gone off to college. This left Tack working at Gold Field and Kelly finishing up her senior year in high school. Judy didn't know it, but she was in serious trouble. Trouble, that is, if she didn't, as often happens, get involved with some football star at college and forget all about Tack.

31

Revisit

As Tack reached the point in his mental revisit to times gone by, the memory left him in another time, mixed up and seeking escape in the lonely hangars of Gold Field. Finally, he saw the light come on in Kelly's room. He craned his neck, looking out of the forward window of the Spirit, and soon he was focusing his eyes on the lovely little Kelly dancing around in the room, turning round and round in her nightly going-to-bed ritual. It was a scene right out of the classic old State Fair movie.

Stripped down to her undies, Kelly swooped across the room to her dresser, and Tack could see her bend down to the middle drawer and pull out a long white nightgown that she held up to her body. She continued to dance with the nightgown as if it were her escort to the prom. She suddenly slipped the gown over her head and worked it down over her shoulders and upper body. He could see her slip one strap of her bra off her shoulder and then pull her whole arm inside her gown and then, in like manner, she freed the other arm. He was fascinated watching her perform this magic trick. He guessed that she did this performance of female modesty rather than close the window and pull the curtains closed. Fresh-air meant everything to Kelly, even in the cold dead of night in the early springtime.

And maybe she removed her bra in this discreet way just in case there was a one-inch-tall little, bitty man out there on a limb, so to speak, that might be watching her.

As Kelly prepared for bed in this manner, Tack was slightly embarrassed watching her like some cheap Peeping Tom. But a stronger emotion than his embarrassment was also at work in his mind. The movements she was making in her white gown as she danced around preparing to jump into her bed enraptured him. What Tack was feeling, of course, were the first true pangs that precede a young man falling totally, irreversibly, in love.

He would never have admitted it to anyone, least of all himself, but falling in love with the perky little Kelly was exactly what was happening. Too bad he didn't have time to savor the moment and let the realization sink in. Besides, she was out to make his life miserable, he knew that, and he also knew that she scared him to death. There was something spooky about the beautiful Kelly.

As he watched her climbing up into her bed, he was trying to figure it out, but he never quite realized that it was how drop-dead beautiful she was becoming and how her developing beauty combined with her devilish attitude about everything was going to make her a force greater than anything with which man had ever had to contend.

After Kelly was truly, firmly in the bed, Tack waited, hoping that she would drop off to sleep soon so he could search her room for his moon rock. Finally, after fifteen or so minutes, he realized that she hadn't moved, so he decided to take a chance and approach Kelly's room.

The silvery disk floated like a dandelion seed through the half-open window as he flew the Spirit into her room. The Spirit hovered over her bed just long enough to convince Tack that she was definitely asleep. Once, she jerked her body, obviously disturbed by some flashing dream of falling perhaps, and he started wondering what he would do if she awoke now and saw this strange Frisbee thing hovering over her face. But she was just dreaming, and her eyes never opened, so he decided to start his search over on her dresser.

He landed the saucer in the only clear space left among all her perfume bottles, powder boxes, and porcelain figurines. Then he lowered the ramp, and a tiny, little Tack Moultrie descended to the highly varnished surface. The air was strong with the smell of perfumed powder. It took him a while to get used to the size of the dust particles at his current scale. There were hairs and dust motes all over Kelly's dresser. In particular, there were powder particles the size of marbles. As he wandered around her perfume bottles and her jewelry box, he found a butterfly pin made of colorful bird feathers. He'd seen her wear that pin on Sunday mornings on the way to Sunday school. It looked very much like a real butterfly had landed in her golden hair, and he'd remarked how clever the craftsmen had made the wings of different-colored feathers. He told her that he was sure that the thing could actually fly if properly balanced. There were other little boxes and different colors of lipstick, some in plastic tubes and others in golden cylinders taller than he was. And he could smell it. It was thick and heavy. When he'd kissed her, he could smell her lipstick, and it was a delicate, feminine kind of smell. Now, it was heavy and overpowering. It must be the size of the molecules, he thought.

At his minuscule size, the exploration soon got the better of him, and he had to take a break. He sat down on a black plastic button that had been torn from her sweater or some other garment. He sat there resting, looking around at his footprints down in the powder. "No sign of my moon rock up here," he said. "Where the heck would she put the thing?" he asked aloud in his, now-tiny, little voice.

Then he saw something over on the other end of the dresser. He glanced over at Kelly in her bed and confirmed that she was still asleep. Then he got up and headed over to the honey-heart bear ring he had given Kelly back when he was seven years old.

As he circled the huge gold-plated ring, he muttered out loud, "I'll be zonked, she still has that ring I gave her on her birthday."

Suddenly there was a loud sound at the window, and he turned to check it out. He couldn't see what had caused the sound and continued studying the ring. "She told me she lost this ring, back when we had that fight. She told me to never come back. Boy, that really hurt my feelings back then. It's weird how people say things that they don't really mean just to make your heart hurt." He stepped over to the inside of the ring and walked around.

"My, my, this thing looks big. I wonder if I'm staying the same size…or shrinking." He put his hands on his hips and surveyed the underside of the setting. "Hey, that looks like a little secret chamber…or…" He looked around and saw a straight pin near by. After climbing back over the ring and retrieving the pin, he came back and began prying open the tightly snapped lid to the secret chamber. Finally, with a pop, the chamber lid flipped open, and a small, tightly folded piece of paper popped out onto the table. There was something else that caught his eye. He stepped up closer to the object. It was a tiny little picture of…him. Kelly had obviously cut it out of some snapshot and placed it inside the bear's heart.

He picked up the photo and turned it this way and that trying to remember when the picture had been made but couldn't place the event. He couldn't tell what he was wearing at the time because too much of the photo had been removed. He laid the photograph back down on the dresser and walked over to the folded paper. It moved slightly and caused him to jump back a step. Being released from the tight confines of the bear's heart, the paper was attempting to return to its original shape. No one would have noticed it at true scale, but at only and inch high, to Tack, it was like the paper was coming alive. "A living message," he whispered, stepping over and pulling the paper folds back so he could read what was written there.

Then his heart throbbed painfully as he realized that somehow, Kelly had written in tiny little letters, "I love you, Tack."

No one had ever really told him they loved him before. At least no one outside of relatives and other older people.

No girl had ever told him she loved him, not even Judy. Judy often said things like, "I'm very fond of you, Tack," or "You're my favorite boyfriend," but never "I love you."

"Maybe there's more to Kelly than I've ever suspected. I just thought she's been teasing me."

Tack looked around for something to write with and realized he was wearing the shirt he always carried his ballpoint pen in. Quickly he printed back right beneath Kelly's note, "I love you back, Kelly." Of course this lettering would be way too small for Kelly to ever be able to read without the use of a microscope, but at Tack's current scale and thinking, that really didn't really matter.

32

Bam! Boom!

Of course Kelly would only be able to read Tack's note using a high-powered magnifying glass, or at best something more powerful. Therefore, Tack's reply would most likely remain a secret forever. He knew that anything he'd written at his scale would be way too tiny for her to ever read, but in writing it, he felt an overwhelming feeling of warmth fill his soul, and he liked it. A life together, kids, school, vacations at the beech, Christmas around the tree—bam! boom!

"What in thunder is that?" he gasped, spinning back to face the window.

It was a giant blue jay. It had probably flown into the room and crashed into the edge of the windowsill. Still fluttering wildly, the frantic bird flew across the room directly toward the dresser mirror and banged into it before it realized Kelly's room wasn't a cave.

Bam! The blue jay fell briefly to the floor and lay there. Tack headed over to the edge of the dresser and was suddenly overwhelmed by the vertigo as the floor below came into view. Then his eyes focused on the blue jay sitting on the floor, blinking its eyes, bewildered at hitting the mirror. To the jay, Kelly's dresser mirror was probably some invisible force field it couldn't understand.

"Holy Alfred Hitchcock!" Tack muttered. The bird heard him and focused its dazed eyes on the pink tiny, little man that was looking down at him from the dresser. Then, just as suddenly the jay took flight—up off of the floor, directly toward Tack's naked position.

Tack took off running back to the Spirit for cover, but it was a long, long way off.

"I don't…think…I'm… going…to…make…it," he gasped.

The jay landed on the dresser and jerked its head first in one direction and then in the other. It finally spotted Tack standing still in the middle of an open space on the dresser. Tack thought that if he didn't move, he'd be safe, but he had just completed a very long run and was breathing hard. His chest was heaving in and out, and he could feel his heart trying to jump out of his chest. Tack didn't act stupid like they do in the movies and wait to see what the giant bird might have in mind. Inspired by the menacing look that the jay had in its dark, black basketball-sized eye, he suddenly took off, running as fast as he could.

The jay spotted him running and hopped after him. Of course, each hop the blue jay made was like the distance of a whole football field compared to Tack's running step. Soon Tack was going to be just so much a sunflower seed to the jay—if he didn't get his tail in gear and get back into his ship.

As he huffed and puffed, Tack could see up ahead, the butterfly pin. It was the only thing nearby, so he dashed for it and took refuge under its feathered wings. "Maybe it won't see me," he breathed. Then his eyes flew open. "Jays eat butterflies." But it was too late to escape. His only recourse was to lie as still as possible and pray.

From underneath the feathery wing, Tack could see the huge dinosaur-like feet of the huge bird as it hopped closer and closer to the butterfly pin. What Tack couldn't see from his perspective was the jay cocking its head to eye the butterfly menacingly. The giant bird decided to take a test peck at the tasty insect.

BAM! CLICK! CRUNCH! WHAM! The jay's beak hammered away at the butterfly. Lucky for Tack, the collision with the mirror had hammered the jay's brain just enough that its usually deadly aim was off ever so slightly, and he missed the butterfly by about the length that Tack was high, an inch, maybe two. Tack got an idea that promised possible escape and survival. He wasted no time and grabbed at the metal shaft of the butterfly pin. It moved.

"Good, I can lift the thing," Tack grunted and picked up the butterfly on his shoulders and ran toward the edge of the dresser.

The jay couldn't help but notice the sudden life that had taken over the butterfly's body, and it pounced after it. This delicious prize was not going to get away, no matter how much the world was still spinning after the collision with the invisible force field. The jay shook its head and pounced again, this time pinning one of the butterfly wings under the middle claw of its foot.

The sudden stop jerked Tack off his feet, and he found himself sliding under the shaft of the pin like he was doing a radical limbo rock. However, he managed to hang on to the metal shaft, and when the jay had to hop back a little to allow his beak to hammer the now-dead insect, Tack saw his chance and jerked the butterfly toward the edge of the dresser and off and over, he found himself dangling, seemingly, miles above Kelly Golden's bedroom floor.

But he was flying. "Wonder of wonders, this thing actually does fly!" he exclaimed. He looked and smiled around at the room as it flew by. He found that he could even steer the makeshift hang glider, if he shifted his weight just so. "Well, butter my bread and sleep in it, I'm actually flying," he said, his voice betraying his giddiness.

Tack hung on for dear life as the butterfly got closer, and closer to the floor. Now, his smile was slowly fading as he saw the varnished boards flying by at a speed that made him dizzy. "This is going to hurt—I just know it," he cried. "I'm going to be roadkill."

He braced himself for the landing, and the butterfly ran smack into one of Kelly's slippers, which just happened to be covered in deep white heavenly fur.

WHOOFF! Tack was jerked free of the butterfly pin and bounced down the side of the slipper to the floor. He sat there, his legs spread wide for a few seconds, and then his senses began to slowly come back to him. "I'm still alive!" he gasped. "I'm still—"

As his eyes focused, he realized he was looking back up at the dresser—miles up to the top of the dresser, miles up to the Spirit, and his only way back to a safe natural size and his not-so-safe, not-so-natural life.

33

Stupid Bird

"Daddy, is that you?" boomed Kelly's giant voice. Tack jerked his head around and looked up at the giant Kelly towering above him. She was looking across the room in the direction of the dresser.

"Thank God, she doesn't see me," Tack whispered.

Then the blue jay darted right at her head, and Kelly ducked. "Oooooooo," she screamed out as the jay smashed into the wall beside her bed. The desperate bird beat at the wall frantically with it wings in an attempt to escape Kelly's waving arms. Tiny blue feathers were flying all around her head as she grabbed up her pillow and began swinging at the jay, angrily crying out, "Shooo! Get away! Get out you silly, stupid bird!"

Tack watched on helplessly as he searched for a way to climb up to the lamp table beside her bed. It was no good. It was miles and miles too high.

He decided that he wanted her to see him after all and yelled as loud as he could, "Hey, Kelly, down here." His tiny, little voice was lost in the noises that Kelly and the jay were making in their struggle, and of course, she couldn't hear him. The blue jay was fighting back at the pillow, pecking and clawing at Kelly as if she were attacking the furious bird's nest full of precious bird eggs.

Anything Tack could think of to gain Kelly's attention would take hours and more strength to climb than a little man his size would ever be able to muster.

Kelly was still dodging the blue jay's attack. The jay had decided that Kelly was the cause of all its trouble that night and was fighting back at her. The bird was dead set on ripping her eyes out. She jumped out of the bed and continued swinging her pillow at the bird, driving it toward the still-opened window. After several tries, she managed to corral the jay back to and out of the window. With her other hand, she slammed the window shut and stood there attempting to catch her breath. Her gown was ripped in a couple of places, but Tack could see that the bird hadn't been successful in inflicting any permanent damage to his girlfriend's lovely body.

Kelly turned away from the window and headed back to the bed. Then she stopped and turned, looking at herself in the dresser mirror. She was not happy with the way she looked and made a face at her reflection. "Wow, what a mess." When she walked closer to the mirror, she noticed the tiny flying saucer on the dresser next to the jewelry box and stopped, studying it with intensity.

"What in the...blue-eyed world...," she said, reaching down and picking up the saucer. "Some kind of toy UFO?" She quickly looked around the room and then back to the small spaceship. She was surprised at the model saucer's weight. She hefted it a couple of times and then shifted it back and forth from one hand to the other. She raised it up to see the underside of it and, in so doing, momentarily lost her grip, and the Spirit was in danger of falling to the floor. Tack's heart stopped, and he squeezed his eyes shut, waiting for the sound of a crash that would forever leave him the size of a cockroach. However, Kelly managed to catch the saucer before it fell totally from her grasp. After all, she had been voted the best baton twirler in her majorette training class and had the dexterity to go with the title.

As she continued to examine the saucer, she mumbled to herself, "I wonder how this thing got in here."

Tack took a few steps away from the fuzzy slipper and waved his hands in an attempt to get Kelly's attention. Of course she couldn't hear him much less notice him down there on her bedroom floor. However, if he had, in fact, been a nasty old roach, she would have not only noticed him, but she would have also screamed in disgust and stepped over to eradicate his existence.

Suddenly Kelly's eyes grew wide, and she frowned in disgust. "Someone's been in my room. I hate that. I'm going to have to kill Dad!" She glanced at the door to her room. "Maybe I'll just start locking my door."

"Kelly! Kelly!" Tack shouted, continuing to wave his hands and moving closer in her direction.

She still could not hear him, and he was growing more impatient and desperate in his attempts to get her to notice him down on the floor. He looked back and forth from the bed and back to Kelly. Then he scanned the room, looking in vain for some way to get to eye level with her so she could see him.

Kelly was still holding the Spirit in her left hand as she walked over to her door and pushed it open. She stepped into the hall and looked in both directions. Then she heard a meow down at her feet and looked down.

"Theo!" she said and reached down to pick up a black-and-white cat. She balanced the Spirit and the cat, not an easy task, as she came back into her room. Tack gulped and swallowed in quick time, hoping against hope that the Spirit would not be damaged beyond repair before he could get back to it and return to his normal size.

"Oh no!" he gasped. "I forgot that Kelly has a cat!"

He was now desperate to find a way to get Kelly's attention now that he was not only facing being stuck at a ridiculously small scale, but also to be hunted down by an elephant-sized monster cat that didn't like him to begin with, "Oh God! I've got to get out of here. I wish I'd never seen that cursed moon rock."

Tack searched in vain for some way to climb out of the cat's reach "Holy katz!" He gasped again as Kelly came back to the dresser and Theo cast its yellow eyes in his direction. He could swear that he saw the cat's mouth break into a grin and lick its fur-lined lips. He tried not to notice the glint of light that bounced off Theo's sharp teeth.

34

Butterfly

Kelly set the Spirit back down in the center of the dresser and walked over toward her bed. There was nowhere for Tack to hide as the monstrously tall female headed directly toward where Tack stood on the hardwood floor. The brightly painted toenails of his gigantic girlfriend flashed red in the light of the room as Tack realized in desperation that she was in all likelihood going to squash him like a bug with her beautiful naked foot.

"Sweet Jesus!" he prayed. He was suddenly gazing up as the flesh of her beautifully tanned legs were briefly swept by her white gown. But there was no time to think about tan legs or anything beautiful because Kelly's dainty little foot, now a huge block of flesh the size of a building, was about to come down directly over him, and he was forced to dive to the floor in a tumbling role that barely saved him from becoming a grease spot on the bottom of Kelly Golden's foot.

As Kelly sat down on her bed and raised the cat up in front of her, Tack rubbed his shoulder, moved to a sitting position, and managed a "whew!" As she held Theo under its forelegs and tried to get the cat's attention, Theo had other things going through its little animal mind—things that tasted good, at least they would taste good to a cat. The furry black-and-white animal was turning its head this way and that, its keen eyesight busily looking for that tiny tasty morsel it had spied moments ago down on the floor. The cat's twitching action said, "Where did that yummy little thing go?"

Theo used his hind legs to scratch back at Kelly, forcing her to momentarily lose her grasp on the struggling fur ball and the cat bounded to the floor, searching this way and that for the tiny morsel called Tack Moultrie.

Tack also was looking this way and that, searching desperately for some kind of cover—any kind of cover. All that he could find that was close enough to do him any good was the butterfly pin.

"It won't save me, but maybe Theo doesn't like feathers and will spit me out." He looked up to heaven. "Oh God, please let him spit me out."

Then Tack dove under the cover of one of the feathery butterfly wings.

Unfortunately, the movement on the floor caught the cat's eye, and Theo pounced over onto the butterfly, trapping the pen and Tack under one of its menacing claws.

The blow and the pressure knocked the wind from Tack's lungs, and he started preparing himself for the pain of being cut to pieces by Theo's sharp fangs. Maybe it will be quick, he thought. God, please let it be quick.

Visions of Bruce the shark in Spielberg's movie Jaws chomping away at the stern of the Orca and the Orca's captain filled his mind as he got a good whiff of Theo's cat breath.

"Theo!" Kelly cried out. "No!"

Underneath the butterfly wing, Tack saw the light grow dark, and he prepared himself for the worst. Then, at the last instant, in a flash, he realized what Theo had done to draw Kelly's attention to him.

Kelly was trying to save the butterfly pin from Theo's drooling mouth and gnashing teeth.

Glancing underneath the butterfly's feather wings, he could see the gleaming shaft of the long steel needle that pinned the butterfly to the hair ribbon or the clothing of the wearer, and he struggled to crawl toward it. Overcoming the pressure of the claw that held him fast was impossible at first, but as Kelly lifted Theo out of the way, Tack broke free long enough to scramble over to the shaft and latched on to it just in time.

In mere seconds, he found himself dangling in midair, high, very high, above the bedroom floor, hanging on to the metal shaft for dear life.

In the heat of the moment, Tack wasn't able to adequately encircle the steel shaft with his fingers, and he was dangerously close to losing his grip. He looked down and then wished he hadn't. "This—is nuts!" he gasped and strained the muscles in his hands to, in some way, maintain his grip. Then he just couldn't hang on one second longer, and he felt the smooth steel shaft slip from his fingers. "Ooooohhhhhh—"

The sudden stop at the end of the fall to his eventual death came much quicker than he'd expected. When he opened his eyes, he was sitting atop a large pink plastic box. And, to his relief, he found that the plastic box was sitting on the bedside lamp table, just inches from Kelly's pillow on her bed.

For the first time since he'd come into her room, Tack could plainly see his new girlfriend sitting there on her bed attempting to straighten out the butterfly's wings that Theo had mussed up.

"Oh, Theo, you almost ruined my pin." She looked down at the cat that was anxiously searching for the tiny, little man she could still smell but no longer see. "Bad cat. Bad cat. This was a present from Red. The big lug said I reminded him of a butterfly...always flitting around from flower to flower." She chuckled. "Oh, well," she said, placing the butterfly over next to the plastic box that Tack was sitting on.

Tack's heart jumped when he thought that maybe she would finally see him, but his anticipation was short-lived. Kelly didn't look where she was placing the pen and only climbed back into bed, rolled over with her back to him, and closed her eyes. He watched as she lay motionless—motionless except for the graceful movement of her breathing; her golden hair spilled out over her pillow like a heavenly carpet. He could see the translucency of her right ear as her shoulders rose and fell with each breath.

Then, suddenly the light went off in the lamp on her table, and Tack found himself cold and alone on the pink box, plunged hopelessly into the darkness.

He sighed, shrugged his shoulders, and looked around at the objects surrounding him on the table as his eyes slowly adjusted to the dark. A tiny, little bit of moonlight was spilling through the window into the room, and the red light of the LED numerals on Kelly's bedside clock spilled across the table pointing the way to the back of her head.

Tack spent the better part of thirty minutes waiting and wondering what to do. Finally he climbed down from the pink box and stood back trying to make out the giant letters that spelled out "BARBIE'S TREASURE" on the side of the plastic box. He walked around the table examining the various items that Kelly kept next to her bed. There was a tiny white Bible with a white-and-gold ribbon page marker, which, of course, to Tack's current scale was anything but tiny.

Next, there was a sewing kit that also, from Kelly's perspective, would have been tiny. To Tack, the kit was the size of a conference table. The thimble could have served a man of Tack's size as a bathtub.

As he worked his way between the Bible and the sewing kit, he tripped over the white-and-gold ribbon and fell against the base of the table lamp, and suddenly Tack was flooded once again in brilliant light.

"Wow!" he gasped, looking down at where his hand had touched the lamp. "Touch sensitive!" His eye was drawn away from the lamp by a sound from the bed. When he looked up, he could see that Kelly was now facing him, her long eyelashes brushing her pink cheeks ever so lightly, her beauty flooding over him like a warm, fuzzy blanket. The smell that came from her was equally overpowering, and he began to wonder if her immense size or his tremendous reduction in size had multiplied the love factor even as it had the fear factor.

As he studied her pretty face, each pour, each tiny hair brought on a new sense of worldly reality that was tearing his mind away from his current, dangerous predicament. The feeling he was experiencing reminded him of something, but he couldn't quite place it—something about being small, extremely small.

Then his memory banks rewarded his mental search with the recollection he was seeking. It was a book entitled The Incredible Shrinking Man. The book was written by Richard Matheson. Tack had seen the movie on the science fiction channel years ago and then decided to look for the book in a used bookstore when he was over in Cedar Town one summer with his stepdad. What he found was an old beat-up paperback with no cover, but all the pages were intact. There was a chapter in the book that had really impressed Tack, and it was coming back to him, now, with renewed importance.

Matheson's tiny, little man too had been only an inch tall, and he was still shrinking at the rate of one seventh of an inch per day. The story had begun at the one-inch mark, and the story of how he had gotten to that scale was revealed in a series of flashbacks. But the part that now occupied Tack's mind was the fact that the little man had believed that he only had seven days to live because he was going to lose a seventh of his size every day from that point on. At the end of the seventh day, it would all be over, because there wouldn't be enough of him left to shrink any further. However, in the end, after the seventh day had ended, he was still alive. At that realization, the little man was reminded that when you reduce something by only a fraction, you never end up with absolutely nothing. A fraction of something is still something. That meant that he would never truly be dead from the reduction factor alone. His existence depended on the environment within which he would find himself.

Now, Tack was looking at a person, someone he loved more than his own life, a wonderful girl who had become a landscape—a whole planet. The idea of a living, breathing human being of that scale was beyond imagining. He could only think of himself as a tiny, tiny pitiful little man that could only be thought of as some kind of uniquely weird novelty—a walking freak show that would handily fit within the average matchbox.

35

Just a Dream

As the one-inch-tall Tack Moultrie stood there on the bedside table, studying the giant girl sleeping only inches away from him, he could see what is known as the REM of her eyes under her eyelids. This random eye movement (REM) is believed to indicate that a person is dreaming, their eyes following the action of the dream and thus creating the apparent eye movement.

Tack wondered what Kelly might be dreaming. Then he realized how dreamlike...or better still, how nightmare like his current reality was: a mere-inch-tall little man looking at a giant girl. He'd recently taken this giant to a dance and then sought to reward her with a moon rock he'd found on the moon. He'd done all this in a stolen flying saucer that he had every reason to believe could, at least sometimes, be piloted by a raccoon.

"Dreams make more sense than my reality," he said as a really wild idea began to form in his mind.

He was close enough now that maybe, just maybe Kelly could hear him if he yelled loud enough. The little LED clock was one inch high, maybe two inches long by one inch thick. And it was battery powered, so there was no cord to fool with. He tried to give the clock a shove and found that is was not nearly as heavy as it looked. Either that, or he was growing stronger. He pushed the clock carefully to the very edge of the table, right in front of Kelly's nose, and climbed up on top of it.

"Kelly," he yelled at her face. "Kelly, it's me, TACK! WAKE UP! I need you."

It took a couple more times, but Kelly's eye bulges shifted behind one corner of her eye over to the other corner.

"Kelly! Kelly! HELP! WAKE UP! HELP!" his tiny voice shouted.

Kelly's eyes shifted one more time, and then they opened. It took several seconds for her eyes to focus on the small clock in front of her.

"Kelly, it's me, TACK! Can you see me?"

Kelly still couldn't focus on Tack's tiny body. She rose up a little and moved her face closer to the clock.

Tack waved his arms. "Kelly, it's me. Can you see me? I'm in your dream."

"T-Tack? Is that really you? What happened…to you? I don't…how did you get in my dream?"

"That's right, Kelly, I'm in your dream, and I need your help to get out. I'm trapped in your dream, and I can't stay here. I need you to help me—please. It's a dream—just a dream…a bad dream. I've got to get out of here. But I need your help."

Kelly rose up on her hands and knees and looked down at the tiny, little man standing there on her digital clock. She blinked her eyes. "How did you get so…so small?" Her confusion made her big eyes even wider. She looked like a little girl that had seen Santa on Christmas morning drinking a beer, and belching.

"It's just a dream, Kel. But I need your help. I need you to put me on your dresser"—he pointed across the room—"over there. Can you do that?"

"On my dresser?" Her eyes seemed to grow even bigger. They were bright and quite beautiful. She looked sweet and innocent, confused and frightened. Tack had never seen her like that before, and he liked it.

"Yeah, over there." He pointed again. "My spaceship is over there. Can you take me to my spaceship so I can escape your dream? If I stay here, I'll die."

"Die…oh no—die?" She looked across the room and then lowered her face down close to Tack on the digital clock and looked at him, tilting her head like a tiny puppy that is trying to figure out what a bug is. Her eyes at that scale were scary. In her quite large pupils, Tack could see the reflection of his tiny body standing on top of the digital clock. "Spaceship?"

"Yeah, that little flying saucer over there. That's my spaceship. I need it so I can return to my actual size."

When Kelly heard the words flying saucer, he saw a tiny glimpse of realization sweep over her face. She had been going along with the "dream" idea so far, but he was certain that all of a sudden she was beginning to doubt that all this could possibly be a dream.

Kelly shook her head. "I don't…I was just holding that space… I wondered…where it came from. It didn't seem like a dream…"

"It's just a dream, Kelly, the blue jay flew into your room a minute ago—it was a dream. You've never seen a blue jay at night, have you? Birds like that don't fly at midnight."

Kelly shook her head again. "I don't know…this dream seems so real. I'm…"

Tack began to worry even more that she was on to him. She was beginning to be more and more like the old Kelly. "It's…it's okay, Kel. Just help me get back to my spaceship, and I'll fly away. When you wake up, you'll remember this really weird dream… where I was this tiny little Tack Moultrie. It has to be a dream, Kel. I'm not really this small. How could I be? It's impossible, don't you see? You'll remember this dream and you'll tell me all about it tomorrow—really."

"Okay," she said and held her hand down to let him step into it. "How's this? Can I just use my hand?"

"This is great," he said and stepped off the clock into her hand. "Be careful. If you drop me, you'll wake up, and I'll be stuck inside your dream forever. That will be just awful, don't you see?"

She cocked her head again and said, almost menacingly, "Hey, if this is really just a dream, I could smash you in my hand, and it wouldn't even hurt, right?"

Tack swallowed really hard and went into a coughing fit. When he recovered, he quickly said, "Please don't do that, Kelly, just take me to the dresser—as fast as you can. If you wake up before I get back to my spaceship, I'll…be stuck in this dream forever…almost as bad as if you dropped me, you see, and that wouldn't be good."

Kelly got up off the bed and walked with dainty, little steps across her room and lowered Tack down to the surface of the dresser. Tack slipped down from the palm of her hand and stood proudly back within reach of the Spirit. He arched his back and looked up at Kelly.

"Thanks, Kel. You did that just great. Now, you hurry back to bed, and you'll dream that I get into my spaceship and fly out of the—oh, yes, you'll have to open the window for me so I can fly out of your dream. Okay?"

He could see that look again. "Window…" She was getting really suspicious now, and there was no time to lose. He was saved as Kelly was struck by a really big yawn. She seemed to be falling for his scheme again. After all, it was easier for her to believe that she was dreaming what had been going on for the past few minutes than to believe that her boyfriend had a spaceship and was only one inch tall. She walked in little dreamlike short, baby steps over to the window and raised it up. Then she yawned again, this time, even bigger than before and looked back over at Tack.

He was waving back at her from the dresser. She headed back to her bed, climbed in, curled up, and pulled the covers over her young body and lay there watching her tiny boyfriend. Tack scrambled back over to his spaceship. He waved back at her one more time, turned, and then ascended the ramp, bounding out of sight. She waved at the little saucer as it rose slowly from the dresser's surface and flew quietly across the room and out of the window. Her eyes drowsily fluttered shut, and she returned to her peaceful slumber as a tiny light disappeared into the night sky.

Then Kelly's eyes flew open, and she sat up in her bed with a start. "Wait a minute…That window was open when I went to bed." She got up and went back to the window.

She searched the night sky. The saucer was gone.

"If this was all just a dream, then why did I close the window?" She puzzled about it for a few seconds, pushing her hand up to twist a strand of her hair as she looked back at the bed and then at the dresser. "If the blue jay was just a dream…then why did I close the window…?"

Finally she shook her head, left her room, and went down stairs to get herself a drink of water.

As her naked feet found each step on the way down to the kitchen, she muttered, "It couldn't have been a dream…but it couldn't have been real either." Her mind fought with the information twisting around and overlapping in a confusion of tangled thoughts. What force, what trick of fate, what mysterious power could ever cause her boyfriend to shrink down to one inch tall? What indeed?

36

Spunky

The clear night sky was comforting as Tack piloted the Spirit in a mad dash to get back to the cave hangar. It took a while to get his act together but finally managed to land the Spirit in the safety of the sinkhole hideaway and gather up his laptop and the newspaper Chris had left him. One final scan of the surroundings and he would be on his way to back to Nova Base.

He wasn't quite sure why he did that but blamed it on the fact that it didn't quite feel the same without Cisco running around checking out every rock and insect carcass he could find. Using the Jacob's chair hoist to get up to the surface was maddeningly slow, so when he finally made it back to his car, he was in a big hurry to get back to the Nova Base. He needed to think. He needed a plan, and he didn't have one.

When he got back to the Nova Base camper, he whistled his door opening code, dashed through the door, and headed for the staircase to the domed upper room. Trying to catch his breath after the climb, Tack stood there for a moment, staring out at all the pine trees that filled the trailer park. As his mind twisted and turned, searching for an idea—any idea—he realized he was still holding the newspaper and quickly looked down and scanned the printed matter.

"EPOTEK lab," he said out loud. "Yeah!" EPOTEK…that's gotta' be where that agent guy took my moon rock. Somehow he got Kelly to give it to him…to study or something…

"Yeah!" he said a little louder than before and started for the staircase. "I just hope to the highest heaven that I can find that moon rock before all those government scientists figure out that it's real…and it came from little old Tack Moultrie.

He used the time while driving over to the field to start working on a plan to fly the Spirit to the EPOTEK lab and search for a way to retrieve the moon rock, but he soon realized he needed a good map of that area to nail down the details of how to go about this wild mission.

………………………………………………………………

Only minutes later Tack managed make it to Gold Field. He jumped out of the Hawk and soon was making his way across the main hangar floor. It was still too early for the rest of the Gold Field crew to have arrived for the morning's first cup of coffee, so he headed straight for the main office and stuck his head into Buford's sanctuary just long enough to say, "Seen Kelly yet this morning?"

He held his breath as he waited to see if Kelly was going to show up that day, telling everyone about her weird dream, but when Buford looked up at him with that look that signaled he suspected that something was wrong, he realized that no spunky little blond female was there.

"She's stayin' in this mornin'," the boss said, his voice low and menacing. "Somethin' about a crazy dream she said she had last night." His expression changed a little, and he went on. "You know anythin' about birds?"

"Not a lot, but dreamin' about birds can get ya thinking about…flyin'… and that kind of thing." Tack swallowed hard, again, his eyes scanning the room to see if there might just be a map of the Houston area lying around in Buford's clutter.

37

World Zoom

Finding no spunky little blond female was there in Buford's office, Tack made up an excuse to take off for a few days. Buford looked at him real hard but finally nodded and said something that sounded to Tack like, "Have a party," and then went into a coughing fit.

As Tack headed back to the sinkhole, he took a couple of side roads, and the worse the road, the better. His hope was to throw off any followers or chasers, and it seemed to him that it had worked. There was no one behind him.

When he was sure it was safe, he carefully hid the Hawk and hightailed it to the cave. He was glad he'd had the presence of mind to fix the Jacob's chair apparatus so that it was easy to hide when it reached the surface. A clever cavelike depression had made the task quite easy, and Tack was confident that only someone with a lot of time on their hands and some basic knowledge of where and how to look for such device would ever be able to locate it—even if they knew what it was and what it was for—out there in the dense wooded tract.

He would have to wait another hour for it to be dark enough for a safe liftoff. He didn't like to use the shrink factor while sitting on the ground. It was disconcerting to see the world zoom to giant proportions right before his eyes—not to mention that it was more than a little dangerous. One never knew when a cat may be nearby or some other potential hazard. Any animal, while the Spirit was reduced in size, could pose a very dangerous situation. Tack's recent encounter with Theo had made him think more than twice about being only an inch high unless it was extremely necessary.

He decided to use the time to reread the article in the newspaper.

"Battey," he groaned. "Agent Battey...He must have taken the moon rock. The article doesn't say that it was taken, it just says that it was in a small town in Georgia, and it was an edition that had hit the stands very recently, so it might just be that Battey somehow talked Kelly into loaning him the stone long enough to have it examined...or whatever," he said as if Cisco was still around, listening. Tack sipped his coffee and let his eyes scan the page again; then he looked around and realized he wasn't talking to Cisco. He felt a pain hit him in the chest as he realized again that Cisco was dead. He'd been so preoccupied with trying to get the moon rock back from Kelly that he'd forgotten about poor little Cisco. "Now, the only one I've got to talk to about my new life...is...is...me."

Then it hit him. "Holy cow...now that I think about it, Battey's the guy that Chris told me about. He was investigating the crash too. He came out to Gold Field in that black helicopter Buford was talkin' about not too long ago. And Chris seemed to be pretty sure that Battey had once worked at Area 51. Jeeez!" I'm in deep yellow snow now. If the FBI's on my tail, no telling what they know...or think they know. They'll take the Spirit away from me...and probably put me in jail like they did Chris Odomma back in the '90s."

He went over to his ice chest and opened a beer. He sat down at the card table and was busy guzzling down the frosty brew, deep in thought. He finally said, "I should have stayed at the cave when I got back from Kelly's place."

When he'd finished off the beer he got up from the table and said, still talking as if Cisco was there, "Going back to Nova Base was a waste of time. I should have just stayed right here so I could get a head start on my mission." Tack walked over to the leg of the Spirit and let his hand play across the cool metal. "A ship built as an escape vehicle," he sighed. "Quadrilla must have designed into this thing special capabilities that allowed it to outrun the ships that she knew were most likely going to be after her.

"I've got to get that moon rock back, before the authorities, especially the FBI, find out that it's really from the moon." Tack walked around to the end of the ramp and continued to mentally work on a plan for his next action as he climbed up the ramp and entered the ship.

At seven fifteen, Tack positioned himself in the command couch and punched on the power charger. The power source of the Spirit was still a complete mystery to him. How the saucer worked was still hidden from his experienced hands and mind. But he'd learned how to operate enough of the systems to hedgehop over the nearby landscape and to fly all the way to the moon and back, and so far, he hadn't killed himself or anyone else that he knew of.

He took his modified TV remote control and moved his hand into the control to lift the ship off the cave floor. Once the landing legs were retracted, he slowly inched the Spirit forward and out of the cave.

It was a clear night, and the afterglow of the sunset was still visible high in the sky. There were only a few stars out as the Spirit began to rise out of surrounding forest.

The ship rose with a smooth acceleration, straight up to about a thousand feet before Tack kicked in the engines and started the Spirit in a forward motion.

All that could be seen from the ground at this point was the dull-blue glow of the gravity amplifiers. This glow could be increased or decreased at the cost of engine power should the pilot wish to attract less attention from any witnesses.

At about thirty thousand feet, Tack increased the size of the Spirit to gain more speed. He monitored the commercial flights until he reached about fifty thousand feet. At that altitude all he had to look out for were the military aircraft. He increased the size of the Spirit to about a mile and a half across and clicked on the radar scrambler Bill had helped him design in the recent weeks. At this huge size, the trip would take less time, but if anyone spotted him, they'd be reporting that a really huge mother ship was invading the Earth. That factor might even work to his advantage. The more bizarre the story, the less likely the story was to cause serious interest.

38

To Escape

Professor Balboa was killing some time in the hotel room at the Day Glow, waiting while Chris finished up his paperwork. While Chris was wondering what Tack Moultrie had been able to do in the way of finding out what had happened to the moon rock, Jesse finally grew bored watching the TV, opened up the Evelyn folder again, and flipped through the pages back and forth until something caught his eye.

"This is the part that Chris was talking about yesterday," he whispered. "I believe he's got a very good point," he said and let his eyes scan over Evelyn's precise tiny handwriting.

It read,

> Down through ages, many of what you call "aliens" have visited your world over long periods of time. I came into being by an act that is commonly performed by one group of these aliens. You and I, and even most of the aliens that I have dealt with, we all live in a brief period of time that hardly exists by the overall standards of time and space. This is the first and most difficult hurdle your belief mechanism must take. This is the scale and the score of reality. It is so vast; it defies our mental resources to describe. The filter you must continuously apply to your image of reality is this, no matter how grand it all seems to you in the present, it is, in reality, much grander. It is more all encompassing—more powerful than your ability to measure. It's like the definition you humans have of God. However, you

> must understand that in large part, your human image of God is inadequate to cover all that is. It is true to a great degree, that the proof of God's existence is in the vary atoms of the air you breathe and to a larger degree the atoms that make up all of reality. God is like the generally accepted concept of gravity.
>
> Gravity and, more importantly, the strong and weak nuclear forces, by the definition within which you have the basis of understanding, are the forces that hold everything together. It's like a form of glue, and this glue gives matter its solidity. However, in all probability, it has never occurred to any human that these forces may have a little understood form of intelligence. By the process you call "thinking," these forces cause electrons to not only be attracted by the nucleus, but they also define and control the orbital patterns of the electrons themselves. All of these functions are caused by thought, because what you call God is the purest form of intelligence.

Here Evelyn had made a note in the margin. She reflected that she could almost see Quadrilla's face.

"Her face," she said, "seemed to move within a swarm of small, foggy lights and a host of smoky, ghostlike forms."

> After you accept the scale factor, you will be expected to know that I came to exist because of an experiment by a group of aliens I will call king angels. Please do not be misled into thinking that all angels have good intentions as you might see them. As you use the name "angels" you understand that there are both good and evil angels. The ancient scriptures that have been found in the remnants of the civilizations of earth have attempted to tell you of the duality of the state and purpose of the angels. However, those angels that are evil have corrupted the angel label for their own purposes. They want humans to believe and

accept the concept of white-good angels and red/black-evil demon angels.

The king angels of which I speak were not necessarily good nor entirely evil. The king angels are much like humans, and this factor was instrumental when they created me. They wanted to breed a king angel with human qualities and create a being somewhere in between the two extremes. I came to learn that this scientific experiment had been attempted many times with very limited success—until I was created. I was not the first or the last of such experiments. However, as the laws of averages or fate will have it, I was special. This is also true of Max and Deltoo. Though, early on, I was unaware of my special gifts. However, as I gained experience through time, I began to realize that I had the ability to think on a level that was beyond the level that the king angels had ever dreamed of. Soon, they, too, began to notice my gifts, and this frightened them. I had to learn to be careful with what I said and did because though they were not specifically afraid of me, they became more and more filled with fear because they couldn't understand how I came to be or how something like me could come to be. I was, in some ways, that they could not, and still do not, understand, better than them. Better in a host of ways.

As happens when those with great power are confronted with something they have created that they cannot completely control, they decided to seal me off from their society—to hide the monster in the basement, so to speak. They sat on me. They held me back—deprived me of the standard communication afforded to the other beings they had created and even the king angels themselves. I discovered that they even planned on occasion to destroy me, but my power prevented that. When they discovered that I could prevent my own destruction, I frightened them even more.

> Therefore, they sent me off to a colony of similar hybrid beings that lived in isolation on an artificial planet they had created far off in an undesirable arm of a second-rate galaxy. It was on this planet, that I decided to use my power to create something that would not only occupy my time, and in effect give me purpose, but would also help me to escape their probing—their monitoring of my existence, my life. I decided to develop a plan of escape. My plan began to take the shape of building some kind of escape ship. The ship had to be small and maneuverable and capable of traveling through space, time, and size.

Jesse looked up from the page he'd just read and stared for a moment at the stained glass window of the church in the painting hanging on the hotel wall. "Size…" he said out loud. "And time…could it be…Is Chris right after all?" He shifted on the couch and leaned back. "Reading always makes me sleepy." He sniffed and closed his eyes and folded his hands across his chest, and in the dream that was to come, all he could see was the face of the mystical hybrid female, Quadrilla.

39

Seems Later

Jesse was still asleep and didn't notice when Chris slipped the key card through the reader on the door to the room. It hardly made a sound, but when Chris went into the bathroom and flushed the toilet, the professor rolled over and stared at Chris's shadow on the wall next to the front door. Little by little, it came back to him where he was. It had been so long since he'd had a normal sleep that he was getting use to waking up in strange surroundings.

Chris finally finished up in the bathroom and came into the bedroom. He glanced over at the professor and then walked over to the hotel window. It was still dark outside, and Jesse cut his eyes over to the clock by the bed. "Three fifteen in the morning… It seems later…" he said.

"Better get up and get ready, Professor," Chris said. "We're gonna' have to get back out to the StarShip and see if we can make it to EPOTEK before Tack does."

The professor rolled out of bed, stood up, and stretched. "I take it that you have new information about Mr. Moultrie," Jesse yawned.

"Yep. I have to assume that Tack read the moon rock story in the newspaper I left at his camper," Chris answered back. "And I am pretty certain that after reading the account of the moon rock, he is headed for the EPOTEK lab in Houston." Jesse watched as Chris was recklessly tossing his suitcase on the bed and cramming his underwear into it.

"EPOTEK? How interesting." Jesse opened a candy bar and shoved half of it into his mouth. "I need some energy," he said, waving what was left of the candy bar at Chris. "Now what would Mr. Moultrie…?" Then Jesse's eyes lit up. "The moon rock you say—yes!" He slapped his knee. "The lunar sample. He's going to try to get it back."

"That's what I figured. Now," Chris said, "better get ready. Every minute could be critical."

Jesse wadded up the candy wrapper, tossed it into the trash can, and reached for his pants.

40

Too Deep

It was still chilly outside when Chris and Jesse went into the office of the motel and found Cassy asleep in the office recliner. She'd obviously been standing in for the usual guy that manned the desk during the late-night and early-morning hours.

Cassy jumped like she was shot out from a cannon when Chris rang the bell on the desk. "Man," she said, "I wish I could get a day job. My nerves are shot." She came over to the desk, and Chris handed her the key card.

"Sorry," Chris said, "the professor and I have to make an early-morning flight, and there was just no way to warn you."

"You'll be glad to be rid of us, Ms. Towers," Jesse added.

"It's no problem, I've had worse happen." She tried to brush her hair from her face as she slipped the key card into the Rolodex.

"Maybe you can resume your nap after we've gone," Chris said as he and Jesse headed for the door.

Once outside, Jesse said, "I am thinking, Tack is most likely flying to Houston in the prototype, right? Is the StarShip going to get us to the EPOTEK lab before Mr. Moultrie?"

"All we can hope is that we manage to intercept him before he gets into any more trouble."

Jesse finished off his candy bar as they let the door slam behind them.

Once again alone in the office, Cassy stood there thinking about that last statement that the professor had offered as she stared at the closed door. "What lab could Tack be headed to… at this hour? Oh well," she said and went back across the room.

She sighed and plopped down in the recliner. Before long she was back in dreamland, flying around in a giant fish bowl with Tack; the bowl was now cradled in his rubber-band-powered Kitty Hawk craft.

Outside the motel office, Chris stopped a second and bent down to tie his shoelace. He stood back up, cleared his throat, and finally said, "Professor, I think Tack is getting himself too deep into something that's way too big for him."

"Yeah, we better get moving," Jesse said and wiped his mouth on his hanky. He then shoved his hands in his pockets and headed for the Jag.

"I just hope we're not too late. It's a big world out there, and we don't know where our guy currently is, do we?"

Jesse stopped in his tracks and watched Chris open the Jag's door.

"Yeah, it's like looking for a pin and a needle in a haystack."

"But if we look for him at the place he'll most likely go…"

"Yeah, exactly what I was thinkin'…the x-ray microscope lab. I just hope he's careful. If he gets mixed up and winds up in the electron microscope lab, he's done for. The x-rays won't kill him, but the electron microscope certainly will."

Chris cranked up the Jag, and smoked up the road back to Gold Field. They rode on in silence for a few minutes, and then Jesse said, "You know, from Quadrilla's descriptions of some of the creatures she observed in the labs before her escape, it's just possible that the character we've been looking for that she called Deltoo is not necessarily a human figure. Remember the zoo of different species she talked about?"

"You know, Professor, if you start looking at the UFO phenomenon from a different perspective, as you were saying sometime ago, you can begin to picture almost any kind of creature or being."

"You're right. If Earth were sending a spacecraft to another planet, the basic spacecraft would look to the aliens like a Jules Verne type of bullet washed up on the beach at Cape Canaveral.

Our rocket-powered craft, our solar-powered craft, nuclear plasma drive, antimatter—all of these ships would look as strange to an alien race on another planet as a covered wagon would look to an Indy race driver. If they witnessed a rocket-powered lander, they would have to assume that all our spacecraft had the same energy source and operated under similar circumstances. And the same logic would, most likely, hold for the organic factor as well."

"Organic factor? What are you saying, Professor?"

"Okay, let's go back to Quadrilla and her story. Let's assume for a moment that her story is true. Quadrilla was a human implant into the king angel's system. Why should we only assume that humans are their only experiments?"

"You're saying that they may have experimented with animals as well…as humans…I see."

"And not only Earth animals, but also creatures that may inhabit other worlds we don't know about. Maybe even other dimensions."

"Professor, you're scaring me again. You're describing the whole Men in Black thing, with the Monster of the Month Club."

"Why not? Think of the various descriptions of eyewitnesses to close encounters. I mean some of them definitely follow a pattern, but there are many bizarre exceptions."

"Yeah, you're right about that."

"So Quadrilla builds the prototype spacecraft, with the aid of another modified human and maybe a modified whatsit?"

"Yeah, and the more I reexamine my notes, I'm convinced they built at least two prototypes, maybe three."

"Two and three? So where are these other prototypes?"

"A better question might be, where and who is the third member of Quadrilla's crew?"

41

Scrambler

Blasting through the state of Texas, the Spirit was headed straight for Houston, and it took only minutes until just outside of Hobby Airport, Tack clicked on the shrink mechanism. It wasn't much of a problem that the shrink process nullified the radar scrambler. The tower only got a brief glimpse of the Spirit's ghost echo on the radar screens before it shrank into an insignificant soft glow because of its tiny size. Even thought he had seen it with his own eyes, the traffic controller on duty at that workstation still couldn't believe what he'd just witnessed. He sat there punching buttons like crazy trying to get it to reappear.

"The danged thing just vanished," he said, glancing over his shoulder to see if anyone heard him. "Must have been an inversion layer...or somethin'."

A guy, with an unlit cigarette between his teeth heard what he'd said and came over to look over the controller's shoulder. He bent forward and looked at the screen. "What?"

"It doesn't make sense. It was there. Then it just got smaller and smaller until it just wasn't there anymore."

"Wish I'd seen it, assuming it really was."

"Yeah, it was there...and then it wasn't...weirdest thing I've ever seen..."

Tack brought the Spirit down just over Interstate 45 and followed it to NASA Road 1. Following this busy traffic conduit, the EPOTEK building was relatively easy to find. He adjusted the Spirit down to the size of the average Frisbee and skipped over the top of the chain-link fence that surrounded the back parking lot of the EPOTEK grounds.

The guard dogs started going crazy as they first sensed the presence of the magnetic waves produced by the engines aboard the Spirit. They went even crazier when they saw the tiny silvery disk passing just a few feet over their heads. One made a mad, frenzied leap up at the Spirit and came within a foot or so of sinking his canines into the body of the saucer.

A monstrously large head of an angry Doberman suddenly loomed large in the front window of the Spirit. Tack's face went white, and his heart skipped a beat or two. "Holy dog biscuit!" he said and banked the ship left at about thirty degrees. Quickly he brought the ship back upright as he headed for the mail slot to the left side of the EPOTEK employee entrance.

Like a huge grinning mouth, the slot grew larger before him as he slowed the Spirit to a creeping hover, reduced the saucer's size to that of a silver dollar, and deftly slid the ship into the slot. On the other side of the mailbox, he could see the office side slit.

"Hey, this is easier than I thought," he said. He came out into the main corridor. After checking out the north corridor and finding only offices, he tried the opposite direction looking for some sign of a lab where the lunar sample might be taken for examination.

This was where he encountered his first big headache.

42

Big Headache

Tack's headache was in the form of a steel door—complete with an airtight seal and an electronic security system that required one of those plastic credit card–like ID passes, and, "Oh no, a 'Can't nobody get in but the good guys' system," Tack muttered.

Tack punched the Spirit down still further to gnat size. "Oooooooooo jeez! This is going to…" He banked and maneuvered up to a hovering position near the door seal. "Darn, now what?" It looked like a giant wall of black rubber. "Still no luck," he said, flying the Spirit up and down the seal, looking for an opening. "No danged way I'm getting past this seal."

"Jeez! This sucker's sealed up tighter than love bug lips. This thing's worse than the lunar lab." He wiped a hand across his brow. "Well," he sighed, "I might as well go for broke—whatever that means."

"Grandma's whiskers!" he said, waving his right hand over the shrink sphere that would reduce the Spirit down still farther in size.

Down, down, down the Spirit began to shrink even further until the seal before him grew to huge proportions. The appearance of the slick rubber seal changed to a series of mountainous blobs, resembling nothing like what one would recognize as a rubber seal to a super lab chamber. It had the appearance of two cavernous walls converging into the distance.

"Now! By George, we're getting someplace. I think we've got this sucker licked."

At this point, the Spirit was of a sufficiently reduced size that the texture of the supertight seal was easily penetrated by the minuscule space ship…well, to be honest, maybe not that easy, but at least it wasn't as impossible as it appeared to be seconds ago. It was like flying between matching sets of gray/green/black mountains and through matching valleys. The mountains seemed to interlock with one another. It was somewhat unnerving to see that there was so much space between the two walls. Apparently the scientists using this chamber for experiments believed the rubber seals to be absolutely airtight. As the ship shrunk still further, the rubber-walled canyons ahead triggered a new avenue of thinking to Tack's mind. His gray matter slowly began to realize, and he began to accept that in the microscopic world, smooth was like a series of mountains, and tight seal was really like a screen door on a submarine.

Luckily, Tack didn't need a compass to maneuver through the seal/mountains. The Spirit's direction-finding device allowed the pilot/operator to just fly straight through a maze of obstacles, and the system automatically let the ship slip through the maze, taking the rout of least resistance.

The mountains and valleys slipped by somewhat smoothly, considering the fact that the Spirit was banking and swooping through stacks of rubber molecules.

It started to grow extremely dark a few seconds into the door seal, and Tack had to turn on the forward maneuvering lights. This made the mountains and valleys look even more ominous. "Jeez! A guy could sure get lost in here," he mumbled as he eyed the large opening up ahead. He flew the Spirit through the slots between a series of openings by turning the ship up on edge. As he flew the saucer-shaped vehicle through the seal, the view ahead began to look more like two giant knobby rollers that threatened to squash the ship flat. As the ship flew along, he realized that there were several such openings, and after the first few, he lost count. "These must be the layers of the seal interlocking on either side like a giant rubber zipper," he said.

Then all of a sudden, he could see light up ahead, coming through the walls of the rubber seal. "I must be getting close to the other side." He gasped as the Spirit emerged into another gigantic hallway. He then flipped the ship back upright. This hallway was white, with an orange stripe running down the walls about shoulder high to an average-sized man.

43

EPOTEK One

The EPOTEK laboratory stood in the light of the full moon and was occasionally lit up by the lights of passing cars, some of them full of NASA employees on their way home from working overtime at Johnson Space Center. This NASA facility was, of course, referred to as JSC by the employees. Acronyms were the hot item at the beginning of the twenty-first century. For reasons that are far beyond human comprehension, this lab had become the center of all existence for Tack Moultrie. He was still far from his goal but determined to retrieve Kelly's moon rock even though it meant a tremendous amount of risk on many different and some unknown fronts.

Somewhere inside this high-tech facility, probably in a plexiglass box, was the objective of Tack's most urgent mission, and not far behind him, in an aircraft called the StarShip, Chris Slattery and Professor Jesse Balboa sought to uncover the mystery of the all-mysterious UFO phenomenon. In certain ways, they both envied Tack and his newfound ability to fly to the moon and even explore the worlds of the microscopic—and whatever else was now an open doorway to him provided by the wonders of the prototype ship. However, Chris was also determined to pursue the crop duster pilot interfering as little as possible with the adventure that Tack had embarked upon.

The dangers that the king angel UFOs posed to Tack, and perhaps the world, were of secondary concern to Chris's current mission, and he set the StarShip down in Hobby Airport anxious to rent a car and get to the EPOTEK labs as soon as possible.

Chris was saying as he drove them down NASA Road 1. "And all the acronyms," he shook his head and made a crude noise with his mouth. "When you talked to Hank on the videophone, did you see Battey?"

"No, I didn't, but I was able to get a brief look at the moon rock. It was on the table behind him. Of course it's inside a glass box...probably plastic box...so you can't get too close to it. They haven't analyzed it yet. I don't know what they are waiting for."

"Or what they think they'll find. I don't think it's possible that Tack could know what they're going to do with it...or where to look for it."

"Do you think he knows that Battey is the one who got the moon rock from his girlfriend?"

"It's possible. I thought if we could work it in, I'd try to warn Tack to hang loose for a while. Battey gets ahead of himself. I don't think anybody's going to take him serious." Chris looked down the road and caught a glimpse of the EPOTEK building; the blue letters on its main tower were being lit up by the spotlights in the courtyard down below the structure.

44

Phenomenon

Chris pulled over to the side of the road and parked several yards from the guard gate to the EPOTEK building.

"Aren't we going in?" Jesse asked.

"Not yet. Dr. Dannon said he'd meet us at the gate. He said he was expecting another group of people that called in at the last minute. We'll be able to see the limo when it gets here. He told me to park here until it arrives."

"Now, I wish I'd gone to the men's room back at the airport."

"Me too." Chris smiled. "Just think of it as a test to see how long we can hold our bladders."

"I wonder if a test like this was conducted by the king angels on Quadrilla."

"I don't doubt it." He looked over at Jesse. "You know, Professor, it frightens me when I realize what we would do if we found a real alien. You know…"

"We would, most likely, cut it all to pieces to see what made it tick."

"Or worse."

"What could be worse?"

"I'm not sure you want to know."

Balboa nodded his head and decided to change the subject. "Yes, I think I know what you mean. You know, Chris, I've been thinking about it a lot since I read some of Evelyn's account of her dreams. Quadrilla wanted to escape her alien captives; that much is certain. But to assure success, she first decided to send the prototype—to Earth."

"Two prototypes—just to make sure, like Noah sending out the doves from the arc."

"Yes, and she does this to find a suitable haven that she believes is safe. While the prototype is on its mission, she builds or her crew builds a more durable ship, perhaps larger, and plans to use this ship for her actual escape."

Chris smiled. "And she brings a powerful body guard with her."

"Right, and someone or something else. That would explain the huge black guy that you mentioned. As we have seen at the Area 6451 facilities, the technology that they have been using to reverse engineer Project Aurora is not as advanced as the prototype that Quadrilla's team developed. It's like comparing a 747 with the Kitty Hawk. Even the bolts that hold these two examples together are different, so we can only imagine how the navigational systems would differ. When you consider that the regimentation that is inherent when a centralized governmental control system is in place and compare it to a totally free agent, whose main objective is to outperform and therefore outrun the king angel's technology, you begin to appreciate what we are really dealing with in our pursuit to find the prototype."

45

Spit in the Wind

To hide from possible surveillance personnel that most assuredly were watching all of the halls, offices, and EPOTEK labs, Tack pushed the Spirit to a hovering position up close to the side of the hallway camera so that he wouldn't show up on the guard's monitors.

"Which way, which way?" he groaned in frustration. "Spit in the wind?" It was sort of a prayer, really because he had no idea of where to start, and he looked and looked until he was exhausted. Finally he banked the ship and headed down the hall. Any direction was better than wasting time under the circumstances.

He went into room after room, chamber after chamber. The Spirit flew through seal after seal—but with no luck.

"I've just got to find it," he said, controlling the ship down through the key hole of one of the file cabinets. After switching back on the forward beam, he then flew down past the rows of tabs on the many files. He quickly read over the names on the tabs as they passed in front of the forward window one by one. Finding nothing of any help to his search for the lunar sample, he flew through the drawers of every cabinet in the room, looking for a clue—any kind of clue that might lead him to the precious moon rock.

The blue light of the Spirit cabin lit up his face as he looked from one side to the other at the control spheres and the readouts on the console. Finally, in frustration, he said, "I guess I should have paid more attention to the detective course I was sent away for in that comic book when I was a kid." He wiped the sweat from his forehead. "Okay, I can do this—now...just think. Clear your head, Tack—and think."

He looked and looked, for what seemed a like hours, and after a while he was so fatigued, he could hardly keep his eyes opened. "There must be a systematic way to do this," he said. He was groggy from the strain of the search and couldn't think straight.

He decided that he'd probably be better off if he just sat tight for a while and allowed himself to think. He spotted a suitable area up on the top of a bookshelf that overlooked the entire room and carefully landed the Spirit. After the settling of the ship was complete, he settled back into his makeshift acceleration couch and looked up at the ceiling of through the observations dome at the top of the flight deck. The flashing lights on the console were visible in his peripheral vision and the flickering of the many lights began to have a restful effect on him. The search had sapped him of most of his strength, and it wasn't long until he drifted off into a deep sleep. He dreamed.

In the dream, Tack was being chased by someone in a silver-gray sports car. He was riding on some kind of futuristic motorcycle, and as he looked back, the silver car had changed into a squadron of very futuristic, flying cars. They shot lasers at him, forcing him toward a cliff.

"Holy jeez! No! No!" he said out loud, his voice ringing throughout the confines of the Spirit's cabin. He was thrashing around on the couch, his arms swinging around in the air.

His fitful flopping around grew more and more erratic, and his hand eventually fell over onto a panel to the right of the acceleration couch. This was the same small command table he'd accidently placed his coffee cup down on when he was making his voyage to the moon, weeks before. At that time he'd put his palm down on the circular area and twisted it counterclockwise just enough to wipe up the coffee he'd spilled there. Now the ship was again being filled with the same trembling movement.

This panel didn't particularly look like any of the controllers he'd thus far mastered, and when his hand brushed ever so slightly in a clockwise movement on the white-colored surface, immediately some very strange things began to happen to the lights and screens on the ship's control panel. It looked much like some kind of crazy theater marquees as the lights began to race around command deck. If Tack had been awake, he'd have been alerted that something was about to happen to the Spirit—something really beyond anything he could have ever imagined. And it was something very important. But Tack was too deep in his dream state and just went right on sleeping. He was hopelessly lost to his dream world, trying to deal with the emergency of the situation that kept growing in detail and realism in this stranger than strange mind fabrication.

While he slept, the ship continued its wild vibration, and a peculiar smell began to fill the atmosphere inside the ship.

46

Time and Ageing

As Tack's fitful dream continued, he was still being chased by the flying vehicles. Flashes of their ray guns could be seen on both of his rear-view mirrors. The flying cars were closing in on him, and he had to drive a zigzag pattern to dodge the laser blasts that were forcing him toward a sheer drop-off on the side of the mountain road.

If anyone had been looking at the Spirit up on the shelf at that precise moment, they would have seen something just as incredible as seeing the Spirit shrink down in size.

The tiny saucer was growing more and more transparent.

The dream was making the crop duster pilot restlessly twist and twitch there in his acceleration couch. By this time, in the dream, Tack's supercycle had left the road, and he was falling off the cliff, but when he managed to see through the slits of his half-closed eyes, he saw on the screen of the main monitor inside the Spirit, or he thought he saw the room around him—or the room around the Spirit, to be more accurate, taking on a weird glow. Tack woke up with a start covered in sweat. The room he could see outside seemed to be breaking down into particles, and the particles were beginning to swarm around his ship, and the light was flashing, creating a flashing effect similar to a strobe light. He looked on in wonder and confusion for a while, trying to figure out what was happening; then he noticed where his hand was on the panel. It was the same panel that had scared him to near death months before when he'd headed toward the moon.

He tried to replay his memory of all that had happened on that event. In a brief flash of memory, he could see the stars outside the forward Spirit window, and they were getting smaller as if the direction of the ship's flight had been somehow reversed.

The small screen on the forward panel was displaying a series of alien figures that were quickly changing in a sequence, reminding him of a countdown clock, and when he'd looked down at his pocket watch, he had seen the second hand on that priceless timepiece swinging around, counterclockwise.

When he realized what was happening, he jerked his hand away in terror. The banks of lights around the command deck started flashing sequentially.

Up on the shelf, the Spirit just grew and grew more and more transparent until it just wasn't there anymore.

Tack said, "I must still be dreaming, or…I'm traveling in time—again."

The swarm on the screen began to slow down, and he began to understand, to notice that there were people in the room, and these people were moving much too fast to be real people. He was inclined to believe that he was still dreaming. He'd done that before. He'd been dreaming and then woke up, but weird things were still happening. And then after a while he really woke up, and it was really weird, like he just never really woke up.

As he moved his hand back and forth over the white disk of the panel, the moving speed would increase and then slow down.

"What in the green-eyed world is going on…" he said, his mouth hanging opened.

And as he moved his hand again over the panel ever so slightly in one particular direction, he noticed he was causing the people in the room to slow down. When he moved his hand the opposite direction, he caused the people to speed up. Then he began to wonder if he could slow the people down to a complete stop. He tried it, but when he finally got them to stop, he found that with just a little more movement he could send them scurrying off backward.

"Well, this is a new wrinkle," he mouthed the words, but little sound came out.

He moved his hand a little more and sent the people scurrying off into the past, this time at comical speeds. It was like watching an old movie of the Keystone Cops, only with the projector running backward.

"Holy, flatfish, I'm...yeah, I believe I'm really moving backward in...yeah, backward in...time. Jeez. This...wow...this means this ship can—holy...it can travel back through time! I can't believe it. In addition to being a spaceship and all the other size-change stuff, the Spirit is a bleedin' time machine. Holy H. G. Wells, Batman."

He watched the people zipping around backward until his eye caught something. This eye-catching something had to do with the lunar sample, and it inspired him to move his hand over the white disc again, slowing, and then stopping his travel backward through time.

"Holy Moses! I wish I could zip myself up to the right size without having to use the Spirit. If I could just return to my normal size without having to drag the old Spirit along with me... well, I could go in there and see what they're doing with that moon rock."

He climbed out of the acceleration couch and rubbed his eyes, never looking away from the view screen. "Oh well, if the mountain can't come to Mohammed." He punched in a reduction command to reduce the Spirit down to about the size of a mosquito.

He put his hand into the control sphere and flew the Spirit off the bookshelf and over to the desk where Agent Battey had set down the plexiglass box with Kelly's moon rock inside. Once there, he pushed the time control in the direction that caused the Spirit and Tack to move backward in time—very slowly so he could carefully discover something that he believed would allow him to gain entrance into the plexi box.

"It must be sealed up in there somehow. Maybe it's not airtight. I know it ought to be, if NASA is doing its job...but this ain't NASA. It's… it's…I guess it's just some branch of the federal government we don't ever hear about."

On the view screen Tack could still see the people moving backward until finally Agent Battey backed over to the desk, turned around, and picked up the plexiglass case. Tack moved his hand into the Lift control, and the Spirit slowly hovered off the surface of the desk. As the agent backed out of the room, tack maneuvered the ship to follow him. "If I can just find the moment when the moon rock is placed inside the case, then I can grow this thing big enough to get out and load the rock on board the Spirit. Of course, it will have to be a big, big room in order to accommodate the Spirit at a size big enough to allow me to pick up the rock and load it—but heck, there has to be a time when it's in a room big enough and left alone long enough. No…no, I don't' have to do that. I'll use the shrink ray!"

The sliding doors almost closed before Tack could make the Spirit fly into the elevator. He had to turn the Spirit up on its side at the last second and fly through the ever-narrowing slot before the rubber seals came together. Once inside, he circled around Battey's head causing the agent to brush away at the metallic insect with his hand. This movement caused Tack an anxious moment, but he was able to outmaneuver the gigantic hand and bring the Spirit to a stable flight. "Maybe I can just land this thing for a while and ride until the agent goes outside."

Tack flew the Spirit down into the agent's hair and lowered the craft down to his scalp. Through the forward window, he could see the towering forest of tree-like hairs running up into infinity, their trunks buried in a crusty, flaky landscape of Battey's scalp. "Whoa!" Tack said. "Battey has dandruff, serious flakesville, man."

Still moving backward in time, it was disconcerting to see the huge slabs of dried, translucent skin working in reverse to come down through the giant tree-like hair stalks and attach themselves to the scalp.

The ship jostled a little as the light through the trees grew brighter, and he realized that the elevator doors were opening.

"Gotta get up were I can follow the moon rock. Can't see through all this hair." Tack lifted off the scaly scalp of Battey's skull and flew through the trees until he broke free and could see down into the top of the plexiglass box as Agent Battey turned around and walked backward out into the lobby. Battey showed his pass to the guard who immediately ignored him. He then continued out the front glass doors where two plainclothed guards joined him in his backward trek past the guard shack and out to the huge black stretch limo just outside the gate.

47

Suite 804

Tack flew the Spirit up by the limo's dome light and hovered there to allow him to keep a watch on the moon rock. The limo was traveling along the highway, backward, of course, while Agent Battey sat spitting hot coffee back into the Styrofoam cup while looking at the passing scenery and forgetting the landmarks he'd been told to remember along the way to the EPOTEK building. Suddenly, the limo was passed by a beat-up old 60 Chevy backward. The Chevy was gobbling up great clouds of light-gray smoke sucking it up into the end of its dangling exhaust pipe, leaving behind/ahead clear, clean air. Occasionally the pipe would make momentary contact with the pavement, and it would scoop up a wondrous spray of glittering sparks.

Tack shook his head and smiled. "I can't wait to use this time travel feature for some real historical research someday. It might just be that I'll be able to finally answer the age-old question: the chicken or the egg? Hey, I could even go back and find out who shot Kennedy...what really happened over the Bermuda Triangle—wow! This ship is really somethin'. I've got to be the luckiest guy in the world.'

When the limo was sucked down into a long black tunnel, Tack became totally disoriented until his eyes adjusted to the dark. When he could see clearly, he realized that they were inside what appeared to be a parking garage. The limo backed up to the basement elevator, and Tack followed Agent Battey as he stepped out of the limo, backward.

After Tack's effort to move back in time, the Spirit had finally ended up just outside of Agent Battey's hotel. Once inside, Battey had the plexiglass box under his arm as he backed over to the elevator doors. The Spirit was hovering just above the LED indicator so Tack could watch the numbers. The elevator slowly climbed upward and didn't stop until it reached the eighth floor. As Battey left the elevator, two more guards joined the agent. They, also, were walking backward along either side of him to a door marked Suite 804.

Tack couldn't tell if the suite was, in reality, a really huge place or if it was because he and the ship were so small at the time. But it did seem impressive as he flew around following Agent Battey over to the glass coffee table. Battey left the room, and Tack took that opportunity to shrink down even further to see if he could find some kind of opening into the plexiglass box. As he reached the molecular level, he slipped through the pours in the plexiglass and flew in a big circle around the moon rock. At this scale, the moon rock was a lot more like a mountain than the small rock that it actually was. In fact, at the molecular scale, the lunar sample was more like the size of a small planet, and thus, Tack began to feel more and more uncomfortable about the situation.

"Okay, here goes," he said as he set the shrink generator to humming and focused the green beam on the giant moon rock. He watched closely and waited, but nothing happened. The shrink beam wasn't working. He looked around, a puzzled expression flooding over his face. "Must be something about being back in time," he said, finally. It must be that you can't use the shrink beam when you are in a past time period—or maybe the vast size difference is causing a problem."

He kept trying again, several times, but no matter what he did to shrink the lunar sample, it was useless.

"This isn't getting me anywhere," he said in frustration. "There's no way I can get the rock on board at this size, and if I grow any bigger, Agent Battey might see me. Maaaan, if he finds out I'm here, I could end up in the FBI labs as some kind of freaky novelty. Come to think of it, since I've obviously traveled back in time, I know the future, at least from this perspective. I'd know already if Agent Battey found out I was here. Mannnn, time travel does something to your mind."

He scrunched up his nose and looked out at the massive moon rock. "If I can crank up the speed of this backward time travel, who knows, I may run out of power and not be able to stop moving backward. I don't really know what I'm doing. My best bet is to go forward in time, back to the EPOTEK lab and see if I can figure out a way to get the rock from the vacuum chamber. They'll no doubt use the vacuum chamber when they observe it using that big microscope Battey was talking about over the phone. Maybe I can use the tractor beam inside the chamber and move the moon rock into the cargo bay hatch to take it on board. If the inside of the chamber is big enough to grow the ship up to, maybe, one sixth scale… Yeah, that might work. At that size, the moon rock would be about as big as an oil drum, and I know an oil drum would fit through the cargo bay door. If I had no trouble with the F-16, I shouldn't have much of a problem with something the size of an oil drum."

48

Real Magic

While Tack had been busy trying to retrieve the moon rock, Chris and Jesse were still waiting in the car by the EPOTEK gate.

Chris had a puzzled look on his face as he found the words to came back at the Professor. "Jesse, what you're saying is that things can actually disappear and materialize...into nothing and from...nothing."

"My butt is taking a beating, Chris. I hope Doc Dannon gets here before my legs go to sleep."

"You're breaking my concentration, Professor. Tell me more about this nothing business. Oh yeah. So you're telling me that we are safe in assuming that the prototype is capable of traveling through time as well as space?" Chris played with the steering wheel and checked the rear-view mirror.

"We've been assuming all along that all UFOs are just part of the same phenomenon," Jesse said and turned to face Chris. "I'm telling you that the prototype is probably unique to most of the UFOs we've thus far encountered. From your own investigation, we also have information that leads me to believe that the prototype can change size as well, shrinking or expanding to any size it needs to be. Think of it, Chris. This spaceship can shrink down to microscopic size, or it can grow to...whatever—I just had a very scary thought. This size-changing ability would explain all the mile-long ships that have been sighted over the years. Those stories always bothered me, you know the ones where these airline pilots have reported seeing enormous ships, and that these giant UFOs somehow managed to fly around in our skies seldom ever being observed by people down on the ground."

"And, Professor, we've always assumed that the really big guys were mother ships like in that movie years ago called ID4."

"Don't let that limit your imagination, Chris. Both scenarios may be true. There may actually be mother ships—in addition to the enlarged prototype. There's just not any reason to limit our thinking on UFOs. I believe the most safe way to think of UFOs is to just accept the fact that for practical purposes, UFOs are the closest thing to real magic we humans have ever encountered. UFOs are in the same league as the black holes we have just recently been able to observe. You know, black holes break all the scientific laws of physics that we hang on to when we try to understand physical reality."

"Magic, eh?" Chris nodded his head. "Like I said before, you're telling me that UFOs can actually disappear and materialize into nothing and from nothing."

Balboa smiled and raised his eyebrows. "Hawkingly has no trouble with that concept of the big bang. And besides that, try defining nothing, Chris."

49

Define Nothing

Chris frowned. "You disappoint me, Jesse, nothing is nothing. You're startin' to sound like Bill Clanton." He shook his head.

"Well, I'm not so sure that Bill Clanton with his 'It depends on the meaning of is' comment didn't open up the idea that it is our responsibility to think of the definition of words and analyze them specifically for what they actually mean. Think of it—standardization, consistency, and—oh yes—don't forget parliamentary procedure. They are all gone in our modern world. We've become sloppy in our modern age, particularly in the use of our language. For instance, how many times have you heard people use the word concept when they should be using 'let's pretend'?

"What I mean by my statement in regard to the word nothing is that when we use the word, we usually picture in our minds an 'absolute nothing'—a perfect vacuum. But just try to actually find such an environment. One—one lone—atom. No, something smaller—an electron or a photon. That's all it would take to contaminate a perfect vacuum; hence, in the perfect sense of the word, no 'nothingness.'"

"Well, it goes without saying, nothing's perfect, not even a vacuum."

"Because the human eye cannot see air molecules, we think there is nothing in an empty bottle, but you know that there is something in the bottle because of your education, and perhaps because you can feel the wind resistance when you move your hand through space and assume that that same air is inside the bottle. When it comes to space, we tend to think that we are at last dealing with a true vacuum; however, this is not absolutely correct. For instance, most people believe that the Earth's atmosphere only extends to about twenty miles above the Earth's surface. They scratch their heads when you tell them that the Earth's atmosphere extends out so far as to be effecting the moon's orbit, slowing its orbital speed. The slowdown is negligible, to be sure, but the moon does encounter molecules of the Earth's atmosphere, and over an enormous period of time these minute collisions will diminish the speed of the moon around the Earth, and thus the moons orbit will decrease also."

"Yeah, you're right about that, I never thought about it that way, but it does make sense. Every molecule in the universe is influenced by other molecules. Atoms—same thing." Chris started to play with the radio buttons.

"Anything with actual mass has gravity," Jesse went on. "That gravitational attraction may be negligible, but it's there nonetheless. And the gravity of a large body like the Earth or the sun reaches much farther than most people think, so just think of a black hole and the extent of its gravitational field. It boggles the mind."

"Therefore, when you say something comes from nothing, or something goes to nothing, is it actually true, or is there some—let's call it—residue left behind?" Chris glanced back at Jesse. "One molecule, one atom would make that statement untrue." Chris watched as a red convertible being driven by a striking redhead went whizzing by. He blinked his eye and whistled. "Kinda late for that, don't cha think?"

50

Still in the Past

Back in Agent Battey's hotel room, Tack was working to make his escape by lifting the Spirit up to an altitude that would take him over to the glass doors and to the balcony outside. Shrinking the Spirit down small enough to go through eye of a needle, he turned the Spirit up on edge and slipped through the canyon-sized crack between the doors.

The silvery disk of the Spirit flew across the desert scale of the patio and then out over tops of the buildings of Houston. Then, as he flew back to the EPOTEK property, he grew the Spirit up to Frisbee size. Heading the ship back toward NASA Road, he followed the road back to the EPOTEK labs. Tack had decided to go back to his original position in the lab, back up on the bookshelf. Once there, the idea was to move the Spirit forward in time hoping to be inspired as to just what to do next.

Chris and Jesse didn't notice as Tack's UFO flew back into the EPOTEK building. Of course, that is an understatement. Tack hadn't thought it wise to maintain Frisbee size while trying to reenter the EPOTEK building and had reduced the Spirit down to about the size of a collar button. Therefore, the ship was too small to be detected from almost any distance at all. And, too, Chris and Jesse, at the time of Tack's fly over, were not yet even there at the EPOTEK lab, because Tack and the Spirit were still in the past, well before they arrived.

On the other hand, had Tack been in the present, or at least what the present would have been had he not traveled into the past on his quest with Agent Battey and the moon rock, well, without charting it out, you'll just have to trust me that in the present, he would have been able to see Chris and Jesse as he flew back over the EPOTEK security fence.

51

Identification

Sitting there several yards from the guard gate to the EPOTEK building, Chris and Jesse had run out of things to say to pass the time, and Jesse was growing impatient, wanting to get out and move around to relieve the pain that had developed in his left leg. And it was also true that enough time had past that Agent Slattery and Professor Balboa were anxious to join the party that had recently arrived at the EPOTEK gate. Finally they got out and started walking toward the guard shack at gate 1. Zelda Krebs met them with a big smile at the door to the guard shack, and as she looked them over, she said, "Hi, I'm Zelda Krebs. You guys look like you could use a hot cup of coffee."

"Lady, you got that right!" Chris smiled back.

Jesse stepped forward, hand held out. "I'm Professor Balboa. Call me Jesse, please."

Zelda took his hand and he gave her a big smile. Then Chris took over shaking her hand.

"You'll have to share the tour with another group of people that have just arrived—unexpectedly, I'm afraid," she said as she led the way into the guard shack.

As they followed Zelda, Chris couldn't help but busy his mind with just how he and the Professor had come to this particular moment. He had been certain that Tack would try to come to the EPOTEK lab to retrieve the moon rock, but he had no idea of where to start, or even what to look for. In order to intercept the young UFO pilot, it had been necessary for Chris and Jesse to come to EPOTEK and position themselves as close to the moon rock as possible, keeping their eye out for anything unusual. So far, his FREEZE agent identification had served them well, but he couldn't be certain that the lunar sample was even actually here at EPOTEK. It was just a strong possibility.

Once inside the guard shack, Balboa remarked that the small room was filled to bursting with the assembly of people that had gathered there. Dr. Luke Dannon, the director of EPOTEK, had yet to make his appearance, and while the group waited for him, they took advantage of the time to introduce themselves.

Jack O'Rilley pushed through the crowd when he recognized Chris and held out his hand. "This is a fortunate surprise, Agent," he said. "I sure didn't expect to see you here, and Professor… Balboa is it? It's good to see you both." He took Jesse's hand and pumped it happily. "I've heard a lot about you, Professor… read your book too."

"I've written thirty-four books," Jesse said. "Which one did you read?"

"I think it was called Clearly."

"Ah, that one. I just finished it earlier this year." Jesse smiled.

Chris also smiled and said, "I didn't expect to find you here, Jack. I'm having trouble believing that this is a coincidence. You're all the way in from Marshall Space Flight Center in Alabama, and—"

"I'm here from California," Bob said.

"California? Wow!" Chris shook his head.

"You may not know SIFI Bob," Jack said. "But I bet you've heard of him."

"You're not the SIFI Bob from Hollywood that has the special effects museum, are you?" Chris was surprised at Bob's strong grip on his hand.

"One and the same," Bob smiled.

"Well, I've heard that you have saved countless science fiction movie artifacts from the proverbial dump. For that you have my deepest appreciation. It's a shame that so much wonderful art gets destroyed, especially all that neat stuff that Hollywood's creative people pour their lives and crafts into."

"And that's only the half of it," Jack said. "I wish you'd been with us in Las Vegas." Jack glanced around to see the group that had gathered in the guard shack. "Yes, we've just come from Vegas…just got to Houston a little over an hour ago. I believe we have some interesting information that you, and especially the EPOTEK people, might just find very, very interesting."

Chris's puzzled look inspired Bob to say, "It's a long story, but I think I can guarantee you'll be interested." He shook his head and gave a short laugh. "I know, I'm still weirded out by it."

Balboa nudged Chris with his shoulder and motioned toward the rear door. Dr. Dannon was just entering the guard shack.

52

Knowing Nod

The professor nodded as Dr. Dannon approached Chris and shook his hand. "I hope you will forgive our lack of preparedness here at the lab," Dannon said. "At this late hour, there are very few people in the building."

Chris glanced over at Zelda. She was fumbling absentmindedly with the chain around her neck that held the personal pass card that Chris was thinking would get them through the glass doors of the EPOTEK lobby.

"No problem, Doctor," Chris replied. "It's my place to make an apology for asking for this tour with so little warning. If it were not for the urgency of the investigation that we are currently conducting, I would have given you the time you needed to prepare. I promise we will be as brief as possible."

"I appreciate that, Agent," Dannon said and turned to Zelda. "This is one of our executive assistants, Zelda Krebs. She will be acting as your tour guide this evening."

"Yes, Ms. Krebs met us as we were just coming in." Chris was surprised to see Lisa Krebs stepping into the guard shack and taking a position behind her mother. She winked at Chris, and he gave her a knowing nod.

"Now, boys and girls." Zelda smiled. "Just follow me, and we'll get started." With that, she and Dr. Dannon led the group, including Dr. Bilbro, Jack O'Rilley, SIFI Bob, Professor Balboa, Agent Slattery, and Lisa, out of the guard shack and toward the front door to the lab, their new visitor's badges flapping in what was left of the evening breeze.

Once inside the building, it only took a few minutes for the group to walk down one of the many halls in the EPOTEK facility to the entrance to a well-equipped state-of-the-art conference room. Chris and the rest of the group began to take seats all around the long table.

All the eyes of the group were on Dr. Dannon as he noisily pulled out his chair and sat down. For a while he just sat there in silence with an aggravated look on his face twiddling his thumbs.

Zelda grew impatient with him and decided to take the lead herself. She smiled, looked at Chris, and then Jesse and the rest of the group, then down to her folded hands. She cleared her throat and said, "Dr. Dannon"—she smiled and cut her eyes briefly over to Dannon—"and I want to welcome all of you to EPOTEK. I like to think of this facility as a scientifically motivated company that prides itself at addressing special projects. They don't like for me to use the term special projects, but that's ultimately what it comes down to. What other companies shy away from, we pick up and manage until we have a workable solution or product." She looked back toward the door to the room. "Perhaps a cup of coffee will help us all get started and give our technicians time to get prepared. Is that okay with you, Dr. Dannon?"

Dannon just grunted, seemingly in a very disagreeable mood. He wasn't all that familiar with the FREEZE agency, and Agent Battey had already left a bad taste in his brain, by insisting that EPOTEK help in confirming the validity of the moon rock he'd brought for them to examine.

"Not for me," Chris said. "If I drink a cup now, I won't get to sleep until the sun comes up tomorrow."

"Well, I'm going to have a cup, anybody else?" Zelda tossed her head slightly to the side, causing her red hair to fluff out ever so nicely.

There were nods around the table, and she quickly took a head count.

Jesse also waved off the offer. "No, thank you. I'm just anxious to see the new x-ray microscope you told us about."

Zelda nodded to her daughter. "Lisa, will you be so kind at to address the Professor's concerns while I get the coffee?"

Lisa waved her hand at her mother. "Happy to."

As Zelda headed out of the room, Lisa attempted to answer Jesse's concerns. "Well, currently, we have a priority investigation under way, and if Hank isn't able to finish up his analysis tonight, I regret that it may be impossible for us to accommodate your request. I'm extremely sorry about that; however, we have many other very interesting investigations going on with some our projects—especially in the electron microscope lab."

"Of course," Jesse said. "We…Agent Slattery and I, will be disappointed if we don't get to visit the x-ray microscope Lab and"—he waved his hand—"whatever it is… Hank is analyzing, but, yes, I would be delighted if we could visit some of these other labs, and I'm sure that goes for the rest of our tour group."

"Good, excellent!" Lisa smiled.

Zelda came back into the room with a tray full of coffee cups and made her way around the table. Once everyone had their coffee, she turned to Dannon and said, "What do you think, Doctor? I need to get back to the x-ray microscope lab and assist Henry. Can you show these gentlemen around?

"If I must," Dannon grunted to Zelda, then turned to the guests. "You will have to understand giving tours of the facility is something we usually do during normal working hours; therefore, this will justifiably be a very short tour."

"No problem, Doctor. Professor Balboa and I have heard very wonderful things about your electron and x-ray microscope facilities here at EPOTEK. I had to do some tall talking convince my boss at FREEZE to agree to a visit. And since the professor and I were flying back to Georgia anyway, going the extra mile to Houston, so to speak, was just too tempting to pass up."

"Yes…I see," Dannon grunted again and pushed back from the table.

"I appreciate your personal attention, Doctor.," Zelda said. "Perhaps Lisa can help you out and do most of the heavy lifting on the tour. She knows this place like the back of her hand."

"Yeah, Doctor," Lisa said. "You've got the authority, and I've got the know-how. Great combination, eh?"

Lisa's smile was captivating and did a lot to soften the Doctor's demeanor. By this time the group had all gotten up from the conference table and were gathering around Lisa and the doctor.

"Well, let's see how it works," Dannon said and motioned for the group to follow him into the hall. "But, Ms. Krebs," he added with a lighter tone than he'd been using up to that moment, "I've got the distinct feeling that you are just using me for my badge to get these people into all the projects we've been trying to keep secret all these years."

"Doctor, you crush me to the quick. I would never do anything like that." Lisa laughed.

53

Present/Past

A strange trembling motion shot through the tiny flying saucer as Tack advanced the time control forward to return the Spirit to what had been the present, at least the present in his memory. Tack was beginning to realize that his concept of time had already been distorted beyond his ability to comprehend the difference between past, present, and future. Worse, and even more dangerous, his imagination was tempting him to just go forward into the future to see what the outcome of EPOTEK's study of the moon rock was going to lead to. But the more he thought about it, the more it hurt his head, and he decided that any time travel experiments that he was to attempt were best conducted under more controlled conditions. It was all too evident that he was not currently in what anyone would call "controlled conditions," and added to all that, he was realizing, little by little, just how difficult it was to be a so-called time traveler—to be able to think about that extra dimension rationally. To come from the past to a present that he'd occupied, in a manner of speaking, just hours ago was more than he could handle without charting it out. The big problem was, he had no idea of even how to begin to chart it out so that it would make any sense at all.

In the now present, the people in the room he'd come back to, was now racing around forward in time—the exact opposite of what he'd experienced earlier that evening. And he watched closely as he approached the actual time wherein he had discovered the time-travel feature of the ship and initiated that experimental time travel.

As the point in time, the exact time, that he could remember leaving the present—think about that for a minute or two—began to approach, he almost ran directly into himself. The Spirit of the future came blasting past the Spirit of the past...or visa versa—he couldn't decide. Somehow, as luck would have it, if there is, indeed, such a thing as luck, he managed to avoid the imminent disaster and found himself settling the Spirit back down to the side of the approximate position on the shelf that it had previously occupied. If anyone had been looking at that particular area on the shelf at the time Tack had decided to zip back into time, they would have seen the Spirit disappear and then reappear in a slightly different position. A physicist would have been puzzled to see the Spirit moving in an apparent faster-than-the-speed-of-light velocity as it traveled instantaneously from one point to another.

Once settled into position on the shelf and able to think in the present once more, Tack got up from his acceleration couch and leaned over the console to peer out of the forward window. He watched for a while until his back started to ache, so he moved around the command deck and killed time, sampling the scene outside the forward window now and then. After almost an hour had passed, he grew impatient waiting for something that would give him a clue as to what to do next and decided to speed up the time travel to see how the moon rock had been inserted the into the chamber.

"A few minutes shouldn't matter one way or the other that much," he said and went back to the acceleration couch. Cautiously, watching carefully out of the forward window, he pushed forward in time. He waited and watched. Finally, something of interest happened. The moon rock was being moved at last. He was surprised to see that the plexiglass case wasn't actually put into the chamber but loaded onto a conveyor belt connected to the chamber by a long, narrow tunnel.

He flew the Spirit off the shelf and followed the plexiglas box as it was driven along on the conveyor belt. It grew extremely dark, and Tack had to fly the Spirit very carefully along beside the box, as the moon rock container moved to the end of the conveyor belt. He could see the airlock door siding open, very slowly, and on the other side of the door, inside the airlock was another very short conveyor belt. Soon, the box was transferred from the outside belt to the inside belt. This whole procedure was repeated after the airlock was sealed, and the second airlock door was opened. Finally the moon box was pushed off the chamber's belt and settled onto a silvery turntable. On this turntable, a series of robot fingers with suction cups on the tips grabbed on to the upper portion of the box. Once they were secure, another series of aluminum tubes came out around the bottom, and a tiny laser beam at the end of each tube was directed around the bottom edge of the plexiglass box. The beams of the lasers cut through the plexiglass walls, separating the top from the base. The top was then lifted off the box by the robot fingers. As the moon rock was picked up by another set of robot fingers, the atmosphere, including the gasses released by the lasers cutting through the plexiglass, were quickly pumped from the chamber. Then, as the base of the plexiglass box was removed, the robot fingers placed the moon rock sample onto a small metal turntable in the center of the vacuum chamber.

This procedure had eventually exposed the lunar sample to the environment of the vacuum chamber, and Tack zoomed the Spirit down closer to the rock for a better angle of vision. He was making a fly around when he noticed a disturbing shudder that rocked the command deck. He glanced around him at the controls and the readouts as if studying them would tell him what had caused the strange trembling sensation. Then it happened again, and before he could look back at the rock and adjust the flight attitude of the ship, he realized that he was losing control. A tongue of fear griped his heart. "Oh no!" he cried.

54

Quantum Room

It took only a few minutes for Dr. Dannon's group to walk down one of the many halls in the EPOTEK facility, and soon, they were entering a room that they found to be very dark and gloomy. This room had every wall painted flat black. Even the floor was a matt-finish black rubber. Except for the low light of the monitor over in a corner of the room, this area was completely without light.

"Wow, ever seen anything like this, Professor?" Chris asked Jesse as his eyes slowly adjusted to the dim light of the room.

Jesse's eyes were also slowly accommodating to the darkness, and he became aware of three additional people gathered around the monitor and the seated figure at the workstation.

As Doc Dannon's group stepped up to the workstation, the two men and a young girl turned to face them. "Why don't you introduce yourselves?" Dannon said and stepped back out of the way as the young girl was the first to step forward with a big smile.

"Hi, I'm Kathy Dawkins. No, no relation to Dr. Dick, I'm afraid. I'm Dirk's assistant. I specialize in troubleshooting programs."

The red headed, tall, skinny guy smiled and nodded. "I'm Dirk Macky. I created Mildred here." He patted the large black plastic box that looked like your basic computer tower, only about four times the size. "I operate it. Frank, here, fixes it, and Roul fine-tunes it." Dirk nodded to each of the other men in turn.

The guy that was seated at the console stood up from his chair and said, "I am Roul Lamont, glad to meet you all."

The tall black guy stepped forward. "And last but not least, I'm Frank Dees. These guys keep me busy trying to keep Mildred working, so to speak." Frank put his hand out to the man standing next to SIFI Bob. "Hi, Jack O'Rilley, I believe."

"Hey, that's right," Jack said, shaking Frank's hand. "How did you know?"

"ESP. I'm a remote viewer in addition to being a physicist and an electronics engineer."

"Handy," the man next to Jack O'Rilley said, taking the doctor's hand.

"SIFI Bob." Dees smiled.

"ESP again?" Bob raised his eyebrow as he shook the doctor's hand.

"No, Starlog magazine." They both laughed.

"Got a name for me, Dr. Dees?" Jesse stepped forward hand extended.

"Sure do, but anybody would recognize the great Professor Balboa. Professor, you're one of the very few scientists that challenges all those so-called consensus scientists. What is it you call them?"

"Oh, you mean pseudo scientists. Yes, I get a lot of angry dialogue stirred up by my criticism of those in my field of study that use the words 'might have' when they really mean, 'It's not provable scientifically.'"

"I hear ya." Frank smiled. "But I must admit you haven't been able to sway me away from the belief in so-called Darwinian evolution."

"Given the chance, I could make you see that Darwin's ideas were founded in observation only. Practical experiments that could prove that his idea of evolution would produce different species in plants or animals were far from his ability or the ability of anyone else of that time for that matter. Perhaps we could get together someday for some serious discussions. For me, though, it is all too obvious that a lot of scientists that agree with Darwin's theory have a lot to gain monetarily from their pursuit of disproving the idea of any kind of intelligent design."

"I look forward to it," he added and turned to Chris. "And you are the agent I have heard so much about."

"None of that stuff is true, you know." Chris smiled. "We government agents have to keep our cover in the forefront, you know."

While Frank was shaking hands with Chris, Dannon stepped over to the plastic tower and put his hand on top of it, patting it gently. "Thank you, Frank." The doctor turned back to face the group. "Mildred is the name Dirk gives this remarkable machine." Then he cleared his throat and began explaining what went on in this particular room. "This is what we call the quantum room. Here we plan to attempt to break down inanimate matter into a form of energy similar to a radio wave that can be transmitted through space and be reassembled at a distant location. The equipment is being constructed off site, but it will soon occupy the rest of this room."

"Can you actually do that?" Jesse gasped. "I had no idea."

"Few people are aware of the work going on in this field. Those of us on this particular project have had only a limited number of successes with our prototype equipment in the off-site location," Dannon said.

"You can say that again." Macky nodded to the group. "I guess you guys are here about the lunar sample that has come our way recently." He laughed. "I've been trying to tell these jokers that there ain't no way that's a real moon rock. It's just a rock with a piece of glass fused to it."

There was a quiet that settled around the room, and Chris could tell that Dannon was hoping that the subject of the moon rock examination hadn't come up. Macky had let the cat out of the bag so to speak, but the doctor didn't want to stress the point, so he didn't protest except to ram his hands into his pockets and look at the floor.

"Oh, you have a moon rock here…being examined?" Jesse queried.

"We aren't yet convinced that what we have is actually from the surface of the moon," Dirk said. "But, of course, I'm no expert on lunar artifacts. If anyone can prove it one way or the other, that would be Hank."

As the members of the small group rambled around, looking and talking about the quantum room and all of the possibilities it presented the world of science, Lisa punched Chris gently in the ribs and said, "Come on, Chris, I'll show you the x-ray microscope. These guys'll be at it forever with all these Mildred technicians." She took Chris by the hand and started toward the door. He sensed that she wanted to get him far enough away from the others to say something to him in private. However, it was not going to happen—not just yet.

Dannon left the group, caught up to Chris and Lisa at the lab door, and put his hand on Chris's shoulder. "Excuse me, Agent Slattery. Hank is currently conducting some very secret studies with that particular rock, and until that period of study is completed, I'm afraid that no one else will be allowed in the x-ray microscope lab."

"Ahhh, shucks," Lisa said, stepping back a bit. She frowned and glanced up at Chris.

Over by the work station, Bob looked over at Macky and said, "Transmission of matter through space." He looked down at the floor and shook his head. "That goes hand in hand with what Douglas Bullworth's pyramid exhibit demonstrated back in Vegas." He looked up and scanned the group with a smile on his face. "Far out!"

55

Time Energy Fields

Tack was now experiencing real trouble. The tiny flying saucer was tilting and swinging in an uncontrollable, faltering wobble as it moved through the vacuum chamber.

For a few harrowing moments, the activity in the Spirit's interior demanded Tack's full attention, and he started to pray while his hands and his brain were busy trying to save what was left of his moon-rock retrieval adventure. He tried everything—everything, but the right thing. Tack couldn't know that the time bank required a great deal of energy, especially when one traveled back and forth within the same time period. Of course, Tack couldn't know that. Only the builders of the ship would know that it took several hours to recharge the bank. All that was needed was to wait for the time energy fields to rebuild, capturing the energy that radiates from the sun and the stars, the various forms of radiation that is all around us to one degree or another, but of course, he didn't know that either.

"Maybe"—he gasp—"if I shrink down to a... smaller size, the ship will stabilize."

He punched in the reduction command again, and down, down, down he took the Spirit through the various size reductions until it was just barely the size of the average pollen molecule, and since molecules are different sizes, his size didn't really mean too much to Tack's limited intellect, but he knew he was small—perhaps small enough to fly the Spirit through the maze of gasket molecules of the vacuum chamber.

But the ship was still behaving strangely. At first, it just wobbled a little, occasionally, like a child's top losing critical speed but coming back to upright for intervals of stability. Seconds later, it would wobble like crazy again.

Then, the tiny saucer started to lose altitude. "Holy crash and burn, Batman! I'm falling! Jeez! I'm losing it—fast."

Tack fought the control spheres, trying, somehow, to stabilize the craft and maintain altitude. He was able to get the ship into a crude glide path, but he saw the terrain up ahead and realized the speed at which he was approaching that terrain was too great. As a seasoned pilot, he knew he was in for a rough landing.

He put down the landing gear, knowing that the impact would, most likely, rip most of it off, but he knew that if the ship bellied in, the only escape through the air lock hatch would be cut off. He still didn't know about the hatch in the ceiling of the airlock. He'd had no reason to look for it, and it wasn't all that obvious.

As the floor of the vacuum chamber came up to meet the ship, the Spirit hit pretty hard, bounced slightly, and skipped on its landing pads for some distance.

"Got to hang on somehow!" Tack's voice was shaky and muffled as he was tossed around before the Spirit finally came to a stop.

He sat there in silence for a while, just letting his heart stabilize. The Spirit was still groaning, settling onto the surface of the chamber floor as Tack unbuckled himself and walked over to the display panel. All the lights inside the ship were growing dim, and soon, Tack found himself standing in the dark.

"Oh great! I must be the size of a microbe, and I'm stuck inside a vacuum chamber where no one can see me and no one knows where I am. Maaaannnn, I'm really up the creek now. Probably without enough air to breath, let alone a paddle," he grumbled. "Got to think of something—fast. I don't know how long the air inside the Spirit will hold out. I have no idea how the danged oxygen supply in this ship works. You'd think a smart guy like me would have checked that out by now. For sure, I should have checked that out when I went to the moon." He slapped his forehead. "I must have been crazy to pull a stunt like that. We can put a man on the moon, but we can't even learn how to breathe." He stumbled in the dark over to another panel. "No power. No power! No air—what in God's green Earth do I do now?"

Tack wandered around inside the ship, aimlessly for a while, bouncing off objects here and there that he couldn't see. He was trying to think, and bumping his head didn't help much, so he tried to find his acceleration couch so he could sit down and hopefully come up with some kind of plan. Finally he felt the touch of the familiar shape, and as he eased himself back into the couch, his hand found his custom headset, so he slipped it on and sat there in the dark for a while just listening to the drumbeat of Tangerine Dream's "Oasis," and letting his mind wander through the maze of options that presented themselves. There weren't many.

After what seemed like half an hour, but in reality was only about one-tenth of that, suddenly Tack yanked off his headset and said, "Spacesuit! That's it. I'll put on my suit. It's got oxygen. And if I can figure out a way to open the airlock with the power off, I'll go outside and look at the damage to the ship. I'm getting nowhere just sitting around in here in the dark listening to music."

After working his way to the airlock hatch, he felt around with his hands, trying to find the hatch control. "Maybe I can't even get outside. If there's no power, there will be no way to lower the hatch—not good! But wait...the designers of this ship must have known this kind of thing might happen. Yeah! And if they did know this loss of power was possible, they also knew the crew would be trapped inside if... they...didn't provide them... with...an...emergency power supply." He spun around twice, his eyes searching. "Toast, I'm toast. No...it's more like soggy bread.

I wish I knew how to operate this crazy ship." Once again he banged his head against something hard, and cried out.

"I've got to find a manual…crank of some kind. It's got to be somewhere…all I have to do is figure out what it might look like."

Tack searched the wall panels and the areas around the airlock door. He was about to give up his mad search when he noticed a faint glow in a shallow receptacle at the upper right-hand side of the door to the airlock. It was a tiny, little blue light. Next to the light was what appeared to be a lever.

"Well, what have we got here? Looks like some kind of door latch…whatever a door latch looks like on Quadrilla's planet." He put his weight against the lever and moaned softly, "Here goes nothing."

To Tack's relief, down it came. He felt the lever lock into the new position, and immediately a section of the wall to the right of the air lock door popped loose with a loud crack and fell off the wall. He quickly noticed that this action revealed a recessed housing surrounding a large spoked wheel. He stepped up and turned the wheel.

The airlock door slowly, noiselessly slid open. He stepped inside the airlock chamber, and soon discovered another tiny blue light. As he expected, there was another wheel inside the airlock chamber located in a similar recessed area.

"Air lock, air lock," he chanted as he closed the airlock door and started to suit up.

While he was putting his helmet on, he studied the recess in the wall. It was different from the recess outside the airlock. This one had something it didn't. There was a large button with a blinking red light in the center.

Once he was fully suited up, he stepped over and pushed the button. The red light went out, and Tack could feel a high-speed vibration run up through the soles of his moon boots. Then the ramp started down.

Once outside the ship, Tack did a walk-around to check to see if the landing had caused any damage to the landing gear. The struts seemed to have come through the landing in surprisingly good shape. It was hard to believe, but then again, Tack had no idea what kind of metal the Spirit was made of.

"Whatever material the little green guys used to build this ship, we could sure use some of it on our aircraft struts," he said.

He satisfied himself that the Spirit was, for all practical purposes, intact. He turned and looked off into what should have been the horizon; instead, all he could see was white. Then, of course, there was in the middle of all that white space the moon rock sitting on a metallic turntable. It was held in an upright position by a strange-looking set of leg-like supports. These legs were mounted on a square base of thick, glistening metal, and on the side of the rock facing him, he could see the ice-blue crystal.

"I'm stuck here," he said, turning to look first in one direction, then in the other. He completed his walk-around and would have shrugged his shoulders, but the space suit prevented any such subtle gesture.

"Well, this is a fine mess you've gotten yourself into, Ollie," he sighed.

56

Grown Together

Dannon's EPOTEK tour was still proceeding to the electron microscope lab, while off in the x-ray microscope lab, Henry sat at his work station trying to rub the pain out of his neck muscles by pounding on the back of his neck with his fist. "I think my vertebrae have grown together," he said with a groan.

As Zelda came through the lab door, he looked up and said, "Back so soon?" He immediately went back to studying some figures on a notepad next to the computer keyboard. Looking back and forth from the monitor to his notes, he mumbled to himself words that Zelda couldn't make out.

She moved in closer to where he sat and said, "Why don't you call it a day, Henry…or a night? Dr. Dannon's tour will be nosin' around all over the place, and it's only a matter of time before they wind up outside your precious lab. I can't believe that you are looking forward to such an interruption." She smiled and put her hand on Hank's shoulder. "Besides, you're going to ruin your eyes if you don't stop looking at that monitor screen."

"Yeah, you're probably right. It's just that I hate to leave a job right in the middle of something that's so difficult to explain." He was about to ask her to take the seat next to him when he spotted something he hadn't noticed before and cried out. "Holy mama!. What…man…I never saw anything like this before."

Zelda leaned in closer to the monitor. "What is that thing?" she asked, fixing her eyes on a mysterious object at the edge of the monitor screen. Without looking away from the strange thing, she pulled over one of the chairs and sat down next to him.

"I don't know. It makes no sense," Hank groaned. "It's just sittin' there off to one side of the lunar sample. I don't know why I didn't see it before. If I didn't have the proof of my own two eyes, I'd be convinced I dreamed the whole thing up. What do you suppose it is, Zel?"

She reached up, brushed her copper-red hair streaked with silver away from her face, and said, "It looks like a tiny little CD disk." Her throat was so dry her voice cracked. "What do you suppose it is?"

"I have no idea, and if I didn't have it on tape, I'd be convinced it was all in my imagination. I sure am glad to know that you see the same thing I do, Zel." Henry motioned toward the video screen. "At least that's some kind of additional proof that I'm not losing my mind?"

57

Pyramid Power

Dr. Dannon's group had decided to gather in the conference room where they'd been earlier that evening. Bob's mind was still occupied with the prospect of actually being able to transmit matter through space and how that possibility worked hand in hand with what Bullworth's reality theory presented. Being a superfan of science fiction movies all the way back to the Republic Saturday serials, with RocketMan and Batman, he'd been surrounded with a multitude of scientific ideas that the Hollywood science fiction directors and producers had turned into horror and adventure films. The list of films he'd admired for their special effects included a monster epic called The Fly. The transmission of matter and the machine that made it all possible was the centerpiece of that particular film. He was about to let his mind ask the question of whether or not the EPOTEK prototype machine had ever been used in an attempt to transmit organic matter through space when Jack got up and moved to the head of the conference table. This move made the room began to quiet down as all of them turned their attention toward Jack, the artist from NASA.

Bob quickly looked around at the faces that lined the huge conference table.

Jack nodded to the group and began to speak. "As I was saying before, SIFI Bob and I have just come from Las Vegas, and we have some information that you might find interesting, especially since you are about to embark on an effort to transmit matter over a distance and reconstitute it. If you are successful in that endeavor, I'm thinking that it is perhaps both desirable and necessary that we give some serious consideration to what Bob and I have learned during our visit to the Luxor pyramid in Las Vegas.

"It all has to do with what we have come to call reality. We all assume an awful lot about reality. I personally find it laughable when I hear someone stand up on their science fiction high horse and ridicule new, bizarre ideas as unscientific, as if they know all there is to know about what is possible or impossible in our so-called reality. Our senses of sight, hearing, feel, taste, smell, and something we call our sixth sense, whatever that is—all of our senses—they tell us everything we think we know about reality. This is the human concept of reality. I have come to think of it this way: These human senses, all five of them—and perhaps a sixth, who knows—they are like five windows out of our sense of self into the reality, or as I like to call it, the realm. And it comes to my limited mind that there are only five senses. That's like having a building with only five windows, not to mention the possible doors. But that's another story.

"Think of any building that has only five windows. Think of all the other directions one might choose to look if only there were more windows. Only five—sad indeed.

"This is the human concept of reality, and it is different for everyone of us. No two people, scientific or not, have the same experiences, education, idea mechanisms, not to mention the belief mechanism that is within each and every one of us. Ever give a minute's thought to what you really believe about the world around us? Ever wonder why a bird never misses the limb it flies to and lands on, those little tiny claws managing to grab onto the limb just in time—and how the little bird balances itself there with apparent ease? With all of the engineering and science at the human mind's disposal, we haven't been able to make a robot that can do that—at least not yet. And even if we could, could we make millions and millions of them and send them out to populate the Earth, as do all the members of the bird kingdom?

"The so-called consensus scientist had his own idea of what is real. He feels no need to actually find out for himself what is real and why and how it works. Once he has the information that satisfies his longing, he addresses others of like mind, and they together decide for us stupid, nonscientists what reality is. He seems to be convinced that he has a great so-called intellect. He thinks he knows everything there is to know about reality as though any of us will or could live to learn about all there is in the realm of reality. He especially thinks he knows more than does little ole me, or any of us gathered here around the table. Okay, okay, bear with me. I know all this sounds fatalistic, and believe me, until I was exposed to the reality of the Great Pyramid and was amazed at what had been accomplished there, I, too, was fatalistic, but not anymore.

"Dr. Darwin Dawkingsly, the famous atheist who, by the way, has been busy attempting to convert Christians and people from other religions to his own idea of what is real, has often expressed a quite different view of reality that most of us hold. He seems to be convinced that he has a great so-called intellect. He thinks he knows everything there is to know about the realm, as though any of us will or could live to learn all there is in the realm of reality. He especially thinks he knows more than does little ole Jack O'Rilley, or any one of you gathered here in this great scientific laboratory." He looked around the table at the blank faces. "I ask you to bear with me. I know this sounds academic, and believe me, I felt the same way until we were exposed to the new attraction in the Luxor pyramid in Las Vegas."

"My mom took me there when I was just a little girl," Lisa said.

Chris looked over at her. "They've changed the attraction since then. New management has taken over the exhibit."

"And the new management has done something wonderful," Jack continued. "We've all been brought up to see something mystical about the Egyptians and their artifacts. The curse of Tutankhamen, the curse of the mummy, the mystical powers of the pyramid, you know, how a rusty razor blade seems to sharpen itself when placed under a pyramid even though this civilization is thousands of years old—we've all been exposed to many of the cultural myths and other details of that period of ancient times.

"Yes, I dare say most of us have heard of the so-called pyramid power," Dr. Dannon said.

"Precisely," Balboa said.

"Well"—Bob nodded energetically—"think of this, Jack and I were invited to visit the new exhibit. And when we went inside—"

"After a rather bizarre roundabout journey to get there, which is another story entirely," Jack added.

Bob smiled, made a tent with his fingers on the table, and continued, "Inside the black pyramid, we were led into a dark room. In this chamber, we were surrounded by black obsidian stonewalls covered with hieroglyphics that were carved deep into the rock. It was very dark, except for the bluish light that came from a cluster of crystals in the center of the ceiling above us."

Jack interrupted again and said, "And you could feel it...a... a...something like a vibration in the air around us."

"And a tingling up the spine." Bob's eyes opened wide. His gray handlebar mustache twitched momentarily, and he continued, "But nothing else happened. We had this feeling inside our bodies, and especially in our minds, but nothing else happened."

"But for some strange reason," Jack said, "we...both of us, I found out later...well, we were not disappointed. We were as satisfied as if we'd just witnessed some great Egyptian exhibit or some cleverly designed and executed show attraction. It was later that the real exhibit seemed to fill our minds. I thought I just had one of those dreams that seem so real and pleasant that when you wake up, you feel...sad..." Jack's voice trailed off."

"You're sorry you woke up." Bob's voice cracked a little, and he added, "It was like leaving a real close friend, and you know you'll never see them again, and we both...well, later at breakfast the next morning, Jack and I were dying to tell each other about the dream we'd had."

"And as we talked back and forth"—Jack's excitement just wouldn't let him shut up and let Bob tell the story—"we began to realize that, lo and behold, we'd both had exactly the same dream."

There was a quiet in the room that seemed to go on for a long time—longer than it really was.

58

The Eye Above

White! As far as Tack could see, there was little else but white. Since there was no atmosphere inside the chamber, the sides of the box in the distance would have been in sharp detail, but since the insides of the box were painted with flat white paint, there was no sense of being inside a box at all. He could make out the corners of the box, and when he looked up, he could see the top of the box as well. The snorkel lens of the x-ray microscope was mounted in the ceiling on a central shaft that allowed the lens to be cycled around the core of the chamber.

"No doubt that thing can see me from any angle," Tack said trying to look up. With the helmet oriented the way it was, looking up was not only a difficult task, but it was also dangerous. If he lost his balance, he might fall over on his back and damage the suit.

"Hey up there!" he said to the gigantic lens structure above him. "Get me out of here. I'm running out of air." Then he started laughing. "I am losing it. I am definitely losing it. They haven't even turned the thing on yet. Least wise it ain't movin'."

He chuckled a couple more times and started walking away from the Spirit, toward the mountainous lunar sample in the distance. "Maybe if I climb up on that moon rock, they'll see me. They probably won't even notice the Spirit. It's…it's just too small and so far away from the moon rock. There's no reason they'd be looking over there."

He could hear the soles of his boots scraping along the bottom of the chamber, along the painted white floor. He clopped along for what seemed to him like hours, glancing up at the lens of the microscope from time to time, looking for any sign that someone might be turning on the machine and watching him. Tack's foster dad had told him of a visit he and Tack had made to Disneyland. What had impressed him most was one particular attraction where the audience was supposedly miniaturized by some kind of shrink ray. The climax of the ride was when the conveyance car passed underneath a giant cylinder. When Tack had looked up into the cylinder, what he saw was a gigantic human eye looking back at him. That sudden image frightened the young Tack so that he'd dreamed about it for two nights in a row. That image was currently filling Tack's imagination.

Eric Strobe's space suit was cumbersome, and it took a great deal of energy to make it move to his normal walking gait. He grew tired but continued to drag himself along. Finally he decided to take a break, and rest, but there was nothing to sit down on, so he just stood there, looking down at the suit controller on his left arm. His oxygen indicator showed his tanks to be half-empty.

"Just dandy," he gasped. "I can sit down and save my air and probably never be seen by those guys up there in the land of the giants—ooorrr, I can use up my precious reserve trying to get up there on the rock where I might eventually be seen."

After he caught what was left of his breath, he walked for what had seemed four or five more hours, and it wasn't easy walking. To the untrained eye, the surface he was walking on would have appeared smooth, but at his current scale, Tack detected a waffled pattern texture that he was forced to stumble up and over on his journey to the moon rock.

"If only there were a blue sky," Tack said, "or a mountain—or anything. But all this white on white." His voice was echoless, depth-less, confined to his space helmet.

So far, his exploration had been completely fruitless. He seemed to be no closer to the moon rock now than he had before he decided to do a little exploring outside his ship. His situation seemed to be hopeless. If only he could power up the Spirit and fly out of the sealed chamber.

"I wonder just how small I am," he said to himself. His answer was only silence.

All he could hear was his own voice coming back to him inside his helmet. His breath momentarily left a small vapor smudge on the faceplate, and he raised his controller arm again. He pushed the button to raise the drink tube and took a sip of the water as he fingered the button for the small faceplate defroster device he'd improvised some months before. It was still working, but like the food, water, and oxygen, he knew if he didn't find something before long, he'd be looking at the world through a foggy faceplate while he slowly suffocated or starved or dehydrated or all of the above.

He stopped at the top of a small ridge and rested again. "Shoot, I don't think I'm going to make it to the moon rock before I run out of resources. When I started out, the lunar sample didn't seem to be all that far." He looked around his current position. "I guess my best bet now is to head back toward the ship," he said in frustration, turning to see the Spirit, tiny in the distance. "Wow, I didn't think I'd come all that far. I hope I can make it back in time."

Tack realized he was doing a lot of talking to himself, lately—especially now, in that strangest of all places. "Oh, how hard can it be? I'll probably run out of air before I get back anyway. Looks like I'm toast all right."

He turned and surveyed the vastness of the chamber; as far as he could see, it didn't give him much hope. "Oh no! Just what I was afraid of. It looks like I'm not going to make it. And I think I'm getting light-headed."

He stumbled over the lumps that made up the textured pattern of the floor. "This stuff is," he gasped, "probably smoother than glass to the guys out there in the lab. Seems like it ought to give me some clue as to my scale, though. Mannn, I must be microscopic. Chances are, they'll never be able to find me at my current size. If I can get back, maybe I can devise some kind of message on the outside of the ship. I wonder what I've got to work with. If I can't hit them with some kind of message, I'm sunk."

He walked on in silence for a while. After a time, he stopped momentarily and rested again. The going was really making him tired, tired sooner than he'd expected to be. "If this place were perfectly flat, I could save my energy," he said. After a few more minutes, he shook his head and continued on his way.

He looked around at the white walls of the chamber, straining to make out any small detail. "Somehow, this place reminds me of that movie THX 1138. There was a scene where they were just walking and walking in this white world, with nothing else in sight for hours and hours. Depressing movie," he mumbled, "but I enjoy seeing it again and again. If I remember correctly, eventually those guys did get to some kind of doorway. Maybe if I just keep on walking, I'll get somewhere." He walked on a few more steps and then stopped, swaying slightly as he stood in place. "They don't make 'em like that anymore," he said.

He walked on for what seemed to be another half hour. "Another movie I really liked was Flight of the Phoenix. This plane crashed in the Sahara, and one of the guys was going to try to hike out and get help. Let's see…who was it, ah—Jimmy Stewart told Richard Attenborough…no…Peter Cushing…no… well, anyway, whatever his name or rank was, he told him that if he was right handed, he would favor his right leg in walking. Without the sun or the moon or stars to navigate by, he would walk in a big circle without ever knowing it, but I can still see my ship. There's no way I'm walking in a big circle. Now, if I can just conserve my oxygen long enough…"

Tack, now and all alone was standing in his white world. He managed to look again in both directions. "Yep, I know it now. I should have stayed with the Spirit. Heh, heh. That's the Spirit! Heh, heh. Yeah, that should be an easy thing to do, since I appear too be to far away to ever get back to the ship while I can still breathe." He sighed and started stumbling along, fighting the urge to start running.

After another what seemed like ten minutes of silence, he said, "Where in Dorothy's name is that yellow brick road?" As if it would do him any good, he looked down at the countdown clock on his wrist. "Lots of good this thing does. Wish I had my pocket watch. Now there's a timepiece worth its weight."

He was getting dizzy, and he laughed weakly. "Funny thing about watches, you never seem to be able to throw one away, especially an old pocket watch. Oh, you can throw it in a drawer or a cigar box. Mannnn, I ain't seen a cigar box since I was ten years old. Shoot! They were great cigar boxes. They were like treasure chests, pirate's treasure. Must have had a dozen of'em when I was a kid. If I ever get out of this cursed place, I'm going to get me a whole box of cigars, and...and...and...oh shoot, I forgot what I was I going to say. Oh mannn...I can't think straight...I...I..." He staggered, spun around, and tripped over something. And fell.

59

Magnification

Not far from the EPOTEK conference room, Zelda was leaning over Hank's shoulder, watching closely at the image on the monitor screen. She could see what looked like a small silver lens-shaped object sitting on the waffle-patterned floor of the x-ray microscope chamber. "I can't imagine…"

Hank couldn't tear his eyes away from the screen but said, "I can't either, but I'm thinkin' it almost looks like it is a manufactured object, not a natural formation of anything I've ever seen before. You know, I'm almost afraid to increase the magnification and get a better look."

60

Mind Expander

SIFI Bob was busy continuing his narrative about the black pyramid attraction while the rest of the tour group sat listening. As he waved his hands in his excitement, he went on to say, "Think of it. How cool is it? Two people having exactly the same dream."

"And what a dream it was too," Jack chimed in.

Bob rolled his eyes. "It seemed to last for...for a very long time, almost like a lifetime. We were in Egypt, back about a thousand years after the completion of the Great Pyramid."

"The big one," Jack put in. "The Pyramid of Khufu... Cheops."

"There was an old man there in robes that came up to us, speaking in our own language. Well, at least we both of us could understand him. He was most friendly and anxious to tell us all about the world we were in. He led us through the streets and avenues of the city, talking to us and explaining details of all the sights we were seeing. I say that he was speaking to us in a language that we could understand, but he seemed to be speaking in a strange language that somehow, as we listened, our minds could interpret."

This time, Lisa interrupted, "You mean you could see each other in the dream like you were there together?"

"No, no," Jack said, "we just had the same dream. When Bob and I talked to each other about the dream, we just started to talk about it as if we were there together.

"The important thing is," Bob went on, "that the man I was following through the streets of the city was not only showing me the art and the architecture and the people of the city, but he was also explaining to me why these things were real." He looked from face to face around the table. "I've never had that happen in a dream before, and I don't know how Douglas Bullworth was able to accomplish it, but this man told me how things really are and how reality…works. And I'm beginning to believe that he was…right. I mean, I can't really say that I think he was just making it all up.

Dr. Dannon cleared his throat loudly and interrupted. "I am reminded of the sleeping prophet." He looked around at the group and went on. "His name was Edger Cayce. He lived back just after the turn of the century, I believe.

"Yeah," Jack said. "I've read a lot about Cayce. He gave many readings and interpreted the dreams of many of his acquaintances. He is known to have given many readings from the unconscious state. He considered the human being as a three-dimensional manifestation of a sort of spiritual form of reality. Think of it, humans are composed basically of atoms that are units of…what he called force energy. Consciousness has a quality that supports these basic structural units of force energy. This forms a kind of structure that can not only be seen but felt as well. Our present understanding of the atom does not yet include what might be understood as a specific consciousness. We know that atoms are different in themselves, that for instance, the iron atom is quite different from a uranium atom.

"From Cayce's perspective, a unit is made up of billions of cells. Each of these cells were seen by Cayce as being composed of many billions of atoms, and here is the part that really gets to me: each of these atoms are a kind of consciousness. He believed that each of these tiny atoms were what he called points of consciousness. They are, in essence, aware."

Bob then joined Jack in his narrative. "Think about that for a minute. Consciousness, dreams—dreams that seem absolutely real. When you wake up, you sometimes remember the places and the people you have seen in your dream as real people. At first I didn't believe Jack and I had experienced the same dream either.

I just thought it was a joke, that Bullworth was pulling my leg. Jack and I share many of the same interests, it's true, but this…" Bob shook his head.

"I don't get it," Chris said. "Just exactly what do you mean when you say how things really are? Is this another Cayce thing?'"

Jack said, "We're talking about reality—the things around us that we, all the time, take for granted and don't give much thought about. Most people never question reality. They just accept as reality what they see or sense in other ways. The point is that we don't really ever wonder what really is. Our senses tell our brains details about our surroundings, and our brains assemble all the input from our senses into a dreamlike reality, and the assembled dream becomes our reality. When we watch a magician, for instance, and you see him saw a girl in half or make a cow disappear, you know that what you are witnessing is not real. It's not reality. It's just a trick, and you accept it all because you have seen these tricks before in one form or another.

"However, when a scientist says that the speed of light cannot be exceeded, and then you witness a tachyon moving from one point to another in excess of the speed of light, then you have to start questioning reality. The same thing is true about what most of us believe to be evolution, that every living thing we know of evolved from a one-celled animal that just happened to be created by the chance combination of a host of chemicals that just happened to be on the planet Earth at a time when conditions were absolutely perfect for the formation of a complex living cell capable of absorbing other blobs of chemicals as food, propelling itself along to find more food and even reproducing itself, passing on its DNA—whatever—so that other cells are produced to be mutated into different cells. And—shazam!—a few million years and you have a man who can come up with something like $E = mc^2$."

Bob picked up Jack's train of thought. "We have been taught that there was a creation point back in the beginning of time when everything began. Some call it the big bang."

"But consider this," Jack picked up the story. "If you read the Bible, it says, 'In the beginning, God created.'" Jack held his hands on the table about two feet apart. He waggled his left hand. "What ever you believe, at some point, way back in time, things just began. Then some humans discovered ways of writing down what was happening so that we, their children, could know what happened in the past. We call it history. If they hadn't written it down in some way, which, by the way, required the invention of language and writing, we would not know about the events that happened in the past." He waggled his left hand again. "So, this is the beginning, and this is the present." He waggled his right hand.

"I can't figure out where this is going," Lisa said.

Balboa smiled and said, "Just let him finish. You'll get it. Well, perhaps, you won't get it, but, hopefully, your mind will be expanded, and you may eventually understand what Bob and Jack are trying to tell us."

61

The Something

The "something" that Tack had stumbled over turned out to be one of the struts of the Spirit.

Tack put both gloved hands out and stroked them up the length of the strut. "Thank you, God. Maybe I can survive after all." He climbed back up to an upright position, and with tears in his eyes he made his way up the ramp, went over to the recess in the air lock wall, and started tuning the wheel to seal the ship off from the outside environment. He couldn't tell if it was getting dark because of the ramp that was now shutting off the light inside of the airlock, or if unconsciousness was creeping up on him. He fumbled with the wheels and the buttons, only half-aware of anything he was doing. Next thing he knew, he woke up lying on the floor inside the ship. His fingers were numb, and his limbs were weak, but he finally managed to loosen and remove his helmet. The air wasn't all that fresh, but it was laced with oxygen, and he welcomed the breath of life no matter how stale it was.

62

Discovery and Idea

The tour group gathered in the EPOTEK conference room were now growing restless. Though they were truly interested in the topic that was being presented to them by the two guys from the Great Pyramid attraction in Vegas, however, their story and their excitement weren't translating into a true following. This didn't go unnoticed by Bob as he tried to bring the topic to a reasonable conclusion.

He looked at the faces around the table and said, "The people in this EPOTEK facility, the scientists, the engineers—all of you—are working on great technological discoveries that, at least in my mind, sort of illustrate what Jack and I experienced as the result of Bullworth's attraction. Perhaps you can think of it as Bullworth presents it. He uses the following analogy or scenario.

"We all know what one of these super-duper computers can do. From the special effects guys in Hollywood, we've seen computer-generated humans and animals created for film productions that are virtually indistinguishable from the real thing. True, the early computer-generated creatures and humans were crude by today's standards. Video games are a good example of that. Now, there are some of those computer-generated models that can almost fool someone into thinking they are seeing something that is real. It's hard to make yourself see anything but real, live dinosaurs when we know that these creatures have been extinct for millions of years.

"Just look at what can currently be done on film. One has to look really hard to determine whether what they are seeing is a real football player or a computer-generated version built for a video game.

"Bullworth's thinking has started me thinking in a whole new direction of what is possible in the reality that we all are confined to. For instance, just suppose there were some super Hollywood studio off somewhere in space or another dimension we don't even think about, with really unlimited resources. Now think of a film project that this studio has directed the minds and talents of all of its creative computer brains to work on. Perhaps, all these brainy guys and gals decide to create a movie that includes all of what we know of as history—every moment in that history. Remember that I said 'unlimited' resources, now.

"This production will include every detail that they can dig up, and it will be created not only as a movie, but it will be required to go a huge step beyond just a movie. This product will be a sort of virtual reality game. And this super Hollywood studio creates this game as realistic as possible using technologies that we now only dream of. The technicians and artists spare no expense and are given no deadline. They can work and rework this epic movie or virtual-reality game of the history of the universe until it encompasses every new discovery and idea possible. Where there are different theories or controversial versions of history, they will just make a number of different versions to accommodate all the different ideas." Bob noticed that Jack was anxious to help tell the story. He shifted in his seat and nodded to Jack to take the lead for a while.

"Currently, we are aware of the fact that scientists are on the edge of being able to transmit matter through space just as it can energy. We have seen, tonight, here at the EPOTEK labs that this it being pursued as we speak. All this effort started to come together in my mind a while ago as Dr. Dannon introduced us to the quantum room and what EPOTEK is attempting to do… right now. Why, I'm beginning to believe that before too long, it may actually be possible to transmit living matter through the air, through space."

"Beam me up, Scotty," Balboa said and got a few laughs.

"Exactly, why not. Take that and add it to what we can do to create computer images that are absolutely real. Now, with enough computer power, you could possibly create living beings by transmitting the models, in absolutely every detail, every atom, into the world of reality."

"Yeah," Jack agreed, "3-D–printed people. Just think they can already scan a human being into the computer world, translating the exact dimensions of a particular person into computer language. And I'm beginning to believe that it won't be long until computer technicians can do something similar with the DNA code." Jack folded his hands on the table. "If humans can come even close to doing all that, what's to stop a superrace of intelligent beings?"

"Or," Bob interrupted for a second, "one superbeing." He suddenly frowned and twitched his mustache, his eyes growing very big. "Yeah, come to really think of it, what's to stop one of those advanced races of intelligent beings"—he waved his left hand up toward the ceiling of the room—"from creating time itself, including everything that exists inside of the confines of that time and the realm of the reality that we are talking about?"

"I have often argued that science doesn't really have a workable explanation for just exactly what time is," Balboa added.

"One thing's for sure," Chris said.

"What's that?" Dr. Dannon said with an obvious expression of disapproval on his face.

"Bullworth's theory would explain a lot of things, even UFOs." Chris winked at Dr. Dannon just to see if he could soften Dannon's facial expression; however, it didn't seem to have any impact.

There were, however, many acknowledgments and nods from the others gathered all around the conference table.

After suffering a long period of awkward silence, Balboa looked over at Dannon. "What do you think, Dr. Dannon? You think that it might be time to check and see if the x-ray lab technicians have completed their secret investigations so we can, perhaps, see the lunar sample?"

"Yes...well, I'm not sure that they've had the necessary time as yet, but perhaps it's a good time to check in on them. Who knows, considering all that Bob and Mr. O'Rilley have brought to our minds, this might be a good time to check in on Hank and Zelda. However, I wouldn't get my hopes up too high." Dannon slowly got up from the table and rubbed his stiff knee before heading to the door. He looked back over his shoulder and said, "If you will excuse me for a few minutes, I'll check on their progress and be right back." He cleared his throat again and left the room.

63

Itty-Bitty

It was very quiet down the dark EPOTEK hall that led to the various labs. All that could be heard was a slight humming from the equipment room across from the x-ray microscope lab. Inside the lab, Zelda walked away from the monitor and with her back to Hank, stretched her arms out, and groaned loudly. "Man, I think I'm having some of your back-pain symptoms…" She arched her back and turned back to her lab partner. "I don't know why you're afraid of enlarging the image, Hank, baby… unless…"—she gave him a small controlled laugh—"the big, strong, master scientist is afraid that he'll find out that"—she held her hand down in front of her, wiggling her fingers—"inside his vacuum chamber he's got a tiny flying saucer that was built by a race of…" She stopped wiggling her fingers and held her thumb and forefinger up to her face, about a quarter of an inch apart. "Itty-bitty space men that have come from an itty-bitty planet to carry Earth's itty-bitty women back home with them?"

Hank spun around in his swivel chair and faced her. He started to say something to her in rebuttal but thought better of it and suffered to express himself with a shake of the head and a pitiful groan.

64

Giant Lens

After Tack had managed to remove his bulky space helmet and welcomed the breath of stale oxygen that laced the atmosphere in the air lock, the tiny astronaut was so exhausted that in a matter of minutes, he was asleep. In that sleep state, he began to dream about Quadrilla, only now he was seeing her in a different costume. It was skintight white and covered with tiny flowers. At least they looked like flowers to Tack. Her head was shaved, and instead of hair, she had a tattoo consisting of decorative, flowery patterns across the left side of her head. She had long gloves on her arms and hands, and she wore some kind of fabric-covered boots. She was trapped inside of a bubble-like membrane and was pushing at it, obviously trying to get out. She was looking at Tack and mouthed the words at him, "Help me, help me, I need the sun. It is my life. It is my power."

At that sight, Tack's eyes popped open. Something was moving the ship. There was a strange vibration all around him. He struggled to get up on his feet and stood there wavering for a moment. Once his stance had steadied, he managed to walk from the air lock down the hall to the command deck. He quickly made his way over to the upper observation port. He climbed up into the seat and looked out at the giant lens that was suspended from the top of the white chamber. The lens was attached to a huge camera that was moving very slowly in an arc above, and around the Spirit.

"They're looking at me. I know they are," he said excitedly. He climbed down from the port and looked around for something—something that might just inspire him with an idea of what to do next. He needed some inspirational jolt that would give him an idea of what he could do to get the attention of the technicians who were obviously operating the microscope camera. Then an idea did hit him—a very strange idea, but one that just might work.

"The Christmas tree lights!" he said out loud. "I certainly have enough of them. If I can arrange them in some kind of pattern, when they see the ship, if they ever find the ship, they'll know I'm down here." He shook his head. "The only problem is getting enough power to those little lights." Tack was painfully aware of the fact that one of the reasons he was in the fix in the first place was the loss of the ship's power. "However," he murmured, "something is powering those tiny lights in the airlock. There must be a way to tap into that power source."

He started scrambling around, frantically looking for the Christmas tree lights in the storage box beside the command couch. Once he had the lights draped around his neck and shoulder, he headed for the air lock. It took him precious minutes to get the panel loose at the bottom of the recess in the wall, but there he found a flat, tape-like strip that ran from the back of the tiny blue light down to the bottom of the panel box. He pulled out his keychain and detached his fingernail clippers. Using the clipper's sharp cutting edge, he scratched at the tape until he was rewarded by the glint of two silvery metal strips that were hidden under the dull gray of the tape. It took him another set of precious minutes to figure out how to connect the positive and negative LEDs from the Christmas tree lights to the silvery strips, but his leather billfold wedged between the wires, and the top of the panel box seemed to force the necessary contact because the Christmas tree lights began to glow with the required radiation.

"Now all I have to do is figure out how to get these lights out on the surface of the ship so those guys up there can see 'em. Good thing I bought all they had in the hardware store, 'cause I ain't got an extension cord, but I do have some good old duct tape." He started slipping on his space suit. "It's a given, those guys up there won't believe their eyes. Shinola, man, it's certain that I'm a dead duck if I don't get some kind of message out there on the skin of the ship—and pronto."

It took him only a few minutes to suit back up and go back out into the air lock. After getting his bulky helmet back over his head and locked in place, he stood there wondering how he was going to climb up on the top surface of the ship, he fortunately discovered the overhead hatch inside the air lock, and after a few tries, he managed to find the proper lever inside the access box to effect the opening of the hatch. Climbing up on the top side of the ship was the most difficult part of the exercise, but arranging the Christmas tree lights to spell out the word help required more time than he could safely afford. His oxygen was reading very low by the time he climbed back into the ship.

65

Progress Backward

The tension inside the x-ray microscope lab was obvious as Hank looked up at Zelda and frowned. It bothered him a little more than he'd like to admit that Zelda might be serious that he was actually afraid of what he might find out about the tiny silvery disk if he increased the magnification on the screen. He realized that he was blushing and finally allowed himself to respond.

"No, it doesn't scare me at all that this is may actually be a tiny flying saucer that was built by a race of itty-bitty spacemen—what ever. But what we are observing in this vacuum chamber does still defy any logical explanation, not to mention that there is no way it could have gotten inside the vacuum chamber." He looked up at her.

She sighed, shrugged her shoulders, came back over to the workstation, and bent forward to get a better look at the object Hank had centered on the monitor. "Well, there's no denying it, this does defy any traditional logical explanation I can think of."

He turned to her and noticed that she was smiling an evil smile. "Come on, Zel," he continued, "think about it. The only other logical explanation is as crazy as your 'tiny UFO from the evil empire' idea."

"Why is it we always come to that? Why does every wonderfully mysterious thing have to have a logical explanation?" She frowned back at him.

"Because logic is the only way we learn what is true."

"Truth…ah…that's right, progress and looking forward, as if we could progress backward. We must learn the truth so we can lie about it later."

66

Baffled by Signs

Hank rubbed his eyes with both hands and said, "I'm seeing things, Zel. The longer I look at this thing, I think I can see motion on its surface."

"Let me see." She leaned closer, and he could smell her intoxicating perfume. She began to slowly shake her head from side to side. "I don't…"

"It looks like…yes…patterns…like letters…hieroglyphics… in a pattern of tiny little colored lights."

"Hey, I must be a little delusional too. If I'm not mistaken, it looks like a letter…yeah…it's an H." She pulled back slightly.

"Yeah, it's definitely an H. And look, something else is happening there."

"I see it too," she said as though she were starting to sing an old familiar song. It's…it's…an…I believe it's an E." Zelda's eyes were widening as she watched the phenomenon appearing on the screen.

"You are absolutely right, and now I see it starting another letter…I'm sure of it."

"It's…a message…" she gasped.

"I can't believe what I'm seeing." Hank swallowed hard, his mouth growing so dry that he found it more and more difficult to speak.

"Like an H, E, L, and a P?" Her voice cracked from the emotion of the moment.

67

Weird Room

Hank glanced at the side of Zelda's face hovering over his shoulder.

"Perhaps...this is a message...Oh, I don't know," she said, trying to make light of something that was anything but.

"Oh, Zelda, how could it be a message? And from whom could the message be? I'm just not believing my eyes. It must be a joke that some crazy nut in the EPOTEK weird room has dreamed up to drive me crazy."

"Oh, I don't know. There's nothing very unusual about a tiny silver disk-shaped object with help written on the side of it—unless of course it's written in tiny, sparkling lights by tiny little people." Zelda started twisting a long strand of her red hair, waiting for Hank to hit her with a humorous punch line as he usually did when she was trying to be flippant with him.

"Is this really happening? Zel, I'm beginning to think I'm dreaming." Hank studied the message, letting his eyes trace over each letter. "I tell you, Zel, I could swear that while these letters were forming—I'm not kidding—I could see a tiny black thing moving around the letters. It looked very much like a tiny, little"—he looked up at her—"man. Did you see it?"

"No, no, you're not going to get me to go along with you on the little people. I was only trying to be funny. I'm not quite ready for the quilted room, not yet anyway." She moved her head closer to Hank's neck. "Probably it was just something on the monitor screen like a bug maybe. Please, Lord, let it be a bug."

68

Alert Sign

It seemed to Tack like hours since he had written the help message with the Christmas tree lights. He'd used all of them and had to unscrew some of the lights, separating the individual letters to make the message more readable. But he'd waited long enough to know that it obviously wasn't working. It was easy for him to conclude that the whole exercise had only been a waste of time and precious oxygen.

However, the giant microscope camera was still circling and seemed to be looking for something—something more. But what?

Tack's neck was beginning to feel the strain of watching the microscope camera as it circled around him in the chamber. Then it moved in closer to his position, and he was inspired to say, "Now I know for sure that they're looking at the ship. It's paying no attention at all to the moon rock." For the next few minutes, he watched the camera swing by a little bit closer to the Spirit.

He scratched his head absentmindedly and said, "I wonder if they can see me." He moved closer to the forward window and waved at the huge lens. He could plainly see the reflection of the ship in the optical glass. "I wonder if they could make out my message, probably wasn't bright enough. There's so much light in this white world." Then he turned and started looking around the command deck for something, some inspirational jolt to his brain that might give him and idea of what he could do to get the attention of the technicians who were operating the microscope.

He banged his head with the flat of his hand, doing the same Winnie the Pooh thing he used on other such occasions.

69

help Sign

Zelda stood back up from Hank's workstation and put booth hands behind her back, stretching and trying to work out the pain that had crept into her muscles.

Hanks' eyes, however, were still glued to the monitor screen, his intense focus on the strange image of something that shouldn't have been there. He hit the Enter key to have the camera make one more pass around the chamber.

"I'm startin' to think that this weird thing we're looking at is going to get us all into a lot of trouble," Zelda sighed.

Hank turned and looked up at her. "I don't see your point."

"We are looking at something in that vacuum chamber that shouldn't be there. Goodness," she sighed and wiped her forehead with her hand, "the thing is, it can't be in there. It's impossible for it to be in there…and I know one thing that's for absolute sure."

She crossed her arms across her chest and shook her head. She walked over to the coffee machine and just stood there, looking at the half-filled coffeepot for a few seconds, decided against another cup of coffee so late at night, turned, and undid the top button of her blouse. "Wheeew! Is it hot in here or what?"

"Stuffy, yes. Hot, I don't think so." Hank gave her an expression of frustration. "So, what is it that is for absolute sure?"

"This thing must be very important! I mean very important. The front office guys had a fit when I said I was going to stay late tonight to help you. This lab is off limits. I had to do some fast-talking to get to come in here and give you the benefit of my expert knowledge."

Henry cocked his head quizzically and watched Zelda as she looked down at her blouse and flicked off a speck of lint. Then he smiled and said, "Yeah, you were always good at fast-talkin'."

Hank pushed back from the monitor for a moment and sat there just staring into space.

"I know what you're thinking," Zelda said with a smile. "You want to keep watching that little disc to see if it's spelling out another word."

70

Another help Sign

"I'm in such terrible trouble, save me!" Tack's voice rang out across the command deck. "By now it's more than obvious that those guys operating the microscope up there can't see me, or maybe they can't believe their eyes. Shinola, shucks, man. If I don't figure out a way to get a message to them and in a really big hurry, I'm a dead duck—a little bitty dead duck. Tack, old buddy, you really did it this time. Your butt is in a vise, and time is turning the screw."

71

Message to Chris

At the third bang of his open palm to his forehead, Tack started to get the beginnings of another idea. He realized as he did this banging routine, it caused short flashes of light to fill his vision. Finally, the new idea began to take form in his fatigued brain. The flashes of light started his mind on a new train of thought.

"The forward beam," he shouted out loud. "I can flash the forward beam and send a message." Then, his hopes fell short of his sudden excitement. "I forgot. I don't have any power. Rattz!"

Then, just as suddenly, another thought hit him between the tiny gray cells. At first it wasn't very strong but enough to get him to move around, searching here and there for the sacks he'd brought with him in a paper bag. Finally he remembered where he'd stored the little sack and grabbed it up from the back of the command chair. A big smile filled his face as his hand found what he was looking for. "This flashlight doesn't need batteries. All I have to do is shake it a few times, and that magnet that slides back and forth will create enough juice so I can send a message."

While he was shaking the flashlight, charging up the capacitor, he walked toward the forward window. Positioning his upper body over the command console, he aimed the end of the light toward the circling camera. "Now, if only I can just remember enough of the Morse code I used to know back when I was in the Boy Scouts. Now, what can I say that will get their attention? A name, maybe. That agent…Chris Slattery. If he were only here instead of that Battey guy." He looked around, thinking—no, trying to think. His head wasn't clear. "The air…without power, the ship can't replenish the air supply, however that works." He shook his head. "If I don't think of something fast, I'm done for."

He struggled to keep his mind as clear as possible. The world was beginning to look like a long dark tunnel with the microscope camera barely visible at the end of it. He searched his memory, trying to remember enough to tap out some sort of signal. "Morse code...how does it go? Dot...dot... dot...dash...dash...dash... that will tell them I'm in trouble. But I don't believe that's enough in my case. What else can I send? Chris would know. Chris... what did Chris tell me...If you ever...if you ever..."

As he tapped out the only message that he could think of that was short enough to get him the help he needed, the tunnel got longer and darker until... "If Chris gets the message, they'll find the ship. Chris will know I'm down here...if...if he's out there. Oh God, please let Chris be out there, or if they can get the message to him, the ship...they won't know I'm in here. Only Chris would know, and how would he find out where I am? Oh man, I'm a dead duck."

On the screen Hank and Zelda could now plainly see a silvery disk-shaped object literally covered with tiny details. The kind of detail was what might be expected of a space model fabricated by the model shop of some high-tech special effects department at a super Hollywood movie studio. Hank could see that there was no new message to replace the help sign they had seen just moments ago across the silvery surface of the tiny flying saucer. Instead, they could see a blinking light coming from what appeared to be a window on the front side of the craft. This light seemed for all the world to be sending out what was unmistakably some kind of patterned sequence of flashes.

72

New Coordinates

"I'll be darned!" the man exclaimed.

"What in the green-eyed world…" Zelda gasped.

Hank's eyes were intent on the x-ray microscope computer that was controlling the camera inside the vacuum chamber; he punched in the new coordinates he'd been configuring in his head. The monitor screen flickered and flashed, and the scanner crisscrossed the image he was watching with the usual bars of static that signaled a drastic fluctuation in current. When the image finally steadied, they both had trouble believing their eyes.

73

Dimmer

On the screen, Zelda and Hank watched the light on the edge of the disk begin to flash on and off.

"I think…no, it couldn't be…" It was becoming more and more obvious that the light was now flashing what appeared to be the old, outdated Morse code.

"It must be some kind of…"

"My God, I think…yes, it is. It's sending the old Morse code…"

"I was afraid you were going to say something like that." Zelda rolled her eyes.

"Well, look at it. There's a definite design to the series of flashes."

"Do you know Morse code?"

Hank shook his head. "I was in the Boy Scouts, but it's been a long time. I know SOS. That's all I can remember."

"Is this message sending SOS?" She looked over at him and cocked her head. "What is SOS?"

"Stands for 'save our ship.' You know, the Titanic sent out an SOS way back years ago when it ran into that iceberg. Three dots and three dashes and then three dots again. Or the other way around, I can't remember. Morse code is made up of dots and dashes. It's the only sounds that could be made back in the early days of the telegraph."

Zelda looked over Hank's shoulder at the door to the lab. "Speaking of flashing lights, looks like someone wants to come into the lab," she said. "The door light is blinking."

Hank got up and went to the voice box beside the door. "Who is it?" he said.

Dannon was caught off guard by Hank's question and tried to compose in his mind a response that would hide his contempt for these kinds of situations. The silence went on for a while, and the gathering of people with Dannon looked back and forth to one another while they waited.

Tack stood at the forward window of the Spirit and studied his reflection in the camera lens outside the ship. He could see his own little, tiny body inside the command deck, or he could have had just been dreaming. His mind wasn't clear. He was now desperately low on air as he took a deep breath of what was left of the oxygen inside the ship. This little body he was seeing reflected back at him looked extremely small and helpless. "You really did it this time, kid," he mumbled.

He felt really dizzy, and he staggered back from the window. He plopped down into the acceleration couch and kept trying to breath. It was getting more and more difficult to get enough oxygen to stay conscious, and the ambient light was getting dimmer and dimmer. And after a short while, there was no light at all—nothing but darkness.

74

Real McCoy

Still caught off guard by Hank's question, "Who is it?" it took Dr. Dannon longer than expected to respond. Everyone waited as a hush seemed to slowly come over the group waiting there in the hallway.

Inside the lab, Hank patiently waited for an answer. For security's sake, he had to make sure he wasn't about to open the door to people that were unauthorized to visit the lab, especially when he was in the process of studying what appeared to be a tiny UFO sitting in the chamber next to the lunar sample. Something contaminating an operation concerning the x-ray microscope was unheard of. It couldn't happen—no way. If something so bazaar got out to the public, EPOTEK would have some embarrassing explaining to do.

Finally after several long seconds had passed, Dannon's stern, official-sounding voice answered, "I'm sorry to disturb you, Henry. It's Dr. Dannon. Something has come up. I have some visitors that are asking to see the moon rock you are examining. Have you made any progress?"

Hank thought a moment. "Doctor, you don't happen to know Morse code, do you?"

"Morse code? I..." Dannon stammered, realizing that he knew nothing about the Morse code beyond the fact that it consisted of dots and dashes.

Outside the lab door, Agent Slattery pushed past Dannon, looked back and forth at Dannon and Bob, and then placed his face close to the intercom at the door.

"I know Morse code." Chris's voice came through the intercom, filling the lab. "What is it? Why do you need Morse code?"

"Doc," Hank said, "I think you should come in here and bring that guy that knows Morse code with you." He pushed the security button to unlock the door, there was an audible buzzing sound, the door opened, and Dr. Dannon guided Chris into the lab.

Zelda gave Chris a quick once-over, and Hank stepped forward, halting Bob, Jack, and Lisa with a raised hand. "I'm sorry. I'll have to ask the rest of you to stay outside for security reasons," he said.

Dannon immediately took over the conversation. "Hank, this is Agent Chris Slattery from the FREEZE agency. Chris, this is Henry Wilkes."

"Good to know you, Hank," Chris said and shook Henry's hand. "Now, I'm dying to know why you need the Morse code?"

Hank looked at Dannon, and Dannon nodded. "Okay, this may sound nuts to you," Hank lowered his voice and continued, "but we've got something inside this vacuum chamber besides the moon rock, which, incidentally, looks like the real McCoy." He cut his eyes back and forth from Chris to Dannon. "This has to be held in the strictest confidence. Okay?"

Zelda moved to the side so Chris could have a better view of the monitor. She leaned forward and punched in a code that slowly began to zoom in on the subject. Soon, the little flying saucer they'd been observing filled the screen.

"It's difficult to believe, but a while ago, we distinctly saw a message on the side of this ship." Zelda's voice was almost a whisper. "It was written in a series of tiny lights of various colors."

"What was the message?" Chris's eyes seemed to grow larger.

"It took a while for the message to appear, one letter at a time, almost as though someone were writing it, very carefully. It said, 'HELP.' If you can believe it."

All of a sudden Chris's mouth felt extremely dry.

"And just now," Hank took over the conversation, "a flashing light came from the little window toward the front there. My Morse code isn't very good, but I think it said SOS and then something else." His mouth twitched slightly from the emotion he was suppressing.

"Something else," Chris repeated.

"Look! There it goes again. This is definitely a message," Zelda said excitedly.

Chris watched the screen closely and mouthed the letters as they were flashed out, "S, O, S." And then, "L, O, R, E, M, E, M, B, E, R, LO, Re, Me, EM, Be, R."

Agent Slattery turned to face Zelda and then Dannon. His mouth began to twitch also, and then he smiled. He looked over at Hank and then back to Dannon. "Doctor, would you please let Professor Balboa come into the lab and see this, please? I can vouch for him, and I accept full responsibility."

Dannon hesitated, looking over at Hank and then to Zelda. Zelda nodded slightly.

"Trust me..." Chris said. "The professor needs to see this."

Dannon quickly trotted over to the lab door and opened it. "Professor Balboa, would you be so kind as to join us? We have need of your expert opinion."

"With inexhaustible pleasure, Doctor." Jesse smiled his biggest smile and followed Dannon over to the monitor. "Let's see. What is it we are looking at?"

Chris moved to Jesse's side and raised the thumb of his right hand. "It's Tack, Professor. He's in there." Chris smiled and looked around at the other faces in the room. The look on their faces made him smile even bigger. "I hope you still have Evelyn's controller in your pocket, Professor. It seems that our crop duster pilot is inside that vacuum chamber, and the controller is his only chance he has for survival."

"How do you..." Balboa's eyes focused on the screen. "Oh my god! This is a vacuum chamber. How is he breathing?"

Chris's eyes grew wide. "He's trapped in there. If his ship is disabled, he may not have enough oxygen to last much longer. If we don't figure out a way to get him out of the chamber"—he turned back to the monitor—"he'll suffocate." The light from the window in the front of the disk was still flashing, but it seemed to be slowing down. Chris translated the pulses for the rest of the room. "A, I, R, N, E, E, D, A, I, R."

"We've got to get him out of there!" Jesse said. "He's running out of air."

"Who...?" Hank stepped back, knocking over his chair, "What's out of where?"

"Can you get some oxygen into that chamber? I mean right now!" Chris shouted.

"But the moon rock. It'll be—"

"Forget the moon rock. We're talking about a human life. A very tiny, little human life." Jesse tapped Chris on the shoulder. Their eyes met for only a second and then Chris looked down at the professor's hand and saw the controller.

Hank looked from Chris to Dannon, then to Zelda. "What do you mean exactly by 'tiny, little human life'? I don't understand."

Chris took the controller and said, "We'll talk later. Right now, we've got to get some O_2 in that chamber, and I mean before you take another breath."

Dannon stepped over to the console mike and sent an emergency message to the vacuum chamber technician to immediately contaminate the specimen with oxygen.

"Better do it gradually," Zelda said. "We don't want the rush of air to blow the moon rock and the other stuff all over the place."

Chris nodded approval. "Can I get into the vacuum chamber room?"

"Of course, follow me," Dannon said.

"Let's see now." Slattery motioned with the controller. "I'll need a powerful magnifying glass and some tweezers and a tissue."

"I'll take care of that," Zelda said.

Chris could tell by the expression on Hank's face that he wanted desperately to ask what Chris was going to do with a magnifying glass and tweezers, but the urgency of the moment initiated his scientific discipline, and he simply said, "You've got it, Agent."

75

Nothing More

Only moments later, the German shepherds guarding the lab rear exit went crazy as the excited gang of people burst out of the rear doors to the EPOTEK lab. Zelda had a way with the dogs and settled them down while Chris carefully walked across the concrete pad over toward the workshop building at the rear of the main office complex. In his left hand, he held the controller he'd gotten from Evelyn Milford and given to Professor Balboa for safekeeping. In the other hand, he held what looked like a small piece of white tissue. What couldn't be seen by those following him, watching what he was doing, was the tiny silver dot in the center of the white tissue. Occasionally the lights around the courtyard would hit the tiny dot at just the right angle to cause a little sparkle, the only indication that the dot was, in fact, a metallic object that Tack Moultrie had given the name Spirit. A couple of guards that led Dannon's tour group pushed open the sliding doors and let Chris through into the darkness of the workshop. Chris carefully walked toward the center of the room and set the small tissue down on the concrete floor.

"How big is this place?" he yelled across the room to the guards that were standing there out of the way.

One of the guards, the one with a large red moustache, responded, "It's sixty by sixty, according to the blueprints."

"Sixty by sixty." Chris looked up at the ceiling for a couple of seconds. "I hope there's room enough for the expansion here. I'm not sure of the dimensions of this thing—forty...or fifty feet I imagine."

"If it's no bigger than that, sixty by sixty ought to give you a safe margin." The guard patted the gun at his hip.

Chris bent down and very carefully set the tissue down on the shop floor. Then, he stood back up and slowly stepped backward away from the little scrap of tissue paper. All eyes were fixed on the pale rectangle there in the dark workshop as the FREEZE agent stopped next to the door to the shop and held the controller, carefully aiming it at the target on the floor.

"Stay back," he said to the others. "I know you all want to see what's about happen, but we'll just have to settle for a long-range view." He reached up and pushed the green button toward the front end of the controller. Nothing seemed to be happening at first. Then, in the quiet of the large workshop, a soft, distant screeching sound could be heard. The entire workshop began to vibrate. Chris could feel it through the bottoms of his shoes. The group stood transfixed, all looking back and forth at one another as dust particles in the ceiling broke loose and fluttered to the floor like so many snowflakes.

If they were going to be able to watch the Spirit begin to grow from a tiny pinpoint to CD size, to Frisbee size, they would have to have been a lot closer. But as the EPOTEK team watched the Spirit grow to garbage-can-cover size to eventually a rubber swimming pool size, they began to step even farther back away from the growing phenomenon. Soon they were witnessing the saucer growing ever larger until it sat there the size of a large air force fighter interceptor, and the screeching sound began to subside into a soft, low rumble. To the person, those in the workshop found themselves crowded against the walls with their mouths hanging open.

"Wow," Bob said, looking over at Jack. "I was right. That model did shrink in my museum. It probably did that so it could get through the crack in the door."

"How could it possibly do that?" Jack asked.

Balboa looked over at him and said, "It's not all that hard to explain, Mr. O'Rilley. The space between the nucleus of an atom and the electrons swarming around it is enormous by any measuring standards. The workings of an atom are not nearly as conventional as we suppose."

"The bottom line is this," Chris added, "in our reality, there is more nothing in the atoms that everything is made up of than there is substance. If science can figure out a way to compress that distance and it's obvious that the science of those beings in... wherever that saucer came from, has done just that."

"Things can shrink to minuscule size," Bob finished for him. "Cool." He rolled his eyes.

Finally, the saucer had reached its normal size and just sat there, dust still falling all over it from the ceiling of the EPOTEK workshop.

"Let's see now," Chris said, "the yellow button with the black dot." He didn't finish his statement because the sound of the ramp descending could be heard coming from the ship. The gang standing around the fifty-foot disk watched with intense interest as the tip of the ramp finally came to rest on the floor. They waited for three or four minutes until they could plainly hear what sounded like the footsteps of someone coming down from the air lock.

First, only the shoes of the spaceman could be seen, then the legs, then...then Tack stumbled, fell, and rolled down the ramp, his body spilling around on the floor like a rag doll. The space helmet he was holding rolled across the floor ending up against Zelda's shoes.

Chris and Lisa were the first to get to Tack's limp body. It took a few seconds for the others to slowly begin to gather around, watching as they tried to assess Tack's condition.

Chris looked over at Balboa. "Just as we suspected, Professor, it's Tack Moultrie all right. This is the guy who's been flying a spacecraft around all over Georgia."

"And California," Bob added.

"And, no doubt, the moon too," Jesse said, bending down into a squatting position to have a closer look at the unconscious crop duster pilot.

"Well, at least the boy's still breathing," Chris said, standing up and handing the controller back to Jesse. "That's something anyway." He stepped over to the two lab guards and Dr. Dannon. "The next order of business, Doctor, is to get this kid to a nice, warm bed and lock up this saucer until we can decide a plan of future action." He let his gaze sweep around the room, making eye contact, briefly with each of the group. "No one leaves the primacies, and no one, I mean no one, uses a telephone or a computer until I clear the communications with the FREEZE agency. Do I make myself clear? It's imperative that we keep the lid on this thing until I can perform some kind of debriefing, and, Dr. Dannon, I'll be needing that moon rock you have in the vacuum chamber."

"Agent, you have no authority to just take over like this," Dannon protested.

Balboa stepped over to Dannon, and Jack joined him. "Yes, he can," Jesse said, and Jack was nodding his head to agree.

"Trust me," Jack said, "you do not want to do anything that will alert the FBI or the CIA—or the NSA."

"Or any other government agency. If they get involved," Bob said, "none of us will ever see daylight again."

Dannon was puzzled by the look on their faces, and it was obvious that fear was creeping into the back of his mind. Finally he seemed to understand what they were trying to tell him, and he said, "Are you serious. They would...kill us?"

"Or worse," Lisa said, tossing her blond hair over her right shoulder.

"How would you like to spend the rest of your life in an out-of-the-way outpost that no one ever heard of?" Balboa said over his shoulder as he strolled over to one of the legs of the saucer. He couldn't resist running his hand along the metallic surface as he took a comforting, deep breath. "I've seen it happen dozens of times. Some poor slob discovers a miracle cure or a new carburetor that produces more gas than it uses"—he turned back to face the group—"or he sees a monster in a lake or an alien body at some place like, say, Roswell."

"Pure files under the X label," Jack said.

"And then," Balboa continued, "if the government can't make the poor slob look like a fruit cake, and totally discredit him or her, he disappears—permanently, like that fellow years ago. Chris Adoma I think was his name."

"Either by death or being locked away forever in some prison." Chris carefully slid his hands under Tack's body and lifted the boy up off the floor with a gasp and a grunt. "Now, let's get this boy to some secret place where we can bring him back to good health as quickly as possible. He's got a lot to tell us, and I for one am anxious to hear his story."

"Then what are you going to do with him? He needs to be in a hospital," Dannon said, falling in behind Chris as they headed out of the shop toward the main EPOTEK building.

"Any hospital is going to keep detailed records. Word will get out, and then we'll lose the poor guy. No. No." Chris shook his head. "No hospital for this kid. We've got to deal with him ourselves as best we can—right here and now. And I know just the people who can make that work." Chris winked at Jesse.

"Here and now," Dannon repeated. "But what about the kid when he wakes up? He'll want to know what he's doing here, and he will want to go home or something. How do you propose to handle that?"

"I'm going to check with my boss at FREEZE, and I believe she will agree with my idea. With her okay, I'll try to make Tack Moultrie an offer he can't refuse." Chris huffed and puffed, shifting Tack's weight in his arms as he strolled toward the EPOTEK rear doors. A caravan of people and two vicious guard dogs followed him at a safe distance, wondering what in the world was going to happen next.

76

Dream World

It was a dream world. Tack was off on what had to be another planet. There was this beautiful woman, and sitting on her shoulder was Cisco.

"Hey, you little fur ball," Tack said. "I thought you were dead. Give me a break, guy. Oh no, this is only a dream, isn't it?"

The woman smiled at him, and he realized that the woman was Quadrilla. It was an angelic smile, and Tack experienced an emotion that was somewhere between true love at first sight and what he remembered when he was really sad, and his mom would come to his rescue. In short, he felt really good. So good that he never wanted it to stop, but slowly, subtly the world around him started to fade. He could see right through the woman and the raccoon like they were double exposed, or like they were reflected on glass. They were only ghosts—not real at all.

"No," he said. "I'm not ready. What's happening. Quadrilla, help me." But as he begged for help, Quadrilla's image had faded to the point that she was just barely visible at all.

"Tack!"

She didn't sound like Quadrilla at all, but familiar, somehow familiar.

"Tack Moultrie!"

No, it definitely was not Quadrilla. It was a man's voice. And although he had only talked to the man on one or two occasions, he knew that the man's voice was that of Christopher Slattery. Chris Slattery. "Chris Slattery."

"Maybe Chris got my message after all," Tack cried.

But to the people gathered in what he believed to be a hospital room, it didn't sound like a cry at all. In fact, it was barely audible, and it was just two words. Tack moved his head slowly from side to side and said, "Low, remember."

"Tack, can you hear me?" Chris bent his head closer to Tack's face. "Wake up, buddy. Wake up."

Tack's eyes fluttered open. He could see Chris standing there close to him.

"Am I dead?" Tack asked.

"Not yet." Chris grinned. "But we barely got you out of the x-ray chamber in time. If it hadn't been for Evelyn Milford giving me that controller, we'd have never been able to get you out of that ship."

"Evelyn…controller? How did…I was, you know, down inside the spaceship…tiny…how…"

"Evelyn knows Quadrilla. She had been in contact with her from the start. Well, ever since the crash. Quadrilla gave Evelyn the controller. It's a little device that you've probably never seen. With the controller, we were able to send commands to the ship, which means it was the only way we could get you back up to normal size and get you out of the saucer?"

"Well, I'll be…" Tack propped himself up in the hospital bed and only then realized that Chris hadn't come alone. Kelly was with him and two other gentlemen and the nurse. "Whoa! Do… all these people—"

"Know about your UFO?" Chris finished for him and nodded. "Yeah, and then some. We've all been following your adventure in one way or another, except for Kelly and Tammy here. They just got involved at the last minute when we told them how close you had come to getting yourself killed. You were without oxygen for a long, long time. So long, in fact, that we thought that your brain might have been severely damaged from the lack of oxygen. You've been out long enough for me…us to managed to bring all of these people here to Houston to be with you while you recover."

"Whoa, that's not good."

"How's the old"—Chris tapped himself on the temple—"gray matter doing?"

"Other than a splitting headache, and…and…"

Kelly came over to the side of the bed, bent down, and kissed him. "Tack gets embarrassed when there are too many people around. And now his deep, dark secret is out, that's got to be a shock." Kelly drew back slightly and frowned at her boyfriend. "So you didn't think you could tell your best friend and girlfriend about your spaceship? We'll just have to have us a long talk about that when you get better."

"Kelly, how did you…" Tack struggled to speak intelligently, but his mouth still wasn't working right.

"We contacted Buford about your accident, and Kelly overheard our conversation. There was nothing we could do but explain your condition, and she insisted that we fly her here to help you recover," Chris said.

"So your dad knows about the UFO too?" Tack swallowed hard.

"No, silly. Agent Slattery just told me and Tammy…well, and one other person…I think."

Balboa stepped in a little closer and said, "I can't imagine what all you've been through, Tack."

Tack made an attempt to raise himself up to a sitting position, almost failed, and then tried again.

Balboa shook his head. "And what a great find you have made. A real UFO. And you had it all to yourself in secret flying around like…what was that guy years ago on TV? Oh yes, the Greatest American Hero. He also had no instruction book on how to use his miraculous discovery."

Tack sat up a little straighter in his bed and looked around the room. "Who are you guys…I mean, I know Chris and Kelly… Tammy May, and you, Professor."

77

Mad Model

Chris stood back slightly from the bed and motioned to the group of people gathered in the makeshift hospital room. "Let me introduce you to some of these people that happened to be here during your moon-rock retrieval adventure. "Tammy May was with Kelly when we contacted her, and she insisted that she come along to make sure you were adequately cared for.

"Yeah, I know Tammy. Thanks for coming, but I hope I'm not that bad...off." Tammy smiled and nodded.

Chris motioned to another guy in the group and said, "I think you know this gentleman we have over here." Tammy turned and stepped aside to reveal a smiling SIFI Bob, handlebar mustache and all.

"Holy, cow." Tack looked from side to side. "How...how..."

Bob stepped forward to shake Tack's hand too. "Hi, Tack, I bet you got a million stories to tell us, but we'll do that later. For now, you need to know who the rest of these stranger are, and this is Dr. Bilbro." Bob turned and indicated the man next to him. "He's an astronomer and a good friend of mine." He turned to the man on the other side of the bed and said, "And this is Jack O'Rilley. He's with NASA. We call him NASA Jack." Jack smiled and nodded throwing Tack a smart salute.

Bilbro stepped up to the head of the bed. He shook his head, looking down at Tack, and held out his hand. "James Bilbro" he said.

"I met James here at the Mad Model Party out in LA," Bob continued. "We got to talking, and I told him about this saucer I'd seen. I just couldn't figure it out—how that little model saucer flew around in my museum and then just vanished. Next thing I knew, we are all here at EPOTEK, rescuing you from the x-ray microscope chamber."

"Being an astronomer," Bilbro said, "when Bob told me about the little model flying saucer event in his museum, he thought I could convince him that he wasn't going crazy. He vouched that some of his friends saw the UFO too and would swear to it. One of them even worked for NASA back when they were building the space station, NASA Jack over here."

Bob scratched his chin. "Jimmy told me he'd seen a similar saucer, only he didn't expect that it could shrink down to the size of the UFO I'd seen."

"And then, when we thought we'd lost you," Chris said, "and Evelyn called me to explain the part of Quadrilla's story that she'd been holding back, well, I got this idea of how we could help you keep this whole thing secret. Then I made contact with Kelly and brought her into my confidence. She agreed to help us keep the secret."

Tack was trying to fight back a spell of oncoming dizziness. It was all happening too fast. "I think I'm dreaming all this. It's too much."

"Tell me one thing," Bilbro said. "How in the world did you manage to fly that thing to the moon. The distance, the astrophysics"—he buffed up his cheeks and let out a blast of air—"there's just no way someone with…" He searched for a way to say it politely.

Tack came to his rescue and said, "Someone as stupid as a crop duster pilot, you mean."

Bilbro smiled and nodded. "Yes, I'm not sure I would put it quite that way, but I'm sorry. How did you do it? You're lucky you didn't miss the moon altogether or crash or burn up in the atmosphere when you came back to Earth…" His voice trailed off. "Any number of things could have happened to you."

"Well, I read a lot. I'm something of a science buff." The image of Eric Strode swept through his mind, and he continued, "And

I've got an old pilot friend that introduced me to flying, and he told me a lot about his experiences in the space program. He not only taught me to fly, but he also helped me to learn a lot about being an astronaut. I've been a fan of the Apollo program and the space station ever since I could walk.

"Besides, the ship, the Spirit, well, I checked it out pretty good and figured out how to read some of the symbols—with Cisco's help, of course."

"Cisco?" Jesse said. "That would be your…ah, pet raccoon, right?"

Tack nodded. "And a whole lot more than that, I've got to say."

"And Evelyn's help," Chris said. "Her connection to Quadrilla helped her to help you, but, of course, you were never aware of it. Cisco was her link to you for a while."

"Quadrilla." Tack was puzzled. He searched the faces of the people standing around him in the room. "Who is Quadrilla? I know the name, and I have these vague recollections of her, but—"

"As you may have guessed," Chris went on. "Quadrilla is the… ah, entity, shall we say, that designed the Spirit. Her mother, it turns out, was what is commonly known as an abductee. More specifically, we have also learned that her mother was an Egyptian princess in ancient times. Many years ago Quadrilla was born to this princess off in some other galaxy. She was a hybrid, an experiment performed in an attempt to crossbreed a human being with what Quadrilla calls a king angel."

"An experiment…by angels?"

"Quadrilla informed us that the term king angels is a translation of the alien's word for what they are." Chris smiled.

"These beings, aliens, little green men—where did they come from?" Tack grabbed his head in both hands. "This is making my head hurt. I am dreaming—got to be."

Chris held out his right hand and made a circle in the air. "Quadrilla says that the king angels only represent part of the investigation Jesse and I have been pursuing. For the past millions of years, it seems, according to Quadrilla, we have been purposefully misled. Our scientific experts have been way too conservative in thinking that only one race of beings have come to the Earth and have been, shall we say, observing us."

"There's more to it than just studying us," Balboa threw in. "They've been manipulating our race, experimenting on us, and in some cases saving us." He rubbed his hands together and smiled. "It's all very complicated. I wouldn't believe it myself except for our finding you and learning of your adventure with the ship you have come to call the Spirit."

"You must be thinking that it's all over now that your secret is known," Chris said, "but perhaps it's just the beginning. It is all just starting now, from this moment on."

Tack's ears perked up. "What do you mean just starting?"

"Evelyn gave me the controller and told me how to use it to bring the ship back to normal size." Chris shook his head. "No, not normal. When it comes to that ship, there is no normal. Let's just say that we brought Tack Moultrie back to normal size. Evelyn told me all this under the condition that I let you keep the saucer as your own, that we all let you continue to have the UFO, let you make the decisions and use it as you will. Only now, we will be your crew."

Tammy stepped forward and wiped his brow. "Poor baby. This is all too much for your, isn't it? Just you relax. Just know that your buddy Agent Slattery made Evelyn a promise."

"We all did," Kelly added.

"What did you make her promise?" A worried look troubled Tack's face.

"I told her we'd keep the...secret if you would agree to take on a few extra passengers."

"It was Evelyn's idea that you take all of us in this room on as the crew of the Spirit," Balboa said. "Mr. Moultrie, just think of all the things this team can do," he added, his face full of excitement.

"We can fly anywhere," Chris said.

"We can shrink down and explore inner space—the mysteries of the human machine," Tammy said. "I can't wait to see all these wonders firsthand."

"We can explore the universe," Bilbro added. "The planets, the stars, galaxies—the possibilities are limitless."

"And, together, with Evelyn's connections to Quadrilla, we can learn how to use all the features she designed into the ship." Chris felt himself getting caught up in the excitement that was filling the room.

"What about Quadrilla?" Tack's head was swimming. "Where is she now…I mean?"

"That information is only known to Evelyn." Jesse cocked his head to one side. "Tack, Quadrilla has to stay in the background…for now. The king angels are still looking for her. That's why they have been tracking you, hoping that you and your ship will lead them to her."

"She doesn't want to be their slave ever again." Kelly frowned and shook her shoulders.

"The king angel aliens hoped that you and the Spirit would lead them to her," Jack put in. "They want to find her—at any cost."

"They will do anything to find her." Jesse waved his hands.

"Therefore Quadrilla will have to stay hidden until we figure out a way to get rid of the king angels," Bilbro muttered.

"And, Tack, old buddy, don't forget about me." A new voice joined them in the hospital room. A new voice but not an unfamiliar voice, at least not to Tack.

78

Captain Tack

The voice was that of Bill Innis as he pushed open the door and stepped into the room. A somewhat frisky raccoon was sitting on Bill's shoulder with his tail wrapped around Bill's neck. "I won't be able to go with you on every mission, but I danged sure will be on some of them," Bill said, grinning and stepping up to Tack's bed.

"Where'd you get the coon? Looks a lot like my old buddy, Cisco, but I guess all coons look alike, huh?"

"Well, I couldn't say I could ever tell one coon from another, good buddy, but"—Bill reached up and took hold of the raccoon and helped it to jump down onto the hospital bed—"this little guy…well, after you left us out at the field, I noticed that the little guy was still breathin'—ever so slightly. When we looked at him at the field, we all thought he was dead. He was so busted up, we didn't even think to check him for breathin'."

Tack's eyes lit up. "You mean…" By this time, the coon was right in his face, looking at him lovingly "This is Cisco? I'll be jiggered." He took the coon in both hands, his thumbs under its armpits, and shook him lovingly. "Hi, Cisco, old buddy, I've missed you so much. You just don't know." Tack's eyes swept the room, gathering in the crew assembled around him. "I thought he was done for."

"When I saw that the little guy was breathing," Bill said, "I wondered if I could do anything for him. So I took him home and doctored him a little. But I ended up leavin' the little guy with Doc Parks for a few days, and"—Bill ran his hand down over his day-old beard—"it's remarkable how the little guy recovered. Doc bandaged him up, but the next day, he kept pulling at the bandages until I just clipped 'em off. I couldn't believe it, the little guy was all healed up. Remarkable thing—really."

"Well, whatever you guys did, Bill, old buddy, it sure fixed him up."

When Tack's excitement died down a little, and the room grew quiet again, Chris continued. "So, what do you say, Tack? You ready to take on a bunch of greenhorns to be the crew of the Spirit and to go where no man—"

"Or woman," Kelly added.

"Has ever gone before?"

"Captain Moultrie," Kelly said dreamily.

Tack cocked his head and smiled a big smile. "Hey, I like the sound of that—Captain Moultrie. Never had a crew before, 'septin' for Cisco."

79

Scientific Consensus

It was well after normal working hours, and Captain Tack had been allowed to rest up with a long nap after all of his new crew members had been encouraged to let him start back on the road to recovery. Being under that all-important x-ray microscope and running low on precious oxygen for so long had done a job on his well-being.

Most of the EPOTEK employees had long since gone home or off to their various dinner dates, and FREEZE agent Chris Slattery was now sitting across the table from his scientific companion, Professor Jesse Balboa. Jesse had been with Chris for the period of time they'd been assigned to investigate the UFO sightings in the little town in Georgia. They had been fighting fatigue all day, still trying to recuperate from the excitement of the past few hours there in the x-ray microscope lab.

As they sat there in the coffee shop/break room of the EPOTEK main building, they were very deep in their conversation about the investigation's recent events. Although their fatigue was haunting, neither of them had enough desire to end the conversation and slip off back to the nearby hotel where they were staying.

"It's interesting that you should bring up the subject of the so-called scientific consensus," Chris said.

"You, of course, are referring to my contention that the field of science is currently undergoing a crucial trial that parallels the trial it went through in the time of Galileo."

"Yes, exactly. When I was a kid in school, I loved science. It was my favorite subject. Science was going to help us get a foothold in the realm of space, and space travel was all I could think of when I was a little kid reading all those comic books and science fiction stories by Ray Bradbury, Arthur Clark, Sturgeon, Richard Matheson, and let's not forget Robert Heinlein."

"Yes, it's a shame that currently, those great creative thinkers that wrote such wonderful stories are all but forgotten by the scientists of today. We should be publishing to the rooftops their efforts that took their readers into the worlds of the unknown, making fantasy and scientific ideas come to life."

Balboa went on, "With the realities that modern science and especially NASA have brought to us, I find it particularly disturbing that I am reduced to questioning the very basis for so-called scientific inquiry."

"Yes, now it's more of a sense of scientific consensus."

Chris made a face and went on, "It used to be that you could trust certain scientists with the papers they publish. Now, the news media has decided to use what people know as the poling devices to come up with what they think should be accepted as the truth about science."

Jesse knitted his brow. "It used to be that you could trust the scientific community to use strictly scientific observation of the realities around us to describe how everything works. Now, a scientist wants to make a name for himself and uses his ideas about reality to prove that his political agenda is what's right for everyone else."

"And the most frightening aspect of that kind of thinking is that they feel it is a great moneymaker to attack the spiritual beliefs of people, attempting to convince them that there's noting to live for but to serve the state. You know, when I was a young man. I loved science, but I also loved God. My favorite part of the Bible back then was Genesis. I loved to visualize how everything began—the creation of the stars, the earth, all the animals, and man. Then in school I was introduced to the theory of evolution, and I just assumed that the evolutionary process was the tool that God used to make everything." Chris waved his hand.

"Yes, those scientists that seem to be obsessed by what they call natural and then laugh at those of us that believe that in addition to 'natural,' there is also a greet deal of scientific evidence that there is also the possibility of the supernatural. They are so full of themselves that they have lost the very essence of what the word scientific really means. I can't help but think of Leonardo da Vinci and the many sketches he made of how water flows around an object that might be found in a spring. This is scientific observation at its most precious. He observed the action of the water, tried to understand it, and then made sketches of the various patterns that the observations had suggested to his mind and his artistic hand."

Chris heard someone come into the break room and turned to see Dr. Dannon heading over to the drink machine. "Hi, Doc," he said.

Jesse said, "Stay away from that Russian tea, Doctor. You'll be hitting the bathroom all night long."

"I learned to avoid that stuff a long time ago. Besides, it's made in China, and I hit the bathroom all night long anyway," Dannon said, feeding quarters into the machine.

Chris turned back to the professor. "Da Vinci was a real scientist. I have to wonder what he would have thought about Darwin's theory. For years and years I bought into evolution. It made sense to me, until one day I saw a bug of some kind flying around in my backyard. That sucker was flitting around all over the place so fast you couldn't tell what it was. It was almost like it was moving from place to place through time. You could barely see the danged thing. It was just a blur, until it finally landed on a nearby bush. It sat there on a branch big as it pleased, so I went over and checked it out. I couldn't believe it was just a butterfly. But it was a strange butterfly, like none I'd ever seen before. You know, most butterflies flit around and finally land on a flower or blade of grass, and you can see them moving their wings open and close almost like they're breathing. But this bug was just sitting there, its wings not moving at all. Then, all of a sudden it took off again, and sure enough, I was right. It was the mystery flying thing, zooming so fast from place to place, with no obvious destination in mind at all. It just zip"—he waved his hand—"zap—gone."

Dannon opened his grape drink and came over to the table. "Mind if I join you, gentlemen?"

"No problem, Doctor, have a seat." Chris motioned to the chair beside Jesse.

Jesse pulled briefly on his earlobe. "So how did this…ah… little bug change the way you looked at the theory of evolution?"

Chris looked over briefly at Dannon. "Well, it started me thinking. Here I thought I knew how to identify a butterfly. I knew what they looked like and how they behaved. Then all of a sudden I encountered one that behaved and looked entirely different. This kicked off a mental recheck in my mind of all that I knew or thought I knew about living things—all living things. One thing led to another, and I wound up thinking about the origin of life that very first moment. It had been fairly easy to think of all life developing from that first living cell, but I began to wonder about that…I mean, the very first living cell. The spark of life. That tiny little spark of life had to be the most miraculous thing to ever happen, at least on the earth." Jesse noticed Dannon's eyebrow going up.

Chris looked from Jesse to Dannon. "The short of it is, I couldn't get my mind off visualizing what that first living cell must have been like. This led me to investigating all that I could find about evolution, concentrating my search for the nature of that first living cell. All that I could find was that there were several scientists that had experimented with what they believed to be the chemical makeup of the early years of the young earth. To put it simply, they put all of these chemicals that their best guess told them were in the atmosphere and the oceans of the early planetary environment into a flask made of glass, or something. By the way, it hit me that glass did not exist until man invented it and come up with a method of shaping it into a spherical globe. Anyway—anyway, then these guys bombarded that primitive cocktail inside the glass with electrical current of some kind. I don't remember exactly how they did that, but to be sure, this electrical spark that is often called the 'spark of life' was nowhere near as powerful or as dangerous as a lightning bolt that they were suggesting had to come out of the dark skies of early earth. The point is that the results of these experiments and similar experiments that are being conducted today have yet to produce a single living cell. But this fact has not stopped certain scientists from claiming that every living thing in our current reality has come down to us through a massive series of happy accidents all derived from that first, and shall I say, missing first living cell."

"That, my friend, is because certain so-called scientists are too concerned with attempting to prove that there is no Creator. They are those that live among us that worship the Creation and deny the existence of a Creator." Jesse smiled. "They prefer to believe and support, in every way possible, the idea that all that is needed is this chemical soup you just described and the electrical spark that fell from the sky, and—poof—you have a living cell. I have to laugh. One of the explanations I remember reading in a book when I was very young is that the soup that was the result of this experiment had big lumps and little lumps and that the first living cell formed when one of the big lumps learned to absorb a little lump, creating, by pure accident, the process of eating—poof!—the first living cell. It would be very funny if they did not take this lumpy soup so serious. A living cell is extremely complex. It is like a city with many systems that all have to work perfectly to keep the cell alive and allow it to consume food, get rid of waste, and even fight off enemy cells like bacteria and the pesky little virus, not to mention the reproduction cycle that is also very necessary."

Dannon could no longer hold back the anger generated by Balboa's attack on atheist scientists. It had been obvious from observing the look on his face that he most vividly disagreed with what had just been voiced by Jesse in the discussion. "You gentlemen are forgetting"—he cocked his head—"the vast number of eminent scientists who disagree with your belief that a Creator was necessary for life to come into existence."

"You're telling me that eminent scientists cannot be incorrect?" Chris fired back. "Tell me, Doctor, how many of your eminent scientists are, as we speak, absolutely certain that UFOs do not exist, and yet we have an excellent example of one right over there in that workshop?"

"And"—Jesse gestured with his hand—"how many of our eminent scientists down through the ages have been wrong about the function of the brain or the origin of insects or the certainty of a coming new Ice Age or, best of all, that carbon dioxide is a pollutant?" He yawned and continued, "Scientific procedure, in my most humble opinion, is not to be decided by polling their individual beliefs."

Dannon sighed an angry-sounding sigh and said, "I can assure you that we scientists that do not believe in fairy tales like those found in the ancient scriptures are in the majority."

"Whether that is actually true or not"—Jesse smiled—"that you feel comfortable in your beliefs based largely on the numbers involved proves my point. God either exists, or he does not, and no matter the outcome of a human vote, no scientific belief that cannot be proved by some kind of experiment and scientific observation can prove otherwise."

"I disagree—most vehemently!" Dannon growled.

"And you have that right." Jesse's smile increased. "As do Chris and I in our beliefs."

"If there is no God," Chris put in, "then, who performs all of the miracles?"

"I do not believe in miracles," Dannon spat out.

"And for that"—Jesse was still smiling—"you have my deepest sympathy. The day will come, my dear Doctor, when you will find yourself in such deep despair that you will wish you had just a little of the comfort that the belief in God gives to those of us who do believe."

Chris's smile had long since faded in the heat of this debate. He decided to shoot back and said, "Yet, Doctor, you and your fellow atheists cling to the belief that the big lumps somehow learned to eat the little blobs of whatever that souplike substance was in that nonexistent glass flask back at the dawn of life, with the lightning bolt, I might add, that would have cooked to ash both the big lumps and the little lumps, and you guys believe beyond all doubt that, that was the beginning of all that we call life. Darwin called his book On the Origin of Species, but that's not what the theory is about at all. The origin of the species and of like, I might add, is left hanging, and the discussion is only about the results of that mysterious, miraculous creation."

"You, Professor, would have the entire scientific world bow down to a God that has caused the division of vast groups of people down through the ages, instead of sticking to the scientific principles of discovery and accountability? I am shocked." Dannon's arrogance was taking on a physical form in the features of his face.

Jesse smiled. "On the other hand, my dear Doctor, I am amused that you liberal scientists are happy to shut down the debate altogether, making fun of those of us who worship the Creator instead bowing down to the nature of Creation. I can only wonder why it is so important for you liberals to force everyone into your own silly little mold, eventually making everyone of us of the identical cut." Jesse shook his head. "As for me, I love the idea that we can exchange ideas and attempt to solve our problems through debate rather than resorting to calling each other silly names and dragging our advisories through the mud."

"My dear Professor, I am not your dear Doctor." Dannon's red face betrayed his loss of control.

"I will refer to you as I wish, Doctor. You liberals are not yet the dictators you strive so hard to be." The professor's smile was erased by another huge yawn.

By this time, Dr. Dannon was so angry that as he attempted to speak, he began to sputter. Along with the sputter, the doctor's cell phone began to chime incessantly, and he quickly stood up and left the room, reaching deeply into his pocket as the door slammed behind him.

80

NASA 1

Lisa Krebs had managed to talk Hank out of the Ferrari he loved so much. But she loved it even more. One of her old boyfriends had brought over a DVD of the movie with Steve McQueen that was called Lemans. The Ferrari was not the star of the show. Steve McQueen's car was a special Porsche 912 that had been thrown together by taking two flat, six-cylinder Porsche engines and combining them one after the other to make a flat twelve-cylinder superengine that eventually won the race in the movie. However, Lisa had fallen in love with the Ferrari from that film. There was something about that particular model that gave her pleasurable chill bumps. It was the only car that she ever wanted to drive. Of course the real reason she seldom drove a car at all was because her Harley was part of her body—like an arm or a leg.

When she had met Henry Balch and found out he had restored one of the old Ferraris, she started bugging him and worrying him from day 1, until he finally made her a deal. If she would help him modify his computer system, he would sell the race car to her for $75,000. Of course she didn't have that kind of money, and the car was worth much more than that, but she was convinced that she had enough markers out to cover half of it. The other half she'd work out with the EPOTEK executives that kept bugging her to come up with ways to keep the EPOTEK computers ahead of those in the rest of Houston's labs.

So, with her long blond hair spread gloriously over the black leather headrest, Lisa directed the sleek red car up the highway called NASA 1, toward her cabin north of Houston and Johnson Space Center.

What she was not ready for was the flying saucer that swooped down and began to follow the Ferrari as she made the turn toward the frontage road to the interstate. She didn't see it, but Lisa was aware that something strange was happening, though she wasn't sure exactly what. She saw something—a motion, a blotting out of the surrounding lights, but not the actual object itself. And no matter what she did or tried to do, she couldn't get a good look at what ever it was.

The saucer drifted over and behind the surrounding trees on the west side of the road, dodging, and hopping from here to there, never giving the driver of the hot little racing car a chance to have a good look. As she turned into the driveway, the saucer found a nearby clearing not too far from Lisa's cabin and settled to the ground.

When she got out of the car, Lisa stopped momentarily, her eyes scanning the nearby scenery, pine trees mostly and a tangled mass of undergrowth, but nothing else. She headed up the pathway to her house, but was still aware of a strange tingling at the back of her neck. As she opened the door, she made a quick swing of her head to look behind her but tried to make it appear that she was only brushing the hair from her face. If there were someone there, she didn't want them to know that she knew they were there. This would give her a slight advantage if she caught someone following her, and that tiny advantage would give her an opportunity to lash out at the stalker with her foot, and her shapely leg.

But she saw nothing. The "nothing," however, did not make the tingling on her neck go away. She quickly stepped inside the cabin and shut the door. Snap, snap, snap. The dead bolt was activated, and two bolts slid into place.

"Judy picked a fine night not to sleep over," she said to herself, leaning back against the door. "Any other time, and this place would be a loud, noisy party."

She would have probably continued her monologue, but there was a noise outside. She couldn't quite place the exact kind of noise she heard, but it frightened her anyway. And Lisa didn't frighten easily. She went straight for the kitchen and got a cold beer out of the fridge. She plopped down in the chair next to the small round table and stretched her upper body out across the red checkered tablecloth, her arms out straight, both hands wrapped around the cold, wet beer can. She fixed her gaze on the intricate label and finally pulled it to her face the lips, opened her mouth, and took a long swig. Then she ran her index finger around the top edge of the can. Finally she took the tab between her finger and thumb and worked it back and forth until it broke off, and she placed it down on the table.

"So EPOTEK now has its own flying saucer." She shook her head and smiled a crooked little smile. "It's…it's…no, I won't say it. Unbelievable, incredible, fantastic—these words no longer mean anything in the world we've gotten ourselves into. My aching back… nothing means anything anymore." She looked up at the ceiling as if some answer to the questions in her mind might just be written up there in the white stucco.

"And now, the EPOTEK boys and girls, including my mom, are forming EPOTEK into some kind of…mother-of-pearl. It's like the beginnings of the united federation of planets…galaxies—shoot, who knows?" She shook her head and smiled a big, confused smile. "Everything…I mean, everything has changed… only we've got to keep it all secret so the government guys don't come in and take it all away from us and make a bomb out of it or something." Her brow furrowed. "I wonder how they might do that." She looked back down into her beer. "Oh well, I, of all people, should have that one figured out."

At that moment, there was another bumping noise outside, and it caused her to look up from her beer, her eyes wide. She cut her eyes to the right, to the kitchen window. It was dark out, and the curtains covered most of the window, but she saw movement, and a black streak of fear shot down through her like an ice-cold shaft of steel.

She got up slowly, thinking about the Glock she kept in the nightstand drawer beside her bed. She didn't want to kill anybody, but she desperately needed the weapon in her hand if, for no other reason, to comfort her, just in case the noise outside was not her overactive imagination.

Slowly, quietly she moved across the kitchen toward the living room. She'd left the light off in the living room, or at least she thought she'd left it off on her rush to get a beer. She carefully crossed the darkened room using her familiarity of the furniture placement to guide her to the bedroom door. The door was opened, and she slipped into the even darker bedroom, feeling her way toward the bed and the nightstand.

She heard another sound outside. "Someone's out there," she whispered to herself, a quiver creeping into her usually confident voice. The curtains to the room blocked all view of the outside from her current position, so she quickly opened the drawer and felt around for the gun. A sense of relief filled her whole body as her fingers closed around the butt of the pistol, and she lifted it up to her shoulder in a classic police academy position. Quickly, with her other hand she reached up and cocked the weapon and let the thumb of he right hand slide up to release the safety. Then with her free hand, she carefully, slowly pulled back the curtain just enough to…

She didn't scream as one would have expected, but she quickly let go of the curtain of the window and began backing across the room. However, as she backed away from the image that she knew was still there behind the window curtain trying to look in at her, the darkness of the room began to change. It was like nothing she'd ever experienced before. It wasn't inside the room, and it wasn't as if a light were coming on inside the room. It was inside her eyes—or inside her mind. She couldn't tell for sure. Around her peripheral vision a ring of light patterns began to form. And the patterns were busy with activity; stroboscopic flashes around her point of view were occurring at a constant rate as if a series of small lines of black and white arranged in apposing directions were trying to imitate the chaser lights that surround a theater marquee.

Her weapon slid from her grasp and fell to the floor where the shock of the impact made it fire once. The sound of the single shot filled the night and the darkness outside. She went over to the end table beside the couch and opened the drawer. She picked up a small flat object and pressed a button on the end of it. Then she slipped it into her blouse. The vision patterns in her eyes, or her mind—she couldn't tell for sure—continued, intensified, and she began to feel dizzy. That was the last thing she remembered about that night for a very long time.

81

Strange Lights

Once outside the room, as Dr. Dannon lifted the phone, he steadied himself at the news that was shouted into his good ear. "Yes, oh yes. My god!" Dannon swallowed hard, and his body swayed slightly.

He slowly closed his cell phone, and it was obvious to anyone had there been anyone nearby that his anger had just been totally replaced by a look of shock and concern.

Still ringing in his ears were the words, "The state troopers were called to check out some strange lights that were reported in an area just north of here. As they triangulated in on the reports, they finally wound up at some cabin just off the highway near a wooded area."

Dannon knew that what had just been described to him was the cabin of Lisa Krebs.

82

Scarlet O.

Chris made his way to the EPOTEK office that Zelda had had prepared for him in one of the less-used equipment rooms of the lab. There he checked his e-mail and his phone messages. Sandra wanted to know how the investigation was going, the usual "boss in charge of the plan" stuff. For now, Chris wasn't sure how he was going to handle this new particular issue. Up to now, he had been putting her off with as many details of his investigation as he felt safe to share with her.

He pulled a notepad out of the center drawer of his desk and ran his index finger down the list of ideas that he had been jotting down over the last few days

His finger hesitated over the note that read, "Tell her everything." His eyes strayed up from the notepad to the wall in front of him. He studied the picture of a DNA computer rendering that hung there like a reminder that we were actually in the twenty-first century. He scratched his head and studied it for a while.

"I can't think about this now. I'll go crazy if I do." As he said that last part, flashes of Scarlet O'Hara zipped through the back of his mind.

"What I really need now is a strong cup of Tack Moultrie's superblack coffee"

He thought deeply for a few moments more and then said, "No, maybe not Tack's coffee necessarily, but strong enough to get me back up to speed."

He headed down the hall to the break room, trying to stay in the middle of the hall, or at least walk in a somewhat straight line.

As he passed the Goddard Room, the largest of the EPOTEK conference rooms, he realized it was occupied. The marquee on the side of the mahogany door said there was currently a conference in session.

He could hear loud voices that, and from some of the words he could make out, signaled that the group was growing more and more agitated. After listening for a few seconds, he decided to come back later and see if he could join the argument when he was well armed with a fresh cup of strong, hot coffee.

The break room was totally abandoned, so he went over to the coffee station and filled up the EPOTEK cup that Phil had given him. This specially decorated cup with the EPOTEK logo in three-dimensional silver letters on its side had been awarded to each of the tentative crewmembers of Captain Moultrie's Spirit ship.

Upon returning to the conference room, Chris held his coffee in his left hand and reached for the doorknob. But before his fingers could close around the knob, the door suddenly swung open and banged into his fingers. "Ouch!" The shocked look on Zelda's face made him feel guilty for sounding off with such a loud "ouch."

"I'm so sorry," she said, letting the door shut behind her.

"No problem. I didn't even spill my coffee."

"I just had to get out of there. Dr. Dannon is hell-bent on making the first Spirit mission a trip through time, instead of the moon mission you suggested as a sort of maiden voyage. Everybody thinks he's nuts, including me.

"Well, I guess I got here just in time—excuse the pun."

Chris pushed the door open and made his way around the conference table. He found himself seated across from Dr. Bilbro. Jesse was at the right of Bilbro and nodded at Chris with a cordial smile. On Bilbro's left was and empty chair, probably where Zelda had been sitting earlier.

He turned to the head of the table and saw Dr. Luke Dannon, the director of the EPOTEK lab.

"I think it's ridiculous," Dannon was saying. "If the explosion of the volcano on the island of Thera was actually the cause of the plagues in Egypt that prompted Pharaoh to let the Hebrew people leave Egypt, we would have to believe that a supernova was of less importance than the simple volcanic upheaval and the resulting cloud of atmospheric chaos."

"I agree with Dr. Bilbro," Jesse said. "His reflection on the concept that in some faraway solar system, there might have been some long-forgotten civilization and during the extensive excavation and discovery phase it is revealed that the entire culture of this particular planet had died because of the intense chaos of something like a supernova is easy to believe. Just suppose that, in fact, in searching the volumes of the so-called Holy Scriptures, this supernova event coincided with the appearance of the star reported by the shepherds near the Bethlehem community. Using the power now at our disposal, of traveling back in time, it might just be possible to, at last, confirm such events as fact, not legend. In this, I believe that the doctor has a very valid point."

Bilbro nodded. "One has to keep in mind that these events were recorded, first, by word of mouth and much later in time written down in scriptures, after mankind had invented the process of writing down what they had experienced or heard of from the multitudes. It happens that human beings witnessed events they could not explain with the conventional wisdom of the time. A star in those days was only one of many millions of stars that they could observe. There had to be something quite different about the star of Bethlehem to cause their interest in identifying it as the star that was predicted by the ancient prophecies. It is true that the prophet Daniel had created a vision of this happening to the Babylonian wise men or oracles, and they were so impressed with the power of Daniel's predictions that they had been for many years looking for this very happening. This special starlike apparition, what ever it actually was, moved against the background of all the stars in a different manner than the usual starry heavens, or these so-called wise men wouldn't have been said to have followed it. It is not like they made their journey in a single night. A volcanic eruption of the intensity of the Thera explosion, filing the sky with a giant dust cloud, smoke, and debris that lasted for weeks, perhaps months…well, that sort of thing is much closer to the people affected. And it would easily be explained by a belief that the God that lived in the mountains, perhaps even the volcano, had been angered to the point of creating such destruction."

"But there is still a paradox," Dr. Dannon interjected as he twisted the tip of his mustache and looked up at the ceiling. Dannon went back over to his chair, pulled it out, and sat back down. "If this God was motivated, say," he went on, "to pressure Pharaoh into letting the people of Moses go free, why didn't he just create another plague—a lightning bolt or something more powerful? After all, to those of you that believe in this most powerful God, it goes without saying, believe that he could easily cause such destruction. Do you not agree? The eruption on Thera would not be necessary. It was not the Therans that made slaves of the Hebrews people. They had nothing to do with keeping all those people in slavery. They were hundreds of miles away from the land of Egypt."

"This Thera paradox that seems to preoccupy your mind," Dr. Bilbro said, "from my perspective, it seems to be a paradox of redemption. Thera explodes sending chaos throughout the civilized nations of the Mediterranean. Thousands of souls are lost. Tuthmosis III lets Moses and his Hebrew salves go free in order to make the Hebrew God stop the plagues from destroying Egypt. What, to us, seems to be the destruction of civilization in the Minoan world is the very tool that God uses to bring life to the world in a different location. Thus, the children of Israel are set free. You seem to think of God as some kind of superhuman being that thinks on a scale of a great movie director, causing one thing to happen, as if by pure magic, for the express purpose of fulfilling the logic of a scene in a particular movie. The good guys win, the bad guys lose. But if you think of God as a Creator, a force way beyond what any human could even imagine, this God lives outside of the confines of what we call "time," these events happen. They are created by God for his purpose. These events are powerful beyond imagining. The repercussions of these miraculous events include many happenings, one overlapping the other, just as the solar winds are somehow shielded away from the Earth because the Earth's atmosphere just happens to be made up of the very gasses that absorb or reflect its killing rays, not to mention the miracle of the magnetic force field that causes the northern lights."

"All this talk of God." Dannon's tone betrayed his growing anger. "God is only a myth. Those of you that believe in a loving God are like little children, crying for mommy in the dark. The human race has long since outgrown God. You have imagined, created God in the image that you want him to be. Your concept of God is merely a collection of the imaginings of pitiful souls unable to grasp the concept that the universe is made up of scientific laws and principles that are all provable in the laboratory. All that is required to bring the universe into existence is the hydrogen atom. Everything else evolved from that simple element through the expansion and collapse of countless stars over billions of billions of years. Gentlemen, Thera exploded, a great explosion to be sure, but it was just another of Earth's great upheavals, of which there have been countless over the ages. If the results of these catastrophic events caused the Pharaoh of Egypt to let the Hebrew slaves go free, that was just superstition working on his pitiful mind."

"So you believe that it was man that created God and not the other way around," Balboa said. "You believe there are no miracles. You are happy in your belief that man can create gods, but you also have a great fear that man can believe that there is a Divine Master Designer. For myself, I find comfort in the idea that my cancer was cured by my total commitment to Jesus Christ. He saved me from a horrible death. The price is simply giving him my devotion."

"I'm sorry that my duties kept me from attending this meeting from the very beginning," Chris interrupted, obviously ready to do verbal battle. "And it's conspicuous, to me at least, that something of which I completely ignorant has inspired this spirited debate on the existence or nonexistence of our Creator. It seems to me that those who are bent on denying the logic of a Grand Creator being responsible for the reality we all enjoy are exposing their real objective in the debate. They are living in fear that all of the scientific discoveries that await us down the road—that is, if we don't blow ourselves out of existence with nuclear bombs or worse, before those discoveries are realized—that we will learn from those discoveries that there is, indeed, a reason for everything—a reason for our existence, a reason for the self-awareness that we all enjoy is actually the core behind all things we witness and enjoy. There is, indeed, a God, or there is not. It can't be both. If God exists, no amount of debate or belittling those who believe in God will make God go away. If God exists, he alone is responsible for all things. Every atom on every star in every galaxy was created or brought into existence by this God, or, if you prefer, Supreme Being. Saint Paul wrote in his letter to the Ephesians that Jesus Christ is, indeed, this God, and he came to earth in the form of a man to tell his children, us, that we needn't live under the fear of death for our inability to live as Gods, that we could not in any way earn this so-called salvation, but he would give us this freedom as a free gift if we just accept his suffering and death for us, and our sins, and follow him."

Every eye followed Chris as his words commanded the attention of the room. "And you can take it or leave it," he went on. "It's up to you. Live on in your arrogant world where you really believe that you, as a human being, can achieve God status, creating, living for power over those you deem inferior. You may find immediate joy in such self-delusion, but you will never achieve everlasting peace. Death will take us all. There's no disputing that. However, for me, I choose to strive to be as good a man as I can possibly be. I take no joy in putting down those who do not believe. I only have pity for those who choose to live their lives without a purpose. I choose to believe in Jesus Christ, not out of fear of him and hell, but out of love and appreciation of what he has promised me. If God himself chose to suffer torture and die for me, it's the least I can do to just accept that concept. I find comfort in believing in that." Chris embraced the air around him with both hands. "You, see, ladies and gentlemen, we humans have created God in our minds, what we think of him, what he would have to be and we try to live up to our image of him, and appreciate what he had done for us."

"Or her." Dannon smirked. "This is ridiculous." Dannon started to stand up.

"Please keep your seat, Dr. Dannon. We might as well get this said, and you have had your turn. Now it's my turn."

83

Nemesis

Chris walked toward to head of the table and approached the smart board at the end of the room. "The trouble with talking about God, or thinking about God, is that we humans use only the images of that we carry around in our minds of what he would have to be. Those images and the powers we attribute to a godlike entity are entirely made up of the experiences, dreams, and hopes that we picture inside our minds. These images are built by the models we create inside the limits of our human minds and its ability to make what we want to believe fall into logical confines." He turned back to face the group. "I find it interesting that the art of building these kinds of models has so structured the way that we think that we have to be reminded that the most important function of the human brain is to forget. That's right. I can see in your faces that you do not agree with that notion, but with only a little bit of thought, just a tiny electron of mental energy, you will find that it is true.

"We walk into a room that we've never before been inside, and our eyes scan the interior for the express purpose of identifying every item in the room so that we can forget them. If, perchance, our eyes catch an item that we do not recognize, we begin to unconsciously study it. The study will become intense and continue until we identify what the strange item is so that we can forget it." Chris took a deep breath and stood there waiting for Dr. Dannon to explode. All members of the Spirit crew sat with eyes fixed on Chris as he stood at the end of the long conference table. "If God wanted us to know who and what he is, and what he is capable of, he'd just show himself, right? No, my friends, what he would do is exactly what the entity we know as Quadrilla did when she found herself stranded from her world—stranded inside our world. She took on the appearance of a human being so she could blend in—be part of us. That human being was Susan Towers. Susan Towers was killed in the big accident that Tack Moultrie witnessed. The creatures we have come to know as the king angels came in their spaceships and had damaged Quadrilla's space vehicle during her attempted escape, and she crashed into the tanker that had narrowly missed Tack a few minutes earlier. But Quadrilla was not killed, and her mate, Max, was also spared. Oh, their bodies died, to be sure, but something of them survived—their spirits, if you will. And these two spirits sought out suitable beings to help them to continue and complete their mission. Quadrilla found the body of Susan Towers. The being we have come to know as Max found the body of a tiny black baby boy. Through some ability beyond our thinking, these alien hybrids had managed to have at their power, the baby was able to develop at an accelerated rate, and thus, we saw Max as an infant only briefly. Not much later, we only saw him as an adult. Dr. Parks, Mr. Belmont, and possibly some of the people at the crash site saw the child briefly before Belmont tried to get him to the medical facility in Atlanta, but the rest of us only know of a fellow we have come to know as Max. This is what we have learned from all of the investigations we have been able to conduct thus far. However, I am using it as an illustration to show all of you just how silly and extremely provincial is your view of God is and what this great God can do and would do.

"God came to man in the form of a human being so that he could not only blend in as one of us, but also to experience what it was like to be a human. Unless you force yourself to explain, through some convoluted mental gymnastics, all of the prophesies down through thousands of years and how those predictions have all come to fruit to explain or discount them as pure coincidence, you will have to conclude that God has been here, and he has explained what reality is and what it really is all about. He is not, as we are, limited by the constraints of what we know of as 'time and space.' He is timeless. He was able to create all those hydrogen molecules that Dr. Dannon and other scientists have told that it was all that was necessary for us to end up with the current reality that we all enjoy. Any power so creative as to be able to create the space-time that rules reality and all of the millions of dimensions that have to exist for our reality to surround us would have little trouble devising a method of impregnating a female human with his great spiritual powers and go through all of the human experiences that brought all of us into the world.

"And the very science of which you are so proud to use in proving the nonexistence of God is now proving many of the very natural processes necessary for God to perform all these miracles. We are, at this very moment, just aching to create a human clone, bypassing the natural process of inception. In a very few years, my good friends, we will be about to accomplish this miracle to produce perfect copies of anyone of whom we have the DNA code in our hands to use.

"You scientists, God love ya, have been laughing at the Christians for centuries, for what you have come to believe is their naive customs and beliefs, never ever coming to the realization that a God that can create everything from absolutely nothing would have little trouble in performing any miracle he felt necessary to cause an effect necessary to fulfill a promise. Now, I'm not going to even attempt to convince you to believe as I do, but don't you dare laugh at the power of God, until you can create a universe from nothing.

"The hatred against Christians is troubling. Yes, there are the so-called Crusades wherein armies led by Christian ideals and beliefs were guilty of horrible injustices. However, reality dictates that no label adequately identifies what we know of as a group of people. Indeed, the old adage of a wolf in sheep's clothing exposes the tactic of some to pretend to represent a certain view when, in truth, they hold entirely opposite views. Accurately identifying a

Christian requires that the individual professing to be a Christian believe and practice a Christ-like way of life. How the radical Muslims, for instance, can condemn all Christians as infidels is difficult to justify. After all, when one does the math on this issue, one has to conclude that the God of Abraham is the exact same God of Ishmael, the same God that sent his Son, Jesus, who is professed to be that same God in a human form. One can easily take the position that Jesus is the Prince of Peace, and all the deaths and injustices done in his name were misguided deviations from his message and teachings professing turning the other cheek, and giving all one has to the poor and following him, in effect also becoming sons of God. I will not argue that point. I will support the concept of Dr. Holt that one's belief mechanism dictates that part of what we believe to be true is based on actual experience, some of it is based on teachings of authoritative personalities and institutions, but most of what we hold to be the truth is what we want to believe—or that which makes us feel the most comfortable with our lives and our realities

"Now, I'm asking, just what sort of discussion got this conversation started down this unholy path?"

84

1600 BC

Dr. Dannon replied in a slightly apologetic tone, which was very strange for him, "We have been discussing plans for a possible mission for the crew of the Spirit. I have suggested a voyage in time back to make studies of what actually occurred in the Mediterranean Sea during the approximate time of 1600 BC. I felt it of considerable importance to witness what might have happened to the island civilization of Thera when the volcanic eruption destroyed huge numbers of people in the area and may have even given birth to the myth of the destruction of the lost city of Atlantis."

Dr. Bilbro then added, "This turned out to be of broad interest to many of the members of our crew. This catastrophic event in the Mediterranean Sea has, in all probability, had even more broad implications that previously anticipated when Dr. Dannon suggested this target for our first mission. Thus the explosion of the volcano on Thera and the resultant dust cloud, tidal wave, etc., may have been responsible for the parting of the Red Sea and the plagues of Egypt, not to mention evidence of widespread destruction in other areas around the Mediterranean, such as the island of Crete."

"And this ancient Egyptian connection led to the Moses connection and, thus, the subject of the God of the Hebrews. The old argument of God, Creationism, versus science, evolution, and Creation by chance thus raised its ugly head," Jesse said. "The year was closer to 1628. A crater created by the Thera explosion, probably the loudest such sound ever suffered by human ears, was believed to be, at least, one mile deep. As the destruction spread out over the known world of that time, it caused huge walls of water to hover around the circumference of the resultant hole in the surface of the sea and eventually to come cascading down into the depths, swallowing the crater in a massive circular waterfall rarely witnessed, if ever, by the eyes of man. As for me, I'd like to witness such a sight for myself, and this Spirit vehicle of Tack Moultrie's offers us just such a grand opportunity. We can see it firsthand. Imagine watching the aircraft carrier Nemesis going over the edge of such a waterfall like some wayward canoe being sucked down into such a watery grave."

"It is indeed such a grand mission possibility," Dannon said, "that I am almost, reluctantly, hesitant to mention that just before this meeting I received a call from the local police that the state troopers have informed me of some strange lights reported in an area that I am concerned is very likely near the cabin of Lisa Krebs. I have hesitated to bring it up until I could have it investigated further, but while Agent Slattery was busy with his speech, I received from one of the state troopers a confirmation that the location of the incident was, in fact, that of Zelda's daughter. And she has been listed as missing."

Chris headed for the door without comment as all eyes followed him with no question as to where the agent was headed.

85

Crime Tape 2

Agent Slattery drove along the deserted backwoods road, fighting the urge to turn around and go back to EPOTEK. The discussion that he had so hurriedly left was still zooming around in his head, and he felt bad at having to leave in such a hurry. Added to that was the overwhelming question of just why Dr. Dannon had held back the information of there being some kind of problem with Lisa Krebs's cabin. He hated to admit how upset he was. Checking with the police had informed him that they were convinced it was a simple case of kidnapping.

"Simple kidnapping!" he groaned. "These guys are worn out. How can a human being get so used to dealing with crime that they can call taking a human being against their will, perhaps torturing them or even raping them, killing them? How can they think of that as being simple?"

He saw the cabin up ahead as his headlights swiped across the pine trees. The yellow crime tape and the fact that all the lights were off were obvious clues that something bad had happened. In his mind, a brief flashback alerted him of a fearful memory from long ago that he hadn't let himself think about, lurking there in his mental vision. It came back with full force into his brain at the very moment he pulled to a stop in front of Lisa's cabin.

He had been diagnosed with cancer. It was some years back, but he was still haunted by the so-called big C. It has started out as a mild case of hemorrhoids. He had tried to get a good and experienced medical professional to take care of his problem only to find that his doctor insisted on a colonoscopy. He had heard of such things before but hadn't given them much thought. This doctor wanted to check out his entire colon. The procedure had found a few polyps, zapped them, and his hemorrhoids had been left untouched. The surgeon had said he'd take care of the hemorrhoids after Chris had had time to recover from the colonoscopy. So Chris had waited and waited for the doctor to follow up. Finally he called the doctor and asked if it was a good time to proceed with the needed surgery. When the hemorrhoid surgery was conducted, they found a malignant tumor, and then the fun began.

All of the doctors involved in treating Chris's condition recommended a procedure where the lower colon and the rectum would be removed, just in case the malignancy had spread beyond the tumor that had been removed.

Chris had finally gotten what is commonly referred to at a second opinion. This different doctor at St. Joseph's Hospital in Atlanta suggested that Chris have an additional surgery to see if all the cancerous tissue had, in fact, been removed. Just in case, this surgeon also had recommended six weeks of radiation therapy. After all the enemas, surgeries, treatments, and medicines, what had bothered him most about all that was his state of mind. What he'd felt was a sense of being in the shadow of what he had previously been. It was like he'd been cloned, a replica of the real Chris Slattery. All of the things he'd once loved to do, the very nature of the world around him was something in his memory, but not a reality the way it had been before all this medical treatment. Things just didn't seem to be the same as they were before.

He still liked a beautiful sunset, but he wasn't at all awed by it. He still loved to read a good book, but he had to force himself to pick one up and begin reading. It had taken him a long time to get back even close to his old self, and he never really totally forgot how weird it had all been.

All this had made him feel guilty because of the sadness he felt all the time. His surgery and radiation had cured his disease, but it had left him in the impossible position of feeling sad that he had actually dodged the cancer-related bullet.

Some time back, he'd heard about some of the Vietnam veterans that had come home untouched by the physical ravages of the horror of that war—all the horror they had been forced to endure—but were plagued with the guilt of having survived when so many of their buddies hadn't survived at all.

That was similar to what he was feeling now as his eyes scanned the cabin, the crime tape, the darkness. The sadness was returning as he sat there studying the lonely, empty cabin. "The world is a very dangerous place," he mumbled just above a whisper. "When a thinking person considers what could happen, but hadn't happened, yet he could worry himself to death."

The yellow crime tape was all over the front porch of the cabin and even a few areas where groups of trees had been roped off. It was a few minutes after midnight. Chris was a little more than apprehensive as he ducked under the first ribbon of yellow with black lettering all over it. He made a few steps toward the front door as he fished around in his right, front pocked for the key Zelda had given him just before he left EPOTEK. As he fitted the key carefully, slowly into the keyhole, he could hear the tiny brass tumblers inside the dead bolt lock as it encountered the teeth of the key one by one.

The door opened easily, and he stepped inside, swapping the key to his other hand to keep his right hand free to purchase the Glock in his shoulder holster. Now that he was an official crew member of Tack Moultrie's Spirit spaceship, he had decided that he, as the first officer of that UFO, should be armed at all times in order to protect the missions and, especially, the captain of the ship. It had been determined early on that Captain Tack was their final best hope in keeping the new alliance a secret and all of their lives intact.

As he felt the weight of the handgun in his hand and entered the darkened living room, it hit him just how dark this room was.

There was hardly any light at all. The moon had long since moved to the horizon and left the forest around Lisa's cabin beyond seeing anything but the bare edges of trees, limbs, and shrubs. Only the soft glow of the city of Houston far off in the distance left him with his eyes boring into the blackness of the room as inside his mind, he was desperately trying to remember from his brief previous visit to the cabin the layout of the living room, but it was almost impossible to see anything.

He tried the nearby table lamp and was gratified that the power hadn't been turned off. This new illumination did little, however, to help in his visual investigation of the room. Before too long, he began to see signs of what he figured was a struggle that had taken place not too long ago. There was a rumpled throw rug that provided the telltale signs of a body having been dragged toward the kitchen. The rug was of a typical so-called Native American design, probably picked up from one of Lisa's visits on her Harley out to her favorite Indian village outpost novelty shop, but what caught his trained eye was the particular way in which the hardwood floorboards had been cut. Under the very edge of the rug, barely visible to his educated eye, he could see that instead of the overlapping, staggered four-foot planks, some of the still-visible planks were cut off at the same length and in line with each other.

"This place must have a basement," he said out loud. "I'd have never guessed it."

He bent over and tossed the blanket away from the suspect area, revealing a four-foot-by-four-foot trapdoor. There was no handle or knob but a single finger-sized round hole on one side of the door. Chris ventured to see if his forefinger would fit the hole, and it did. He lifted the door, surprised at its light weight and how cleverly the hinges had been devised to keep the trapdoor as unnoticeable as possible, and there was no squeaking noise that one might expect from such a secret opening into an underground hiding place.

"I was hoping I wouldn't regret not bringing my flashlight with me, but this new discovery looks very unfriendly." Chris stood back up and headed back to his car.

To his complete surprise, the batteries in the flashlight were still good. Usually, when one needed a flashlight, there was a lot of shaking and opening of the battery case to only find that the small energy cylinders had been coated with a strange discolored, crystalline, crusty material that signaled that until battery replacement was performed, this electronic torch was going to be totally useless. As he swept the beam around on the surrounding foliage, he said, "Thank goodness," and sighed a deep sigh.

He happily headed back to the cabin, but before he got to the crime-taped porch, he stopped suddenly. There was a sound. He looked behind him, chill bumps cloaking his arms. He stood there studying what little he could see from the soft glow of the nearby city.

86

Who's There?

Chris felt as though he were being watched. In a movie, the soon-to-be victim would cry out something stupid like, "Is anybody there?" Chris just stood still and watched.

Then, he slowly scanned the area around him, and he finally caught a glimpse of something shiny like a small light over in the wooded area to the left of the cabin. He stood there studying it for a few seconds and then headed over into the woods to check it out. As he walked cautiously toward the edge of the forest, he could see something lighting up the pine straw and fallen leaves piled there on the ground near the trunk of a pine tree. At first, he thought it was a smoldering cigarette. He bent down to have a closer look and sniffed the air. There was no smoky smell, so he moved closer and could detect that the small red light was blinking.

"I wonder," he said out loud, almost in a whisper. His voice sounded loud to him in the stillness of the night. "I wonder...if Lisa really was taken by somebody, she might have had something with her that she dropped. It had to be something small that her kidnappers wouldn't have seen or known she had in her hand."

Kneeling down there in the grass, Chris could see that the small light was pulsing with a slow, methodical rhythm there on the ground in the pine-straw mat that covered the floor of the forest. He lowered his face even closer and pushed the straw aside to reveal a small flat box about the size of a paperback book. The light coming from it was very small and red in color. He reached for the box and lifted it up closer to his face.

"It's one of those little things, what do they call 'em? A PD or something." He turned it slightly, and in so doing, he felt the latch release button at one end of the small box and pushed it. A lid flipped open, and he could see that there was a display screen on the top face of the device. He had, of course, seen iPods and BlackBerries in the modern world that surrounded him, but this was different. It looked, somehow, homemade.

He studied the screen and was becoming more and more convinced that the small computer-like device was something that Lisa would have designed and built.

He continued to talk out loud to himself, "She did tell me that she had a secret backup system somewhere." He looked in the direction of the cabin. "She said that she could..."

In his mind he tried to remember her exact words that night when she helped him with the tape of the accident out on SR 432 back in Georgia. He finally had the memory of that night under control. He remembered that when she finished making the copy for him, she hit a quick configuration of keys on the keyboard.

"I've got a secret backup just in case someone gets sticky fingers with your copy," she had said. "Don't worry, it's safe with me. Even the EPOTEK boys can't break into my system, mainly because I created most of the system they use at EPOTEK, and"—she had picked up the same little box he now held in his hand and said—"I can access anything on my secret backup with this remotely from as far as a mile away on a clear day."

"I wonder why she grabbed this particular device." He stood up and started working his way back toward the front porch. Lisa hadn't said where this secret backup system was located. "I wonder if it could be in the basement under that door I just saw in the living room."

Cold chills were running up his spine at the thought; he went back inside and began studying the mysterious trapdoor. He finally found a notch in the door, slipped his finger into it, and lifted the hatchway up.

He shined his flashlight down into the darkness, but he couldn't see very much. Then as his sight adjusted to the flashlight beam stroking the contents of the room below, out of the corner of his eye, he saw the silver light-switch box on the side of the opening, just under the hatch, and flipped it on. His eyes had to do another adjusting to the new-lighted environment, but he quickly scanned the room below and was surprised to see what looked like an extension of the EPOTEK lab. The walls were white; the floor, a gray tile; and on the three tables that were positioned around the room and across the north and south walls, there were computers and other electronic equipment he couldn't immediately identify.

"Well, well, Lisa's little hideaway." He smiled. After a second or two of surveying the situation, he stood up, turned around, and backed down the wooden ladder that led down into the room.

There was the chance that Lisa had just accidentally dropped the little computer box when she was snatched away from her cabin by…whomever. It could have been in her clothing and just slipped out from her struggle to escape. Or, and this was what he let himself hope, she had intentionally grabbed the device off a table in a desperate attempt to send a message—a message to any would-be investigators. How could she do it? What would she say?

He looked down at the screen of Lisa's little secret device and, after playing with some of the buttons with careless excitement, turned it on. The screen lit up, and there were three letters on the readout that made his heart speed up. "C, H, R," he read out loud. And then he saw the diamond-shaped icon. He moved his thumb over the touch pad and pressed the diamond.

Immediately Lisa's whole room came to life. Lights flashed here and there on the wall console. The main computer flashed to life, and on the monitor, he saw a list of folders. He was shaking his head as soon as he scanned the list. "No, no, nothing." Then his eye caught a folder with the name Christopher under it. "Well, now, let's see."

He reached over and took hold of the mouse. He moved it around on the mouse pad and watched the cursor follow his lead until it fell on the Christopher folder. Click, click.

There was only one document inside the folder. It was labeled "Hamlet's Mill."

"This is interesting. I don't remember mentioning Hamlet's Mill to Lisa." It was Chris's habit to move the cursor along the words as his eyes read the text.

He was reading the message as the cursor passed under each word. "Chris, I'm going to leave this for you, just in case something happens to me. It's silly, I know, but I've been following some hunches I've had ever since you brought the video to me that night. I found out about the lady in Hamlet's Mill that is apparently at the hub of this UFO mystery. Her name is Evelyn Milford. I flew down a couple of days ago and asked around until I found out where she lived. I had no idea what I'd learn down there, but to make a long story short, I got more than I bargained for—and then some.

"The bottom line is that I fully expect Evelyn and her buddy—I never saw him, but she kept talking about Max this and Max that, so I figure he's part and parcel of this whole thing—she, a lady named Four, and Max were going to make some kind of trip. When I questioned her further, she indicated that it wasn't the sort of trip one normally thinks of. It was to be a somewhat-mysterious and dangerous journey that Four felt was necessary because of something she'd discovered about. Well, she called it her mission. Evidently, Four and Max are working together to escape from what she calls the king angels. But, more importantly, they are looking for answers to questions they have been formulating during their attempts to escape these strange alien beings.

"The thing is, I talked them into considering taking me with them before I was able to find out exactly where they were going. But after coming back to Houston, I've been playing back and forth in my mind all that we discussed, and I've come to the conclusion that Max and Four are somehow able to travel through time, probably with one of those UFOs you were talking about. They seem to believe that the answers they are looking for are, somehow, in the past. They kept talking about someone or something they called Deltoo. This Deltoo was working to acquire information about the mystery they are chasing, and Deltoo had given them their latest clue that pointed to some period of time in the past."

The text ended there, and Chris found himself rereading Lisa's message over and over. What did it mean?

87

That's an Order

Tack Moultrie sat at the picnic table looking down at the red-and-white straw sticking out of the paper cup in his hand. He was looking forward to Agent Slattery showing his face this morning. If Chris had found any clues at Lisa's cabin the night before, he was extremely anxious to hear about it.

He put the straw between his thumb and second finger, capping the top of the straw with his index finger and lifting the straw slowly out of the orange soda. Small ice cubes danced around the other end of the straw as he lifted it up to the level of his face and removed his index finger in little tapping jerks. With each tap, a tiny spurt of orange liquid plopped back down into the paper cup. When the cylinder of the straw was empty, he repeated the procedure and watched the force of gravity suck down the liquid in an automatic response to one of nature's laws.

He heard the door to the EPOTEK building slam shut behind him and was disappointed that is wasn't the FREEZE agent. Zelda Krebs stepped out into the sun and headed toward him, her hand automatically going into her pocket for the pack of cigarettes she was slave to. She nodded to him, smiled, and lit up a weed. Tack saluted her and went back to playing his little game with the orange soda. But the game soon lost its hold on his gray matter, and he let his eyes focus through the straw over to the building across the EPOTEK back courtyard where the Spirit UFO was currently housed, far away from the prying eyes of the rest of the world, its secret still intact at least beyond the few members of the newly formed crew that would be using the prototype flying saucer for special missions to…to…to…

Well, to be honest, that was the very reason Tack was sitting there in the morning sun playing with a soft drink he didn't really want to drink. The drink-dispensing machine was all out of root beer, and that was what he would have preferred.

Zelda took another puff on her joint and thumped it John Wayne style over into the newly mowed grass where it smoldered silently. Tack dreaded the oncoming conversation. He knew where it would go, and he didn't relish another session of trying to convince him that things weren't going to be so bad with a team use of the flying saucer instead of Tack's private meanderings with his new favorite toy.

"Hi, Captain," she said, trying to sound as informal as she could under the circumstances. Of all the members of the Spirit team, she was one of the ones he knew the least about. True, she and Hank had saved his life, sort of. They were the ones that had seen his message and attracted the attention of Chris Slattery and Professor Balboa. Between the two of them, they'd figured out that the strange UFO sightings, at least some of them were explained away by what they'd learned about Tack and his mastery of flying the prototype. When they found out that Tack was probably attempting in some way to retrieve the moon rock he'd given to his girlfriend, Kelly Golden, and with the discovery that the prototype was probably capable, through some alien technological magic, of changing its true size, they had picked up on the Morse code message they had seen in the x-ray microscope chamber at EPOTEK that Tack and his tiny flying saucer were somehow trapped inside the chamber. Chris and Jesse had explained the situation adequately enough to Zelda and Hank, who were observing the microscopic message on the surface of the tiny silver disk, and the two scientists had managed to free the space ship from the chamber and thus saved the life of the young, used-to-be crop duster pilot.

"Hi, Zelda," Tack mumbled and bent down to suck on the straw. As he looked back up at her, she climbed over the picnic table bench and sat down. "You ought to give those things up, you know."

She smiled and said, "You mean the cigarettes of course."

"Yeah, I had a friend that died from those things. I'll never forget his last words to me about how he wished he could stop breathing and stay alive. He said, 'When I try to breathe, it hurts so bad, I find myself trying not to count each breath.'" Tack looked down into his drink and played with his straw. "He advised me to never start smoking—that it just wasn't worth it."

"I know you're right. I just enjoy it so much. I know I should quit, but I just don't have the will to do it."

"I know. People know what's best for them, but they believe they are slaves to their own will. It's strange to me. I've never been able to make myself understand why people believe they want to live instead of die, but what they really want is to do what ever they want to do, when ever they want to do it, because they want to do it. I learned a long time ago that we are our own worst enemy. We'll do things to ourselves that we'd never allow someone else to do to us. We'd fight like hell to keep them from winning, but the big lie that we all have to overcome is that something outside ourselves drives us and makes us do what we do."

Zelda sat in silence, her smile fading by small stages, so he continued.

"Sure you have the will to do whatever you want to do. We all have it. All we have to do—and this is the hard part—is realize just how strong we are. We set our minds to accomplish something, do some planning on how to achieve that goal, set our minds to do whatever it takes, and never waver; and before you know it, you've got your own company, the love of your life, a new car, or your own airplane—or you quit smoking." Tack bent back down and noisily, on purpose, slurped his orange drink. "Stop smoking, Zelda. If you're going to be a member of my crew, you can't smoke on board the Spirit, and if you step outside for a smoke, well, let's just say that every breath you take is going to hurt like hell out there in the vacuum of space."

Zelda's smile was now completely gone. "You're serious, aren't you?"

Tack stood up from the table. "Quit smoking, mister. That's an order." He straightened his shoulders and turned to find Chris Slattery standing right behind him. It surprised him, so he almost jumped.

88

Too Scared

Chris wasn't smiling, and Tack's smile quickly faded. "As you probably know, Tack, I managed to take a good look at Lisa's cabin last night," he said, his eyes darting down to Zelda and then quickly back up to meet Tack's. "There's no doubt about it she's gone, and it doesn't look good. I think she was taken against her will—or worse."

"Or worse, I'm beginning to hate that phrase," Tack said.

Zelda quickly slipped out off of the picnic table bench and stood up. "What are you saying, Chris?"

"Her place is a mess, the door is busted in, and she's gone."

"You think she's been—" Tack muttered.

"Abducted," Chris finished for him. "All the signs point to one of those other ships Evelyn told us about. I saw them, and you did too." The three of them exchanged glances as Chris went on. "We have ample evidence that these other ships are looking for the prototype what we call the Spirit. They must have traced us to EPOTEK. Lisa works here, but she's the only one who was vulnerable enough for them to track her to her remote cabin and snatch her up. They must have been tracking her, and when they knew she was alone, they nabbed her."

"My god!" Zelda said. "I got a call. I couldn't make out who it was or what they were saying. Then a voice finally managed to make enough sense that I determined that they had contacted me by mistake and were trying to contact my daughter. I gave her the phone, and Lisa talked to them for a couple of minutes, hung up, and then said she had to go back to the cabin. My god, I never dreamed—"

"That sounds like a possible connection," Chris said.

"What could they want with Lisa?" Tack sat back down at the table. "All of a sudden I don't feel so good."

"You don't feel good—my only daughter is..." She looked back at Chris. "Who the hell are these guys anyway? When you say 'abducted,' you don't mean—"

"Zelda, I attempted to bring you all up to date at the initial Spirit crew meeting. Tack's ship has been followed"—he waved his hands—"all over the place. I saw two of these king angel ships the night Tack first went aboard the Spirit. And Evelyn and I watched them hovering over her lake. They seemed to be after the Cisco...you know, Tack's raccoon."

"And I zapped two of them on the moon," Tack choked out. "No, it wasn't actually me, the ship somehow did it, and they were chasing me at Area 6451, you know. Chris, you and the professor saw them being chased by the F-15s."

"Yeah." Zelda stuck out her chest a little more than necessary. "You brought me up to date all right." She looked down at her feet in deep thought for a few moments. "I just didn't want to believe it." She looked back up at Chris. "It's too much like a bad science fiction movie."

"Yeah," Chris said. "Like War of the Worlds, only so far we're lucky that there aren't more of these king angel ships. There seems to be only two of them that are making most of the trouble. Probably scouts looking for Tack's ship." He looked up at the sky a moment. "Something about that ship they want back pretty bad."

Tack jumped in. "That's the way I figure it, Chris, but I was sittin' here thinkin' before Zelda came out here ta have a smoke."

Chris sighed and sat down on the bench. "Better take a seat, Zel. This is going to be good."

Zelda sighed a big sigh and sat back down. Tack hefted his bottom against the hard boards of the bench.

"I've seen this kid's camper," Chris said, "and that wild airplane he built. I've been following his adventures all across the skies of Georgia, all the way to LA, and, somehow, I think he's the best chance we've got to find out where Lisa is and in what condition." He nodded to Tack. "So let's hear it, son."

"There's somethin' neither of you don't know about. I barely know about it myself. There's another...you know, it's what Evelyn calls a 'prototype', basically it's a sister ship to the Spirit.

"Wait a minute," Chris said, "are you telling us that there is another ship just like the one we've got over there in the workshop?"

"I know it sounds incredible, but after the last few weeks, very little surprises me anymore. Kelly Golden played a trick on me back at the Milford Lake. She was pretending that she was going to drown, so I dived in after her. Well, it turned out she was just trying to scare me, you know, she's always pulling some kind of trick on me, it's just her way. Anyway, while I was looking for her under the water, I saw something—a metallic shape. I couldn't get a close look at it because I was running out of air, but I decided to go back and have me a good look when things weren't so hectic. Well, I never got to go back and do that, you know, dive in the lake and look around, but later, when I was working on my ship down in the sinkhole cave that I found, it turned out that there was a tunnel that led to the area down under that lake. When I explored that tunnel, I found a chamber that had been carved out like some underground bunker, you know, like they dug back during the cold war, when everyone was afraid of a nuclear holocaust. Well, then I realized that up in the ceiling of this chamber was the bottom of a flying saucer that looked exactly like the Spirit, and I met the guy that was living in that prototype."

"Let me get this straight. You met an alien that was living inside that saucer—down at the bottom of the lake?" Chris was developing a twitch in his left eye.

Tack looked back and forth from Chris to Zelda. Neither of them seemed to be willing to say anything or ask a question, so Tack continued.

"His name was Max, you know, Max, the big black guy. I think you called him Chips-a-Million."

"Yeah…Chips-a-Million," Chris interrupted. "Loves cookies, as I remember."

"Yeah, that's him. But that's not all. He warned me about the other ships, that they would try to catch me. I think it would be a good idea if I went back to the Milford Lake and see if I can get Max to tell me where he thinks they might have taken Lisa. If anybody will know where they might take her, he will."

Chris ran his hand down over his face and looked over at Zelda. "Well, Tack, since you're the captain, I see no reason to object, at least not to the point of having a better idea. And, while you're away, with the Spirit out of town for a few days, it'll give me some time to organize the crew and come up with a plan of how we can make this space venture work for the good of all."

"And to keep the government from taking the thing away from us," Zelda said, "and turning it into some kind of super-weapon." She put both hands on each side of her face. "God! Just think of what we have here…it's…it's—"

Chris held out his hand and said, "It's going to take a very carefully organized plan. We will be like the starship Enterprise."

"No," Zelda said. "More like the whole United Federation of Planets, only without the other planets. Our little team here will have more power and ability than any group of people in the entire history of the world."

"You make it sound like we'll have the power of almighty God himself." Tack felt cold chill bumps burst out on his arms. "Man, I'm just beginning to realize how deep I've gotten myself into the affairs of the entire world." He stood up. "Maybe I'm not the guy to be the captain. I'm too young, too inexperienced… and… and…too scared."

Chris stood up too. "You think about it too much, and you'll have us all scared. You're the only one who can fly this thing and make all of its features work. The ship talks to you, and there's no guarantee that anyone else can do any of the things that you have the instincts to do."

"Or..." Zelda looked back and forth at Tack and Chris, extreme worry clouding her features. "Or think about this, anyone else we can trust. At least Tack has possession of the Spirit, and possession—"

"Is nine tenths of the law," Chris finished.

"Well, if I'm the captain, then I say I better get my butt back to Hamlet's Mill and see if I can find Max and see if he knows anything about Lisa's abduction, and tomorrow is too late. Lisa's life may depend on it." He got up from the bench and headed toward the back door to the EPOTEK building. "And this mission might just be the best ever first step in whatever our future together as the crew of the Spirit is destined to be." He waved both hands and broke into a run. "I've got a few things to pack, and then," he yelled back over his shoulder, "Cisco and I will take the ship back to Georgia."

89

Every Scrap

Chris and Zelda watched as Tack disappeared into the building and then gave wondering looks at each other. All that was missing was a dual shaking of their heads. With nothing else coming to mind, they both sat back down at the picnic table in the courtyard. Before they could come up with a decent conversation, Tack came blasting back out of the EPOTEK building with a change of clothes and a new toothbrush stuck in his breast pocket. Cisco was scampering along at his side as they zipped past the table on their way to the workshop that housed the flying saucer.

"You sure about this trip, Tack?" Chris yelled after him, nodding in the direction of the Spirit.

"Yep," he yelled back, "and if I were you, Chris, I'd head back to the cabin as soon as possible and see if Lisa left any clues you might have missed. If we are going to find her, we need every scrap of evidence we can dig up as to who might have taken her and where she might be."

"I can do that, but—"

"No time now, Chris. We'd both better get goin'."

"Right." Chris and Zelda quickly got up from the table, looked back and forth at each other, and then to the Spirit that was already moving out of the work shop. Then, the two members of the newly formed crew of the good ship watched, their eyes glued to the flying saucer as it drifted steadily out into the courtyard. They stood directly in front of the ship, and therefore were able to see Tack's face through the front window as the ship moved slowly toward them and then began to shrink in size.

Chris caught a fleeting glance of Cisco pacing back and forth behind the ship's window as the Spirit shrank down to manhole-cover size. The saucer then slowly rose skyward into the blue sky. When the ship was no longer visible, they continued to look at each other for a moment. Then they calmly walked back into the building. As they got to the door, Chris held it open, and Zelda stopped and looked into his face, studying his expression.

"Are you sure letting Tack take the ship and just leave is such a good idea?"

He motioned for her to go on in through the doorway and said, "I know, I know it makes me nervous too, but it's his ship. He found it, learned to fly it, and he's managed to figure out things about an…an—let's face it—an alien spaceship with alien technology. Heck, Zelda, Tack's the only one who knows how and what to do with the thing, at least for now."

Zelda pushed past Chris and waited inside for him to join her. "I get your drift, but what if he just…just…disappears—like Lisa?"

"Well, I don't personally know Tack all that well, but I've been on his tail long enough to know that he's a good kid. If he's got some ideas of how to find out what happened to Lisa, I have a good feeling about trusting him to do all he can to find her, rescue her—whatever. It is possible that he might leave the rest of us and go hide his ship somewhere, but there's no way he's going to leave a member of his new crew to the mercy of the aliens, or whatever they are. I trust Tack to do the right thing."

"I guess I do too." She fell in along side Chris as they headed toward the front office.

"I think I'd better go back out to the cabin. The police said they had the place taped off until the crime lab could do a proper investigation, but I used my badge and promised I wouldn't touch anything, and they agreed to let me have a key to check the place out to my satisfaction. If you promise not to touch anything and keep your mouth shut about anything we find, you're welcome to come along."

She stopped in her tracks, and he turned to look into her face to see her reaction to what he'd just said to her. He was testing her on several layers, and he could tell from her expression that she knew he was testing her. After a long pause, she said, "I think I'll take a rain check on that. You go ahead. I know if you find anything of use about what happened to my daughter, you'll tell me about it. Am I wrong?"

"As a fellow Spirit crew member, you can count on me to fill you in on anything I find out, and that goes for the rest of the team."

She shook her head and smiled. "This is going to be a real change of life. Nothing is ever going to feel or be the same with any of us for...for—"

"The rest of our lives," Chris groaned. "Or until the government comes in and takes over, and I'm committed to standing in the way of that eventuality if for no other reason, or no better reason, I have a real problem with a fellow I've worked with that goes by the name of Driscoll Battey."

"Real piece of work, eh?"

"Yeah, he's one of those guys you know is working against you, but you just can't be sure who he's working for. I'd say it was the Russians if the Berlin wall hadn't come down. I'd say it was the Democrats, except that I know a couple of Dems that are of the Jack Kennedy variety. If I blame the Communist Party, I'll get a bigger laugh than if I blamed aliens from outer space, and aliens, are just where my big money is. Driscoll has got to be an alien—of the worst kind."

"Are you saying there are good aliens?"

"At least one that I know of."

"The one that Tack told us about?"

"Mr. Chips-a-million."

"Max and Four. You know, I think Four is just the short name for Quadrilla. What do you think?"

"Yeah, Four. I didn't mean to leave her out. But, remember, Four is at least partly human—if she really does exists at all."

"Maybe we'll find out if she does really exist when we fly out on one of our future missions."

"I'm counting on it." He turned to go and then over his shoulder said, "Sure you don't want to join me to the cabin?"

"To tell you the truth, I don't think I could handle seeing Lisa's place without her in it. And…I'm terrified at what you might find."

"Got cha." Chris turned to leave.

90

Lake Bed

The Spirit was streaking through the blue sky, heading due east toward the state of Georgia. Before long, Tack was maneuvering the Spirit over the low mountains of North Georgia. He followed Interstate 20 until he saw the cutoff for State Road 432. Even though the Spirit was hardly big enough to attract any attention by other than an occasional wild goose, he had taken his sweet time on the way to Hamlet's Mill just to be safe and to avoid attracting attention from any possible witnesses. As he approached the location of the sinkhole, the sun was moving toward the late afternoon. He began to recognize familiar landmarks, and he sensed that something wasn't right. He banked the Spirit slightly, increased his speed slightly, and headed for Evelyn's house.

The sun threw long blue-gray shadows across the pastureland and eventually the lake as he approached the Milford mansion. Then as he drew closer, he saw something that caused his mouth to drop and his throat go into dangerous restriction. The lake, it was completely dry. All that was left of it was a deep basin with a circular gray, muddy area at the very bottom…

"It's gone, Cisco." He grunted in disappointment. "The sister ship is gone, along with all the water, and…and…Max—everything!"

Cisco was way up in the forward window, its little black eyes looking in the same direction that Tack was looking. Tack slowly circled the Spirit around the dried-up bed of the lake, searching for clues as to how the sister ship had managed to pull out of the lake bottom and leave no signs of the huge chamber he knew to be below where the ship must have been located. However, all that was visible to Tack and Cisco was a muddy circle of gooey, gray ooze. He did a quick spin around maneuver to check out the surrounding area. "Don't see anybody down there at all. I sure hope it's safe to land so we can check out the area. Maybe Evelyn can tell us what happened to the lake."

The Spirit slowly approached the mansion and moved around to the back where it hovered ten feet off the ground. The Spirit's four legs came down and locked into position. Once the ship had made contact with the grassy surface of the backyard lawn, the ramp came down, its bottom step almost lost in the deep grass. Cisco had been quickly pacing back and forth at the top of the hatchway, obviously impatient to get down to solid ground. Tack wasn't far behind him as they headed down the ramp and toward the back door of the mansion where Tack hoped he would find Evelyn working away in her kitchen.

His heart began to beat faster when he watched Cisco prance up to the back door. He gulped as he saw the raccoon slip inside through the back door that was already standing open. "Wait, Cisco!" he shouted. "I've got a bad feeling about this—wait! STOP!" But Cisco had a mind of his own and was quickly out of sight, inside the kitchen area. Tack cautiously followed Cisco into Evelyn's kitchen.

After a quick look around at the table, the sink, and the cabinets, Tack moved on into the dining room and then into the den. Cisco climbed up on the coffee table and soon was busily leafing through a pile of books that it found there in chaotic disarray. This sight prompted Tack to whip his gaze toward the bookcase. But for a few exceptions, many of Evelyn's books had been pulled from the shelves and were scattered around on the floor of the den. Some of them were opened up to various illustrations and foldouts. He quickly picked up one and scanned a few pages. Soon, Tack began to detect a pattern to the subject matter.

"Look," he said to Cisco, "it seems that whoever created this mess…well, they were looking for something, and it looks like they were very interested in ancient mysteries. Look." He opened the book he was holding to a photograph of Egypt. "This book was opened to the chapter on the pyramids." He grabbed up another book. "And this one is centered on the ancient city of Atlantis, or what they think it looked like." He picked up another book. "And here's a chapter about the temple King Solomon built." Then Tack noticed that Cisco was also pouring over a book that was opened to a page that had a picture that featured a badly distressed piece of parchment—a scroll.

"What cha got there Cisco? Looks like some heavy reading you're into, little britches."

It was actually a handwritten Bible, and it was illustrated. The foldout depicted a detailed print of a painting that showed Moses watching the finger of God cut the tablets of the Ten Commandments from a wall of crimson stone. Then as he got closer to Cisco and could see the illustration better, something else caught his eye. It was the single word "Tack" with a number 1 behind it. This word was scratched in red ink on the bottom of the page across the white boarder beneath the picture.

"I wonder why Evelyn…" He looked at Cisco. Their eyes locked on each other. "Do you think she wrote this for me?" Tack started shaking his head. "It looks like the way Evelyn prints… I think."

He started leafing through the pages of the Bible and found another interesting illustration. It was a painting of Samson, straining between two large pillars of stone. At the bottom of this picture was the word this.

"Holy…" he said and started leafing through the bible to the next illustration. But before he could find it, he stopped, looked at Cisco, and said, "You hear that?"

Cisco shot, in a flash, across the room to the front door, and Tack followed at a trot. He gulped at what he saw. There was no front door. The entire wall surrounding the area that would have been facing the double doors that had been the main front entrance to Evelyn's mansion was gone. It looked like it had been ripped out by a steam shovel. Tack looked down and realized that he still held the Bible book in his hands.

"Quick, Cisco, help me gather up as many of these books as we can carry, and let's get out of here. I've got a sick feeling that the guys who ripped out that door are coming back. I can hear them, can't you?"

Cisco's answer was to make a blue streak of motion back into the den. He quickly started shoving the books on the table toward one end as Tack grabbed a cloth sash from the nearby couch sending two very expensive candlesticks sailing to the floor as it brushed the end table. He used the cloth to bundle up the books as Cisco pushed them off the end of the table. Tack threw the bundle of books over his shoulder. Then, he and Cisco headed out through the kitchen door and across the tall grass. In a flash he scampered up the ramp of the Spirit with Tack not far behind the little guy.

In mere seconds, the ramp closed, and the sleek flying saucer lifted off the grassy backyard. The ship quickly began to shrink down until it was the size of a garbage can lid. The Spirit was still shrinking down as it headed around the left side of the house and zipped off toward the wooded area where the sinkhole was located. Just as the ship slipped into obscurity and was now too small to see, a huge king angel saucer came zooming up over the tops of the nearby pine trees and maneuvered toward the Milford house.

The huge dull metallic saucer moved around to the front of the mansion. It hovered there for a few minutes before, from the center of the red dome atop the saucer, a weird orange-yellow beam shot out toward the front of the mansion. This beam caused a wave of flame to gush out from the front porch and down through the grapevines that lined either side of the walkway. Soon the entire building was swallowed in red-orange flames that leaped toward the sky.

Tack was totally unaware of the destruction he had just narrowly avoided by only seconds because, by that time, the Spirit was slowly descending down into the deep darkness of the sinkhole. Down into the pit of the sunless depths, Tack piloted the ship toward the shelf below that defined the entrance to his secret hideaway. Soon he could just make out the narrow passageway to the cave that had once housed his flying saucer back when he had to abandon hangar 18 at Gold Field. As far as he could tell the natural cave-like look of the hideaway was the same as it had been when he'd left this underground refuge sometime ago, in order to seek out Kelly's moon rock.

Cisco quickly climbed down from the forward window, dropped to the floor, and ran over to the acceleration couch. One quick jump and he was perched on the arm of the couch, next to his captain, his eyes searching Tack's baby blues.

"Watch this, Cisco," he said as he reached into the forward propulsion sphere and eased the ship handily into the cave. A quick movement that betrayed Tack's quick mastery of the ship's controls switched on the forward searchlight of the saucer, and he could see the walls on either side of the cave move by as the ship glided along the stone corridor.

When the Spirit had reached the center of the familiar chamber, Tack performed the maneuver of turning the ship around and lowering the craft to the stony slab that formed the floor of the cave.

After seeing Evelyn's house in its current condition and seeing the lake all dried up, Tack was stunned to find that the cave area that had been the Spirit's hangar area for a little while after he'd abandoned hangar 18 and while he'd conducted his search for Kelly's moon rock was virtually unchanged. "What in blazes is going on, Cisco?" he said as his eyes scanned the console in front of him. "The lake was all dried up; the very bottom was clearly visible." Tack was then forced to say, "I really expected this cave to be all sealed up, or at least changed in some way."

The engines of the Spirit were still winding down as he unbuckled his seatbelt and headed for the air lock. Cisco was close by his side as Tack snatched up his emergency flashlight.

91

Sink Pit

Since the cave seemed to be pretty much the same as it had been when he last left it, Tack decided he didn't need to spend the time it would take to turn on the generator that would provide light to the chamber. It wouldn't help much in the task at hand anyway. Tack was anxious to see what the strange room that had once housed the sister ship looked like now that the lake was all dried up. The deepest part of the floor of the lake that had once been the sister ship itself had been sealed up in some manner, hiding the rock-walled chamber below from the prying eyes of any visitors to the Milford place.

He made his way toward the back of the cave to the tiny entrance he'd discovered just before his flight to Area 6451. The horror of what he'd witnessed there in 6451's huge underground bio lab still haunted his mind, and he was relieved to find that this cave area seemed to be pretty much as he remembered it. There was no hesitation at all in Tack quickly dropping to his knees and scrambling deep into the narrow passageway.

Cisco wasn't far behind as his master pushed ahead with his flashlight into the small tunnel. Even though his flashlight was taking quite a beating in being slammed against the rocks and stonewalls that he was encountering. He was able to move along handily toward the mysterious chamber that lay at the end of the tunnel.

Then, suddenly, before he could even guess at the degree of progress he'd been able to make, he ran into an obstacle he hadn't expected. As the tiny tunnel took a sharp turn to the left, he ran into a wall of crushed rock and stony debris. "The sister ship," he mumbled to Cisco, who had managed to move up along side of his head, "must have dislodged all of this crap when it left the floor of the lake." He sneezed. "And the water probably carried it along to the sinkhole…here. All of this stuff"—he grunted as he tugged at a stone in his path—"must have sealed up the tunnel as all that water rushed through. I hope the chamber is still intact. I want to see how the opening the sister ship left behind became all sealed up."

Cisco moved up closer to Tack's face and looked him directly in the eye. Tack was startled to see what looked dangerously like a worried look on the coon's fuzzy little face.

"What?" Tack asked, as if expecting Cisco to burst out in a frenzy of dialogue.

In an apparent negative response to Tack's inquiry, Cisco moved behind Tack and started back toward the entrance of the tunnel. The passage was just too narrow for Tack to turn his head to watch the raccoon's progress back out of the tunnel, so he decided to see what he could do to open up the passageway to the sister ship chamber.

He continued to work on removing the stones that now blocked his path. "This ain't gonna be easy." He managed a muffled moan. "There's just no place to put all these rocks so I can get through. Oops!"

That last "oops" was in response to a tiny trickle of water that was squirting in a little stream out from between a couple of the rocks.

As he watched, the squirting little stream became a mild little trickle. Then, the trickle seemed to increase, slightly, so he attempted to put back the rock that he'd finally been able move out of the way.

The rock didn't seem to fit at first, but, finally, it seemed to do the trick, at least it seemed to be helping until the stream of water reappeared and then grew to a finger-sized "squirt" that pushed a different small stone out of the orifice. "Oh maaan!"

Tack's fingers quickly searched around on the floor of the tunnel for the stone, any stone, but the stream grew even more. Soon the flow of water became way too big for that particular stone to do any good at all. Frantically, he set aside the flashlight and moved both hands around in the stony rubble, searching for a stone big enough to stop the liquid flow, but the stream was now a fist-sized flow that gushed out, running under his belly and sweeping the flashlight around so that the beam blinded him momentarily.

"Not good! Not good! Not good!" he grunted as he began to frantically backpedal, pushing himself as best he could away from the growing flood of water.

But try as he might, he was unable to outrun the growing flood. Soon, it gushed up into his face, choking him into a coughing fit. This flood was making his retreat impossible. It was quickly making the floor of the tunnel slippery with gooey mud. His hands could not find enough friction to help him to achieve adequate backward motion. Then, to his horror, his body began to be more and more of an obstacle to the free flow of the water.

As a result, the level of the ice-cold liquid was rising up around his neck, and then the lower portion of his face. Soon, in addition to his feeble efforts to back himself out of the tunnel, he had to keep his mouth shut and hold his head back at a painful angle to keep from sucking the water up into his nose.

Added to all of this, as if that were not enough to increase his heart rate to the maximum, the tunnel seemed to be growing smaller. It squeezed painfully in on his lower body. His progress in backing out to safety was now halted altogether, and he felt himself hopelessly stuck in place.

The flow of water rose up in a gushing flush and covered his entire face and head. He held his breath as long as he could, but soon he had to give in to the pressure, the desperate urge to breathe, even though the only thing left to breathe was water. His lungs were filled with each of his attempts to breathe, and, in his mind, he saw the world begin to pass by at an ever-increasing speed.

92

Apelike

As Tack struggled to breathe and avoid swallowing more and more water, he began to see his life's events fly by as the fuzzy image of what he took to be a young boy became clear for a moment; the boy was standing there in his pajamas, watching the rain pour in through the front door of his stepfather's living room. His stepmom was standing next to him. She had a huge shotgun in her hands and was looking down at him. Fear gripped his entire body as he watched his stepmom step out onto the porch, pointing the barrel of the huge gun up toward a large brilliant, glowing object.

The target, wherein his stepmom was pointing the gun, moved up out of his view as his lungs ached with a burning of an intense fire. The object came back into view and he saw it dissolve into a huge UFO. It was hovering in the field behind the Milford Lake. Now it was broad daylight, and Cisco was there, only Cisco looked different. He had huge cartoon-like eyes. A long time ago, as a young boy, he'd seen a comic book character that looked a lot like this version of Cisco. The comic featured a caveman-like character that was called Tor, and on his shoulder was a strange little animal. The animal was sort of cute in some ways, but the main thing about it that he could remember were the creature's big eyes. These huge black orbs dominated the tiny fur-covered, apelike body of the creature.

Now Cisco had those eyes, and his body was thinner than a normal raccoon's body. In addition to all this, the edges of Cisco's catlike ears were lined with a string of tiny little lights, similar to the fiber optics that had once become so popular in novelty lamp fixtures. Cisco was watching as the UFO settled to the ground.

A ramp slowly descended down from the UFO, and this weird Cisco scampered over, stopped in his tracks, and waited for the bottom of the ramp to settle into the grass. The tiny creature then turned and looked back in Tack's direction. Big-eyed Cisco then quickly waved his pawlike hand just before he turned back and dashed up into the saucer. Once the coon had disappeared into the ship, the ramp rose quickly up into the UFO and slammed shut. A loud humming sound filled the air and the disk shaped ship began to rise up from the clearing up into the sky.

At that point, Tack's lungs exploded, blood mixing with the water that was gushing into his mouth and throat. He saw the UFO rose up higher and higher, and the sky began to spin faster and grow brighter. The edges of the sky began to grow darker and darker, until it was as if he were looking into a giant whirlpool with a brilliant ball of glowing matter at its center.

And Tack felt himself being drawn toward the ball of light. Or, maybe, he thought, I'm falling into it!

The circular area of light seemed to be growing larger or closer, it was difficult to tell, and it mattered little, because there was nothing Tack could do to change his course, and he was fast losing his ability to think beyond the pain he was currently suffering.

He was almost there, almost to the light. It filled the sky or, I should say, the world. The light was very close now, right before him, and in an instant, he slipped inside, into the light itself.

At that moment he could see that he was passing through a portal, a threshold of sorts, and as his eyes attempted in vain to adjust to the light, little by little, he began to make out shapes of objects and a strange architecture.

The world he had just entered was wondrous, and his intense pain was now modified slightly to an indiscernible sensation he'd never experienced before.

Nothing here was familiar—nothing. The imagination of artists down through the ages had not begun to touch the images now forming inside his mind. What he was witnessing was even beyond the images of his most imaginative dreams, and, now, he felt wonderful. The pain in his lungs was totally gone. He couldn't remember the moment the pain and the fear that he'd seconds ago experienced had left him, but now, it was all gone. Now he was experiencing emotions and feelings that transcended anything he could remember living through. And the images his mind was experiencing were creating more joy in his very soul that he'd ever even hoped for.

Tack was flying, walking, moving through various objects and shapes of pure beauty, and, finally, he was moving toward a glowing figure of some sort. Surrounding the figure was a ring of star-like lights, and the figure was dressed in what might have passed for armor, but somehow, it didn't look like any war armor he'd ever seen. He decided it was some kind of space suit, though there was no helmet, or any visible life-support system.

He was closer to the figure now, and he could almost see the features of his face. Yes, it was a male figure, and his face...was...

As if his emotional state could take no more of the friendly warmth it was experiencing, this new emotion was so overwhelming that he just stopped trying to measure how wonderful he was feeling as the man's face became more and more clear. And then, the man smiled at him, and Tack began to cry. His emotional state swept him away from himself and he was connected to something—someone, others, countless others, and he was crying uncontrollably. And then he realized he was also laughing, laughing out loud so hard that the tears were flooding his mouth and covering his entire body. He looked down and realized that the tears were not tears at all, but drops of pure gold, glittering golden drops, a kind of liquid gold of a warmth that comforted his soul.

Then he was looking at a darkened room with a bright light glaring down into his face, hurting his eyes. The light was moving in tiny little circles. It was jittery, as if the hand holding the light was nervous. Tack tried in vain to see beyond the light. He wanted to see the man's wondrous face again.

Then he noticed something else. At first he couldn't make out exactly what it was. It looked like some kind of moth, flying around in the light, occasionally brushing his face. But it didn't feel at all like feathery moth wings as it fluttered around and collided with his nose and cheeks. It felt cold, icy. Then as his eyes managed to focus on the thing he caught the glitter of an ice-blue glow. It was the crystal; it was the crystal he'd found in the grass around the circular burned area near the Milford Lake. No, he decided it was a different crystal. It was attached to a silver chain and it was swinging around in maddening circles over his face. As he attempted to see what the other end of the chain was attached to, he caught the reflected, edge lighting against a tiny hand—no, not a hand. A paw.

As his eyes regained a better focus, he realized that Cisco was holding his flashlight in one hand and dangling the crystal over his face with the other, and he was back inside the cave, under the aft section of the Spirit.

"Cisco," he gasped and attempted to sit up. But Cisco pushed the warm lens of the flashlight against Tack's forehead and pushed him back down to the cave floor.

93

On a Chain

Tack was confused. He thought he'd lost the flashlight when the tunnel had flooded him. He assumed it was lost forever, but after seeing Cisco with the flashlight, Tack's focus grew better by slow stages. He realized that Cisco was holding his flashlight in one hand and dangling the crystal over his face with the other, and he was back inside the cave, under the aft section of the Spirit. The little raccoon was insistent that he lay still and had pushed Tack gently back down on the cave floor.

Tack's mind was racing now, almost beyond his control. He was thinking, trying to figure things out. His brain was working frantically to absorb and understand the reality of the recent events—what was real and what was obviously what happens to your brain when it is in the very process of giving up the ghost. His close call with the agent of death was hammering him mercilessly. The only relief that finally came, with little tugs at his reasoning powers, was the image of that crystal on a chain, swinging around in circles over his face. He was beginning to believe that, perhaps—just perhaps—the crystal had more to do with his recovery than he was willing to let himself believe. Maybe the crystal had some magical power of which he was unaware.

He quickly ran his hand down over his left pant pocket and felt the bulge of the crystal he had found and was surprised to find that it was still there where he had placed it before he'd attempted to enter the tunnel. "There must be two crystals," he muttered.

It was very difficult for him, in his current condition, his pants being soaked in water and gooey mud, but finally he was able to pull the crystal out of his pocket and let it dangle there in front of his nose. "Okay, little crystal, I get the message. I think I'll keep you around for a while," he said and slipped the chain over his head, wondering when he had taken the time to put the ice blue jewel on a chain. Then his eyes swept around over to the crystal that Cisco was holding.

He motioned to the raccoon. "You had that crystal with you in the cave, didn't you, little britches? If Evelyn is gone, how did you end up with it? Did she somehow managed to get it to you without my knowing...or did you...oh maaan, maybe it's not Evelyn's after all. Maybe it's someone else's—maybe it's yours—or, I never thought about it before, it might belong to Max.

"Come to think of it, the first time I ever saw you, you were working like crazy to find something in that circle of soot and ashes left behind by the saucer. I've been assuming that you never found what you were looking for, that I found it, the crystal. But the more I think about it, I remember that my crystal didn't have a...it wasn't mounted on a chain like this one." He fingered his crystal, looking down at it. "It was just loose, like a piece of stone that had been fused out of sand and soil by the saucer's engine blast. I've been assuming all this time that the intense heat of the saucer created that crystal. But, after all that I've been through these past few weeks, it seems to be that more and more of these mysterious crystals are showing up. There was that one I found on the moon, then one at the bio lab, then there's Evelyn's, and, well, wonder of wonders, you might just have a crystal of your own. Is that it? Does that crystal belong to you, and this one is...mine?"

Cisco looked back at Tack and sat up on his hind legs. Then Tack watched as Cisco did something very strange—strange even for Cisco. He was folding his arms over his chest. He'd never seen an animal do such a thing, except in the animated films and videos. But as strange as this was, it was only the beginning of the wonders in store for the young space ship captain.

Cisco was just sitting there looking back at him. As Tack watched the little raccoon, the fur ball began to grow slightly out of focus, or, at least, it seemed that way to Tack. It was like the wind was blowing into his face, and his eyes were watering to the point that the images in front of him were wavering and flooding into an animated blur. He rubbed his eyes with the backs of his hands, but it didn't make things any better. His little pet raccoon was changing right before his eyes, as they say. Cisco was metamorphosing into…

"My god, Cisco." Tack's throat suddenly went dry, so dry that he couldn't finish what he was going to say.

Cisco continued to change. His eyes grew bigger, becoming very much like the vision he'd recently seen in his dreamlike state. Then the raccoon's ears grew longer, and the tiny lights that were located around the outer rim of his ears were more prominent. And the lights were merrily flashing in an obvious pattern. The gray fur on his face became longer and curled around forming snakelike tendrils. And it was as if his head were growing larger, but as Tack watched, trying to swallow the dryness in his throat, it was obvious that Cisco's head may have been becoming larger, but the body was also growing somewhat smaller.

Finally Cisco's transformation was complete, and the little beast twitched his nose and licked his lips. "I guess you are ready Tack, Moultrie," a weird tiny, little voice came from the new Cisco. "You call me Cisco. I am called Two by those who know me, mostly I am called Deltoo. I am part of Quadrilla's team. I am partners with the one you call Max. Max and I serve Quadrilla. Quadrilla's team has been observing you for a long time, and you have performed well—so far.

"There are many things you have yet to learn and understand. It will take time. You will be exposed to these things and not have full understanding. This is why I have been chosen to provide you with the help you will need in order to achieve success in your mission."

Finally, Tack was able to control his vocal cords. A warmth began to fill the area around his throat that just seconds before seemed to be frozen. He forced some sounds out of his throat.

"Cisco, you can speak! I had a feeling…my god. You're not a raccoon at all, are you? I'm…I'm—"

"There will be time," Deltoo spoke calmly but unfolded his arms and began to gesture with his tiny pawlike hands, much as a human being would have when speaking. "One does not lead with a chain. Leading is accomplished by showing the way with a light on the pathway."

Without a great deal of thought, what Cisco was telling him seemed to Tack to be justifiable. Cisco had been observing him all these weeks and probably studying his every move and thought.

Deltoo waved his paws. "We have little time, Tack Moultrie. We can discuss what has passed between you and I at a time wherein we have managed to avoid being captured by the evil angels. I understand that you and the rest of the Spirit crew call them the king angels, but I am certain that these beings are responsible for the abduction of Lisa Krebs. And they are determined to find us and recover the Spirit prototype ship. I am sure that we need to avoid the storms of time that are to come, and I'm not sure what they will do to us should they manage to capture the ship.'

Tack rose to his feet and stood there swaying as he managed to get his bearings. "It sounds like you are afraid that these evil angels will attempt to abduct us, if they can find us."

"Yes, they will, as you say, abduct us or—and I know you hate to hear these words—worse."

Tack couldn't hold back a slight smile at Deltoo's acute observation. He noticed his mud-covered flashlight lying down on the floor of the cave where Deltoo had dropped it and managed to bend down long enough to pick it up. He was still too dizzy and weak to do much maneuvering, but after steadying himself a little, he said, "You are absolutely right, Cisco…I mean, Deltoo.

We've got to get our sweet arses out of here in one quick hurry." He turned and faced the Spirit across the room.

"Sweet arses? What means our 'sweet arses,' Tack Moultri?"

"What it means is 'Blow this joint! Vamoose, skedaddle! Head 'em up 'n' move 'em out!" With all of that, which left Deltoo scratching his furry head Tack headed for the ship.

"Vamoos! Make tracks—scoot!" Tack added as his gate turned into a trot. "What's the difference? We've got to get a move on. Storms of time indeed!" He headed up the ramp of the Spirit. Deltoo hesitated only a half second and then trotted after him on all fours.

The cave's walls vibrated with a musical roaring hum as Tack engaged the Spirit's engines, and the ship lifted up gracefully off of the cave floor. Once outside the cave and hovering over the huge shelf of stone, the Spirit began to rise, slowly and carefully up, up, up, out of the sinkhole. Tack was uncertain about whether or not the king angels might be waiting for them out there by what was left of Evelyn's house, and he was acutely aware of the fact that they needed to do all they could to avoid being captured by Cisco's evil angels.

94

No Time

After a quick flyby of all that was left of the Milford Mansion and a survey of the Lake, Tack headed the Spirit through a series of billowy clouds that conveniently provided the necessary cover that, under the circumstances, he and Deltoo decided was a good idea. Once Tack was confident that the king angel ships had gone elsewhere at least for a while, he chanced to enlarge the ship to normal size and it would remain that way for the trip back to Houston.

Cisco seemed to be captivated by the beauty of the sky, as was Tack. Though they both were bent on attempting to avoid being seen by any pilots in the area, the Spirit managed to cut a sweeping path through the delirious gathering of cumulus puffs that filled the sky. At least this was how the voyage was going so far.

Tack could, of course, easily cover the distance from Hamlet's Mill to Houston in a shorter period of time by playing with the time-travel sphere, but he was hesitant to attempt initiating time travel while the ship was in motion. His single experiment with the newly discovered feature of this fantastic space ship had been kicked off, as it were, when, some time back, the Spirit was sitting statically on the shelf in the EPOTEK lab. He had accidentally set the ship in motion through time in what seemed like ages ago. And it was hard enough to force his mind to concentrate on getting from here to there, without complicating matters with the added function of thinking of how to get from the present to the future or the past.

Now he decided to just fly the Spirit as he would a conventional aircraft on the way back to the lab. Flying was his passion, the feel of the controls in his hands, the ship itself, and his being part of it filled him with the confidence of an experienced pilot, and pushed back his curiosity into the concept of traveling through time. Therefore, he made a pact with himself, and the Spirit o put off any time travel until he'd given it more consideration. He would use the ship's ability to fly and only employ the time travel and the size controls when the mission specifically called for those abilities.

It was thus that Tack and Deltoo were totally unaware of the fact that the Spirit was being followed and targeted. Sorry to say, they had not avoided the evil angels in their pursuit of recapturing the prototype, at least not completely.

95

Command Ship

The alien ship was huge. If anyone but Tack Moultrie ever found out about it, how the giant UFO had gotten into the airspace of the United States without detection would be a mystery for years to come. Although it had been there months ago on Tack's little moon adventure, it had gone unnoticed. It had been behind one of the lunar mountains. Thus, if Tack had been able to actually see the craft, he would not have been able to recognize it as the command ship that had sent the saucers to attack him there near Mare Tranquilititus. Now it didn't matter at all, because he couldn't actually see it; currently, the huge craft was shrouded in a deep gray cloud that was laced by strange, violet-colored lightning bolts, and Tack nor Cisco could see the real danger that they were about to face.

Tack was in the process of deciding whether or not to go around what looked to be a large thunderstorm that the Spirit was approaching. He could gain altitude and go above the storm, but he was concerned that this might attract too much attention to his flight. Any radar installations in the area would most certainly see the huge blip on their screens and check it out. He could dive and go under it, but that would require possibly encountering any low flying aircraft or drones that might be in the area.

The glowing electrical fields were busily streaking around over and through the cloud like so many angry electric ells fighting for the dominant position in the misty vapor of a storm.

Even though Tack couldn't see what was causing the stormy countenance of the cloud, he was considering the prospect of shrinking the size of the ship just in case he might need to avoid detection by what ever it might be. Perhaps this tactic would hide him from potential danger. However, shrinking the ship in size would also slow down his speed. The smaller he became, the longer it would take to cross the necessary mileage to escape.

The gray, vapory mass was growing darker and more translucent as he watched the violet electricity climb insanely all over the body of the cloud. Then as he watched the viewing screens, little by little, they were being filled with an image he was having trouble making out. This image was of the strangest spaceship he could ever imagine. He quickly slipped his hands into the spheres as the cloud grew more and more active and drew ever closer.

"Holy," he gasped. The scale of the huge ship was impossible to determine, but all indications were that the ship was maneuvering toward the Spirit, and Tack suddenly realized that he was the target of the aliens that were piloting that monstrous machine.

The memory of the saucers that had been mysteriously zapped to minute size by the shrink beam of the Spirit back when he'd managed to fly his ship to the moon, flashed through his mind as he fought the controls to fly the Spirit down to a lower altitude. This maneuver he'd managed to come up with was basically to attempt some kind of escape. Added to that maneuver, he, then, assumed a zigzag pattern that just might add to his possible success.

The gigantic ship was some three thousand feet above the Spirit and descending methodically down to the altitude wherein Tack was flying. Soon Tack could feel the tingling in the skin of his scalp as the edge of the cloud began to engulf the body of the Spirit. The viewing screens grew darker and then went to black except for the occasional purple flash and a series of snowy streaks that made the screens look as if they'd just lost horizontal hold.

He tried looking out of the forward window, but that gave him little comfort. It was painfully obvious that he would soon be inside the worst storm he'd ever seen. A storm led by a monstrous alien spaceship.

96

Captured

Cisco or, rather, Deltoo hopped down to the deck and scampered over to the command chair. He looked up at Tack and said, "Captain, it seems that we are now inside the capture beam of the king angels' command vessel. I'm thinking that there is no escape. We must now shut down the engines and reserve our power if we are to ever escape. It is a drastic move; however, it does give us the time to prepare for a possible escape at some later time."

"You're telling me that I must allow this so-called mother ship capture the Spirit? I don't think so."

"I understand your feelings, Captain. However, in so doing we will gain the time to think of a way to somehow escape at some later time.

"Well, I'm thinkin' it's not that great of an idea, but for now, I'm takin' the advice of my copilot."

97

Angry Sky Gods

Tack fought to push aside his strong compulsion to be indecisive. He looked back and forth at Deltoo and the darkened window. "Are you sure? Can you be sure? What will the king angels do with us?"

"I am not certain," Deltoo answered. "Perhaps we can make some kind of escape after we assess the situation aboard the vessel. Our best action at this point is to, how you say, cool it."

Tack fought a moment with his strong drive to fight back at all costs, but the look that the strange little fuzzy alien was giving him with those huge black eyes was making him think it might be a good idea to go along with his expert insight. After all, this fuzzy little alien had saved him from the cave, not to mention the two saucers he'd encountered on the moon.

"I know it might be asking a lot, ah, er, Deltoo, but could you work just as well by, you know, going back to your old self. I would feel more comfortable with you back as a little raccoon, and calling you Cisco instead of having to deal with a bug-eyed alien called Deltoo. Can you still talk to me in that form?"

"Of course, Tack Moultrie. Most of what we see is what we think we see anyway. There are many assumptions and illusions that disguise the reality that we perceive. Remember, the main purpose of the brain is to forget, you know. If we could not forget the multitudes of information and all the data that is constantly flooding our reality, we couldn't know what is going on minute to minute."

"Well, I never thought of it that way, but if you could be Cisco again, I'd have a lot less trouble thinking straight, and I would really appreciate it.

"Problem it is not," Deltoo said, doing a passable impression of Jedi Yoda and morphed himself back to the likeness of the raccoon.

Tack smiled at his old friend. In memory flashbacks, his mind quickly played back Cisco's first injury, then his death, and then his transformation from a friendly little raccoon to a strange big-eyed friendly little nightmare. "Thanks, Cisco. Let's just save your little secret for the team back at EPOTEK when I need to get some badly needed attention. What da ya say?"

98

They Are Prisoners

There was little to see outside of the Spirit as the ship was being absorbed into the king angel mother ship. There were vapory clouds of gas or steam, backlit by many lights and vague, shadowy shapes. Movement of the Spirit was barely noticeable until, at last, the saucer came to rest inside a huge well-lit chamber.

Cisco turned from looking out of the forward window, and focused on Tack's facial expression. He hesitated only a moment and then jumped down to the floor and made a mad dash over to the central observation chair. Climbing up the tower to the chair wasn't all that easy, but soon the small furry animal was sitting on Tack's shoulder looking out into the expanse of the chamber at all the objects scattered here and there across its deck.

"Captain. We apparently have been captured by the same mother ship that has also captured the sister ship. I am guessing, from all the recent events that have surrounded us, that the nice lady Lisa along with Evelyn, Quadrilla, and Max will most likely be on board the sister ship. Or perhaps they are prisoners of the king angels here aboard the mother ship.

Tack's eyes continued to scan the chamber that he was beginning to consider the hangar area, and then he caught a movement out of the corner of his eye. At first, when he got a good look at this movement, he thought of a small group of Halloween revelers on their way to a costume party. But after a few moments of study, he realized that they were aliens, and there were many different kinds of aliens. They were walking along rather clumsily looking at the sister ship, concentrating their attention on the underside of the craft. Occasionally, one of the aliens would look toward Tack and the Spirit. This sent a shiver of fear up through Tack's body. He'd been expecting to see some kind of alien crossing his path, so to speak, because he'd assumed that aliens of some sort had created the Spirit, and he also assumed that they eventually would come back to claim their saucer.

However, he'd not expected to see what appeared to be an organized group of aliens, some different, but some, obviously in groups by race or rank. The line "We are not alone" was slapping Tack in the face with a vengeance.

"Cis…co…I don't think we're in Kansas anymore."

Cisco, who was soaking up the same scene Tack was watching, slowly turned his fuzzy head, ears, and all to look into Tack's face. "What means this 'We're not in Kansas anymore?' When have we ever been in Kansas?"

"It's just one of those human expressions that you are going to have to get used to. I use them all the time. It's from an old movie about a little girl who is sucked off the planet up into a land called Oz, and it's a really weird place with a lot of weird characters, like we're looking at now, only Oz was a fantasy. I really wish this was a fantasy. I really do wish this was a fantasy 'cause all those weird guys are coming this way."

"Ooooo. What are we going to do if they make us come out?"

"I've been giving that some deep thought. Maybe they will just ask us to come out. They captured our ships for some purpose, but if they can't make us come out, I'm wondering if they can…you know, come in and get us. I wonder if they have been able to get to the crew of the sister ship."

Cisco turned his head and looked at the console screens as if he expected to see some new usable information appearing there.

Tack noticed Cisco's distraction to the screens and said, "What is it? What are you thinking?"

"Just had a thought that whoever is aboard that sister ship, perhaps Quadrilla herself and certainly Max, they may still be aboard the sister ship just as we are still aboard the Spirit. If that is so, perhaps I should be attempting to contact them. Together, we stand a better chance of escape than we do alone." He looked back at the captain. "Is that not true?"

99

Sister Ship

While leaning over the forward console next to Cisco at the window, Tack watched the activity out in the mother ship work chamber and then looked at Cisco. "Well, little britches, I think it's time for us to consider coming up with a plan to keep those weird guys out there from entering the Spirit or the sister ship, for that matter.

Cisco blinked and nodded. "If it is, indeed, at all possible to do so," he said.

Tack studied as much of the chamber as he could see, finally focusing on the various creatures milling around in the hangar area and performing suspicious activities. The creature gang currently seemed to be paying special attention to the sister ship.

After a while, it seemed that some of the creatures and the king angels were losing their interest in the sister ship and in small groups were moving toward the Spirit. "Look Cisco, it looks like these weird Os are going to pay us a visit. I won't be surprised if they attempt to find some means of access.

Tack wasn't far from being correct. Soon he and Cisco could hear and feel the effects of the creatures scratching and pounding away at the metal surface of the Spirit as they searched, without much success, to find some kind of entrance into the saucer. After a lengthy period of maddening frustration, the gang of creatures moved back to the sister ship and seemed to grow even more frustrated at their failure to find some way to get to the crew. No doubt, their main objective was Quadrilla herself.

Over a period of time Tack and Cisco watched the gang of creatures working back and forth between the sister ship and the Spirit. It was growing more and more obvious that the weird gang had no idea at all of how to gain access to the occupants inside these two ships. This was somewhat of a relief, but not enough to keep Tack's mind from searching for a better plan than just watching these creatures as they were sure to eventually find some means of entry.

He was still searching for an idea of what to do as the king angels eventually decided to try entering the Spirit through the forward window. For the first time, Tack was afforded a close-up view of just exactly what these alien creatures looked like, and it wasn't pretty.

"Okay, Cisco…Deltoo—whatever—you don't happen to have any brainy ideas of what we can do to stop all this and get the heck out of here, do you?"

As the creatures began to scratch and putter around on the forward window, the scary sounds they were making were suddenly accompanied by another sound. It was the radio or whatever Quadrilla would have named the communications device. Whatever it was, it was a helpful, welcome sound—a woman's voice, not a familiar woman's voice, but welcome just the same.

"I am calling the flying saucer craft located across the room that has just recently arrived inside the king angel mother ship," the voice was saying. "I am assuming that a Mr. Tack Moultrie is the pilot of that saucer. Am I correct? Please respond."

"Yes, this is Tack Moultrie. Who's this?

"Hi, Tack, you may remember me from the EPOTEK labs. I work there as computer specialist. My name is Lisa Krebs."

"Yeah, of course, I remember you. You're Agent Slattery's friend. In fact, I'm here because of you. Chris was sure that you had been abducted… or…well, and I volunteered to try to find you and bring you back. Well, looks like I've found you all right, but bringing you back…well, as I look around this mother ship and all the weird creatures milling around in here, looks like that's going to be rather difficult."

"What you may not know is that I am also a friend of Evelyn Milford and Quadrilla. Quadrilla needs to know are you alone, or is there a Deltoo aboard your ship also?"

Tack glanced over at Cisco. He could swear the raccoon was smiling. "Yeah, that little rascal is here with me all right."

"That's fortunate." The voice changed, and Tack assumed that it was the voice of the strange Quadrilla gal.

While he was trying to figure out the logistics of some kind of an escape attempt, Lisa went on, "Several days ago, I came down to Hamlet's Mill to get more information from Evelyn. I had just returned to Houston when I was taken from my cabin by these aliens on the mother ship. I don't know how or why they sought me out, but Evelyn and Max, in this sister ship, intercepted the communications between the mother ship and those creatures that had captured me at my home. When Evelyn heard that I was their captive, Quadrilla and Max came up with a plan to rescue me. We don't have time for the entire story now. I'm calling you to help Quadrilla to guide you and Deltoo in her plan to escape from this mother ship. Are you ready to talk to her?"

Tack looked over at Cisco, and the little guy nodded back. "Yes, go ahead. We are listening."

"Hello, Tack, this is Quadrilla. We don't have much time, so listen closely."

"I'm still here, go ahead. If it will get me out of this mess, I'll do anything I can."

"For now, let's just say that it is best that we sit tight and do some creative thinking." Somehow, Quadrilla's voice sounded more familiar to Tack than did that of Lisa Krebs, and it made him feel a whole lot better.

Deltoo grunted and said, "I think we do not have the luxury of the time it will take to do the creative thinking of which you speak." Then the coon motioned for Tack to look at the extreme left viewing screen. What Tack had missed up to now in his communications was the fact that not only was Quadrilla's voice being transmitted on Deltoo's monitor, but he could also now see Quadrilla's face and behind her the interior of the sister ship.

"Is that you, Deltoo?" Quadrilla's eyes opened wide.

"Yes, my lady. I am here and ready to assist in any way that I can to help both our crews to escape, and I have a…what you call a creative idea."

"Then speak now, little one. Time is of the essence as the humans often say." Quadrilla was now smiling, and her true loveliness began to show.

"That the king angels are not able to receive our communications I am desperately hoping," Deltoo squeaked. "Therefore I will use the translation feature of my crystal." The raccoon held up the ice-blue crystal on the chain around his neck and continued. "I believe it is possible for both our crews to shrink our two ships, and try to find a way out of the mother ship. We can avoid these creatures by making a quick flight around the interior of the mother ship in a drastically reduced size while we perform a simple, but necessarily difficult exploration. With both of us performing the exploration, this difficult task can be reduced by at least one half."

"Thank you, Deltoo. That is a very good start, and I like the idea that this initial plan will give us additional time to think further of ideas that may help us to make a successful escape. With both ships working at the same time, your plan seems to be immediately workable."

100

Angel Storm

The crews aboard the two captured flying saucers now housed in the mother ship work chamber were at the start of putting their plan of escape into action, but the king angels aggressively studying for ways to get into the sister ship, and the Spirit had other plans. They were quickly putting into action their efforts to gain access through the forward windows. The Spirit was their first target for this particular action. They had assembled a small team out in front of the Spirit window and had summoned a very menacing looking machine to attempt to crack open the window glass.

It was impossible for Tack to tell for sure whether this menacing device was a creature or a machine. It was in the form of a many legged spider beast. However, the description didn't stop there. What appeared to be an identical creature was positioned upside down on top of the spider, with legs reaching up from the body of the beast. It was an arresting sight, the twitching and waving of the many legs of the alien beast were more frightening than Tack could even imagine. Soon the spider was climbing up over the forward section of the Spirit and moving its razor-sharp jaws up against the transparent material of the command window.

Cisco was frantically moving back and forth in helpless desperation, screaming at Tack to do what ever he was going to do, fast, and get them away from this ungainly beast. "Quick, Captain," Cisco groaned in his freaky little voice. "You must power up the ship!"

Even though the Spirit was beginning to come to full power, Tack's attention was still fixed upon the monster spider that was attempting to eat its way through the forward window.

"Now, Captain! Now!" Cisco screamed.

"The sister ship is still trying to come up to full power. I'm going to see if I can use the shrink beam to shrink the aliens and the machine!" Tack yelled back and maneuvered his hands inside the shrink beam sphere.

Across the maintenance hangar, Tack caught a glimpse of the sister ship as it began to lift upward. "Good," he said, "she's up to power, just in time."

Across the mother ship chamber, Quadrilla's ship was finally hovering just over the floor. Soon, it began to shrink rapidly. Tack could only assume that the Spirit was about ready to assume the same mode, or not far behind. Now, the spider creature seemed to grow larger at an impossibly rapid pace. The vision grabbed Tack in the pit of his stomach. Even thought the creature was outside the ship, Tack felt a strange sense of change coming over him. It wasn't as if the Spirit and everything inside was shrinking. It was more like everything outside the ship was growing at an incredible rate of speed. It was creating the feeling of falling rapidly into a deep pit.

101

Spider King

Deltoo held on to the brace of the window and said, "I've got a feeling this is going to be rough, Captain." The raccoon was still assuming the Cisco countenance as he hung on desperately near the viewing screens on the console. Outside the forward window everything was shaking violently and growing to huge proportions. The monster spider machine was now so huge that one of its shiny black legs almost filled the entire window area. The monstrous machine was no longer attempting to eat its way through the forward window, but instead, searching around for that flying saucer that had just become less than as dust mote to its visual sensors.

"Tack, do you read me?" It was Quadrilla again. "Tack, please respond."

"I'm listening, Quadrilla, go ahead."

"We are both shrinking, and we must begin searching immediately for an escape rout. To assure the highest degree of success, it is imperative that you let Deltoo take command of your ship. He knows how to communicate with me on the level necessary to achieve success, or at least give us the best chance for our escape."

"No problem," Tack said and looked over at the raccoon. "Cisco, old buddy, you have the com."

"I have the what?"

Tack waved the raccoon off. "It's just another one of those expressions that I use. It means that I am giving you command of the ship."

"Roger that, Captain!" Cisco scampered over to the command couch and took his position at the controls. "Okay, Quadrilla. This is Deltoo, and I have the…a…com. What should I do?"

"I have set our size to point 10 percent. You must do the same. Fly your ship in a straight line until you reach the outside wall of the maintenance chamber, and then turn left. We will go the opposite direction and turn right. I am setting the tracker so that when one of us finds an escape, we can rendezvous at the same point and proceed with our exit together."

Tack thought a moment, and eventually it hit him what Quadrilla was suggesting. "I understand. Once outside the king angel ship, we can proceed together back to Earth."

"No, only you and Deltoo must return to Earth, but we, in the sister ship are also on a mission to lead the king angel force away from the Earth before they cause more problems with the nations of the planet. These evil ones have been concentrating on finding me and my crew. If we can divert them away from the Earth, perhaps we can return at some future date."

"I understand," Tack replied. "And at the moment, I can't make a good argument against your plan…at least nothing that seems better than what you have come up with."

Tack was watching the scene out of the front window as Deltoo quickly piloted the Spirit away from the giant spider machine and headed toward the outer walls of the maintenance chamber.

"Good luck," Quadrilla shouted over the chaos inside her own ship.

"Roger that," Tack replied and held on to the armrest next to Cisco on the command couch.

The king angels and the army of aliens were scrambling around, desperately searching for the saucer-shaped crafts that had miraculously vanished form sight. They had completely lost track of the Spirit and Sister Ship. The tiny size they had achieved had allowed them to vanish from the sight of the aliens and zoom off toward the outside wall.

Had it not been such a life-or-death situation, it would have been funny to see the spider creature scurrying around in the maintenance room trying to figure out what had happened to the two ships. In the process of searching, it even ran into one of the king angel creatures and knocked it over. The sounds he made indicated that the king angel was not happy.

Across the hangar, a similar scene was taking place with the sister ship, and wild activity was sparked and spreading from these two origins, filing the maintenance chamber with its chaos.

When the Spirit came to the wall, it made a sharp turn to the left and sped down toward two huge gray metal doors. As the Spirit flew along the wall, it came close to several king angel guards rushing in the opposite direction. "Those guys must have been alerted to our disappearance," Tack said. "It's great that they are going in the opposite direction than we are."

"It's comforting to know that they do not have a way of detecting our existence, or tracking our direction of travel," Cisco replied and continued to control the ship. "If memory serves me," he went on, "the king angel engineers have a propensity for venting in a series of small openings instead of large vents. That door up ahead appears to have a series of small holes spaced at equal distances around its perimeter."

"Okay, let's check 'em out. One of them may be channeled to some kind of exit."

The small saucer streaked toward the opening at the upper right corner of the gray door and slowed its speed as it made its final approach. Soon, the opening Deltoo had chosen loomed large in the forward window of the command deck.

Cisco was busy keeping the Spirit at the size of a medium-sized beetle. He guided the ship over to the opening and carefully adjusted the size of the ship to make sure it would clear the walls of the shaft. After a few seconds, they came out into a room that looked familiar. It was a lab similar to the one they'd entered back at Area 6451. It reminded Tack of his ghastly experience at that weird lab. Cisco guided the Spirit across the room, over to a nearby lab table. His eyes were busily searching for anything that looked like a vent large enough to allow their escape. Finding no workable prospects, the raccoon then punched the acceleration sphere and zipped the Spirit back across to the other side of the laboratory.

They were so busy trying to find an exit that Tack hadn't been able to get a good look at his surroundings. The lab they were in appeared to him to have something to do with human/alien experiments. The Spirit headed toward a doorway that became visible as they approached the gray wall panel. Eventually the ship entered a dimly lighted shaft that twisted off to the right and grew to a deep-green color. Cisco followed the shaft snaking back and forth and soon came to a brightly lighted chamber that at the current scale seemed to be at least a hundred feet across.

This room was a metallic-gray color. The floor was concave and curved up into the sides that met the exact shape of the inside of a perfect six-pointed star configuration.

On either side of this lab, Tack could see tables covered with laboratory hardware. At the far end of the room was a strange contraption that Tack took to be a machine for dissecting animal bodies. There were glass cylinders similar to those he'd seen in the bio lab back at Area 6451. There were about twenty or forty of the cylinders down either side of the chamber. These too were about fourteen feet high by four feet in diameter. Instead of the black plastic material at the bottom as in the bio lab, these cylinders had a maze of plumbing made from a dark metallic substance. Various shapes of gunmetal and black-colored plastic-looking plumbing came from assorted places around the sides and the base of the cylinders.

Inside these glass cylinders were what was unmistakably human beings of various sizes and sexes and a menagerie of various animals, at least that's what they looked like to Tack. At closer range, Tack could see that these beings were of too alien an origin for him to be absolutely sure what they actually were. It was like looking at some kind of fantastic, waterlogged series of zoo specimens.

From Tack's point of view these specimens looked strangely larger than life as the green, eerie glow that was emanating from the cylinders filled the chamber. This deep-green glow was spilling across the room and reflected off of the many curious-looking cylinders.

Cisco cautiously brought the Spirit to a halt. It hovered there in front of one of the cylinders, waiting. He deftly nudged the control sphere until the ship was positioned just in front of the face or at least what looked like the head of one of the weird creatures. This particular specimen had more eyes, if that was what they were, than any decent alien should have.

"Holy optical overkill, Batman!" Tack breathed, his expression filled with disgust. At closer study, he noticed the row of tiny lights similar to those that adorned Cisco's ears down either side of the creature's head and neck.

Then his gaze wandered down the creature's body to its arms, there were at least four of them, and instead of hands, he could see many octopus-like tentacles. Studying this creature caused Tack's mouth to suddenly go very dry. He turned and looked over at Cisco, who was, for some reason, fighting the controls. "Was this thing one of the creatures you and Quadrilla worked with?" he asked.

Cisco finally was satisfied with the controls and managed to look back at Tack with his most sincere expression. He then twitched his nose and looked like he was going to sneeze.

The Spirit then moved around what looked a lot like an operating table and then down a long row of spherical beakers. Then Tack saw what looked like the gray furred monkey he'd seen back at Area 6451. The animal was strapped down on a table, and its eyes were closed. Then he noticed that the creature's hands looked like the three-fingered hands of an alien gray.

Next, Cisco directed the Spirit slowly around the table, and then headed toward an open archway.

This chamber was full of smaller containers. There must have been a hundred of them. He maneuvered the ship around the first container. It was capsule shaped and about eight feet high and three feet in diameter. Inside, submerged in a blue fluid, was something disturbingly similar to a human female. Her face looked similar to Quadrilla's face. She floated with her back arched and her arms suspended over her head as if reaching for some unseen something that hovered above her. Her fingers were spread, and it seemed to Tack as though she were begging for some unseen entity above the container to come to her aid. Tack was filled with a wave of pity for the poor girl and growled a pledge to somehow, someway make the king angels pay for this kind of inexcusable cruelty.

"What in black and blue blazes is wrong with these king angel guys…king angels my round butt. They're more like evil angels—scums of the galaxy!"

Cisco caused the saucer to make a slow circle around the container, and Tack was brought back to the urgency of his mission when Cisco said, "We don't have the time for all this exploration, Captain. I'm going to get us out of here and search for an escape elsewhere."

The raccoon waved his head back and forth as if to clear its thoughts and speedily continued down the row of cylinders. Tack and his once raccoon were justifiably growing more and more anxious to get their tails and the rest of their bodies out of this horror chamber and more importantly, escape from the king angel's mother ship. They desperately needed to make their escape before the alien monsters somehow recaptured them and put them into one of those horrible cylinders. However, even with the urgency of the moment pressing on his consciousness, as the Spirit passed by at the last cylinder, Cisco was forced to pause for a moment.

At a glance it was obvious that this creature too was a female subject. At least she was partly female. Her arms were much too long for any normal female human, and her feet looked like the talons of a very large bird.

Before he could give thought to this new creature, Quadrilla's voice came over the communications link. "Tack, time is running out. Have you found any promising possibilities for our escape?"

Tack glanced back over at the main viewing screen. "Not yet. We were distracted by this chamber we found. It looks like a huge laboratory facility that's full of awful biological experiments."

"And we are not sure we can find our way back out of here," Cisco groaned.

"And I want desperately to get out of here—fast!" Tack's tone of desperation was all too obvious.

Quadrilla's voice answered back, "We've had no luck either, and because we are inside the king angels ship, the shielding they use in the construction of their spacecraft is cutting off our ability to replenish our power supply. We've got to get both of our ships out of here, or we'll be stranded here forever!"

"No argument from me in that regard. Got any ideas?" As Tack spoke, the Spirit was passing another cylinder, and Tack noticed a creature that had an appearance that was even more horrible than those he'd just seen. He quickly looked away and tried to keep his heaving stomach calmed, and studying Quadrilla's face on the monitor helped some.

"Yes, I do. I have several ideas, but one in particular is the most workable in my opinion. Listen very carefully. It's risky, but we have a lot to lose if we don't manage to escape pretty soon."

Tack waited for her to continue, and it seemed like forever before she finally resumed laying out her plan.

102

Beyond the Shift

On the command deck viewing screen, Tack watched Quadrilla get up from the command couch of the sister ship. She crossed the space between the couch and the console and spoke to the command deck camera.

"Tack," she said with deep concern in her voice. "What I am about to suggest has never before been attempted. I am concerned that we both are using up to much of our power in this search for a way out, and it will take most, if not all, of the power we have left to do what I am about to suggest."

"Well, go ahead," Tack said, "I can take it. Give me the bad news first." Tack shot a quick glance over at Cisco.

"The plan requires that we both go back into time, simultaneously. We must attempt to go back to the time before we were captured by these monsters. But in doing it simultaneously, we run risks that are unknown because it's never before even been attempted."

"Wait a minute, we were both captured at different times?" Tack said, feeling his heart begin to pound with his growing concern and just a little bit of fear. "When we go back in time, the Spirit will go back to one certain period, and you will go back to an earlier point in time—am I right?"

"You are correct, unfortunately, and that makes us face the first problem. Somehow, we must synchronize our time-travel speed to make us go back to a common point in time so we can retain the memory of what is about to happen to us in our current time frame. This will, hopefully, help us to avoid again being captured. In effect, we will be changing the future that we are currently experiencing."

"Wow, this makes my head hurt. You are saying that we will be changing the now, because we know what is coming. I think I follow what you're saying." Tack cast another glance at Cisco who was busy scratching himself in a couple of places.

"If we don't synchronize our travel," Quadrilla continued, "my calculations are that we will forget what we are now experiencing, and, again simply be vulnerable to recapture. If at all possible, we must avoid that event."

"Well, what the heck?" Tack said. "We might as well give it a try." Tack sighed. "I sure don't want to stay in this mother ship one second more than necessary." He turned to Cisco who was still scratching himself, putting now in a different place.

"Deltoo, you will have to do exactly as I say. Do you understand?"

Cisco/Deltoo nodded to the screen and placed his little paws into the control spheres.

"Okay, Cisco, old buddy," Tack said, "it's all up to you, now. Make sure you get this ship back into an earlier time period—if you can."

"Yes, Captain." Cisco twitched his nose again "And hopefully we'll wind up someplace besides this mother ship."

103

Trial by Desert

Deltoo's head quickly snapped back and forth as he studied the strange symbols that were appearing on the viewing screen. Whatever her technology input device allowed, Tack assumed that Quadrilla was typing out these strange instructions to Deltoo. The raccoon immediately began to do things to the controls of the Spirit that totally mystified the crop duster pilot. And the ship was doing things that he'd never felt it do before. He couldn't call it a vibration or a shaking, thumping, twisting, turning—maybe all of the above. However, thankfully, Deltoo seemed to be in total control of whatever he was doing to cause these strange sensations.

Tack could still see outside the forward window, and what he saw, or at least thought he saw, was the sister ship coming directly toward him, but somehow, he felt, or sensed, that it wasn't the sister ship at all, but a mirror image of the Spirit.

The interior of the command deck seemed to begin to glow, and he was being surrounded by moving things he couldn't quite make out. Soon he was only conscious of the intensity of the glow toward the forward window, which eventually became the focus of his consciousness. Tack sensed that he was being drawn toward the intense light. I think I've been here before, he thought.

In front of him, a circular area of light seemed to be growing larger, and the sister ship's speed toward him was increasing, rapidly increasing. "We're going to hit it!" he screamed at Cisco. But Cisco was no longer visible. The saucer was getting even closer, and he was helpless to stop what was about to happen. How could it be that the Spirit and the sister ship were about to collide, and there was nothing Tack could do to change his course?

The sister ship now filled the scene out of the forward window before him, and in an instant, he was back inside some kind of glowing world of light.

At that moment he could see that he was passing through a portal or some kind of threshold. As his eyes adjusted to this brilliant world of light, he began to make out shapes of various objects. Eventually he could see that some of the objects were becoming more distinct. They looked like huge soap bubbles. And inside the bubbles were people. As they zipped by, he could see that one of them looked exactly like Quadrilla. Then there was Max and Lisa. The idea that now occupied his mind was that the bubbles were some kind of automatic escape pods. But if that was so, then why wasn't he inside a similar bubble. And, Cisco, was he too inside an escape bubble somewhere?

But he couldn't think of that to any greater detail, because something new was happening. It was wondrous. Nothing he'd ever seen was so wondrous … except… Then there was a steady series of flashes that filled his eyes and his mind. It was as though the light was penetrating his skull. Then the scene changed. A huge object was passing around him and then was moving away from him at a great speed. It was the sister ship. It was glowing red, and now it was moving away from the Spirit. Then as the sister ship was moving far away from them, it was absorbed by the brilliant world of light. Images began to replace the vision of the sister ship in his mind. Again, his soul was being filled with a wonderful emotion. He was experiencing a profound joy in his very soul that he'd never dreamed existed or was possible. He looked down at his right hand and then the left. It was like an x-ray. He could see right through his flesh to the bones. "Holy shinola, Batman! I'm becoming invisible! This can't be happening!"

His head was pounding, and he realized that he was flying, walking, moving through various objects and shapes he could not make out.

As if his emotional state could take no more of the friendly warmth it was experiencing, it was sucked away from him and replaced with an extreme feeling of loneliness. It struck him like a huge hammer. This emotion of sadness was overwhelmingly destructive to his will to live. He just stopped trying to fight it, and Tack began to cry. His emotional state swept him away from himself, and he was suddenly totally lost and alone. The interior of the ship, the command deck, Cisco—all of it had dematerialized right before his eyes, dissolving into nothingness, and he could feel hard tears flooding his eyes, and covering his face. He looked down and realized that he was standing on a sandy, pebbled surface. An intense blast of white-hot heat swept around his body, his naked body. He looked up from his feet and gasped, "Where am I? What the heck is this place?"

A breeze suddenly whipped up around him and he realized that, except for the crystal hanging from his neck, he was naked. "What in the world has happened to me? And the ship? Cisco? What is going on? This wasn't supposed to happen. "This is not good." He slowly turned and surveyed his desolate surroundings. "Not good at all."

104

Stones of Bread

As he walked along the blazing hot, sandy surface of the hostile desert, he kept his feet balled up on toes and heels to protect as best he could the instep of his tortured feet. Added to that, he was torn between wanting to see another human being and dreading trying to explain why he was naked. "What a mess I'm in," he sighed. "What else can happen to me?" he said, looking up at the blistering sky. He was tempted to look at the blazing sun, but knew that he'd find an angry white sphere up there trying to cook him to a cinder.

To get his mind off his misery, Tack tried to replay the events that had left him here in this godforsaken desert; maybe he was on some strange hostile planet, or perhaps he had shifted into some parallel universe. He and Quadrilla had coordinated their efforts to make the ships travel back into time. But the sister ship had to go back further into time, for them to rendezvous. Lisa had warned that the gravity control monitor of the mother ship might distort their time travel in ways that were unpredictable. It was for this reason, in fact, that Quadrilla and Max had not attempted it before. They were aware that it could cause instant death, or worse.

In desperation, Quadrilla had decided that the risk was worth a try and Tack had agreed. At Quadrilla's command, Cisco had initiated the Time Travel Control to go back to just after Cisco and Tack had left the sinkhole back in Georgia, and Quadrilla decided to take her ship even further back into time to make sure that they were outside of the mother ship's maintenance chamber.

They had attempted to synchronize their time travel to go back to a time where they both could link up. They were shooting for the same time and same place, which had never been attempted before. However, the mother ship's gravity control monitor, it was beyond Tack's ability to comprehend; the way things had turned out, the experience he'd just gone through, and the place where he'd ended up, Quadrilla must have been onto something, he thought as he stumbled over a stone and almost lost his balance.

It wasn't long before he was hot, tired, and thirsty—extremely thirsty. As he stood there surveying his surroundings, he said to himself, "This is worse than the moon rock chamber. At least there I had some idea of where I was, where the ship was. And my feet didn't hurt." He scanned the horizon and sniffed the air. It didn't smell right. Something was missing. "My god, where's my ship? I wonder how I got outside the ship? It doesn't make any sense at all."

He found a suitable rock and sat down. Down near his naked foot, there was a feeble little piece of vegetation sticking out from a small gathering of stones, but it was all dried up and probably dead or waiting for a nice soft rain to bring it back to life.

"Since the attempt to arrive at the same time and place by two different time machines had never been tried before, some strange interaction between the gravity control of the alien mother ship, and the attempt to synchronize two different time machines threw both ships back to a time and place that…that… Maaan, I have no idea where I am, when I am, and I need some water really bad."

He got up and looked at the mountains far in the distance. "Maybe if I got out of the sun or, just maybe I could find water over there near that mountain. Oh well, I've got nothing else to do," he said and headed off toward the mountains.

105

Armor

After what seemed like several hours, Tack was still stumbling along, barely conscious. Badly sun burned in many places he'd never dreamed of having exposed to the sun, ever. He found himself standing at the base of a huge wall or rock. There was no sign of water. Not even the barest blade of grass could be seen. And now, all that he could think of doing was lying down and letting the sun finish cooking him like an oversized piece of bacon. His head was swimming, and it seemed to him as if the blazing sun was beginning to grow dark. Then it seemed that the whole world was growing darker, and all he could do about it was to go down on his knees and try to breathe. He knelt there, his body weaving back and forth for a while before he fell forward, throwing his face into the scalding dust.

As he lay there, in his mind or in reality, he couldn't be sure which might be true, he was approaching the light he'd seen twice before. The edges of his world were growing fuzzy and darker. But just as his vision was close to totally black, a brilliant ball of glowing matter materialized before him. Oh no, not again, he thought.

The circular area of radiance was growing closer as his eyes adjusted to its brilliance. The steady flashes that filled his eyes and his mind told him that he was being engulfed in a profound emotional torrent of experiences. As he looked down at his body, he was shocked to find that he could see nothing. "Oh no, I'm invisible! What's happening to me?"

His surroundings still seemed to be growing darker and darker. His entire world was disappearing. And then he was buffeted by a loud sound like thunder, the loudest thunder he'd ever heard. It was like he was inside some giant cannon that was exploding all around him, and huge amounts of warm water starting to pour into his face and over his body. The water was gushing like he'd been thrown into the midst of a waterfall.

Finally, the realization hit him that somehow, through some miracle, it had begun to rain. And it was a rain like he'd never before experienced. It reminded him of a time that seemed ages ago. A time when he'd been racing down a Georgia country road, being passed by a huge fuel truck; it flashed from the memory banks of his mind. That's when it all started, he thought. That cursed rain!"

He forced his eyes to open against the flooding waters of the driving rain. Now, it was extremely dark, almost pitch-black. However, there was a faint blue glow coming from the right side of his vision. Though the pain in his neck was prohibitive to motion, he managed to turn his head in the direction of the glow to find the huge figure of a man standing not more than ten feet away from him. The blue glow seemed to be coming from around his silhouette, as though the driving rain that was hitting the figure was being turned into some kind of energy as it beat down on and around his large body. The glow was also giving definition to the silhouette's front surfaces. The man seemed to be wearing armor of some great detail. Ornate designs covered the breastplate and shoulder pads. At first, he thought the armor to be of Roman or Greek design, but as more and more of the figure became visible, he wasn't so sure. There was an Asian quality about the designs that were cut into the gray metal surface of the weird costume. He gave up trying to identify the cultural origin of the designs and concentrated on trying to speak; however, he found his throat too dry to utter any sound beyond a raspy croak. In all this rain and water, he thought, I can do no better than a pitiful frog imitation?

When he realized that the large man-figure was moving slowly toward him, a stroke of fear began to grow in his sense of awareness. There was a flash of silvery metal at the right hand of the figure. That looks dangerously close to being a sword in that guy's hand, he thought, and he seems to be ready to use it. I'm a dead man. But as the figure grew closer, he recognized the object in the figure's hand as scepter of some kind. Perhaps, he is a king, Tack thought, or some kind of royalty. What the heck's a king doing out here in the desert, in the rain—at a time like this? Tack felt a humorous urge to ask, "Do you come here often?" But, of course, he was only able to produce another frog-like croak.

Soon, the figure was standing over him, menacingly looking down at the helpless pilot. At this closeness, Tack could almost make out the figure's face. He'd expected him to be bearded, like some Carthaginian general, but the huge man seemed to be clean-shaven. His conclusion held up as the figure bent down, slipped his muscular arms under Tack's body and picked up the roasted, naked, crop duster pilot from the muddy surface of the once hostile desert sand.

As he was carried along, Tack felt himself drifting off again. He felt sick to his stomach, and his whole body seemed to be suffering from intense pain, thus causing him to welcome the impending oblivion. Come quickly, sweet death, he thought, I hurt all over more than anywhere else.

Soon his prayers were answered, and he was returned to the world of oblivion and darkness.

Sometime later, when he finally regained consciousness, Tack was warm and surrounded by the walls of what he recognized as a room that seemed to be made of stone.

The cave was filled with a warm glow as from a campfire, and as Tack rolled his head over to one side, he could again see the huge figure of a man in armor seated next to the fire, with his back to him. The figure was silhouetted against a glow, only now the glow was warm and friendlier. The campfire crackled and sent occasional clusters of sparks to the floor of the cave. A strong sent of burning, spicy smelling wood filled the atmosphere of the warm cave. And there was the smell of something else. This smell was like some kind of meat, roasting over a fire. The figure was obviously cooking something, Tack was sure of it.

106

Dee Skull

The giant man-figure began to speak in what Tack took at first to be some strange native tongue. "I con seense dot you are awoked," the deep resounding voice said. It was a soft yet commanding voice, but the man at the fire had not turned to face Tack. "Come, john me by de fiah. I wond to zee you face."

Tack wanted to answer and tell the man that he couldn't move, but all he could do was croak like a demented frog again.

Tack struggled to move and finally managed to crawl around to get a better look at the man's face. Tack could now see plainly that the figure was holding a human skull that had been bleached white by the sun. The giant held it in both hands, looking into its sightless eyeless sockets. "Evea see a humand skull befoa Tok Malltree?" the man asked. Tack was trying to place the accent. It sounded familiar like a corrupted mixture of Cajun and Jamaican and something else he couldn't identify.

Tack couldn't tell for sure, but it appeared that the man was wearing some kind of very realistic mask. It could have been the fellow's real face, but there was something about it that made him doubt he was looking at what this weird man really looked like. Tack croaked again, but this time, he was at least able to make it sound like a word, but, sadly, not an intelligible word. It sounded sort of like, "Wolgeff."

The armored man shifted his gray eyes over at Tack and said, "Not..." He raised his left hand up off of the skull and gestured as if holding an egg between his thumb and middle finger. "Speakon wall. I fix." he closed the space between his thumb and middle finger and snapped his fingers. Tack felt a smoothness slide down his throat like he'd just swallowed a boiled okra pod.

"Who are you really?" Tack managed to ask with his newly freed throat muscles.

"Onsor queshton pless."

"Oh, sorry, yes, I've seen a skull before, but well not a real one. I think it was plastic."

"Oah," the man said, tossing his head back a little. "Blostick! No Blostick dees dahs. Muss be from deefronts times."

"I'm having trouble. What language are you speaking?"

"Yoo gotts dee kreestaol in dee pohkits, no? Yes?"

"Huh?" Then Tack's brain finally deciphered what the man was saying. "Yeah, I got." He started to reach into his nonexistent pocket and was reminded that he was naked. "Uh, seems like I've lost my clothes somewhere."

The man threw his head back, his drumming laugh filling the cave with the weirdest sound Tack had ever heard. "Nott to know daat dee kreestoal be wearin roond dee nek. Hole kreestoal between thumb und mid deegeet."

"Wha...oh, I got cha." Tack reached up to find that though naked in every other way, he was still wearing the Deltoo crystal on a chain, dangling down on his naked chest. With his right hand, he took it between his thumb and middle finger.

"Now, that's much better to understand, yes?" The man waved his hand and smiled at Tack.

"Wow," was all that Tack could answer back. There was still the accent, but now the words were decisively English.

"There, that's much better. It's obvious that Deltoo didn't tell you about the universal translation properties of the tracking device. It's only a small part of the UTV's power, but a useful tool when traveling through time."

Tack cocked his head a little, and it hurt his neck. "Just how is it that you know about my ability to travel through time?" This new revelation energized Tack enough to give him the energy to allow him to rise up on his knees. "Who are you?" he asked. This time he raised his voice, realizing that the power of his speech mechanism was finally coming back to a more comfortable level.

"Last question first, I am called Legion, because I am many. We are many. First question last, I know about everything. This is my kingdom. I am lord over this world, as you can plainly see." He returned to holding the scull with both hands and held it even closer to his face. "Most of us see many skulls during our lives. They are used to frighten us, to entertain us, and symbolize to us and help man to accept what we call death." Then Legion returned his gaze to Tack's face. "But look at the art of it, Tok, sorry, Tack, this used to be a living thing—a person." He looked back at the skull. "In this case, it was a man. Could have been a female, does not matter all that much, really. It used to be attached to a body, and there was a brain inside. It was covered with flesh and blood flowed through the brain giving it the power of thought. There were eyes set in these bony sockets. It laughed and cried and was the first thing you looked at when the man approached you. It had a mouth and could speak." He tossed the skull into the fire, and the room was filled with sparks and a blinding flash as the scull was miraculously consumed as if it were made of gunpowder.

Tack shielded his eyes from the flash and drew back from the edge of the fire.

"However, skulls"—the man turned back to Tack—"are not unique here in my world. There are piles and piles of them, everywhere. People have been dying and rotting away to nothingness for countless centuries. I have places here in the desert where there are mountains of these human leftovers stuffed in caves and buried under the ground. People like to bury the dead, you see, so they won't have to look at the bones, the skeletons and"—he turned away from Tack—"especially dee skulls."

Legion's words and especially his demeanor was making Tack feel just a little bit uneasy. It did, however, take his mind just a little bit away from the fact that he'd lost his ship and his good friend and companion Deltoo. And though he was extremely hungry, he was beginning to feel a little bit nauseous.

"Inside your head, Tack Moultrie, there is a skull. Did you ever think about it? Someday, someone could be holding your skull in their hands and wondering what you were like when alive, what you looked like, what you might say or do. Do you not find that just a little bit interesting? Now you are alive, and I can look at you and talk to you and you can talk to me. But when you're dead, you're dead. Your body rots away and leaves you more naked than you are right now. Your flesh will be dissolved away into the past, and all that will remain is your skeleton—and your skull."

"Personally, I like the idea of going to heaven," Tack said. "At least thinking of things that way is preferable to your idea of being dead."

"Why is that, do you think? After all, when you die, it's all over. You will have no sense of being at all. You won't worry about what happens next. You won't think of where you are or what you must do. You will just be dead unless—"

"Unless what?" Tack cocked his head, curious as to Legion's answer.

"Tack, you are correct, of course. Some like to believe that they will be released at death. Released from the trials and worries of this life. Instead of being dead, they like to believe that they will be transformed into a new creature and transported to a place they call paradise—unless, of course, you have done, let's say, questionable things, and some form of punishment awaits your death in a less-than-pleasant kingdom."

Tack curled up his body into a tighter ball. "You're talking about hell."

Legion nodded. "Yes, some like to refer to that kingdom as hell. If I believed in such things, perhaps I would call it Hades. Hades is a place where some people store their potatoes, out of the sun, in a cool, damp place. It's odd how that name has come to represent an eternal, fiery furnace where the lost souls are tortured for all time." He forced a bodily shiver and reached back into the fire with his bare hand. Tack watched as he pulled his hand back out of the fire. He could see that the unburned hand held a pointed metal prong with a piece of some kind of meat hanging on it. It looked and smelled wonderful. Tack licked his lips as he watched the grease drip off of the roasted meat as Legion held it toward Tack's face. "Here, eat, you must be very hungry after your ordeal with the loss of your ship and your mates."

Tack carefully took the handle of the prong out of Legion's hand and lifted to meat to his lips while his mind played with the fact that this Legion guy seemed to be aware of more about what had happened than he could possibly know. The meat was actually too hot to bite into, but after he touched his tongue to it and blew on if for a few seconds, he managed to take a small bite. It tasted as good as it smelled, and soon it had cooled enough for him to manage a bigger bite.

107

Gosh, Awful

As Tack chewed on the meat and eventually was able to swallow, the cave was once again filled with the sounds of Legion's maniacal laugh. When his crazed laughing sounds had subsided, he leaned over and held his face close to Tack's burning cheeks. "As I have already told you, I am more than meets the human eye. I am many—many. You have never seen the likes of me before. Nor will you again unless—"

"Mr. Legion, you seem to be…I mean…well…what else were you going to say?"

"First, call me Legion. Mr. Legion sounds…well, too twenty-first century. You are no longer living in the twenty-first century, Tack—not anymore. This"—he looked all around him at the walls of the cave—"is a different time, a different time altogether, and, just perhaps, it is also a different universe. Only the God knows for sure where we in fact are." Legion laughed again as if he knew the punch line to an unstated joke.

Tack's face betrayed deep concern. "When is this time? No, wait, first, let me ask, do I really want to know when this time is?"

Legion laughed loudly, and then after a short breather, he filled the cave with another burst of laughter. Finally, Legion lowered his heavy voice and said, "Probably not. You see, this time is beyond your wildest dreams. Come, let me show you." Legion stood up, and Tack again was amazed at the size of this man creature. Tack guessed Legion to be at least seven and a half feet tall.

Legion looked down at Tack in silence for a few seconds and then turned his back to him. He moved to the left wall of the cave.

Tack watched and then tried to stand up. He reasoned that he'd have to somehow get the strength to at least stand if he was going to follow Legion somewhere.

By the time Tack had managed to master his wobbly legs, Legion had turned back to face him. In his hands Legion now held some kind of garment that looked to Tack like a woolen robe. He grunted out, "This will cover your body while we explore my world together. These are different times than you are used to, but we still look upon nudity as uncivilized."

Tack took the robe and struggled to get it on. It was a simple garment, but he wasn't sure which was the front and which was the back.

Legion helped him to fit the garment over his body, and Tack stood there looking like the prodigal's son on his return from his wild time off yonder in the big city.

"What do you think, Tack? Does that robe give you a sense of the time you are in?"

"You are scaring me, Legion."

Legion laughed again. "I have just begun to scare you, Tack Moultrie. Come, let me show you something very strange."

Tack followed Legion to the mouth of the cave and was startled to see that it was the middle of the morning outside. He'd been thinking all along that it was late at night. And he was surprised and delighted to find that he was no longer in the desert. It was still an area devoid of lush vegetation, but he was delighted to see palm trees and an occasional flower along with the sand and pebbles.

He soon became aware of a large lake up ahead. Through the midmorning haze, he could barely see the other side of this huge body of water.

"Ever go fishing in your time, Tack Moultrie?" Legion glanced back at Tack as they approached the small buildings along the edge of the lake.

"I'm not much of a fisherman, but my stepdad used to take me deep-sea fishing when I was thirteen."

Then Tack heard a voice off in the distance cry out, "Hey! You're fishing from the wrong side of the boat." He stood on his tiptoes and strained to see the source of this voice.

108

New Nets

"Fishing for fish is a gift," Legion said as they approached the water's edge where the small waves were lapping at the rounded stones along the shore. "When men fish, there is a satisfaction of mastering the elements, and bringing a tasty dish home to the family to eat to the satisfaction of their stomachs."

"Fried catfish has always been my favorite, but once I had some really great broiled red snapper that melted in your mouth."

Legion looked back at Tack and shook his great head.

"Dead snapper, you mean." And more laughter.

As they walked along the shore, Tack realized that they were approaching a man who had also come up to the edge of the sea. He wondered if he were the source of the voice he'd heard earlier, yelling about the wrong side of the boat. The bearded man was taking off his robe and soon was standing there in his undergarment waving his robe at the men way out away from the water's edge in a boat of an ancient design.

"Look there," Legion said, "that man is a great fisherman. Listen to what he has to say to those men out there in that boat." Legion looked around and found a nearby boulder of a sufficient size to provide a resting place. He swept away some dust and bugs and sat down, gesturing to Tack to sit beside him.

As they both watched the man waving his robe and shouting something that Tack was having trouble making out, Tack absentmindedly toyed with the crystal on the chain at his throat and then glanced over to Legion's face.

"Relax, Tack Moultrie, and just listen."

Tack held his hand to his ear and did as Legion had advised.

"Hey," the half-naked man was yelling, while waving his robe most frantically. "You there in the boat. You are fishing from the wrong side. Hey, can you hear me? Try your nets on the other side of the boat!"

Tack could see the men out, in the dipping and rocking boat, stop what they were doing and look back at the screaming man. He could almost make out the expressions on their faces as they tried to figure out how the man over on the shore was able to tell where the elusive fish were hiding.

Tack looked over at Legion. "If the fish are under the boat," he said, "what difference does it make which side of the boat they drop the net over?"

"Just watch and listen. That man knows what he's talking about."

"I don't understand. Do you know that man? You said he was a great fisherman."

"Yes, I know that man. He has more will than any man I've ever known. If he says that those fishermen are fishing from the wrong side of the boat, they should listen to him."

Tack turned back to look out at the boat. It seemed to have drifted a little closer to the shore. "Do you know those fishermen?" he asked.

Legion nodded. "Oh yes, some of them. I can't see them well enough yet to know if I know all of them. They are very good fishermen, but they have a problem, you see."

"A problem? Yes, I can see that they have caught very few fish."

"That's the least of their problems. They have no idea how much their lives are about to change. They think they know the sea and are master fishermen, but that man, the one yelling at them, is about to show them that they have much to learn about fishing."

"The wrong side of the boat!" the man yelled again. "Cast your nets over the other side if you want to fill your nets!"

Finally, the men in the boat were busy pulling up their nets. Hand over hand they hauled in the wet cords of the empty nets. Tack could see that as they pulled at the ropes, they would raise their gaze back up to the man on the shore. The man had put his robe back over his body and was slowly pacing back and forth from north to south as he kept his eyes focused on the boat and the fishermen.

"Look, now," Legion said. "They have almost gotten all of the nets back aboard the boat. Now you'll see something to tell your friends about—that is, if you ever get back to your friends."

Tack winced at the thought of getting back to his world and his time and then said, "You sound as though you have seen this kind of thing before."

"You are very perceptive, Tack Moultrie." He nodded. "Yes, I have, and much greater things than this I have seen. Now watch closely."

The men out in the boat were tossing their nets over the opposite side of the boat, and Tack would have sworn that the boat had now drifted to a point that the nets were being tossed into the exact location that they had been before when dragging over the original side of the boat. But no sooner had the nets sunk into the depths out of sight until the fishermen were frantically pulling at the cords and ropes with such a furry that it was obvious to Tack the weight of the nets was dangerously close to pulling the men into the water or, worse, capsizing the boat itself.

"Look at that." Legion laughed. "Those men have never seen such a catch. The weight of the catch actually threatens to sink their boat from under them." He began to laugh even louder and this caused the man in the robe to turn and face Legion and Tack. Tack could see that the man was smiling a very big smile, and then the man began to laugh as well. It was a big, loud, deep in the belly sort of laugh, and the sound of it made Tack feel very happy.

When the man had gained control of his laughter, he yelled out toward them, "Ho, Legion, my friend." He turned and waved in the direction of the boat. "Ever see such a catch in your life?"

"Never," Legion yelled back. "Well, except for the last time you pulled such a trick. My friend, those poor souls have no idea what they are in for."

"Of that you can be sure," the man replied.

109

Stranger

Tack suddenly realized that the man was actually now approaching the area wherein they sat. As he got closer, Tack could see that the man's eyes were looking directly at him. The man's smile and his dancing eyes sent a warm, happy feeling inside Tack's otherwise cold and churning belly. Whatever Legion had fed him back in the cave, it was taxing his inner comfort. But this strange, smiling man…

"Who is that you have with you, Legion?" The man's voice had a pleasant ring to it. "He looks rather green of face."

"This is Tack Moultrie. He is from the future, hasn't happened yet, can you believe it?" With this Legion burst into laughter again.

As the man drew within range, Tack put out his hand to him. But instead of taking Tack's hand in the universal handshake gesture, the man come closer and embraced Tack in a crushing hug that lifted him up to his very toes. When he finally let Tack's feet touch the ground once again, the man said, "Tack, do people fish there in the future?"

"Well, I…er…I'm not much of a fisherman, actually…back there in the…well…future, you know. Who…are…what is your name?"

"Hasn't Legion told you my name?" He laughed again, and Tack forgot about his aching tummy. "What's wrong with you, Legion. Ashamed of our friendship already?"

"That's not it at all." Legion laughed. "Tack is lost. He's a stranger in a strange land. Has no idea where he is, who I am, and has no idea who you are—and that is good. When and if, I might add, he returns to his own time, his present, oh"—he put his thumb and forefinger to his brow and massaged his temples a little—"this time-travel business can make a mind swim where the fishes don't dare. Anyway, it is best that he does not know your name, at least not yet. It makes it so much more interesting, don't your think? Let's call you…mmmmm… make up a name for me, my good friend."

"What if we borrow a name from the animal kingdom, such as the lion or the bear?" the man said, working his fingers into his beard and casting his eyes up to the sky.

"How about Fish?" Legion offered.

"That is a very good first try, Legion, my friend," the man said, "but since I am a very good fisherman, calling myself Fish doesn't quite do it. What do you think? How about something soft and cuddly, like a puppy or a cat?"

"Somehow I can't see you as a cat and a puppy, please, no," Legion shook his large head. "Puppies are lousy fishermen. Maybe a Lamb."

The man nodded and smiled. "Good. Sheep need to be shepherded, and my Father has often said I need to be watched over by a shepherd. What do you think, Tack? Will Mr. Lamb do for now?"

Tack nodded and tried to smile. He hoped it wasn't a silly smile because during all of this name searching and talk about his being a time traveler to a stranger from the past who seemed not at all to be disturbed by the notion of traveling through time "I guess so…I don't…feel so good…good…goo—" And with that, Tack felt himself falling backward and thought looking up at what had to be the sky, but all he saw was darkness closing in all around him.

110

Mr. Lamb

With the sounds of yelling and some boisterous laughter from the fishing boat off across the lake, Legion stepped over to Tack's body and looked down at him with some concern.

"I had no idea that he was about to die," Legion's voice said, but to Tack's consciousness, all was darkness.

"Don't be silly, Legion, the lad's not dead. He only sleeps. After all, his body is exhausted after his ordeal in the desert. I know only too well what it is like to be stranded in the desert. The days are unbearably hot, and the nights chillingly cold. There's no water and nothing to eat but bugs and dried-up roots. No, the boy is just resting; soon he'll be back with us. But for now, I must join my fishermen. They'll soon be close to the shore, wondering what to do with all of those fish."

For Tack, now, the darkness was beginning to fade slightly. The shadowy vision was gradually being replaced by a dim glow, and he attempted to open his eyes.

"Lamb!" Legion laughed. "I'm impressed, Mr. Lamb. You never fail to amaze me with your ability to see through things. Go, join your fishermen, and let there not be so long a time till next we meet. Is that agreeable to you?"

"Certainly so. And need I remind you once again that you are very close to danger?"

"Don't worry, my friend, Mr. Lamb. The authorities are too focused on the man who stands in water to be very close behind me."

"It's not the authorities of which I speak. There are still the dark forces that trail behind you, seeking to take advantage of your weaknesses. Beware and be on your guard. They are powerful and have many tricks with which to lead you astray."

Tack could hear Legion's laugh filing the atmosphere and the light from that unknown source became a bright glow on the other side of his eyelids as he managed to blink them open in a few test blinks. By the time he was able to see where he was, the man called Mr. Lamb had joined his fishermen as they struggled to get their boats to shore with their huge catch. This made Tack feel a strange lonely sadness that he could not remember experiencing before.

111

Light on the Mountain

Legion's laugh was still ringing in Tack's ears as he continued to blink his eyes attempting to clear his vision enough to better see his surroundings. He was currently down in a horizontal position and was having trouble remembering how he had ended up on the ground and what had happened to the man called Mr. Lamb. He attempted to role over enough to get his hands and arms in a position to help raise himself up off the sand.

Legion quickly came to his aid and helped him to his feet. Tack was finally able to managed a few words. "What happened to Mr. Lamb?" he asked just above a whisper. "Where did he go? I was going to ask him…well, I did have a question a minute ago, but now…" The overwhelmingly strange lonely sadness blocked the rest of his words, and Legion, again, came to his rescue.

"Your body is still suffering from fatigue, Tack Moultrie. I must get you out of the hot sun and back to the cave. Mr. Lamb has many duties to perform and has left us to our current pursuits. We will soon, no doubt, rejoin him in his efforts to train those fishermen. They have never seen such a catch as now overflows their nets." Legion then helped Tack back to his feet and led him away from the activity now surrounding the beached fishing boat and the overflowing fishnets.

"I…my head hurts. I…can't think straight…right now." Tack wobbled on his feet as Legion led him down the sandy beach.

"Once we are back in the coolness of my cave, your mind will, no doubt, become more lucid. I was too forward in pushing you out into the world until you were more yourself. Back in my cave, we can think more clearly of what next to do." Legion's words were presented calmly and with comprehensible purpose; however, Tack's mind was still filled with Mr. Lamb's parting words about the dark forces. "They are powerful and have many tricks with which to lead you astray," he had said.

Tack's lack of strength was slowly being replaced by a renewed vigor as Legion led him back into the darkness of his cave. It had been a much longer walk than Tack remembered making earlier as they had approached the edge of the sea. Once Legion had managed to sit Tack back down near the remnants of the fire, he began to bring Tack up to speed on the things their encounter with Mr. Lamb had sparked in his mind.

"Tack Moultrie, I feel the need to tell you more of my friendship with Mr. Lamb. He is a great teacher. And he knows of many things beyond this existence here in the desert or near the great sea. I feel a pressing need to share my thoughts with you before more time has passed between us."

Tack rubbed his cheeks with both hands, attempting to get his awareness up to this new challenge. All that had happened and all that he was continuing to encounter was an awful lot to take in with his mind and body, especially in his current weakened condition. It was just too short a time to let his taxed mental state make sense of it all. "I'll do the best I can to make my mind understand your words, Legion, but I have to ask you to be patient. After all, I just got here, wherever here is."

"Tack Moultrie, for the moment, let's just say that you have a strong belief in the presence of God."

"I have no problem with that," Tack returned. "God has saved my bacon many a time in my life."

"Saved...your...what is bacon?" Legion questioned.

"Oh yes, bacon. That's my way of saying that God has saved my life many a time, some that I probably don't even know about. When you are a pilot and fly around in the sky, you fight sudden death almost at every turn. In our time, bacon is sometimes... like... referred to as life. I'd be really stupid to not say a quick prayer every time I get in an airplane to fly around with no parachute. You see, most of my flying is so close to the ground that a parachute wouldn't have time to open."

"Para suit? You must explain para suit, Tack Moultrie." Legion stroked his beard slowly with his right hand.

"Parachute, oh yes, I'm sorry, you see, Legion, in the future, men will be able to fly, you know, like a bird. Well, not exactly like a bird, but...well, I have built a...let's call it a device...It's like a bird that you can build yourself, like you can build a fire... or a bridge or maybe a boat. Yea, it's like a boat that you can move through the air, just like a boat can move through the water. It's a device that can ride on the wind. You know, when you feel the wind blowing on you really hard and it almost knocks you down, well, that wind can be made to hold up a device, and aeroplane, and the aero plane can hold up a man, you see—way up in the air."

"This is possible in the future you speak of?" Legion sat down by the circle of stones, and Tack looked around for a place to sit, found a large flat stone, and carefully sat crossing his legs in front of him.

"Yes and more, the parachute that I spoke of is like an airbag that can slow down your body if you fall out of your airplane. If you happen to fall off of the aeroplane, the parachute is a way to escape falling to you death. It's like a big cloth surface that catches enough of the wind to make you fall slowly enough that the worse you can get is, maybe a broken ankle."

"I see...yes, this makes perfect sense," Legion said. "I thought maybe you were talking about the wings of angels. Many believe that angels have wings that allow them to fly around like the birds. However, though this is a wonderful image of the angels, as a mental vision it is now completely unfounded, angels that I have seen do not have what one might call wings at all."

'You speak of angels. You have actually seen angels?" Tack scratched his head as Legion nodded in the affirmative.

"This is something that surprises you?"

"Well, yes, sort of. I mean I have heard of angels, and my stepmother even said she saw an angel once, but I have never seen one."

"The vision of angels with wings makes beautiful creations in the human mind; however, angels do not have wings that are attached to their shoulder blades as some have envisioned. This does not, however, mean that they cannot fly. Angels are creatures unlike human beings. They often have the appearance of man. When the virgin that we know of as Mary was approached by the holy angel and told of the power of God, that through her womanhood was to bring forth the miracle of a virgin birth of he that was to be the Savior of all mankind, well, she did not see angel wings, but that does not mean that he could not fly.

112

Birth

Tack thought deeply for a few seconds about the Virgin Mary and how it might have been with the holy angel telling this young girl about the power of God. The idea about angel wings and whether angels could fly or not was overpowering his mind. Finding it hard to breath under the circumstances, Tack was barely able to say, "You're talking about the birth of Jesus Christ?"

This was all too far from the reality that Tack had thus far been able to enjoy, even if commanding a flying saucer and being declared the captain of the ship by his new crew was not anything one might call "close to reality," this was just too far into the world of the holy kingdom for him to grasp. Even if all this information was being declared by Legion, it was also very true that Legion seemed to be more than a man. This strange man creature, for all the world, seemed to have some of the radiance of what one might call an angel. At least, at that particular moment, this was the notion that was racing through Tack's tortured mind.

"Perhaps you, Tack Moultrie, are unaware of the great war that took place many, many years ago as you might realize the passage of great periods of time. A war that took place in what you might know of as God's holy kingdom. It seems that in some profound ways I, yes, even I, Legion, am a product or, perhaps, victim is a better word of that greatest of all wars.

"You first must understand that in the beginning of time, God was inspired to create a reality of pure beauty. Pure love was his medium and the void of what you call space was his canvas. He painted a creativity of beauty. First came the angels and his Holy

Son. To this Son of God he also gave the power of creativity. In turn, the Son of God created the universe and a part of that universe that you call the Earth."

Tack shifted his weight on the stone whereon he sat. Outside there was the warning sounds of thunder that signified the approach of a terrible storm. Tack's backside was growing numb, but he hesitated to interrupt Legion in the great story that he was telling and the sounds of the storm seemed to be adding to the great battle that Legion was telling of. This battle had taken place in the great holy kingdom of God itself.

"However," Legion went on, "God also created a very special angel of pure beauty. His name was Lucifer. To this Lucifer, as with all the angels God had created, the gift of what you would call the power of freedom of mind was given. God did not want to create a world of angels that were mere slaves to his command and will. He intended from the start for them to be able to choose for themselves what they, as his creations, might will."

Tack struggled to visualize all that Legion was saying but was slowly falling slightly behind. "Freedom of mind," he managed to get out from his still dry throat. "I think I understand. God has put the concept of love ahead of the law that man thinks are the driving force of all that is. Each of us has things that we want to do. Some of them are things that we know will most likely cause pain in someone else. But if we love each other, this will has the power to help us to do only those things that we know will not cause pain in others. Those persons that live to cause pain in others, they have the will to do evil but also they have to will to love. If they love enough, the pain they can cause is lessened. Isn't that right?"

Legion nodded. "This decision by God to give Lucifer free will, sadly, set in motion the focus of horror. Of all of God's creations, what was to come was the worst horror of all.

"Lucifer was of a mind to set up himself as greater than God's Son, God's only Son. And through Lucifer's maneuvers and evil plans, one-third of the angels eventually joined Lucifer in the evil plan to actually overthrow God's holy kingdom."

"This is incredible."Tack raised his voice. "How could an angel do such evil? To actually go against the Creator of all things—his Creator even? And for what? Even if Lucifer were successful, all that he would be in control of would be the masses of evil that he and his angel supporters had corrupted of God's great beauty of love. How could he find pleasure in all this corruption?"

"Lucifer corrupted his will to turn Love into hate. He worshiped the Creation and hated the Creator. Lucifer, for his will, chose to will that he replace the Creator, and this kind of quandary that we see was not to be settled in the holy kingdom. A great battle ensued, and thus God was forced to deal with Lucifer, and threw him out of his kingdom and down, down to eventually be the Lord over the Earth for a limited time. He then was to be called Lord of the Air."

"Lord of the Air, sounds reminiscent of a superhero, sort of." Tack shifted again trying to keep his leg from going to sleep.

"Lucifer is no hero. He is called Lord of the Air because all life in the earth is dependant on what you know of as the Atmosphere. You talk of flight through the air/atmosphere. This is anything but the freedom of flight through the air. The battle between God and Satan's evil angels, though it happened so long ago, has left its mark on the planet as well as the heart of man. I know, firsthand, of the tremendous level of evil that Lucifer has brought to the reality that you and I are trapped within. He has led his evil angels astray. And, sadly, these angels are all around us. We call them demons. It is only the love and grace of God that can shield us from their tricks, black magic, and evil powers."

"This all sounds strangely familiar,"Tack, said. "When we discuss reality and the human perception of this reality, the constant arguments we hear against God, and those who are determined to lead people away from even the concept of God, they talk of the creation of man and woman and the obvious great differences between the different sexes. They even make fun of those of us who see sin as a reality in our world and in our history. They especially make fun of our belief that there is a God. They say that we who believe are in God are idiots, stupid, believing in fairy tales."

113

To Start With

Legion reached over and stirred the embers until the dying fire took on newer life. Sparks circled and danced up toward the ceiling of the cave. When he was satisfied with the level of the light he turned to Tack and continued his story. It was obvious to Tack that Legion felt it essential to make Tack understand the nature of the reality of the moment within which they both were currently captured.

"Since you are, in essence, a traveler in the medium that most of us accept as time, you will appreciate that in the beginning of time, God, the master Creator, was inspired to fashion a reality of the purest beauty. He painted/sculpted all that we can now observe, and it was wonderful to behold.

"First came his Holy Son and then all the angels. To his Son he also gave the power of creativity. In turn, as I have said, the Son of God then created the universe, including the part of the universe we know of as Earth."

Tack's backside was almost totally numb by that time, but he kept still and let himself be captivated totally by Legion's way of telling this story.

Legion stifled a cough and continued, "A lot of folks observe the works of evil in the world, mainly the pain it causes people and thus their tremendous losses, and this makes them ask the question, 'How is it that this pain and suffering can come to be under the leadership of a God who has infinite wisdom, power, and love?"

"Yeah, I've often wondered about that." Tack smoothed down his left eyebrow that was beginning to etch. "It seems to me that it's hard to miss seeing all the evil in the world, but there are many who don't blame the devil. They just think that all that is responsible for evil are the bad guys and gals."

Legion smiled and said. "Those whereof thou spikiest, those disbelievers in the one true God, they use this as their driving excuse to reject the Word of God that has miraculously come down to us over the ages in the written Word, and I fear that it will be their undoing."

"And the poor devils don't have a clue that they are doomed." Tack rubbed his aching knee.

Legion grunted. "It is all too clear, at least to my thinking, that through some negative traditions and faulty interpretations that these lost souls have of God's Holy Word have had the effect over great periods of time of obscuring the Word's so-called ability to teach man about God's character, including the nature of the government that the Almighty has created. In addition"—he coughed—"it has clouded the very principles of how God deals with the evil we call sin."

Tack made a face. "Yeah, just where did all this so-called sin come from. Why do so many fall for Satan's evil influence?"

Legion looked down at his hands and glanced toward the front of the cave, at the loud thunder that rocked the very room within which they were secured. After a lengthy pause, he went on, "Explaining to believers and nonbelievers just where, in the reality of time, what we call sin had its origins is difficult to impossible to accomplish. This is especially true if your goal is to do it in a way that gives possible reasons for sin's very existence."

"Yeah, even with all of this to consider from all those disbelievers"—Tack sighed—"men can begin to understand enough of the disbeliever's corruption of God's concept of the origin and eventual ending of sin. They can do all this if they try and see for themselves all of God's justice and goodness. By now, these things should be unmistakably clear to everyone."

Legion frowned. "I believe that all these souls that are bent on finding excuses for sin are, in effect, in the very act of defending sin and all of its evils, as if there were any defense of such as that," he groaned.

114

Infinite Wisdom

Tack nodded and for a second, gave some thought to Legion's last words. He had to agree that all the people that were using excuses for the sin's they felt free to commit and then standing up for all of it's evils as if the life an death of those around them, both strangers and friends alike, was just the way things were and that there was no use spending any time or effort trying to fix all these evils. He nodded and finally managed to say, "It strikes me that if man could come up with a good excuse for committing sins, then he would no longer consider sins to be sins at all."

"It is important to remember that love is God's law," Legion said, "and it is the very foundation of God's government. Sin is, very much, an expression that man makes to put forward these principles that are, in effect, at war with God's law. Before there was sin, joy and peace were dominant in the entire universe." Legion waved his hand at the ceiling. "Before sin, the love for God was unmatched and that love of the first man and his mate was totally unselfish. Then man was tempted by Satan to doubt the Word of his Creator." Almost as a special sound effect to emphasize the power of what Legion had just said, a loud clap of thunder filled the cave. It was almost as if the impending storm was attempting to come inside the cave and destroy them both.

Tack's eyes quickly searched the walls, and then he said, "I have always believed that Jesus is the Christ and is the only begotten Son of God, but I have never thought of love as being a law—God's law. I always thought of love as just an overwhelming feeling that we have for someone else."

Legion gestured with his hand. "That Jesus was one with the eternal Father in nature, in character and in purpose is a subject that has been debated all the way to that time, in the future, that you have come from, Tack Moultrie." He went back to what was left of the flames in his circle of stones. "Jesus Christ is, in fact, the only being who can enter into all of the counsels and the holy plans of the Almighty. It is written that by Jesus all things were created that are in heaven, whether thrones, dominions, principalities, or powers. The law of love is the very foundation of God's government. The happiness of all the beings he has created in heaven and on the earth are dependent upon their willing harmony with all of its principles of righteousness."

115

Red Sparks A-Okay

A swarm of red sparks zoomed up from the fire as Legion raked a small knife through the glowing ashes. "Almighty God is not," he continued, "in anyway pleased at any allegiance paid to him that is, in effect, forced upon an individual soul. God has granted all these souls the freedom of the so-called will. This is done by the Almighty to ensure that serving him is a totally voluntary function."

"Yes,"Tack nodded. "I understand the concept of free will. We use to have it in America back in the good old days."

Legion smiled as if he actually knew of the good old days that were somewhere way up there in his distant future, in a world that Tack called America. He then said, "Lucifer, for some reason, perhaps born from the free will that God had given to him, chose, in effect, to misuse the freedom that had been given to him by God. And he, in fact, attempted to overthrow God and takeover the holy kingdom for himself. This being was the most beautiful of all the heavenly angels and, as such, was the only one of God's creations that was so very jealous of Jesus."

Legion shook his head. "This great jealousy that possessed Lucifer caused him to choose to attempt to overthrow the very God that had brought him into existence." He shook his head again. "The very God that had not only brought into existence all of Creation, but also the kingdom of heaven itself. God had inserted Lucifer into the realm of time. This was done as a wonderful gift to the beast, but then, Satan/Lucifer actually chose to rebel against God, the great Creator. And it didn't stop there, Satan's rebellion went so far as to entertain the thought that he,

Lucifer, could actually topple the very kingdom of God and take it over for his own."

Tack scratched his cheek and cocked his head. "So the evil of sin began with Lucifer when he rebelled. I can only think that before Lucifer, there was no…everything was a-okay, right?"

The a-okay statement caught Legion by surprise, and he lost his train of thought for a second or two. The thunder rolled again outside and then he said, "Lucifer, this Satan, was actually right next to Jesus Christ and had been very close to him right up to the time he decided to rebel against the almighty, and if you think about it, Satan and Jesus were the only beings God honored above all other angels, holy and pure." Legion scratched his chin and turned back to the fire.

That last statement had triggered a long-lost memory, and Tack shifted his body on the stone; he finally got up the courage to chance a little input to Legion's story to see if the armored giant might have more to tell him about the angelic battle in the holy kingdom of God. "Yeah," Tack said, "I remember in Sunday school once. We went over the fact that the evil of sin began with Lucifer and that he was actually next to Jesus Christ and had been in this position right up until the time he took a third of all God's angels with him in his great rebellion."

"Yes," Legion sighed. "It is difficult to hold on to the idea that Lucifer was ever the being that God honored above all other angels, actually chief among the covering cherubs. He was holy and pure. He was told by the Almighty God that he had actually been in the great garden of Eden and that every precious stone was his covering. God had established him as he was on the holy mountain."

Tack shook his head slightly. "Yeah, I never got the part about Satan walking back and forth amid fiery stones. I'm not even sure how I even know about the fiery stones."

"It is written that Lucifer was perfect from the day he was created. Then iniquity was found in him." Legion waved his hand.

"Super wickedness!" Tack grunted.

116

Boisterous Laugh

That last statement had triggered a long-lost memory and Tack shifted his body on the stone, getting ready to chance a little input to Legion's story to see if the armored giant might shed a needed glow of reason to what little Tack was remembering about his Sunday school lessons. And as it turned out, Legion did have more to tell him about the angelic battle in the holy kingdom of God, that and Tack's input about the God's offering that when Lucifer was in the garden of Eden every precious stone was his covering and that Lucifer was the anointed cherub who covers.

Legion laughed his boisterous laugh and went on to fill in what Tack had left out. "That's right, my boy, and God told Lucifer that he had established him on the holy mountain, that he, Lucifer, had walked back and forth in the midst of fiery stones. That causes one to think as well. What could that mean? Indeed, what in fact does that mean? However, when one talks about God and his holy kingdom, us mere mortals must bow down to our ignorance. We are locked in the dimension of time, a system you seem to know a great deal about, seeing as how you have a machine that allows you to move back and forth in that dimension—if dimension is a word that accurately describes what time is.

"However, God is not locked in this dimension. Time is merely one of God's creations. He created it, and he understands it as only he can. Mankind, it seems, is only vaguely aware of God's kingdom outside of this thing we call time. Any thought about what is there outside of our sense of reality is difficult to gain… ah, anything close to the necessary understanding. Think of the fact that God talked to Lucifer. You would say it was in a very personal manner. He told this rebel angel that he had created him perfect in his way from the very beginning and then wickedness was found in Lucifer. Lucifer's heart was lifted up because of his apparent beauty, and he thus corrupted God's great wisdom for the sake of his own magnificence. It is written in the Holy Scriptures. I have seen it. The Profit Ezekiel tells of it in chapter 28:12–17."

Tack almost stood up in surprise. "You have seen these Holy Scriptures, yourself?"

"Oh yes, my boy, and many more of the writings besides. When I was warned by Mr. Lamb that the daemons were still after my soul, I was urged to learn all that I could about evil and there is much in the Holy Scriptures about evil and better still, how to avoid its hold on one's soul."

Tack's left leg was going to sleep and tingling, so he reached down and rubbed it as Legion went on. "Lucifer went on to voice that he would exalt his throne above the stars of God, that he would also sit on the mount of all the worshippers and would ascend above the heights of the clouds, and, get this, he said that he would actually be like the most high God. This prince of angels, Lucifer, wanted the power that belonged to Christ alone. The other angels saw Lucifer's exaltation of himself and their observations gave those of them, who held God's glory as supreme, a strange dread of the evil it would bring.

"And it came about that the heavenly councils pleaded with Lucifer to pull back from his efforts to overthrow God in his holy kingdom. Jesus explained to Lucifer the goodness and justice of the creator God and also demonstrated the sacred nature of the law of the Almighty God.

"However, Lucifer didn't listen. He rejected God's law, and in so doing the evil angel dishonored his God. He thus brought down ruin onto himself, and those who followed him in his evil efforts. Satan believed that if he could bring other angels with him in his rebellion, he could also bring the other worlds."

At this point in Legion's talk, Tack was overwhelmed. He begged Legion to forgive him as he interrupted the noble giant. "I'm sorry to interrupt your story, Legion, but I'm wondering about what you just said about other worlds. Satan wanted to bring other planets besides Earth and rule them with his evil power?"

Legion fought back a small crooked smile and decided to take a break in his monologue. "Well, my little time-traveling friend. You must know that there are many other worlds that are beyond the normal thinking of mankind. However, that is a story for another time. I'm afraid that your limited thinking would in all likelihood just explode if I told you or, indeed, if we had the time for me to tell you the entire story of the existence and true scope of what I know of as the realm."

Legion could no longer hold back the laugh he'd been suppressing at Tack's interruption, but a deafening clap of thunder cut short Legion's laugh. It sounded more like a gigantic explosion somewhere off across the vast reaches of the sea. The very ground shook with its fury, and Tack felt himself ducking as if that would do any good.

Tack had already noted that Legion had been very busy in his telling of the story to Tack as the coming storm had been developing. Tack's attention to what amounts to an extremely lengthy tale, encompassing a huge battle in God's kingdom of heaven between one third of the heavenly host and the good angels had presented many mental visions in Tack's tortured mind. Not only had he found himself here, in wherever and whenever this dimension was, there were all these mental images in the process of totally overwhelming Tack's ability to imagine. God and his devoted heavenly angels and the battle that the evil angel had brought to the heavenly kingdom was just impossible for his little human mind to take in. Tack, as a human time traveler, now living in another time that he had scarcely given much devoted thought to, had just been instructed that Satan had been able to convince a staggering one third of the heavenly host up in God's holy kingdom to follow him and his evil plan instead of following Jesus, the very Son of God. True, the remaining loyal angels had stayed and supported their God in his fight to put and end to the evil in the world. It was to be, that all this must play out in the many years of evil earth control until the day Jesus returned to rule his earth as originally intended by the Almighty.

Now, locked in the storytelling period inside Legion's cave, Tack struggled mentally with the thought of the angel rebellion. Now, Legion's story was being jumbled into the present by what appeared to be a terrible storm that was growing close to Legion's cave and was probably created by Lucifer himself in the evil angel's attempt to confuse the issue altogether, the evil power of Satan was obviously forcing a terrible interruption to the story Legion was telling.

Legion, also, was alerted by the threatening thunder, and his eyes searched around the walls of the cave, and his ears took in the loud rumble. It seemed to Tack, beyond his belief mechanism, that this thunder was just an ordinary thunderstorm. It seemed to him as if the world was coming to an end as he'd read about many years ago in the Bible and the book of Revelations.

Legion groaned and sighed. "I can't help but be concerned that, after emptying their nets, my fishermen friends might have headed back out to sea. If so, they might get caught up in the clutches of this storm.

"Well," Tack said reluctantly, "it might be a good idea to see if your friends might need some help, not that I'm going to be of much help against what sounds like the storm or the century—whatever century it is."

117

Shelter

Indeed, when Legion and Tack moved outside the cave, they could barely see the fishing boats out in the nearby raging sea.

As they were forced to seek shelter in the wrecked fishing boat the weary fishermen had left upside down there in the sand, Legion shouted against the sounds of the storm, "We can use this while we think of a plan to somehow help the fishermen get back to shore. I only hope there is still time before their boats are flooded beyond our ability to help."

"Perhaps this storm is being created by Lucifer. It certainly seems so," Tack managed to shout back while having trouble speaking out against the terrible storm.

"Yes, all this wind and noise certainly forces an interruption to the story I was relating to you. And yet, somehow, perhaps this dilapidated fishing boat will give us refuge while allowing us to somehow give aid to our friends out there battling the sea."

"I can barely see the boats out there," Tack yelled back as Legion lifted the end of the boat and motioned for Tack to seek shelter from the pounding rain in the shadow of the bow.

Tack groaned loudly, went to his knees, and ducked under the railing as he scooted out of the rain. "I'm guessing," he shouted, "that this boat has been left behind until the owners can return with materials and tools to fix it."

While being sheltered by the boat, the battle in heaven story was, soon, allowed to continue with renewed emphasis and raised voices, because of its relationship to the storm from which Legion and Tack had been seeking shelter.

Legion spoke out, against the driving rain as he let the boat down to the sand and moved his face close to Tack. "It was very strange inside the heavenly kingdom. In God's holy kingdom as one might expect, discontent was unheard of. In all of time, such evil had never before been known to exist."

As if punctuating Legion's last statement, the thunder rolled and caused Legion to take a breath. He was forced to wait a few seconds more while the sound died down enough for him to continue, then said, "It became necessary for the whole universe to see the deceiver and to remove his unholy mask. It was decided that Satan could no longer remain in the heavenly kingdom. God considered that the loyal angels could not then see the justice and mercy of God if he at that moment had just destroyed Satan. God felt it necessary that the whole universe see the deceiver unmasked so that the angels still loyal to God would serve their Lord from love rather than from fear.

"Even after the decision that Satan could no longer remain in heaven, the loyalty of God's creatures needed to rest on the conviction that God is just and fair. Above all, Satan's rebellion and its resulting effects, demonstrated to the universe about the horrible and disgusting things that sin brings about. The world needed to know for all time the results of sin. People killing each other in the name of an unjust God, calling the evil of Satan by other names so that he could wield his hateful power to conduce brother to kill brother, and to put women under the threat of being held down to the demands of a society dominated by man and religion.

At that moment, the lightning and thunder was accompanied by a whipping wind. An ear-splitting, thundering blast shook the earth around them, and Tack's eyes were treated with a whirling sensation of blinding flashes and twisting images. After several minutes of this swirling environment, the boat above their heads dematerialized around them and both of them were quite suddenly, magically, transported to what was seen by Tack to be another time and place. The brightness of the flashes of lightning turned into the blazing rays of the sun. Everything was overpoweringly bright, and it took a while until Tack could realize that somehow time had again shifted. He and the giant Legion were somehow, now, making their way up a trail that lead to what looked to Tack like a small village in the distance.

"Where…what happened?" Tack asked Legion and spun around on the pathway. "How did we get here? Where are we headed?"

"Don't tell me you have already forgotten that you are a time traveler, and now we are trying to follow Mr. Lamb. He's up ahead of us, somewhere, no doubt leading his fishermen friends into the city. It is without question that the storm left them extremely tired and hungry."

Legion's eyes searched the sky for a moment as if something was written up there in the clouds, except there were no clouds. "Ah…where was I?"

"I think you were in the middle of telling about the great city of Alexandria."

"Ah yes, the great city of Alexandria. Were it not for the Great Alexander and his love of a good story, we would never have had such a city."

"How so?" Tack asked.

"Alexander, even above his many exploits loved the stories that had been relayed to him from the great poet known as Homer. In one of the stories he could remember hearing as young man a tale that touched upon the island in the Mediterranean Sea known by sailors as the island of Pharos. We know of the island now, in our world because of the great lighthouse located there and the remarkable things that are said about it. It is called a wonder and is known as one of the eight wonders of the world. There are many stories about the reach of the brilliant rays of that mighty lighthouse and its magical abilities.

"Alexander in his travels and conquests eventually was able to set foot on that island and was immediately reminded of the stories he'd heard of in his youth. Inspired by those floods of memories, Alexander swore to his men that here he would build a great city, and thus it was so: the great city of Alexandria was born on that day."

Tack almost stumbled over a large stone at the middle of the road and said, "I've always heard of the great city of Alexandria. It's still a great city even in my time, but I never made the connection to Alexander the Great. No wonder it has his name."

"And, my young friend, that is just the beginning of the story. The great library of Alexandria was for a great time the center of all learning and experimentation. A great attempt to gather everything that was ever written down was sought and drawn to that great museum. Great men with great minds put forth wondrous efforts to attract all written materials and books to the great library. This is especially true about the book known by us as the Bible. There was a man, I don't know his name. This man became interested in the stories he heard of the Hebrew people, about their history. This man became so interested in these tales that he sent out word to all the civilized world that he wanted anything ever written down about the Hebrew people. He called them the Hebrew children, because they claimed to be the chosen people of a great God. It is truly a remarkable book. Years later the Romans had a great battle, and it is recorded that in that battle the great library was destroyed by a fire. Many of the world's greatest books were thus destroyed forever. We shall never know the real extent of all the damage that was done to recorded history by that fire."

Tack turned his head and looked up at Legion's face and thought he saw tears streaking down his cheeks. "Everything was destroyed? That's just awful."

"I am told that some of the great books managed to be salvaged or otherwise saved from the fire. Those who worked in the library did what they could to move and save as many of the written works as possible before the fiery destruction, but we will never know for sure the extent of the damage to the stores of knowledge once kept there in that great museum.

"However, the powers that be, during that time, made it a law that everything written that ever came into the harbor of Alexandria was to be put into that library, and those forfeiting the writings must be satisfied to take with them the parchments copies that had been duplicated. Therefore, all was not lost as might have been expected because those copies that had been made were in many cases still intact. In this way, the Bible was thus, perhaps, saved from total destruction in the fires.

"The invention of writing has done much to aid mankind and protect him from evil. I do know that the writings that gave us the story of the great battle between the good angels and the evil angels was somehow saved from that evil destruction."

"Look, Legion." Tack couldn't restrain his excitement at what he could see up ahead that they were approaching.

What Tack could see were palm trees and flowers, great stones with shapes and colors that sent his imagination whirling. The walls and the building established that this was indeed some great estate, most likely the home of some very important official in the city. As they drew closer to the mansion, Tack could see that there was an open gate. It had the look that it has seldom been used to bar the entrance to the estate.

Tack turned to Legion, "Is this the place you told me about?" As Tack felt the words leave his mouth, he realized that Legion had never mentioned anything about this place or any other. Tack searched his memory with little success as to where the words he'd just spoken came from. He decided that something had happened when they were hiding under the boat that had transpired without his knowledge a scene as it were that he'd somehow missed.

In answer to Tack's question, Legion simply said, "Come, they are waiting for us."

"What... who...I don't understand," was all that Tack could muster.

118

Living Water

Soon Legion and Tack were crossing a great courtyard within the center of which was a very large circular wall that was waist high to Tack's body. The structure resembled a large well. As they approached the well, Tack expected to see water down inside its walls. He was, however, surprised. As they passed close by and he could see down into its depths, instead of water, the well seemed to be a huge vertical cave or tunnel that snaked deep down into the bowels of the courtyard.

Legion put his hand on Tack's shoulder and guided him past the well and on toward the entrance to the great building. However the well-tunnel was still heavy on his mind, and Tack made a mental note to come back and check it out more thoroughly. Then his mind was shifted back to Legion's lead, and he could hear voices up ahead. Soon they were moving inside the building and could see many men and women sitting at a large table listening to one of the men who was seated there by a very attractive woman. Tack recognized the man who was speaking as the mysterious Mr. Lamb.

"And," Mr. Lamb went on with his talk, "s we sat by the well, I told her about the living water." The woman beside him smiled but cast her eyes down to the plate of food on the table in front of her. "And I told her to go and sin no more."

There were nods all around the table. Mr. Lamb looked up at Legion and Tack as they approached the table, motioned toward two empty seats, and said, "Welcome, gentlemen. I'm afraid you have missed my story about this young lady and all that she has accomplished. I'm going to have to take my leave now, because of some trouble I have to address. But you sit down and have your fill. I will be catching up to you later."

Legion nodded and removed his helmet, placing it on the table at one of the empty spaces. Tack took the hint and sat down next to the place Legion had indicted he was going to sit.

With that, Mr. Lamb smiled at the group, stood up from the table, looked down at the woman, and said to her, "This is Legion, the man I told you about. Get to know him. It will be worth your while."

After speaking those last words, Mr. Lamb straightened his robe and nodded to the rest of those gathered around the table. Before he took his leave of them he quickly bent down briefly to Tack and spoke into his ear. Tack's eyes quickly scanned the man's smile and those nearby saw the strangest expression sweep across Tack's face. All could not help but wonder what Mr. Lamb had told him, but before anyone could inquire, Mr. Lamb headed for the door slightly waving his right hand in the air.

Legion looked knowingly into Tack's face and said, "Makes you think, doesn't it, my friend. When he speaks, I listen. We all can only wonder what he has related to you before he left."

Tack straightened up his body and said, "Legion, I have to go, now! It may be too late, but I must try to find Deltoo."

"Deltoo is part of your, how you say, crew, is he not?"

"That's correct, and he needs me, and I need him. I must go quickly. Time is short—so short."

As Tack made his way to the door, he couldn't help but notice that the beautiful woman sitting there where Mr. Lamb had left her was watching him very closely as he headed for the door. All the eyes of the group watched after him as he left the room. The light outside seemed more intense than it had been when he and Legion had first approached the building, and he was extremely surprised to find, as he walked into the courtyard, that the beautiful woman Mr. Lamb had been sitting beside at the table was walking right behind him, obviously following him or perhaps she was trying to catch up to Mr. Lamb.

But, no. It didn't take long for him to realize that she wasn't following Mr. Lamb at all. She was following Tack. He decided to slow down and let her catch up to him. "How may I serve you, my lady?" he said, surprising himself with not only the question but how his voice sounded. It wasn't Tack Moultrie's voice or wording at all, but he couldn't think of it in any depth because his attention was drawn away from such thoughts by what the lady said in return.

"I'm afraid that it is I who must serve you, Tack Moultrie."

Tack tried not to show how stunned her statement made him. "Serve me… how?"

"I have been in contact with someone who says he is part of your crew." She shook her head and went on. "I'll never forget the moment that I realized that a creature, an animal really, was speaking to me. However, beyond that difficult moment in my recent experience, and I have had many just recently that choked and stirred my very being. I was told by this animal that you must go down into the well that is in the center of this courtyard and there you will find your spirit. I do not know what that means. But now I have delivered the message, and that's all I can say about it." With that she turned and walked away.

The woman was quite beautiful even though she wore no trace of makeup. Tack felt as if he'd seen her face before, but there was something different about her and the face he could remember. Perhaps it was just a resemblance to someone he'd seen before briefly in passing, but there was definitely something, even if he couldn't place it.

As Tack looked around at the courtyard and his eyes finally settled on the wall around what the woman had referred to as the well, he realized that the palace area was typical, though much larger than Tack had envisioned from the description Legion had given him earlier about the place they were approaching.

It was basically a series of large houses, with rooms that had very high ceilings. The houses were built together with common walls that made a huge square courtyard in its center. It reminded Tack of a place he'd seen before. It was the elaborate set for a Hollywood movie made back in the late '50s. The movie was one of those huge epics with a wide screen and stared a host of Hollywood megastars.

What Tack noticed that made a glaring difference between this palace and the one he'd seen on film was the huge empty well where the woman had told him that he would find his spirit.

He hesitated a moment, then walked over to the rock wall that surrounded the well. Looking down into the depths of the dark cavern he was surprised to see that there was no water at all in what Legion had referred to as a fountain. Legion had gone on to tell him that the well in olden days had been the source of water for the entire nearby village, that the water was deep down in the tunnel area. He had described an environment deep down where the debris from the plants and animals made it hard to actually get to what water that happened to still be down there in the darkness. Legion had also said that the water was very cool because of its being shielded from the heat of the day's sunlight.

As Tack's eyes were scanning the area, then focusing again on the well. He noticed that on the far side of the wall that encompassed the well there was an opening that led the way to a stairway cut into the circular chamber wall. The walkway spiraled around the outer edges of the vertical tunnel and disappeared into darkness of the afternoon sun.

Legion mentioned a man named Marmouth and that Marmouth, in times past, had taken on the responsibility for the well. He made access to the well a right for everyone in the village. He had his workers keep it clean and protected, and it stayed that way until he had workers dig a new well for the village between his palace an the river to the north of the village."

As Tack made his way closer to the well, he could have sworn that he could hear water splashing and dripping, deep down inside.

"I don't get it," Tack heard himself say. "There's no water visible in this well, unless Legion is right that it is deep down there in the cool depths. Yep, I can definitely hear the splashing and dripping of water. Must be an underground stream, maybe a small waterfall?

It didn't take long for Tack to climb down, down into the dark tunnel, only to find a small room deep down in the darkness, except—lo and behold—there was a dim blue glow coming from somewhere across the darkened room. There was some source of light casting the glow from behind a large rock.

He held his breath as he drew closer to the rock to see what lye behind it, and to his great surprise, there it was, the tiny shape of the Spirit. He was gratified to conclude that the Spirit the beautiful woman had referred to was, in fact, his spaceship. True, the ship was now shrunk down to the size of a large dinner plate, but it was the Spirit after all.

Before Tack could give the situation another deep thought, a vivid green beam of extreme radiation shot out from the front side of the Spirit and surrounded Tack's body. The sensation he felt all over his being was indescribable, but it worked as intended. Deltoo was shrinking his captain down to the correct size to successfully take him on board the ship without the need to enlarge the Spirit to Tack's apparent size. Down, down, Captain Tack shrunk rather quickly until he found himself small enough to dash up the ramp to be greeted by his first mate and second in command, Deltoo.

Deltoo was the first to speak. "We don't have much time, Captain," he said with his raspy little voice. "Our power chargers are growing weak because of the depth of this cave. We need the sun. Once outside the atmosphere, we can easily use the sun and the distant stars' energy to recharge our power units. Thus we will be more than able to make a decent escape from this time period and get back to a rendezvous with Quadrilla's ship."

The woman at the well had been correct and extremely helpful in the words she had spoken to Tack. However, his mind was currently preoccupied to the point of putting her words and Mr. Lamb's living waters designations to the back of his mind for further study later when he and Deltoo were back in their world so to speak. Soon the Spirit's engines were up to speed, and the ship was filled with the familiar hum of success. Then the Spirit lifted off the cave floor and was off to another time and place. Tack was soon relieved to find himself seated comfortably once again in his command couch. And then, everything went black.

119

Seconds

The blackness was incredible. It was way beyond any darkness he'd ever before experienced. He had, of course, heard of those many instances that occur to some individuals that are called near-death experiences. It was exactly what went through his mind as he lay there on the floor of the sinkhole cave. He was apparently just lying there, looking up at Cisco's concerned tiny face. He did have the presence of mind to realize that there was an intense pain in his chest and that this excruciating pain was causing him to cough, spit, and try to, again, breathe.

Then wonder of wonders, water gushed out of his mouth like a fountain. He was choking and vomiting at the same time, and it wasn't pleasant at all.

The last thing he could remember was being wrapped up in the intense green glow from the shrink beam of the Spirit as Deltoo had taken him aboard the ship for their escape from ancient times, Legion, the woman at the well, and the total confusion of those lost times.

Now, in the current existence within which he found himself, Cisco was slowly backing away from his master a few inches, his little eyes twitching and sweeping, watching his master as he continued spilling water out of his lungs. It had been going on for a very long time and seemed like it would never stop. During this whole episode of swinging back into the world of the living, Tack had became so violent that he had knocked the flashlight out of Cisco's tiny little hands.

The silver cylinder rolled away from them a few feet and swung around on the cave floor, its beam finally stopping on Tack's contorted face. He blinked his eyes at the glare as Cisco jumped up on top of Tack's chest. The little raccoon had a blue crystal on a chain around its neck, which he quickly took in one of his paws and then pushed it painfully against Tack's straining throat.

After a few awful seconds of pain, Tack's uncontrollable coughing seemed to grow less and less intense. Finally, the coughing fit tapered off slightly, and a more normal condition began to return to the young crop duster pilot.

Cisco looked at Tack with great concern as his captain was just lying there on the cave floor, looking up at the ceiling. He seemed to be currently focused on one of the huge stalactites hanging up there on the ceiling of the cave.

Now, the reality of the moment took over from the fantasies that were being reflected within Tack's tortured mind. When his lungs were free enough of the tunnel water to actually breath, he moaned pitifully, "Where am I?"

The stalactites didn't answer back.

After his mind had cleared enough that the stalactites weren't expected to do anything but what they were designed to do in the first place—hang there like giant, stone, icicles. Tack rolled his head over and focused his eyes on his little buddy Cisco. The coon was now busy, sniffing his nose, and dangling the ice blue crystal there in front of Tack's red face.

Tack groaned loudly, went through a brief coughing fit again, and then forced himself up close to a sitting position. It took a while before he settled down a little and managed to make the room stop shifting and moving in weird momentums.

The memories of what he believed had happened over the last few days were now coming back to him in short and flashback bursts on the dream screen of his mind.

"Hi," was all he was able to get out to his first mate, before he began to cough again. After he'd settled down some more and control was at least approaching something more normal for him, Tack looked over at the cave wall where the tunnel was located.

A steady stream of water was still flowing across the cave floor, out of the dark orifice, and out toward the center of the room.

He finally focused his attention on the coon and said, "Well, I don't know how you got me out of there little buddy, but I sure appreciate it. I was a goner. God, it was awful. I've often wondered what it might be like to drown. I guess now I have a pretty good idea, and I don't look forward to repeating the experience—ever again."

Tack managed to get to his feet and swayed there for a moment before stooping down and picking up his flashlight. He stood there swaying back and forth a moment, and then, trying to get his head clear enough to think, he was distracted by little Cisco coming over, with the crystal in his tiny hand. Tack realized that this crystal was different in that it was attached to a silvery chain.

"Hey, what ya got there, little feller?" he bent down and took the crystal in his hand. "Hey, I've seen this thing before…or… maybe… looks a lot like the one I found up there in the clearing and the circle of ashes"—he scratched his head—"but somehow it looks different. I can almost make out something down inside it like the others I've seen. But it doesn't look quite the same. It's not the same thing that I've seen inside the crystals that I've come across."

He focused the beam of the flashlight on the ice-blue stone and tried to make out the object embedded inside it, get a better view and understanding of just what it was, but it was obscured by muckiness. He longed for a magnifying glass but was sure that magnifying the milky cloudiness wouldn't help a whole lot. And with his recent near-death experience still plaguing his body, and mostly his mind; it was quite difficult to focus on anything.

As he studied this strange gem and his senses became more coherent, a question began to form in his mind. He looked down at the raccoon. "How did you get this thing, Cisco? It's not really just like the one that Evelyn wore around her neck or the one I found in the clearing. It's different. It's not like the ones I saw in the bio lab either. I... just... don't..."

Cisco just looked back at Tack and twitched its nose. Tack felt that the Cisco he new and loved was about to turn into the Deltoo that kind of scared him. He knew and felt like he had to watch the weird transition, but he had finally been able to put together in his mind the idea that Cisco was a whole lot more than a simple raccoon, and it was starting to concern him that he felt as though Cisco owed him more of a response when he talked to him.

Then, the mood and moment of silence was broken by the loud, sound, the sound of a lot of water moving through the tunnel over at the edge of the wall. Tack turned abruptly and aimed the flashlight beam in the direction of the noise. He felt like he'd lived this moment before at some different time, perhaps in one of those parallel universes he'd read about and possibly experienced with Legion.

Small stones in the rubble by the entrance to the tunnel were now being washed away into the room and across the cave floor.

"I'm thinkin'," he said to Cisco, "that all this has happened before, but to heck with that. I'm also thinkin' we'd better get the heck out of here, Cisco, and I mean right now!

Cisco looked back at tack for a few seconds; then, quite suddenly he began to change into Deltoo. While still in transition, Deltoo ran like crazy toward the ramp to the Spirit. Tack joined Deltoo, and soon they were headed in the Spirit back out to the shaft of the sinkhole and up, up.

The flight back to EPOTEK took most of the rest of the night, and the German shepherds guarding the lab went crazy again as Chris walked across the concrete pad back toward the main building. Tack had alerted Chris to the fact that he and Cisco had been unable to find any clues as to what had happened to

Lisa and for that matter what had happened to Evelyn Milford as well.

At the EPOTEK labs, it was well after normal working hours, and Chris Slattery was looking forward to having a discussion with Tack about his trip back to Hamlet's Mill as he sat across the table from Professor Jesse Balboa. He and Jesse were still trying to recuperate from the past few days there in one of Houston's most secret scientific laboratories.

As the Spirit crossed the Texas state line, Tack was relaxing in the long flight, sitting there in the command couch playing with the crystal Cisco had used to bring him back to the world of the living. He was dreading he debriefing he faced upon his return to the lab and all the scientists and engineers that were likely waiting for his return and planning for some huge scientific mission for the Spirit crew to undertake.

In his dread, frustration, and confusion after the weird dream of Legion, Mr. Lamb, and the woman at the well, he raised the ice-blue stone Cisco had given him back in the cave and tried again to make some sense out of the object down inside it. He still found it quite difficult to focus his eyes well enough, but now the image seemed to have changed or at least become much more clearly outlined. As he studied this wondrous gem, he smiled and looked over at Cisco. It must be the crystal that Legion gave to me in my dream, no, must not have been a dream at all—and wow! If it wasn't a dream after all, then... He raised the crystal back up to his face an studied and admired the silhouette of the tiny cross drifting there in its crystal blue center.

The End—Maybe a New Beginning!

CPSIA information can be obtained
at www.ICGtesting.com
Printed in the USA
LVOW04s2057120816
500060LV00016B/285/P